Deemed 'the father o   ard
Austin Freeman had   as
a writer of detective fict   f a
tailor who went on to t   a
surgeon at the Middles   , Freeman
taught for a while and join   onial service, offering his skills
as an assistant surgeon along the Gold Coast of Africa. He became
embroiled in a diplomatic mission when a British expeditionary
party was sent to investigate the activities of the French. Through
his tact and formidable intelligence, a massacre was narrowly
avoided. His future was assured in the colonial service. However,
after becoming ill with blackwater fever, Freeman was sent back to
England to recover and finding his finances precarious, embarked
on a career as acting physician in Holloway Prison. In desperation,
he turned to writing and went on to dominate the world of
British detective fiction, taking pride in testing different criminal
techniques. So keen were his powers as a writer that part of one of
his best novels was written in a bomb shelter.

BY THE SAME AUTHOR
ALL PUBLISHED BY HOUSE OF STRATUS

A Certain Dr Thorndyke
The D'Arblay Mystery
Dr Thorndyke Intervenes
Dr Thorndyke's Casebook
The Eye of Osiris
Felo De Se
Flighty Phyllis
The Great Portrait Mystery
Helen Vardon's Confession
John Thorndyke's Cases
Mr Polton Explains
Mr Pottermack's Oversight
The Mystery of 31 New Inn
The Mystery of Angelina Frood
The Penrose Mystery
The Puzzle Lock
The Red Thumb Mark
The Shadow of the Wolf
The Singing Bone
A Silent Witness

The Golden Pool
A Story of a Forgotten Mine

R Austin Freeman

Copyright by R Austin Freeman

All rights reserved. No part of this publication may be reproduced, stored in a retrieval system, or transmitted, in any form, or by any means (electronic, mechanical, photocopying, recording, or otherwise), without the prior permission of the publisher. Any person who does any unauthorised act in relation to this publication may be liable to criminal prosecution and civil claims for damages.

The right of R Austin Freeman to be identified as the author of this work has been asserted in accordance with sections 77 and 78 of the Copyright, Designs and Patents Act 1988.

This edition published in 2001 by House of Stratus, an imprint of Stratus Holdings plc, 24c Old Burlington Street, London, W1X 1RL, UK.

www.houseofstratus.com

Typeset, printed and bound by House of Stratus.

A catalogue record for this book is available from the British Library.

ISBN 0-7551-0361-0

This book is sold subject to the condition that it shall not be lent, resold, hired out, or otherwise circulated without the publisher's express prior consent in any form of binding, or cover, other than the original as herein published and without a similar condition being imposed on any subsequent purchaser, or bona fide possessor.

This is a fictional work and all characters are drawn from the author's imagination. Any resemblance or similarities to persons either living or dead are entirely coincidental.

Contents

1	In Which I Make the Acquaintance of Captain Bithery	1
2	In Which I Set Out for Africa	14
3	I Hear Strange Stories and Vague Rumours	26
4	I Visit a Graveyard and Meet a Blind Man	33
5	I Encounter a Curious Relic	41
6	The Journal of Captain Barnabas Hogg	49
7	I Form an Absurd Resolution	58
8	I Make a New Acquaintance	67
9	I Bid Farewell to my Friends	78
10	I Take to the Road	88
11	I Find Myself Among Enemies	101
12	I Change my Identity	117
13	The Golden Pool	127
14	I am Led Into Captivity	143
15	The Aboási Mine	158
16	I Assist in a Robbery and Become a Fugitive	176
17	The Last of Bukári Moshi	192
18	I Again Become a Fugitive	210
19	I Make my Appearance in a New Character	223
20	I Join a Party of Bohemians	236
21	I Meet With Some Old Acquaintances	250
22	A Catastrophe	265
23	I Make a Curious Discovery	280
24	I Return to an Old Trade	292
25	I Set Out Upon my Voyage	310
26	I Put Out Into the Darkness	329
27	Ship Ahoy!	347
28	In Which I Bid Farewell to the Reader	360
	Epilogue	364

Chapter One
In Which I Make the Acquaintance of Captain Bithery

It must have been a matter of surprise to most of us who have arrived at, or passed, middle life, on looking back through a vista of years, to note what an astonishingly important part has been played in our lives by entirely trivial circumstances. It has, indeed, become a commonplace that "great events from little causes spring"; but we do not realise, until we actually submit our experiences to analysis, how the whole tenor and meaning of our lives has in many cases been determined by some occurrence so unimportant that, at the time, it appears incredible that it should have any consequences at all.

Yet so it is. Not only great and critical events which occupy our attention at the time and impress themselves afterwards upon our memory, but trifling circumstances that pass almost unnoticed and are straightway forgotten generate each its train of consequences; and when in retrospect we retrace our steps through the busy years, we are apt to find the starting point of the main action of our life in some little incident that had long since passed out of recollection until thus recalled by association.

These reflections are suggested to me as I review the series of strange and well-nigh incredible adventures that befell me in the early years of my manhood – adventures which it is the purpose of this narrative to chronicle; for their occurrence is traceable to an event so insignificant that its mention would appear an impertinence but for this connection.

This event was, in fact, nothing more than the mislaying of a matchbox. Yet, but for this trifling accident, not only would those marvellous experiences never have befallen me, but the entire course of my life – indeed, my very personality – would have been quite different.

It happened thus:

On a windy September evening I was standing on the quay of the inner basin of Ramsgate harbour, filling my pipe with the shavings that I cut from a cake of "hard." I had just descended the worn steps of Jacob's Ladder, and still lingered in its shelter until my pipe should be fairly alight, and when I had finished stuffing the bowl with the fresh-rubbed, clammy shavings, I thrust my hand into the pocket of my monkey jacket for the matches. But the box was not there. I hastily searched other pockets, but, as I expected, without success; for I am methodical in small things, and that box had its abode in that particular pocket.

I was somewhat vexed at the loss, although the thing was of no intrinsic value, for it was only a copper case, into which an ordinary matchbox slipped; but it had been made for me by a friendly shipwright from the sheathing of an old corvette (a portrait of which was etched on the copper), and I set some store by it.

As I walked on, sucking the unlit pipe, I tried to recall the last occasion on which I had used it; and suddenly I remembered having passed it to a collier skipper some evenings ago, in the parlour of the "Hovelling Boat" Inn; so thither I immediately turned my steps.

It must not be supposed that I was, in those days, a frequenter of taverns. But to a young man, deeply in love with the sea, the "Hovelling Boat" had special attractions. It was situated in a little narrow street full of crinkled gables and odd bay windows, and blocked at its end by a medley of masts and spars; a street in which anchors and cables sprawled on the pavements, sidelights glared from ship chandler's windows, and suits of oilskins dangled from projecting poles, as if some fisher of men were lurking inside and had just had a "bite."

The inn itself had a coloured lamp, surmounted by a gilded lugger in full sail, and its cosy parlour abounded in all sorts of sea monsters – piratical-looking fishermen from Gravelines in knitted caps and stockings and mosaic breeches, whose principal patches hinted at sedentary habits; jolly Dutchmen from square-bowed schuyts, pale Scandinavians with colourless hair and faded blue eyes; smacksmen, colliers, and coasters from the "West Country": all foregathered here to smoke and drink and gossip in the lurid dialect of the salt sea.

I had pushed open the door and was making for the parlour, when the landlady spied me and held up her hand.

"I think I've got something of yours, Muster Englefield," she said, reaching up to a shelf. "Doesn't this matchbox belong to you? I found it in the parlour last Tuesday."

"Thank you," I said, seizing the treasure and dropping it into my pocket. "I had come to ask about it. It's an old friend, and I should have been sorry to lose it."

I was turning to go out again when she stopped me once more.

"There's a bit of an unpleasantness going on in there," she said, nodding towards the parlour. "I should be glad if you could find time to sit down there for a few minutes, sir. Perhaps the presence of a stranger and a gentleman might keep them in order."

"Very well," I said. "Send me in a glass of grog and I'll smoke my pipe in the parlour, and hear what they have to say."

As I entered and looked round through the blue haze of tobacco smoke, it was not difficult to see who were the parties to the "unpleasantness" for the inmates of the room, about a dozen in number, lounged on the settles, regarding with placid expectancy two men who occupied separate tables near the fireplace.

They were both mariners of the better class, apparently shipmasters; and one of them – a tall, burly Norwegian with the palest blue eyes and a mass of straw-coloured hair and beard –

stood resting his knuckles on the table while he glared ferociously at his antagonist – a thick-set, powerful man, apparently English, whose swarthy face was made remarkable by a deep scar on the jaw, the contraction of which had drawn his mouth and nose somewhat to one side.

"I ask you again," exclaimed the Norwegian, huskily, "do you say I am a liar?"

The Englishman made no reply, but a curious, sour, one-sided smile spread over his face, giving it a rather sinister appearance.

"Whoy don't ye answer the man, 'nstead o' settin' there a-agravatin' of 'im?" protested a jovial smacksman (who appeared to be attired for a dress rehearsal of "Puss in Boots").

"I have answered him," replied the other gruffly. "I have told him that I have got a smashed channel and he has a dent on his stem; he's lost half a jibboom and I've found one – on my deck."

"What's the row about?" I asked a Cockney bargeman who sat near the door, fondling a pewter pot.

"It's all along of a collision. 'E begun the rumpus," replied the bargeman jerking his head vaguely at the fireplace.

"Which one?"

" 'Im," responded the bargee, nodding again. "That bloke with the kink in 'is dial."

This delicate allusion to the Englishman's facial peculiarity appeared to reach the ears of its subject, for he turned sharply and inquired – "What's that you're saying?"

"I was telling this gentleman what the trouble was about," replied the bargee, meekly, evidently wishing he had clothed his ideas in less allegorical language.

"And what the devil has it got to do with either you or him?" demanded the Englishman.

"Why there y'are. 'Tain't got nothing'; but I'm arst a civil question and I gives a civil answer," and the bargee veiled his countenance with the pewter pot.

"As to me," said I, as persuasively as I could, "I hope you won't take offence at my curiosity, which is really not unnatural, you know."

"I'm not taking any offence as long as you don't interfere with what doesn't concern you. If you want to know what the row was about, I'll tell you – "

"Not here," I urged.

"And why not here?" demanded the other, blazing up into sudden wrath. "D'ye suppose I'm afraid to speak before any putty-faced Dutchman that ever trod the rotten deck of a Baltic sea-knacker? I'll speak where I please and say what I like; and what I mean to say is that these damned Scandinavians are the pest of the high seas. Why, devil take it! They navigate their rickety derelicts as if they'd served their time in Noah's Ark. Perhaps one of 'em did, too," he added, with a sour grin all on one side of his face, "and then I'd lay anything that it was his watch on deck when she got ashore on Mount Ararat."

A chorus of guffaws greeted this sally and threatened to bring the quarrel to a crisis, for the Norwegian, who had reseated himself, now rose, crimson in the face and, thrusting his hand under the skirt of his coat, stepped forward, shouting hoarsely: "You are a dommed liar – a cursed, ugly-faced wrecker, and I am going to show you – "

"Here, Oi say, none o' that!" interposed the jolly smacksman at this juncture, for a broad-bladed "green river" had made its appearance from under the foreign sailor's coat. "Do what ye loike with yer fists, but no cold iron without you want to find yer head jammed in the bight of a rope."

"Let me go!" roared the Norwegian, struggling in the grasp of the smacksman and a couple of sturdy colliers, "let me get at him! I am going to show him something."

"Well, let's see what he's going to show me," said the Englishman, pushing forward with a very ugly expression on his unsymmetrical face.

"Don't be a fool, mate," said the smacksman interposing his massive person between the belligerents, adding in a lower tone, "They've sent for the police, I think."

Thinking this a favourable opportunity to intervene, I laid my hand on the Englishman's arm.

"Come," I said coaxingly, "this won't do, you know. For a man in your position – a stranger in the town, too – to be mixed up in a tavern brawl with people like this," and I nodded vaguely at the company in general. I had no idea what the man's position was, but it seemed a politic thing to say, and so it turned out, for he faced me with a mollified growl that encouraged me to proceed. "I'm sure it wouldn't suit you to be involved in any scandal here. Why not come and have a drink with me somewhere else? Come along. I want to hear all about this."

"Perhaps you're right," he replied in a quieter tone, and was turning towards the door when it suddenly opened and a tall elderly man in a peaked cap and black uniform entered.

"Here's Muster Jenkins," announced the smacksman as the newcomer, raising his hand, inquired in rounded oratorical tones: "What's hall this disgraceful noise and riot about?"

"Out you come!" I exclaimed; and without more ado I seized my new acquaintance by the arm and fairly dragged him out at the door, and hauling him up the passage, shot him out on to the pavement.

"Now, leg it before they come out," I commanded, and my friend having by this time awakened to his position, we made off together for the harbour like a pair of quite exceptionally agile lamplighters, and did not slacken our pace until we were halfway along that stretch of quay known as the Military Road. In this secluded spot, with the dim shapes of the colliers' masts looming above us on one side, and the tall black sail lofts on the other, we halted to listen for the footsteps of pursuers, but all being silent we resumed our progress at a more leisurely pace.

"Have a smoke?" asked my companion as he hoisted out of an enormous side pocket a handful of cigars.

"Thanks," I replied; and then when we had lighted our respective weeds with some stinking Swedish matches from the same receptacle, I ventured to ask: "By the way, what *was* all that row about?"

My companion took his cigar from his mouth and laughed a little shyly.

"The fact is," he said, "I opened the ball by making a confounded fool of myself. You must know, I have a pet aversion – call it prejudice if you like – that pet aversion is Dutchmen, or rather, I should say, Scandinavians."

"Why, I thought they were considered excellent seamen," I said.

"So they may be," he replied. "Anyhow, I don't like 'em, and I am more than usually down on 'em just now, for one of the beggars got aboard of me last Tuesday night and played the deuce with my vessel."

"Indeed!" said I, pricking up my ears.

"Ah! It was about seven bells in the middle watch – half-past three in the morning, you know – and as dark as a vault. We were slipping along with a nice little bit of easterly breeze, just abreast of the East Goodwin light, making for the Downs. It was the mate's watch, and, my mate being a careful man, he had a lookout on each bow; the sidelights were burning brightly, everything was shipshape and Bristol fashion, and nobody dreaming of any danger, when suddenly the port lookout gave a shout, and before anyone could stir, a vessel heaves up out of the darkness, with never a blessed light about her, mind you! And bumps right into us amidships. Her jibboom snapped off in our main shrouds and brought our main t'gallant clattering down about our ears, and then she came grinding along our side clawing about half our bulwarks away with the fluke of her anchor, and tearing our shrouds all to rags."

"And what had her skipper to say for himself?" I asked.

"Say?" shouted my companion. "Why, bless your heart! Before we could get about to speak to him he was off into the darkness without a sign; he might have been a derelict – but he wasn't, for we saw a man at the wheel."

"How did you know he was a Scandinavian?" I inquired with my friends' admitted prejudice in my mind.

"Why you see," he replied, "we always keep a lighted lantern on deck to show to any vessel that may be overhauling us; so when she ran us down, the mate caught up the lantern and threw a glimmer of light on her. We could have spotted her by her deck-load of timber and her jolly old windmill, but the mate managed to get a squint at her stern as she went by and, although he couldn't make out the name, he could see that she belonged to Brevig. Now we hadn't been in Ramsgate twelve hours when in comes a crazy old barque from Brevig with half her jibboom gone and a dent on her stem just the height of our channels. That Dutchman in the pub is her skipper, and he swears his jibboom was carried away a week ago by a steamer, but he won't let us try the broken piece on his stump. So now you understand why I pitched into him."

"Quite. But you'll have a Board of Trade inquiry, won't you?"

"Of course, we shall; in fact, it's on now, and that's why I was such an infernal donkey to quarrel with him; and I am very much obliged to you, sir, for getting me out of that pub before anything unpleasant happened."

He laid a huge hand on my shoulder as he spoke and, in the dim light, his twisted face took on a more pleasant expression than I had thought possible.

"Not a bit of it," I replied; "but that reminds me that we were going to clink a glass together. Where shall we go? The coast will be quite clear by now."

"I'll tell you what," said he. "You come aboard with me, and we'll have a glass and a yarn in the cabin, and let the pubs go to blazes. How will that suit you?"

"I shall be delighted," said I, with truth; for I did not care to be seen in the ordinary taverns of the town, whereas a ship's cabin had an alluring smack of romance to a sea-smitten landsman like myself.

As we talked we had been strolling round the basin, and now, having passed over the second bridge on the Crosswall, made for the gates by the Custom House.

"My craft's berthed in this corner opposite the 'Queen's Head,'" said my new friend. "I'm having a new t'gallant mast fitted, and this berth is handy for the riggers."

As he spoke we turned out of the gates into Harbour Street, and almost at once I perceived, shooting up into the black void, a tall and shapely mast that even in that light I could not fail to recognise.

"Surely," said I, "this is the brig that came in from the Downs some four or five days ago?"

"That's so," replied my companion; "did you see her come in?"

"Yes, and, by Jove! what a beauty she looked in spite of her damaged mainmast."

"You're right," my friend responded, "she's a remarkably pretty model, and the owners don't mind spending a few pounds on keeping her up; and then, of course, a vessel that goes foreign has to be fitted out a little differently from a craft like that," and he nodded superciliously at a grimy, battered collier that lay close by, "that's always mucking about in harbours and rivers round the coast. But here we are – mind your shins on this ladder. Anyone on board, Moloney?"

"No, sorr," replied a tall sailor who was pacing the deck in company with a portly black cat. "Misther Jobling and Misther Darvill have gone to the theayterr, and the new stcheward hasn't come aboard yet."

"All right, Michael," said the Captain, for such I judged him to be; "when the steward comes aboard send him to me."

"Ay, ay, sorr," replied Moloney, smartly touching his cap; and having adroitly hoisted the cat some half-dozen paces along the deck with his foot, he resumed his walk, apostrophising his feline companion in a grumbling bass as he went.

"Will ye kape out o' the fairway, ye great, fat, lazy, lollopin' black divil!" But I noticed that the pair seemed on excellent terms despite the Irishman's rather abrupt manner.

The cabin as we entered from the dark companionway, looked singularly cosy and homelike. A large oil lamp which swung from one of the deck beams shed a cheerful light over the little interior and showed it to be in keeping with the brig's smart design and rig. The panelling was of mahogany and bird's-eye maple, the ceiling was painted a dead white; broad, cushioned lockers surrounded the table – now gay with a crimson cloth – and the aperture of the skylight was covered in by handsome red silk curtains.

"This is my little home," said my host, looking round, somewhat complacently I thought, upon the trim little apartment, "and I bid you welcome in it, Mr – "

"Englefield," said I. "Richard Englefield."

"My name is Bithery," my companion volunteered in return. "Christian name Nicholas, trade or profession master mariner, of Bristol City, at present commander of the brig *Lady Jane*, from Hamburg to the West Coast of Africa." As he, half jokingly, furnished these details, the Captain's face again lighted up with the singularly genial smile that I had observed before, in which its trifling deformity was forgotten.

"Sit ye down there on that locker," said he, and proceeded to make the most formidable preparations for a carouse, reaching out of a cupboard in the bulkhead a veritable battalion of bottles – high-shouldered Dutch bottles, tall brown stone German jars, squat bloated bottles of unknown nationality, and lastly a bottle of old French brandy. Then he discharged a cargo of cigars from his coat pocket, and taking a couple of tumblers and a water bottle from the swing tray that hung above the table, he sat down with a sigh of content.

"There now," he said, "out of that lot we ought to be able to get a drink. There's German gin, Squareface, and the Lord knows what else, but if you take my advice you'll stick to that cognac – it's the right stuff."

I charged my tumbler with this highly-recommended beverage and, the Captain having followed my example, we sat and smoked in silence for some time.

"So you like my little ship?" said the skipper presently.

"I fell in love with her the first time I saw her," I replied. "I've never seen a brig at all like her before."

"I don't suppose you have," rejoined the Captain. "Probably there isn't another like her afloat, for they don't build clippers of this size nowadays. You see, our owner is a bit of a sportsman and this brig is his fancy. By the way, you're in the shipping line yourself, aren't you?"

"Not I," I answered, smiling a little bitterly, "I wish I were. No, I'm a clerk in Jobson's Bank."

"My eye!" exclaimed the skipper. "I couldn't stand that. Sitting in a cellar all day counting other people's money. What made you take that job on?"

"Well, it was this way. When I was about twelve my father was offered a post in the bank, so he came down here from London and brought me with him. Then, about eight years ago, he was taken off suddenly by influenza and, as my mother had died when I was quite a child I was left high and dry to shift for myself; so I applied at the bank for some kind of work and was taken on as junior clerk – and there I've been ever since, and pretty sick of it I get sometimes, I can tell you."

"I expect you do," said the Captain, regarding me meditatively through a haze of tobacco smoke. "It must be a dog's life. Why don't you chuck it?"

"What could I do?" I asked.

"Well, what *can* you do?" the Captain inquired by way of a Scotch answer.

"I can write a decent hand," said I. "I can keep books of a kind, can speak French and German fairly – I pick up languages rather easily – I can sail a boat and I can build one, too, if necessary."

"Can ye, though?" said the Captain, pricking up his ears, as I thought.

"Yes. I built myself a little canoe yawl, and I sail her about here a good deal. On Sundays in summer I often take her right round the Goodwins – start in the early morning and come home in the dusk. And I made every bit of her myself in off times: hull, spars, sails, blocks – everything but just the iron fittings."

"Did ye now?" said the Captain approvingly. "Sails and all? You're a pretty handy man then."

"Yes, I'm pretty handy at wood and metalwork and such like, but, of course, that doesn't help one much towards getting a living."

"No, I suppose it doesn't. It's useful though. What should you like to do if you had your choice?"

"Oh," said I, "if I could see a chance I would go abroad and see foreign lands and knock about the world for a time. I've been on the lookout for a billet of the kind for years, but nothing ever seems to turn up."

The Captain remained silent for some time after this, surrounding himself with a dense cloud of smoke and regarding me as attentively as if I had been some rare and curious work of art.

At length he removed his pipe from his mouth and, still regarding me fixedly, said: "How should you like to come with me this trip?"

The question staggered me for a moment, but recovering myself I asked: "Do you mean to Africa?"

"Yes," said the Captain.

"There is nothing," I replied eagerly, "that I should like better, but I don't see what use I should be on board. I'm no seaman, and you don't want clerks on board ship."

"Well, the fact is we do in this trade," said Captain Bithery. "You see, this isn't just a vessel with a cargo consigned to a merchant at a given port. This is a floating shop. The cargo is our own, and we sell it where we can, and how we can, mostly to small native traders, and we trade and swap and chaffer for the produce with which we fill up for the homeward trip. That's where you would come in. Most of the actual trading was managed last trip by our steward, who was practically the purser; but he got typhoid, so we had to leave him at Hamburg, and although we are taking on a new steward here, he will only be a sort of cook and cabin steward – we ship a black cook on the Coast – and he doesn't know anything about the trade. Now, I've taken a bit of a fancy to you, and I think you and I could get on together pretty comfortably, so if you like to ship with me to help me keep the books and work the trade, I've got a spare berth that you can have, and I'll pay you eight pounds a month and a commission on any profits you make; and you shall be at liberty to leave the brig at any time if anything should turn up that would suit you better."

This was unquestionably a very handsome proposal, and so much in excess of any expectations I had formed that, without pausing to give the matter any further consideration, I accepted the Captain's offer with many expressions of gratitude and delight.

"Very well, then," said the skipper, pushing the bottle across to my side of the table, "that's settled. You come with us this jaunt and, as you must have some title on the articles, we'll call you the purser, although that's only what you'd call an honorary title, you understand. So here's a health to the new purser," and as I mixed a fresh glass with a trembling hand, Captain Bithery emptied his tumbler at a draught and slapped it down on the table with a flourish.

Thus was the curtain rung down on the first act of my life's little drama. A few words spoken, like a magic incantation, had changed my identity; and when I scrambled up the ladder on the quay as the harbour clock was striking twelve, I barked the shins, not of Mr Englefield of Jobson's Bank, but of the purser of the *Lady Jane*.

Chapter Two
In Which I Set Out for Africa

It was a soft sunny morning when, some ten days later, I stood on the white deck of the *Lady Jane*, taking, very earnestly, and indeed with unexpected emotion, my last look at the town and harbour of Ramsgate.

The brig lay at the mouth of the eastern entrance to the basin, and already, with the gentle northerly breeze filling her broad white topsails, she was beginning to tug impatiently at the great hawser by which she was tethered to a stone post on the quay. On board all was bustle and apparent confusion. Chain sheets rattled, blocks squealed, coils of rope thumped on the deck, and the branch pilot rushed about the vessel, as Moloney said, "like a dog at a fair"; while on the quay, a stout red-jowled harbour official stood and bellowed unceasingly – apparently from sheer excess of animal spirits.

"Are ye all clear there?" shouted the pilot, darting on to the forecastle to take a last look at the headsails.

"Are ye all clear aft – here, you! leave that trys'l be – we don't want him yet. Are ye all clear?"

"All clear," growled the mate.

"Cast off the sternfast, Mr Giles," roared the pilot, and the official, having deliberately hitched the great bowline off the post, announced that it was "All gone" in a voice like the report of a forty-eight pounder.

As the hawser fell with a splash into the water, the quay with the little crowd of onlookers began slowly to move away – as it seemed to me; and as the brig gathered way the whole scene around seemed to glide past like the shifting picture from a magic lantern. All the familiar objects – the clock tower, the row of freshly-painted buoys on the quay, the sun-lighted obelisk and the tall church steeple, the tide ball up on the cliff and the crowded masts in the basin, began to fade away and grow small in the increasing distance; while a musical tinkle arose from under the vessel's bows, and the water astern began to be dimpled with eddies and tiny whirlpools. Then for a moment the lighthouse loomed up high above our deck, and the grey pierheads, lined with a throng of gaily-dressed girls, slipped quietly by and, leaving the dead water of the harbour, we met the soft swell of the bay, which the *Lady Jane* saluted with a stately curtsey.

I stood by the taffrail gazing, with my heart in my mouth, at the receding land; the clustering town above the white cliff – now grown so strangely dear – and the dwindling harbour, and rapidly reviewing the events that had occurred since my momentous meeting the Captain Bithery.

What a time it had been! How I had rushed off on the following morning to emancipate myself from the thraldom of Jobson's! With what glee I had run up to London, on the Captain's advice, to buy an outfit for the voyage, and how I had swaggered down the Minories with the rolling gait of a seasoned buccaneer, followed by a porter staggering under the burden of a colossal seaman's chest. How the said chest had been triumphantly flung open in the *Lady Jane's* cabin and made to disgorge piles of storm suits, sail needles, palms, jumpers, dungarees, marlin spikes, boat compasses, sheath knives, pistols, until the Captain fell back on the locker and fairly shouted with laughter. All these things surged through my mind until the voice of the branch pilot wishing the Captain a pleasant voyage as he stepped down into his boat, recalled me to the fact that our voyage was really begun and that the wide ocean lay before us.

On the incidents of the voyage it is not my intention to dwell. It was on the whole an eminently prosperous voyage, and for that very reason singularly devoid of incident, although to me, fresh from the grinding routine of an office, every minute of the day brought with it something new, surprising and delightful. For hours at a time would I pace the heaving deck listening to the song of the breeze as it hummed through the rigging or murmured in the hollows of the sails; gazing with unwearied eyes at the ever new prospect of sunny sky and incredibly blue sea that stretched away on all sides like a moving mass of liquid sapphire. The dainty pink "Portuguese men-of-war" that drifted past in endless processions, and the fantastic forms of the flying fish, were wonders that never staled; the porpoises that gambolled around our bows seemed like the creatures from some Eastern fable, while at night, the glitter of the moonbeams on the water and the sparkle of the Noctiluca in the vessel's shadow furnished visions of beauty beyond my wildest dreams.

Yet, novel and delightful as it was to me, the voyage was, as I have said, quite uneventful. The north-easterly breeze with which we started carried us to the chops of the Channel, and then veering round to the south-west gave us a fortnight of what the Captain grumblingly described as "wind-jamming." At length, as we approached the thirtieth parallel, we felt the first breath of the north-east trade wind, and thereafter a fresh draught poured constantly over our quarter until we were well south of the latitude of Cape Verde. In all this time the only land we sighted was the peak of Tenerife, which one day lay on the extreme verge of the horizon and which I at first took to be a bank of cloud.

One morning when we were between five and six weeks out, on coming out of my berth I found the Captain seated at the table thoughtfully contemplating a perspiring slab of corned pork which lay before him, while he slowly stirred his coffee.

"You lazy dog," he said, smiling, pleasantly nevertheless as I entered, and pushing the dish of sliced pork over to the place where my plate was set. "You idle ruffian, do you know that it's nearly two bells and that we made the land at daybreak?"

"Made the land!" I exclaimed excitedly. "Why, I didn't know you expected to see land for another week."

"We might have seen it any time this last ten days, for we've been sailing parallel to the coast ever since we rounded Cape Palmas, and never much more than twenty miles off."

"Whereabouts are we now?" I asked.

"Just passing Cape St Paul. Oh, you needn't excite yourself," for I was rising to go on deck, "there's nothing to see, only a thin grey line with a few coconuts like pins stuck into the horizon. It's a scurvy-looking coast, this."

"When do you expect to make your port?" I inquired eagerly.

"Port!" he exclaimed contemptuously, "there are no ports here, my lad; just open roadsteads with a swell that's enough to roll the sticks out of a vessel, and a surf pounding the beach that would kick the stuffing out of an Institution lifeboat."

"That's jolly," I remarked.

"Ah, you'll say so when you have to go ashore through it. But to return to the 'port' question; we shall be off Quittáh in about an hour – sit down, man for God's sake! and drink your coffee like a Christian – and as a good bit of the cargo is going ashore there, we shall have our anchor down maybe for a week or two!"

I took a gulp at the hot coffee and began to stow away the corned pork and biscuit with a speed that did not escape the Captain's notice, for he remarked with a grin: "Don't gobble your grub like that, Englefield. Africa'll keep, never fear. Besides, lad, I want to have a bit of serious talk with you."

I slowed down my mastication and indicated that I was all attention.

"Well, now," said the Captain, "you remember what I told you about this trip – that our business was more to trade than to carry freight. We've got some tons of stuff for a merchant here in Quittáh – a Portuguese named Pereira – and a biggish consignment for a German down at Bagidá; but more than half the cargo is our own, and we've got to turn our goods into produce by trading on our own hook. Well, you see, most of the trading has got to be done ashore, for the niggers won't bring their produce on board through the surf, nor will they come on board to buy our stuff when there are stores ashore where they can buy, so the governor has made arrangements with Pereira to hire a store at Quittáh by the lagoon side close to the market place, and I have got to stock that store – or factory, as they call it out here – with trade goods and put somebody in charge of it to sell the goods and buy the produce.

"Now, my lad, you're very useful to me on board ship; you can take your trick at the wheel with any of them, and you can go aloft and hand a sail if need be, but, thanks to the Boss we're not short-handed aboard, whereas we *are* a trifle short for the shore work. So I've been wondering whether you'd care to take a spell ashore and look after the factory for a while. It would be a bit of a change for you, and you'd make something in the way of commission, besides seeing the country, which you seem anxious to do."

"Of course, I know nothing about the trade," I objected.

"Of course you don't; but I can very soon put you up to all that you need know. You'll have the store well stocked with Manchester goods, gin, guns, powder, knives, beads and trash of that kind, and you'll have a chest of cash, say a hundred pounds – all in silver and mostly in threepenny bits (for the niggers won't touch copper money, and don't understand anything but a dollar or a threepenny piece) to carry on with. When the bush niggers come in with their produce, you'll buy it at a fixed rate and take all of it that you can get – palm oil, kernels, copra, rubber (especially rubber), ground nuts and any oddments, such as scrivelloes, ebony or copal, that may turn up. Then, when you have bought them out, you'll let 'em browse about the store and look at your goods, and you'll have to keep your weather eye lifting so that they don't hook the toys and mizzle without paying. If you work 'em properly they'll spend all you've paid 'em for the produce, and go off as pleased as Punch with their cargo of gimcracks. I know what you're thinking," he continued, seeing that

I hung back. "You don't consider it quite the ticket for a gentleman to sell gin to a parcel of naked niggers."

I laughed and perhaps reddened a little, for he had pretty accurately gauged my thoughts.

"I expect it's pretty awful stuff," I said evasively.

"There you are wrong," he replied. "Cheap as it is – I shouldn't like to tell you what we gave for it at Hamburg – but it is as good gin as you could wish to drink, supposing you wished to drink any at all. The mystery is how they do it at the price. And as to serving in the factory, I am sure you needn't mind that; every produce buyer has to do it, and there are some excellent fellows in the trade. But turn it over and let me know what you think about it, and let us go on deck and have a look around."

The scene on deck betokened the occurrence of something unusual, for the whole ship's company was assembled, the men gathered in a little knot on the forecastle and the two mates pacing the poop in earnest conversation, all eyes being directed over the port bow where a stretch of low land was visible at a distance of some three miles.

Above the lee bulwark the head of Moloney was visible as he stood in the main chains heaving the hand lead, and his faithful companion, the cat, sat on the rail above him and gravely superintended the operation.

"Whisht!" whistled Moloney as he whirled the lead round. "Will you take that black chucklehead of yourn out of the road before ye get it knocked off;" then as the lead plumped into the water and he gathered up the slack of the line, he sang out in his mellow Irish baritone: "By the deep – eight."

Six weeks of unvaried sea and sky makes the sight of any land welcome, and so we all gazed shoreward with a feeling of pleasure, although we looked upon nothing more than the ill-omened coast of the Bight of Benin.

And an agreeable enough picture it made, with the deep blue sky, the bright yellow streak of beach lace-edged with a white fringe of surf, and the low-lying land covered with dense soft-looking foliage of dark bluish green.

"That's Jella-Koffi that we're passing now," said the Captain, pointing to what looked like a large park or wood, "all coconuts, thousands of palms – we ought to get some copra from there."

"How far is Quittáh from here?" I asked.

"There it is," he replied, pointing to another grove of vegetation a mile or so further east; "we shall open the fort in a few minutes."

We continued to approach the land obliquely, guided by Moloney's probings of the deep and taking in sail by degrees, until the veil of foliage rolling aside disclosed a white building of some size, above which I made out with my glasses the Union Jack fluttering from a tall flagstaff. At this moment Moloney sang out, with some emphasis, as I thought, "Quarter less – six," on which the brig's head was put up into the wind and the anchor chain rattled out through the hawsepipe for the first time since we sailed out of Ramsgate harbour.

That afternoon, as the Captain had to go ashore to transact some business with the District Commissioner, relating to the duties on our part of the cargo, he proposed that I should accompany him that I might see some of the sights of Quittáh and make the acquaintance of Pereira. To this I readily agreed, and soon after lunch the skipper and I took our seats in a couple of Madeira chairs that were lashed to the thwarts of a surfboat that Pereira had sent out for us in charge of his coloured agent, a dark mulatto named Isaac Vanderpuye. By Vanderpuye we were assured that the surf was as quiet as a lamb today, which gave me the impression that the African lamb must be a beast of an exceedingly boisterous temperament, for after being most infernally buffeted and shaken up by the heavy swell we were finally shot out on the beach drenched to the skin with salt water.

The glare on the beach was blinding and the heat terrific, for the dry sand was so baked by the sun that the air rose from it all in a tremble, but after a few minutes' laborious scrambling over the loose shifting surface, we suddenly entered an avenue which, by the abrupt contrast, seemed as dark and cool as a cloister. It was formed by two rows of wild fig trees which, arching overhead, enclosed a species of tunnel, the deep green roof of which was lighted by innumerable shafts of golden sunlight, and from the interlacing branches there hung down great stalactite-like masses of brown aerial roots. As we sauntered up the avenue, gazing around with a seaman's delight at its umbrageous beauty, we passed numerous groups of native soldiers, barefooted ragamuffins dressed in threadbare blue serge, squatting on the ground, gravely engaged in a kind of primitive chess which they played with large beans on squares scratched upon smooth patches of earth with a pointed stick.

The end of the avenue brought us out opposite the front of the crazy, weatherbeaten fort, from one bastion of which the tall flagstaff bent and shook in the wind, and at the wide gateway, where a barefooted sentry stood on guard, I left the Captain to pursue his business while I strolled with Vanderpuye into the town.

As I walked through the streets (if I can apply so dignified a name to the irregular alleys by which the town was intersected) I stared about at the strange and novel sights that presented themselves on all sides with the wonder and curiosity of the raw country bumpkin that I was; for it is to be remembered that I stepped, as it were, straight from the quiet little English seaport into this strange and remote African town with a transition as abrupt as I had been transported thither in an instant by some miracle-working jinn. So I walked on like one in a dream by the side of my conductor – who, I may mention, was tastefully attired in a suit of crimson-flowered chintz and wore a white helmet and carpet slippers – under strange broadleaved trees and rattling coconut palms, past mud-built native hovels and whitewashed stores, pausing now and again to watch the groups of black people under the shady trees and continually questioning the grinning Vanderpuye.

We passed several Europeans – pale-faced, depressed-looking men with square-cut beards, evidently Germans – all dressed in white drill, with pipe-clayed helmets and red cummerbunds, who gazed at me with languid curiosity; but of none of them did my guide take any notice until, turning a corner into a broader thoroughfare, we suddenly encountered a white man of quite different appearance, at whom I stared with renewed astonishment.

He was a tall, elderly man with a fine white beard cut to a point, and a face that was singularly grave and dignified in cast. But his dress, which in another place might have seemed eminently appropriate, was the occasion of my surprise, for it consisted of a suit of black broadcloth with a wide-skirted frock coat, a chimney-pot hat of patriarchal mould, and polished black boots, and he carried a neatly-rolled black silk umbrella. Altogether his appearance was even more suggestive of the agency of some sportive jinn than my own, for he might have been picked up just as he stood in Oxford Street and dropped an instant later in the middle of Quittáh.

"This is Mr Pereira," said Vanderpuye, as the stranger removed his hat with a flourish and bowed solemnly to me.

"You're from the *Lady Jane*, I perceive," said he glancing at the house-badge on my white cap and speaking in almost perfect English.

I replied that I was, and explained that the Captain proposed to join us as soon as he had finished his business with the Commissioner.

"Then," said Mr Pereira, "we will walk to my house and wait for him."

So we resumed our walk through the hot, sandy street amidst crowds of naked, black urchins and groups of small shaggy short-haired sheep, which bleated stridently and quarrelled for scraps of offal – dry plantain skins, shreds of sugar cane, and even fragments of putrid fish – which they disinterred from the grimy, heated sand.

In the course of about five minutes we arrived at Pereira's house, which abutted upon a narrow street or lane, along one side of which a row of broadleaved wild fig trees cast a deep and grateful shade.

The house was a two-storeyed building of whitewashed brick, the lower or ground floor forming the trading store, over which were living-rooms surrounded by a wooden verandah.

At the entrance to the stairway Vanderpuye took his leave, and Pereira and I ascended to the "hall" or principal living-room, where my host handed me, with a bow, into a luxurious easychair; and having blown a shrill blast upon a whistle which he drew from his pocket, begged me to excuse him for a few minutes while he despatched some business that demanded his attention in the store.

Left to myself, I gazed about at my new surroundings with uncommon satisfaction, for, accustomed as I had been to the narrow proportions of the brig's tiny cuddy, the lofty, spacious apartment in which I now sat appeared quite magnificent, and as my eye took in the various details – the floor covered with handsome matting, the wide hospitable chairs, the shining table with its bowl of flowers, the little painted sideboard groaning under huge dishes of bananas, soursops and mangoes, the perspiring watercooler that hung in the open window, and, above all, the charming vista of blue-green foliage, glossy-leafed plantains and feathery coconut palms – I felt that the prospect of a few months ashore was not so alarming after all.

My meditations were shortly interrupted by the entry of a barefooted native servant who carried a pot of steaming coffee. The man grinned amiably as he entered, and remarked, "Mawnin' sah!" having made which concise but irrelevant remark – it being about five o'clock in the afternoon – he laid out the coffee service on the table, fished a tin of crackers out of the sideboard, and with another grin, flopped out of the room. He had barely disappeared when the cheerful notes of Captain Bithery's voice were heard on the stairs, and in another moment that gentleman entered with Pereira.

"So, you've found your way here, have you?" he remarked, slapping me on the shoulder. "Quite at home you look too in that chair. By Jingo! but that coffee smells good! We don't catch any sniffs like this out of the *Lady Jane*'s caboose, hey?"

"No, I expect you do not," replied Pereira, as he filled our cups. "I have tasted ship's coffee, and it was – well, it was not like this." He smiled apologetically and handed the condensed milk to the skipper.

"I'll wager it wasn't," agreed the Captain, smacking his lips and sipping the hot fluid daintily from a spoon; "real good stuff this is. Not native?"

"Grown at Akropong," answered Pereira.

"Basel Mission?" inquired Bithery.

"No. A friend of mine has a plantation there, and I get the coffee from him. I've a couple of hundred bags in the store down below now if you'd like to have some."

A knowing grin spread itself over the starboard side of Captain Bithery's face.

"There's a cunning old fox for you," he said, turning to me. "Before I've been in his house five minutes he begins shoving his wares under my nose and trying to trade. Oh! you're a downy old bird, Pereira."

The old man smiled deprecatingly and shrugged his shoulders, remarking that good coffee was selling very well at home just now, and eventually, after some haggling, the whole two hundred bags were accepted as the first instalment of the *Lady Jane*'s homeward cargo. The conversation now drifted into strictly commercial channels, being chiefly occupied with the disposal of the *Lady Jane*'s cargo, and I noticed that the Captain glanced at me from time to time as he talked, and conjectured that he was wondering how I was impressed by what I had seen of Africa. That this conjecture of mine was correct, was made evident when Pereira presently left us, to pay a visit to the store, for the Captain turned to me and asked a little anxiously: "Well, Englefield, what do you think of Quittáh?"

"It doesn't seem a bad sort of place at all," I replied.

"I suppose," the Captain continued after a pause, "you haven't thought any more of what I spoke about this morning?"

"Yes, I have," I answered, "and I have decided that I don't mind staying ashore for a month or two and working the store."

"Have ye now?" exclaimed Bithery, jumping up and seizing my hand. "I am delighted to hear you say so, for if you will take charge of the stuff ashore, I shall be relieved of a great responsibility. You see, old man, there's nobody else on board that I could trust with the goods and the money, and of course I know nothing about any of these shore chaps; so I take this as really kind of you. I'll tell Pereira that you're going to stay with him, shall I?"

"By all means," I replied, with another complacent glance round the airy, comfortable room; "that is, if he is willing to put me up."

"Oh, he'll be willing enough," rejoined the Captain, and Pereira returning at this moment, the arrangement was completed out of hand, much to the old gentleman's apparent satisfaction.

That night I slept but little, for a variety of causes kept me restless and wakeful. In the first place the large square bed, which was enclosed in a mosquito curtain that flapped and rustled in the wind, had an irritating way of keeping perfectly level and stationary – a state of things that now seemed quite abnormal and surprising. Then the night air was filled with new and unfamiliar sounds. Instead of the rhythmical creaking of a wooden ship, the song of the breeze among sails and rigging, the squeal of parrel or sheave, and the grinding of the rudder, the stillness was broken into by the "churr" of countless insects, the monotonous whistle of a large bat, the muffled boom of the surf, and the shrill falsetto of a native dog. And, lastly, my mind was in a whirl with the thoughts and speculations concerning the new phase of life to which the morrow was to introduce me and which I was indeed still turning over when the bugle from the Hausa lines announced the coming of the day, and the dawn began to filter in between the jalousies of my window.

Chapter Three

I Hear Strange Stories and Vague Rumours

Of the details of my life during the time that I remained in charge of the store it is not my intention to speak, for, although every day brought with it some new incident which interested me then as it does now to recall, yet few of the events of my busy and laborious life had any relation to those subsequent adventures and strange occurrences which it is the purpose of this narrative to describe.

I shall therefore content myself by giving a brief account of my manner of life at Quittáh, and of the one or two events that determined my subsequent destiny.

When I first took charge of the store, being ignorant alike of all the native languages and of the value of both the trade goods that I sold and the produce that I was to buy, the Captain secured for me the assistance of Vanderpuye, who, although a Fanti by birth, had been settled many years in Quittáh. But in a week I was able to manage the business alone, or, at least, with the aid of one native assistant only.

It was a curious life, less distasteful than I had expected, but very hard work, for I had to be in the store soon after daybreak and remained until near sunset, with only a short interval at midday.

I would earnestly recommend any explorer who wishes to attain to an intimate knowledge of the people amongst whom he is dwelling, to open a store and trade with them; for by so doing he will obtain an acquaintance with their language, appearance, dress, habits, tastes, disposition, and the natural productions of their country, which it is practically impossible to reach under any other circumstances. To the trader, as to one engaged in a rational and intelligible pursuit, the native exhibits himself as he is, without any more reserve or deception than the particular transaction seems to require, while to the professed explorer he shows himself full of suspicion and perversity. The mere pursuit of knowledge he neither understands nor believes in, but attributes to the investigator some hidden and sinister motive for his inquiries; whereas the actions and objects of the trader, differing in nowise from those of native merchants, are perfectly comprehensible to him. Hence the trader is treated by the native with a frank familiarity in great contrast to the cautious reserve that is exhibited towards the traveller, the official or the missionary.

It thus happened that, before I had been ashore a month, I had begun to get some insight into the manners and customs of the negro as applied to commerce. My natural facility in picking up languages, too, to which I have already referred, stood me in good stead, for I soon acquired a quite useful collection of phrases in the local dialects, particularly in the barbarous and unmusical Efé language which was spoken around Quittáh, and the hardly more euphonious Adángme of the people who came from beyond the Volta River.

I also began to learn, but in a more systematic manner, the simpler and really melodious language of Hausa, of which Pereira had on his shelves a dictionary and some selections by Dr Schön. This was indeed less useful than the local tongues, but I was not without the means of exercising it, for it was spoken by the native troops, or Hausa constabulary, who were constantly making small purchases at the store, and by the itinerant merchants from the interior, whose visits were somewhat rare, but who, when they did come, were rather extensive buyers.

It was from one of these travelling merchants that I received the first of the series of impulses that finally sent me wandering into the unknown interior. This man, a Hausa named Amádu Dandaúra, arrived at Quittáh when I had been there about two months, in company with his two sons and a small caravan of slaves.

He was a man of some substance, and as he came day after day to purchase goods for the markets of the interior, I used to have a mat spread for him in the store, on which he would sit and make his purchases in the leisurely, chaffering manner so characteristic of the native trader.

But it was impossible to keep his attention fixed on business matters, for, being a perfectly indefatigable talker and having apparently had many strange adventures, he used to collect quite a considerable audience of his countrymen from the Fort and the lines to listen to his spirited narrations. While he was discoursing in this manner I would often, if I had leisure, lounge hard by and listen, trying to follow the conversation but never succeeding, for, not only was my acquaintance with the language insufficient, but, as I presently discovered, neither Amádu nor the soldiers pronounced the words as they were spelt in my books.

But although unable to make out the matter of Amádu's discourse, I succeeded in picking out one or two phrases, which, as they often recurred and were received by the listeners with a great show of surprise, I conjectured to be an important part of the merchant's story.

One of these phrases was "Matári 'n seliki" or "King's treasure house"; another was "Makáfi dayáwa," "a number of blind men." When I had with some difficulty translated these phrases and committed to memory some detached words which seemed to be the names of places – such as Diádasu, Tánosu, Insúta, and Kumási – I had learned all that I was destined to learn of Amádu's story, for my assistant, Daniel Kudjo, spoke not a word of Hausa, and few of the Hausas spoke more than half a dozen words of English; and thus my curiosity, which had been strongly aroused by these mysterious phrases, had to remain unsatisfied.

But a curious light was thrown on the subject by Pereira in the course of a conversation that I had with him one evening.

It was my invariable custom at this time, on returning home from the store, heated and fatigued with the endless weighing of rubber, kernels and copra, and measuring of countless demijohns of palm oil in the glaring compound, or rummaging amongst the bales and cases in the store, to spend the long evenings, after my bath and dinner, lolling in a great chair, pipe in mouth, while the old gentleman reclined in a hammock and entertained me with his reminiscences of life in West Africa.

We were talking on this occasion about the Ashanti war, then just concluded, and were discussing the indemnity of sixty thousand ounces of gold claimed by the British Government.

"It seems an enormous sum," I remarked. "Nearly two hundred and forty thousand pounds. One would not expect the king of a barbarous tribe like the Ashantis to possess such a reserve of wealth as that."

"Probably he does not," replied Pereira, "and probably the indemnity will never be paid. Perhaps," he added with a dry smile, "your judicious Government never intended it to be paid. A debt that cannot be met is sometimes of great use to the creditor."

"Then you think that the king of Ashanti doesn't possess sixty thousand ounces?"

"Who knows?" replied Pereira, deliberately rolling a cigarette. "One hears wonderful stories of the store of gold in the Royal Treasury at Bantamá, but then no one has seen it, and an African's idea of a large sum is so different from that of a rich European Government."

He lighted his cigarette and stared absently at a gecko that was creeping stealthily along the ceiling towards a corpulent black moth.

"It is probable," he remarked presently, after blowing a cloud of smoke up towards the unconscious gecko, "that there are really large hoards of gold scattered about the country, but these are not available for the king's use."

"How is that?" I asked.

"Why, you see, among the African tribes the custom exists of making over certain treasures to particular fetishes. Here a rich gold mine is shut down and given to one fetish; here a river that has alluvial gold in its bed is made sacred to another fetish; here a mountain containing a rich vein of quartz is 'busum' – sacred; here a temple has a hoard of gold raised from the sacred mine, or washed from the sacred river. If you travel in the interior you will constantly meet with fetish mountains – you can see one, the Adáklu mountain, from this verandah on a clear day – and every river of any size that you cross is sacred to some fetish or other; and probably nearly all those rivers and mountains are rich in gold."

"It is a curious custom," I remarked.

"Not so very unlike our own," the old man replied, with a dry smile, that spread out a fan of wrinkles on either temple; "think of the South American churches that your countrymen looted; think of the shrines in my own poor country, and think of the fetish treasures that your king Henry laid his strong hands upon. No, Englefield, man is much the same all the world over – love, war, greed and superstition are the forces that move him, whether his skin be white, black, red or yellow, and whether his house is in the frozen north or the sunny tropics."

I was amused at this philosophic outburst on the part of my host, who, having delivered himself of these truths, resumed his abstracted observation of the gecko.

That reptile, having captured the moth, proceeded to devour it, scattering fragments of its wings down on to the table; after which it suddenly started in pursuit of another gecko, presumably a female, which had made its appearance on the ceiling.

Pereira nodded at the lizard.

"See, Englefield," he said, "even the little housemaster is no different. He has his business to attend to like us, and now that he has filled his belly, he finds leisure to attend to the affairs of his cold little heart."

I laughed at this mild pleasantry, but as the old gentleman appeared to be wandering away from the subject of our talk I gently led him back to it.

"Is the situation of any of these fetish hoards known?" I asked.

"To the natives a good many of them are," replied Pereira. "You see, they are quite safe; no native would incur the displeasure of the fetish by attempting a robbery – not even an invading tribe, for the invader believes in and respects the local fetish. Of course, towards the white men the natives preserve a good deal of secrecy, but still I have heard indirectly of one or two of the sacred hoards."

"Have you really?" I exclaimed.

"Yes. The accounts have been generally rather vague, but one or two were quite clear, although I can't vouch for their truth. It is said, for instance, that by the side of the caravan road from Ashánti to Kong there is a mass of gold sticking up out of the ground like an anthill. Nobody can touch it because it is guarded by a fetish who would instantly destroy the sight of any person who should attempt to seize it; and this, it seems, is firmly believed even by the Mahommedans of Kong. Then there is a queer story about the Aboási pool near the source of the Tano River in the north of Ashánti. It is said that the headwaters gush out of a great rock with tusks like an elephant – whence the name Abo-áse, under the rock – and fall into a still pool, the floor of which is thickly coated with gold dust. Now all this gold is sacred to the great Tano fetish (or abúsum, to speak more correctly), and it is said to be protected from possible pilferers by a bodyguard of huge, ferocious fishes, which swim about in the depth of the pool."

"That sounds pretty far-fetched," I remarked.

"It does," agreed Pereira, "although it doesn't do to be too sceptical, you know. However, the rest of the story is, I must admit, quite incredible. It is reported that near Aboási is a large cavern which forms the treasure house of the Tano fetish, and here the fetish priests live with a number of slaves or prisoners, all of whom have had their eyes put out. Once a month a party of the prisoners are taken on to the lake in a canoe and are made to dredge up the gold-bearing sand in copper buckets, and when they have got up a sufficient quantity they are taken back to the cave. There it is supposed that they spend their time in washing out the gold under the direction of the priests, and working it into ingots or ornaments, and it is said that the treasure accumulated in the cave is enormous. Twice a year the King of Ashánti is reported to send to Aboási a party of his executioners with a fresh batch of prisoners whose eyes are put out as soon as they arrive. Then a similar number of the oldest prisoners are killed as a sacrifice to the fetish, and their bodies thrown into the lake to the sacred fishes; after which the executioners receive a tribute of the fetish gold for the king, and return to Kumási."

"You don't suppose that there is any truth in that story, do you?" I asked, as Pereira finished his recital.

"I certainly do not imagine it to be true," he replied. "But as I have said, we should not be too incredulous, for the longer one lives in Africa the more does one realise that it is a land of wonders."

This story of Pereira's, wildly improbably as it was, made a considerable impression upon me, for not only is it true, as my host had remarked, that Africa is a land of strange and unexpected happenings, but to a newcomer like myself, the novelty of the surroundings, and the total contrast to the conditions of life in prosaic, workaday England, produce an impression of unreality that vitiates the standard of probability. I recalled, too, the mysterious references of Amádu Dandaúra to the "treasure house" and the "blind men" of Tánosu, and bitterly regretted that I had not taken the opportunity of learning from him more about the weird and dreadful cavern of Aboási if such a place really existed.

Chapter Four
I Visit a Graveyard and Meet a Blind Man

I do not know whether in the preceding pages I have made the reader understand what manner of place Quittáh is. Probably I have not, and a few words of description may be useful before proceeding further.

Quittáh, then, is one of a row of towns or villages dotted along a narrow tongue of sand which stretches from the mouth of the River Volta with a few interruptions to the Niger Delta. On one side of this isthmus is the ocean and on the other a chain of large lagoons; and so narrow is the space separating sea and lagoon that, in many places, travellers proceeding along the latter in canoes can not only hear the boom of the surf upon the beach outside, but can see the white crests of the waves over the low-lying shore.

Thus from the peculiarity of its position Quittáh was very much like a small island. From the sea one was cut off by the dangerous surf; from the adjacent villages of Jella-Koffi and Vojé by the loose, shifting sand which it was almost impossible to walk upon, while between us and the mainland the lagoon spread out like an inland sea, right away to the horizon.

This mainland, of which I heard occasional reports from native traders, became to me a source of continually increasing curiosity. From the lagoonside market, where I often stood watching the fleets of canoes unloading their little freights of produce on to the "hard," it was, as I have said, invisible, and the lagoon stretched, an unbroken waste of water as far as the eye could see.

But from our verandah a few palms could be seen upon the other side, their heads just standing above the horizon, while on very clear days one could discern the dim and shadowy shape of the Adáklu – a solitary mountain some seventy miles distant in the interior.

It happened one evening that as I stood on the verandah, telescope in hand, dividing my attention between the cloudlike mountain and the fleet of canoes returning homewards from the market, Pereira came out, and flinging himself into a squeaking Madeira chair, began to roll a cigarette, regarding me meanwhile with an indulgent smile.

"I often wonder, Englefield," he said presently, "what it is that you are continually spying at through that telescope. Surely the lagoon and the canoes and the palms and the pelicans are pretty commonplace objects by this time, and I think they comprise the entire landscape."

"Certainly," I replied, "the outlook is a little monotonous; but yet somehow it attracts me, and I find myself continually wondering what there is behind the horizon there."

"Then wonder no longer, my friend," said Pereira, "but come with me tomorrow and see for yourself. I have to go to Anyáko to visit a branch store that I have there, and as tomorrow is Sunday I propose that we make my business visit into a picnic. But don't imagine that there is anything to see. Conceive Quittáh with pink clay instead of grey sand, with anthills in place of sand dunes; add to the coconut palms a few gum trees and baobabs, and substitute a slightly different stink, and there is Anyáko."

"Any white people?" I inquired.

"Not now," answered Pereira. "There was a mission station there once, but the missionaries died off as fast as they were sent out, so the station was abandoned. You'll see the graves and the remains of the chapel tomorrow."

On the following morning I met Pereira by the lagoonside just as the sun was rising, but early as was the hour, all the necessary preparations for the journey were completed. Half a dozen of the long flat-bottomed canoes (each fashioned from a single log of silk-cottonwood) such as the natives use, were drawn up by the "hard" or landing place, and of these the largest was evidently set apart for our use, for it contained two Madeira chairs, and even as I approached I observed Aochi, Pereira's servant, stowing in the bows a green gin case from which protruded the necks of two claret bottles.

The lagoon at this hour was perfectly still, with a dull, unruffled surface like a sheet of polished lead, and was overhung by a shroud of yellowish rosy mist. A quite unusual silence brooded over the scene – for ordinarily Quittáh with the strong sea breeze, the chattering coconut palms and the boisterous natives, is rather a noisy place – through which the giant pulse of the ocean could be heard booming rhythmically upon the beach.

We had no sooner taken our places than the two canoe men – each provided with a long crooked pole forked at the end – pushed off and began to propel the canoe at quite a rapid rate. In a few minutes the shore had vanished into the mist, and for the next hour we moved smoothly on with nothing to mark our progress but some chance floating stick or an occasional solitary pelican that emerged from the mist, slid across our circumscribed field of view and faded away again before we had time for mutual examination. Presently the sun began to appear through the haze like a disc of burnished copper, and then sea breeze came down, dimming the surface of the water and driving before it row after row of little hollow ripples that slapped noisily on the flat side of the canoe. As the mist cleared there appeared before us a low-lying shore clothed with fan palms and a few lank and ragged trees, and one or two thatched roofs and a single whitewashed building could be seen half hidden among the foliage. Nearly opposite this building the canoe presently grounded in some six inches of water, and the two stalwart canoe men, stepping overboard, proceeded to lift Pereira and me bodily out of our chairs and carry us through the shallows, depositing us at length on dry land.

"Well, Englefield," observed Pereira, stretching himself and stamping on the dry mud, "here we are in your promised land, and here comes Aochi with the chop box. Breakfast, Aochi, one time. We'll have our food first, and then I'll see about my business while you take a walk in the garden of Eden."

We breakfasted in the mouldy-looking "hall" of the decaying mission house, on the inevitable spatchcock and plantain fritters ("pranteen flitters" Aochi called them) from the green box, and then Pereira betook himself to the village, leaving me to roam about in the bush. It was not a lovely spot, I was compelled to admit, but it was new to me and a change from Quittáh. There were bushes and trees and fan palms and actual solid earth of a curious pink colour – a great relief after the eternal loose grey sand. And there were great snails with shells striped like a zebra's skin, and curious vole-like animals, and large birds that uttered sounds like the whirring of an invalid chime clock, and great anthills: in short, there were multitudes of things that I had never seen before, so that I spent a couple of hours very pleasantly poking about among the bushes. Making my way back towards the village I stopped to examine a large and incredibly corpulent baobab tree from whose branches the velvet-covered fruit hung down on long straight stalks. I was about to move on when I perceived among the bushes a low mud wall, and looking over it found that it formed one side of a square enclosure.

"This," I thought, "must be the old mission garden," and forthwith I resolved to explore it in case any of the fruit trees should be still bearing.

Scaling the low crumbling wall, I entered and looked about me. The whole place was choked with a riotous profusion of vegetation. The ground was almost hidden by the feathery masses of the little sensitive mimosa, whose leaves shrink away and close up at a touch; low bushes and small trees were scattered about, and here and there clumps of cactus and branching euphorbias rose out of the tangle. But of cultivation there was no trace.

The most singular feature of the place was the large number of anthills – sugar-loafed structures of bright red earth from eight to ten feet high – of which a dozen or more were grouped quite near together. From one of these I noticed an angular piece of white stone projecting, and, wondering how a piece of stone could have got into such a situation, I drew out my knife and endeavoured to dig it out, when to my astonishment it turned out to be one arm of a monumental cross around which the anthill had been built.

This discovery led me to examine the place more narrowly, with the result that, by dragging aside creepers and bushes and scraping away portions of other anthills, I found no less than seven flat gravestones, each with a marble tablet let into it on which was engraved a name and a scripture reference. All the names were German, and mostly those of men.

So this was all that was left of the Anyáko mission! It was a solemn sight to look upon, and fraught with a suggestiveness that was by no means pleasant; one of those disagreeable reminders with which West Africa is apt to salute the intrusive white man.

I sat down upon a flat slab that I had just cleared, lost in gloomy meditation, insensibly contrasting the bright face of nature with the sad and pathetic relics around; glancing at the blue, sunny sky, the gay vegetation, the gem-like sun birds that hovered round the cactus, and the great blue-bodied lizard that nodded his scarlet head at me from the top of an anthill, and thinking of the "pestilence that walketh in the noonday" amidst all this exuberant life and light.

My reflections were interrupted by the sound of footsteps on the path outside, and looking up, I perceived a figure approaching which, by its tall black hat, long black coat and black umbrella could be that of none other than Pereira.

"Aha!" he exclaimed as he came up. "Meditating among the tombs? And a very fitting occupation for a coaster." He furled his umbrella and leaning his arms on the wall, looked round.

"Yes," he continued, "here is West Africa in a nutshell; a most concise epitome. I knew all these men, Englefield, and the first of them came here less than a dozen years ago. And here they are; and so the world wags in Africa. The white man comes out full of life and energy and purpose. The jungle laughs and covers him up and he is straightway forgotten. Then more come, and the act is repeated *da capo*, and so on. But what have we here?"

I stood up and looked over the wall. Two natives were coming towards us along the path, one an aged woman, white-haired, lean and shrivelled, and the other a middle-aged man who held the woman's hand with one of his and with the other grasped a long staff with which he tapped upon the ground before him as he walked.

There was nothing remarkable in the appearance of the old woman, excepting the fan-like group of radiating scars on her temples which showed that she belonged to the Krepi tribe. But the aspect of the man was most horrible. His body was to the last degree emaciated; his face was so seamed and disfigured with scars as to be hardly human; his neck was covered with a pattern of warty button-like scars; his ears had been carved out into scallops like a cock's comb, and his empty eye sockets were so sunken that his face was like that of a dry skull.

As the pair came up to where we were standing, Pereira addressed them in the Efé language, and I gathered that he was inquiring after the man's health; but although his manner was kind and sympathetic enough, his questions were received with sullen reserve, and after a very brief conversation, the old woman put an end to the interview by abruptly seizing the man's arm and hurrying him away.

Pereira looked after them with a puzzled expression on his face, as the old woman strode along and the man, with chin stuck forward and his stick groping before him, stumbled by her side.

"There goes another African mystery," my friend remarked turning to me.

"How so?" I asked. "What did the old lady say?"

"Oh, she said," replied Pereira, "that she had brought her son all the way from Peki to see the white doctor at Quittáh."

"Well, he does certainly look a trifle off colour," I remarked. "Did the old woman say how he lost his eyes?"

"Ah! that was the question that gave so much offence. Her explanation was that he had some kind of sickness as a child, but she was not inclined to be confidential, as you saw."

"No, indeed. But I suppose there is a good deal of eye disease here as in other tropical countries?"

"Oh, certainly there is; but I suspect that the disease that cost him his sight was somehow connected with a flat iron rod with a hook at the end."

"Good God!" I exclaimed, "you don't mean to say that you think his eyes have been put out?"

"That is my belief," answered Pereira. "Didn't you notice his eye sockets with never a vestige of eyeball left? And did you see his ears and his neck? Those were no tribal marks. That man has been an Ashanti 'donkor' or alien slave. I remember once before meeting a blind man – also a Krepi – with just the same appearance and marked in the same manner, and he was just as reticent as this one; and he, I learned for certain, had been one of the King's slaves in Ashanti, but I never could find out anything more about him."

"And he had had *his* eyes put out?"

"Evidently, although he told the same story of illness in childhood as this one."

"What an extraordinary and horrible thing!" I exclaimed. "Why, it recalls that ghastly yarn of yours about the Aboási cavern."

"I was just thinking the same myself. But come, that villain Aochi will have our coffee ready by now, and we ought to be starting for home presently. It doesn't do to be overtaken by darkness on the lagoon."

During the return passage across the lagoon the usually loquacious and discursive Pereira preserved an unwonted silence, and I surmised that he was thinking of the old Krepi woman and her son. That this was actually the case appeared later, for after he had wished me "good night" and was retiring to his room he paused by the doorway and looked back at me.

"I can't help thinking of that poor blind devil, Englefield," he said. "What fearful sufferings he must have gone through, and what constant terror he must be in lest he should be discovered and dragged back to his slavery. But miserable wretch as he is, he has the advantage of you and me in one thing, if it can be considered an advantage: he holds the key to some of the darkest secrets of this mysterious land."

Chapter Five

I Encounter a Curious Relic

A couple of days after our excursion of Anyáko I received a letter by the land post from Captain Bithery. It was dated from Axím on the Gold Coast, and in it, after giving me sundry items of news concerning the brig and her crew, the Captain went on to say that he proposed to drop down to the leeward coast in about a fortnight to ship some produce that he hoped to obtain. This produce consisting chiefly of palm oil, kernels and copra, was to be collected for him by a certain Cæsar Olympio – a Portuguese mulatto who lived at the village of Adena or Elmina Chica, a beach village some twelve miles to leeward – *i.e.* to the east – of Quittáh; and he proposed that I should proceed to Adena to conduct the purchase and superintend the storage of the produce, leaving my store in Vanderpuye's charge.

On receiving these instructions I made the necessary arrangements with Pereira, and the same afternoon set out for Adena in a spare hammock which he lent me and which was carried on the heads of four of our labourers.

This was my first experience of this mode of travelling, and very pleasant and even luxurious I found it to recline at full length in the springy, swaying hammock as the barefooted carriers trudged over the soft sand. A canopy of painted canvas protected me from the sun during the daylight and from the dew when the night closed in, and by peering underneath it I could look out at the groves of pattering coconut palms on the one side, and on the other at the ocean which surged up almost at our feet.

It was about eight o'clock and bright moonlight when the hammock drew up outside the compound of Olympio's house, and as I scrambled out on to my feet I was saluted by a little yellow-faced man with bright, beady, black eyes and a most persuasive and conciliatory smile.

"You are Mr Olympio?" I said as I shook his hand.

"Quite right," he replied in a singularly soft and musical voice, adding, "I bid you welcome to Adena. Will you please to come in?"

I followed him into the house, a mud-built thatched cottage of three rooms, and immediately became aware of an aromatic and savoury odour, and perceived with great content that preparations – of a somewhat primitive nature indeed – had been made for a meal.

I was not the only guest, it appeared, for, as I entered, a native in European dress – what is locally known as a "scholar man" – rose to greet me. He was the very antithesis of Olympio – big, burly, black as the ace of spades, and full of the boisterous humour and high spirits of the typical African; and as he gripped me by the hand and bid me welcome to Adena his joy overflowed in little gurgles of laughter.

"Glad to see you, Mr Englefield," he said in a deep buzzing bass. "I hear your name plenty time but never see you. Now I see you very fine gentleman. Ha! ha! ha!" Here he leered at Olympio, who keckled softly and rubbed his hands.

"Mr Englefield smell de palaver sauce, hey! Olympio?" continued my new friend, whose name, by the way, was David Annan. "You like dis country chop, sah?"

I replied that I had very little acquaintance with African cookery.

"Aha! no! You no get fine country wife like Olympio to make you palaver sauce. Dis yer Olympio he sabby what be good. He sabby fine chop, fine liquor, fine girl. He very bad man, sah, ha! ha!"

He laughed uproariously, and certainly the picture of the little wizened mulatto in the character of a *bon vivant* and ladykiller was not without its comic side. But these flights of wit were cut short by the appearance of a handsome, light-coloured Fanti woman who carried a deep, black clay dish, and was followed by a procession of small girls and boys each bearing some adjunct to the feast, and soon the little table, with its red and yellow striped cloth, groaned under a burden of delicacies. The black dish was filled with a gorgeous orange-coloured palm oil stew, while smaller but similar receptacles exhibited such dainties as kiki, or okra stew, rolls of fufu, looking like gelatinous suet puddings, stuffed egg fruit, large red capsicums and piles of green and red chillis.

That dinner was a series of surprises, of which I experienced the first when I unguardedly swallowed a spoonful of the orange-red "palaver sauce" and was instantly reduced to tears and suffocation. But the most surprising thing of all was the behaviour of Mr David Annan. He commenced the meal by popping into his mouth and calmly masticating a large scarlet capsicum. He next pinched off a lump of fufu and, indenting it with his thumb, fashioned it into a kind of cup which he filled with the peppery stew and solemnly bolted with closed eyes like a toad swallowing a caterpillar. Finally, he poured out half a tumblerful of Angostura bitters and drained it at a draught. After this my capacity for astonishment was exhausted, and if he had proceeded to quench his thirst with the contents of the paraffin lamp and to swallow the forks it would have seemed quite in character. But he did neither of these things, and the meal dragged on to the end with no further diversion from my sufferings.

Shortly after dinner Mr Annan took his leave, earnestly beseeching me to keep an eye on Olympio and endeavour to restrain him from the wild excesses into which it was his habit to plunge and the little mulatto and I then settled down to pass the evening together.

The proceedings were not as boisterous as Annan's warning might have led one to expect, for Olympio was a shy and silent man, and, moreover, unaccustomed to the society of Europeans; so we sat at opposite ends of the table, with a calabash full of chopped tobacco leaf between us, and engaged in conversation which was so spasmodic and one-sided that it gradually "dwindled away into silence." Then we sat speechless for some time, during which Olympio observed me continuously, and whenever he caught my eye chuckled softly and rubbed his hands, until I became possessed with an instant desire to empty the tobacco leaf over him and bonnet him with the calabash.

But he saved me from this outrage by retiring to dive into a cupboard, whence he returned carrying a biscuit tin and a weatherbeaten musical box.

"You are perhaps fond of music, Mr Englefield?"

"Very," I replied, with an apprehensive glance at the musical box.

"So am I," said Olympio, and he proceeded to wind up the instrument; and having balanced it upside down and cornerwise in the biscuit tin – the only position in which it would consent to go – he "gave it its head."

It had but one tune, but of that it made the most, repeating it in every variety of time; commencing with obscene hilarity, retarding to funereal slowness and stopping in the most unexpected places.

I felt the old insane impulse reviving, and as I had no wish to see my host fly from the room with his head through his own calabash, I brought the entertainment to a close.

"I think, if you will excuse me, Mr Olympio, I should like to turn in. The hammock journey has rather tired me."

"I shall be most delighted, sir," replied Olympio, with less politeness and more truth than he supposed.

"I will show you your room in a moment. Hi! Kwaku! why you no bring Mr Englefield his candle?"

The latter question was bawled through the open door into the darkness of the back compound, from which presently emerged a small boy bearing a paraffin lamp, which he shaded skilfully from the strong sea breeze. Olympio took the lamp and led the way into my bedroom, which opened out of the room in which we had been sitting. He held the lamp above his head as we entered, and looked round the room with evident pride in the resources of civilisation that it exhibited. It was indeed far beyond my expectations, and I hastened to say so, for Adena was but a remote native hamlet and little could be expected there but the ordinary accommodation of a native house. Yet there was a good iron bedstead with clean white sheets and a serviceable mosquito curtain, a washstand with a veritable china basin, and a dressing table fitted with a looking glass fully nine inches square. But the most surprising and unexpected object in the room was a small but massive oak chest of drawers with a secretary top, which I at once perceived, both from its quaint and antique design and the dark colour of the wood, must be of considerable age.

"That is a fine piece of furniture, Mr Olympio," I remarked. "There are not many like it in Africa, I expect."

"No," he replied, setting the lamp on it and passing his hand affectionately over its polished surface. "I have never seen one like it even in the castle at Elmina. It is very old. My grandfather had it in his house at Adáffia when my father was a child, I have heard him say."

"Did he bring it out from Portugal with him?"

"Oh no. It came from a ship that broke up on the beach at Adáffia many, many years ago. I have heard that she was English."

"You don't know her name, then?"

"No. It was long, long time ago – before my grandfather's time I think. I have told Kwaku to put your things in the drawers. I thought you would like it because the chest is an English chest. I don't give it to the Germans who come here."

He smiled shyly and backed towards the door, and when I had thanked him – which I did warmly – for this graceful little act of courtesy, he wished me "good night" and went away much gratified.

Left to myself I made leisurely preparations for bed, ruminating, as I undressed and washed, upon the strange fortunes of the old ship's chest, speculating upon its history, upon the men who had fashioned it, on the old-time skipper who had sat before it to write his old-world letters, and on the bills of lading, charter parties, and other sea documents that had once reposed in its pigeonholes and drawers.

When I had got into my pyjamas I lit a pipe – not of Olympio's tobacco – and taking down the lamp made a more thorough examination of the chest. Its nautical character was now evident, for on each side, near the bottom, was a perforated chock through which a lanyard had been passed to secure it to a ring-bolt in the deck of the cabin. The ornamentation, too, savoured of the sea, for the drawers were enriched by rude shallow carvings of ropes in festoons, coils and hitches, and each corner terminated above in a kind of diminutive figurehead representing a buxom, blowsy sea maiden with a very full bust and a dolphin's tail. The handles of the drawers were of hippo ivory, carved with a knife and now cracked and yellow with age, and the flap that let down to form the writing table had once been decorated with a painted design, but this was now obliterated.

I drew out the sliding supports and let down the flap, intending to stow away my stationery in the upper part conveniently for writing. Here I found a row of drawers, and one of pigeonholes above them, while the centre was occupied by a little tabernacle-like cupboard, the door of which was decorated with a roughly executed painting, very yellow and faded, of a sea maiden, similar to those carved on the corners. When I opened this door there was revealed a set of four very small drawers, all of which were empty; and I noticed, when I pulled out one, that it was only half the length of the drawers below the pigeonholes. Evidently this little nest of drawers masked some secret repository – if that could be described as "secret" which was so artlessly concealed.

Now there is something highly stimulating to curiosity in the idea of a secret drawer or cupboard, no matter how transparent the secrecy may be, and I had no sooner ascertained the existence of his hiding place than I was all agog to lay bare its secret.

First I drew the drawers right out and felt at the back, thinking there might be a cavity there; but the back of the drawer case was quite unyielding. Then I noticed that the nest which held the drawers was a separate and independent structure let into the row of pigeonholes, and not continuous with them; so I took hold of one of the partitions between the drawer spaces and gave a gentle pull, when, sure enough, the whole nest came sliding forward, and I lifted it bodily out of the cavity in which it fitted.

The back of the nest was formed by a panel, which I could see slid in grooves, and I was about to slide it up when I suddenly bethought me that I was perhaps invading the holy of holies of my too-confiding host, who might quite conceivably make the secret drawers behind the panel the repository of his most treasured possessions. However, I considered that, even if it were so, I had no intention of abstracting anything, while most likely the drawers were empty, so banishing my scruples I boldly slid up the panel.

There were no drawers inside, but in place of them a flat copper box which stood upright in the cavity and fitted it exactly. The green, encrusted condition of this box seemed to indicate that it was not often taken out, and when I drew it forth and tried to open it, the close-fitting lid was jammed to so tightly that I had to prise it open with my knife, when I found that it had an airtight flange like the lid of a snuff box. Inside the box, and exactly fitting it, was a small folio volume bound in parchment. This I supposed to be Olympio's book of accounts, but I nevertheless shook it out of its case and turned back the cover, when I perceived a pale and faded inscription on the flyleaf in an odd, crabbed handwriting, but yet adorned with several expert flourishes.

This was the inscription: "The Journall of Barnabas Hogg, Master of the ship *Mermaid*, of Bristol City, 1641–16–" The second date was not filled in, and I surmised that the journal and its writer had together come to an untimely end in the roaring surf of Adáffia beach. This was rendered more probably by the fact that the book had remained in its hiding place, for, had the Captain survived he would presumably have taken his journal with him: a view which received confirmation when I turned up the last entry, which was near the end of the volume, and read:

"16 June (1643). We are still at anchor off Adáffia, but shall not remain here since there seemeth to be little trade with this wild and turbulent people who have brought us but a few elephants' teeth (and those very small and poor) and some teeth of river horses. Moreover the sudden storms of this season of the year do make this roadstead most perilous for ships to anchor in."

That was the end of the journal. Doubtless on the day following, the very danger that the Captain had foreseen overtook the ship, and as for poor Master Barnabas himself and his hearts of oak, they all probably perished in the surf or fell victims to the "wild and turbulent" people of the coast villages.

There was something very solemn in this unexpected meeting with the quaint and musty little volume. On that June evening, more than two centuries ago, the final entry had been written and the book put away by the methodical Master of the good ship *Mermaid*. And there it had in all probability remained, unseen by human eye, its very existence forgotten, while generation after generation was born and passed away, while dynasties rose, flourished and decayed. As I turned over its yellow leaves covered with faded writing I felt like one holding converse with the dead (as indeed I was), and so fell into a train of meditation from which I was at length aroused by the little American clock in the sitting-room banging out with blatant modernity the hour of midnight. So I rose, knocked out my pipe, replaced and closed up the secret cupboard, and, having deposited the journal in my dispatch box, turned into bed.

Chapter Six
The Journal of Captain Barnabas Hogg

My stay at Adena was somewhat of a holiday until the brig arrived, for, although the amount of produce to be examined was greater than I should have obtained at Quittáh in the same time, the actual purchase of it was effected by Olympio, so that I could deal with it in bulk; and then there was no store to look after and no selling of goods to the natives. Hence, I had a good deal of time on my hands, a part of which I utilised for outdoor pursuits, and the remainder I spent lounging about with a book in the shady coconut grove near the beach by day, and in my room at night. I had brought one or two books with me to Adena, but these paled in interest before the manuscript journal, over which I pored, at first secretly, and then, as I found that no one noticed what I read, constantly, until I read the antique handwriting of Captain Hogg with as much ease as Olympio's ungrammatical copperplate.

Fascinating, however, as I found the journal, I shall not inflict upon the reader any of the entries but those that have reference to this narrative. I had read through the whole of the diary for the year 1641; had examined the quaint, rough sketches and charts of the coastline with which it was embellished and amplified, and had made extensive notes of the descriptions and comments of the shrewd and observant old shipmaster, when on a certain afternoon some four days before the brig was due at Adena, I took the old volume out with me on to the beach, and spreading a mat on the dry sand under the coconuts lay down to read at my ease. Commencing with the date "New Year's Day, 1642," I read through the first dozen entries. They contained nothing of interest but plentiful details of the trading transactions on the Ivory Coast, off which the ship was then cruising, details that were now familiar and a little monotonous. This lack of interest in the narrative, combined with the heat and the rather somnolent surroundings, the patter of the palms overhead, the endless murmur of the sea breeze, and the surging of the surf hard by, produced a feeling of drowsiness, and I was just letting the book fall when, recovering myself with a start, I observed on the opposite page an entry of considerable length. As this promised more entertainment that the briefer notes of trade and navigation with which I had been engaged, I plunged into it; and I had not read far before my drowsiness completely vanished and gave place to the keenest excitement.

I extract the entry at length:

"Sunday, 14th Jan. – Dropped down from Bassam during the nighte, keeping a good offing and sounding every five minutes. Passed Cape Tres Puntas in the nighte, and cast anchor soon after daybreak in Axim Bay in seven fathoms. Soon after we had anchored we perceaved a fishing canoe to be approaching from the shoare; it was paddled by three negroes, and two more were sitting near by the stern. When it hadde come alongside we could see that, besides the blacks, there was in the canoe a white man who lay at the bottom and seemed to bee sicke. The negroes climbed up the side on to the deck, but the white man was too feeble to follow them, wherefore we dropped into the canoe a rope, in the end whereof was a bowline or loop; and when the sick man had passed this round his middle we drew him up on to the quarter deck.

"The aspect of this man was most wretched and pitiful. He was quite naked excepting for a loincloth such as the black people use to wear in these parts. His wrists and ankles – one of which bore an iron ring – were all raw and festered; his backe and shoulders were seamed with scars not yet fully healed; his ears were torn and cut with greate notches, and, most horrid of all, the balls of his eyes were gone from their socketts so that his face was as that of a dead skull. Moreover, his whole person was as meagre and cadaverous as though he had been long sicke of some wasting distemper or calenture. At first he was so feeble that he could not stand alone, but after we had fed him with fresh meate and made him drink a cuppe of Canary wine, he revived somewhat, and being sett to rest in a bed in the cabin, he fell into a deep sleep and so continueth.

"Monday, 15th Jan. – The strange man remaineth still very sicke and feeble, but he hath related an account of the circumstances that broughte him to so wretched a condition. This narrative I received from his own lippes, and so set it down, knowing not whether it bee a true relation or made up from a disordered imagination."

"The man deposeth that his name is José d'Almeida, and that he is a Portugal by birth. For many years past he hath lived at the Castle of St George at Mina on the Gold Coast, being engaged in trade with the blacks.

"Two years since, when he was journeying from Mina to Shamah, a party of blacke warriors came forth from the bush and made captives of both himself and his followers. By these men he was carried away far into the country, and after journeying for nine days through a greate wildernesse wherein the trees were so many and of so great a bignesse as almost to shut out the light of the sun, he arrived at a great town which the blacks called Coomassy, which seemed to be the capital citie of the nation who call themselves the Asantays. Here he lay in close captivity for severall weeks in much discomfort of body, and very sad and fearfull, for he was fettered both hande and foote, and his food was both scanty and poore. Moreover, he witnessed many dreadfull spectacles which made him to fear that he shoulde shortly be made away with; for these Asantays have many fearfull rites and horrible forms of worship, and are used to offer up to their Gods sacrifices of men and women. At length there came on a certain day to the hovell wherein he was confined certain men strangely cloathed, and having their hair twisted into a number of rolls or ringletts which hung down round their heads like a fringe and made them to have a very terrible aspecte. By these men he was carried away into the wildernesse, and so for four days they journeyed through the woods until they came to a large river by which standeth a town called Tanosoo. In this river, as the negroes beleeve, there abideth one of their Gods, a strong and fierce devil who keepeth a pack of greate fishes to devour any who shall defile the sacred waters by bathing therein; and Almeida doth say that he saw many of these fishes with his own eyes, and that each of them was of the bigness of a man, and that the wizards or priests do call them together from the bankes, and when the said fishes have assembled (as he affirmeth they constantly do) the wizards cast to them offerings of egges of guinea-fowles boiled hard and shelled, which they instantly devour.

"When the strange men were about to carry Almeida across the river (which they presently did by way of a bridge formed from a single great tree), the chief wizard came and took from each of them his staffe and cast it on to a great pile of staves that is hard by the river, for it seemeth that the River God will not suffer any person to carry a rod or staff across the water. Then they passed over the bridge, and each of the men shook out into the streame a small bag of gold dust for a toll or due to the River God. From Tanosoo they journeyed yet two daies more in the wildernesse, keeping near to the river, whiche they crossed once each day, and on the second evening they came to a place where was a large poole or lake, at one end whereof was a great rock of red stone having two points like the horns of a bull or the teeth of an elephant. From the face of this rock a streame or fountain of muddy, red-coloured water poured into the poole, and so, Almeida thinketh, formed the headwater of the river. At this place, which is called Aboassy, that is, 'the place by the rock,' strange and terrible things befell him; for he was but just come to the shoare of the poole when there came forth from the bushes four men of the most frightfull appearance and advanced to him. Each of these men – if men they were and not devils – was cloathed in a long robe of grass, and his face hidden by a painted maske with bull's horns most horrible to look upon. When the magicians – or devils – had spoken awhile with Almeida's captors, a drum was beaten, and forthwith a great shouting arose, and there came forth from the bushes men, women, and children to the number of three or four score, all dressed fantastically in petticoats of unwoven grasse, and bearing some kind of rattles upon their wristes and ankles. These people formed a ring around Almeida and commenced to chant a stave of musick like a psalm, repeating it again and again and keeping time thereto by clapping their hands and shaking their rattles. All the time they continued slowly pacing or shuffling round like children playing in our country; and the magicians having knelt on the ground before Almeida, nodded their great maskes in time with the musick.

"On a sudden, the four wizards arose and uttered a most dismall howle, and then withoute any warning Almeida felt himself seized from behind, and instantly a leathern bag was drawn over his head so that he could neither see nor cry out, and indeed, scarcely breathe; his armes and legges were pinioned afresh with rope, and he felt himself lifted from the ground and borne away.

"After he had been carried some distance he perceaved the air of a sudden grow cooler as if he had entered some large building, and it seemed that he was borne along some passage or corridor, for once his head struck what seemed to be a stone ceiling. Presently, his bearers halted and some of them seemed to descende a ladder, when the others handed him downe, and so descending perhaps a dozen feet they came to the level and started off again. Anon they came to another ladder and again descended a couple of fathoms or so and off again along the level. Presently the air became exceeding hot and stifling, and wondrous foul-smelling, and in the midst of this heat and stench his bearers halted and laid him on the grounde close by a wall. Then the leathern bag was plucked from his head so that he could breathe somewhat more freely, but he could see little as his bonds restrained him from turning his head; but it seemed he was in some sorte of vault or cavern and that of some size; and that there were others in the place beside himselfe, for he could hear the murmur of voices around and the sound of bellows blowing, and could perceave the glow of fire on the roof and walls. Moreover, there was a noise as of the beating of hammers, and sometimes the splash of water.

"In this place he remained lying without food or water for many houres – a full day and nighte he surmiseth – and all that time no person came nigh him save once, when two men came and examined him narrowly, talking very earnestly the while, and then wente away. And though he besought them most pitifully to give him water, he being consumed with thirst, they answered him not, affecting not to understand his speech, which was that of the Dena negroes. At length the men came to him againe after many hours, and now they brought an earthen jar, full of olde and soure palm wine, and a gourd shell to drink from, and they gave him of the wine as much as he would drinke, which was near upon two quarts. Whereupon the wine being, as I have said, old and heady, he became quite drunk and straightway fell into a deepe sleepe, from which he was violently awakened by feeling some weapons thrust into his eyes, causing him great anguish. But being still besotted with the wine he had drunk, he presently fell asleep again. When he awoke he could feel that a clout had been tied over his eyes (in which he had still much pain) and that his shackles had been lightened. And now his keepers gave him both meate and drink in plenty, although he had but little stomacke for food.

"At length, after many weary days of anguish and sickness, there came certain persons who took off the clout from his eyes and cast off the shackles from his limbs. Then, perceiving that he was blind, he put up his hand to his eyes, and behold! the socketts were empty.

"And now he was told he was to be henceforth one of the slaves of the River God, of which slaves there were in the cavern quite a goodly company, and all, like himself, as blind as so many mouldwarps; and that he should labour constantly to get gold for the River God's treasure.

"And so it befell; for in that noisome cavern he abode for nigh upon two yeares, labouring always to get treasure for his master the Demon of the River.

"Some days he would sit on the ground working a small bellows beside a furnace, and constantly driven with a whip whenever he flagged. Some days he laboured with a greate pestle, crushing the ore in a mortar, and other days he was led with divers of his fellow captives up the ladders out into the sweet air and into a canoe or raft on the pool.

"Here he would drive the craft forward with a long pole, or dredge along the bottom with a small metal buckett on a rope and empty into a large brass pan, which they carried in the canoe, the mudde that came up in the said buckett; which mudde, Almeida declareth, was nearly pure gold dust, especially that from near the fountain in the great rock.

"When the pan was filled with the mudde Almeida and the other slaves would bear it along on a pole, back to the cavern and lower it into the vault or under-cavern. Then the slaves would wash the mudd in gourd shells, while their taskmasters gathered out the gold which Almeida believeth was afterwards melted in the furnaces and cast into shapes for the God's treasury.

"And so Almeida abode in the cavern, as he sayeth, for nigh two yeares. Then on a certaine day he was brought forth, but instead of being taken to the pool he was bound by a rope and an iron collar to some other of the slaves, and led away on a journey. And as he journeyed he learned that the King of Asantay was at war with the King of a nation called the Denkeras and that he was making many offerings to his Gods. So Almeida and the other slaves conceived that they were to be sacrificed to these Gods, whereat they rejoiced in that their miseries should be soone put an ende to. But on the third day of their journey a great tumult arose, and it presently appeared that the keepers of the slaves had been attacked and overwhelmed by a bande of these same Denkeras, who, when they had slain the Asantays, carried the blind slaves away with them to their country. Here the King of the Denkeras, having compassion upon Almeida for that he was a white man and had suffered such grievous wrongs at the handes of the Asantays, caused him to be sent to the coaste and delivered into the handes of the Commandant of the Castle of St Anthony at Axim. And there he abode until some shipp should take him away from the accursed land of the negroes, and so he was brought to oure shipp as hath been related.

"Such is the story of José d'Almeida as he hath declared it to me, Barnabas Hogg, and by me faithfully writ down from his very wordes."

When I had finished reading this extraordinary narrative, which, strange as it was and teeming with marvellous and incredible incidents, yet seemed to me to bear the evident impress of truth, I was singularly affected.

Up to the present I had seen but the outside fringe of Africa, which, with its gin cases, its bales of cotton goods, its bags of kernels and puncheons of oil, seemed prosaic and sordid enough. But yet, even in my brief and shallow experience of the country, there had repeatedly reached me faint echoes of a more romantic and mysterious life enacting in those little known regions on whose blue and shadowy distances I had so often turned a longing eye from the verandah of Pereira's house. And now, like a personal message to me from the dim, forgotten past, came this story of the old-time Portuguese trader, stirring up all that was romantic and adventurous in my nature and awakening in me an irresistible desire to see the wonders of Africa for myself.

When I had paced the beach for a while I returned to the journal to see if it contained any further account of Almeida, but no reference was made to the Portuguese until I came to the 30th January, when I read:

"The man José d'Almeida, who hath been very sickly of late, was founde dead in his bedde this morning. We buried him in the sea about nine of the clock and fired a salute with our small cannon after his corpse had been cast into the water. He seemed a godly man, although, like moste of his nation, a rank papist."

It was late that night before I turned in to rest, for the travel fever that had infected Mungo Park, Denham, Clapperton, Lander and the host of other intrepid wanderers whose exploits I recalled and whose remains rested in this ill-omened but fascinating land, had fairly taken hold of me: and when I at last tucked in my mosquito curtain and blew out my candle it was only to fall asleep and dream that I sat, a destitute wanderer, under the shade-tree of some faraway village in the heart of the continent.

Chapter Seven
I Form an Absurd Resolution

The day following that on which I met with the narrative of Almeida in the old logbook was one of more than usual activity, for a large consignment of produce had just been acquired on our behalf by Olympio from no less a person that Mr David Annan. The "scholar man" had, in fact, rather effectually tapped our source of supply by intercepting the little caravans of "bush people" and clearing them out before they could reach the coast. In consequence, I spent the greater part of the day seated upon a pile of gin cases, tally sheet in hand, watching Olympio and his myrmidons weigh out the kernels and rubber, and measure the palm oil.

It was while I was engaged in this fascinating occupation that Mr Annan himself made his appearance. He seated himself with native grace upon the gin cases by my side and genially entered into conversation respecting the merits of the produce he had sold us, which he declared to be quite exceptional.

"Look dat rubber now," he exclaimed, as Olympio slapped a parcel of it on to the scales, "good sound rubber dat is; no grit, no dirt, no water, rubber all de way trou! Take my word, Mr Englefield, s'pose you want good rubber, you buy him from de native merchant, not from bush people."

"Why is that?" I asked.

"Because," he answered, "black man sabby black man fashion. S'pose dem bush people bring me black rubber all grit and stones, I tell um 'dis no good for me. Take um for de white man factory, *he* fit to buy um.' Huh! huh!" He guffawed with great enjoyment and continued. "Look dem monkey skins; where you fit to buy skins like dat from de bush people?"

There was not a little truth in this, for the skins in the particular parcel that he had sold us were in excellent condition, whereas the few purchased from the "bush" natives at Quittáh were riddled with slug holes and half bald besides.

"Where do you get your monkey skins?" I inquired.

"I buy um mostly from de hunters in de far bush," he replied, adding, with great discretion, "de business of de native merchant is to sabby where to get what he want. No one fit to get good monkey skins widout he sabby de hunters which catch de monkey, and dem hunters live for far bush. Dey never come dis country."

At this moment there appeared round the corner of the shed in which we were sitting a figure so remarkable that my attention was instantly diverted alike from Annan's conversation and the produce on the scales. The newcomer was evidently a Fulah, for he was dressed in the picturesque costume worn by the Fulahs and Hausas; and that he was not of the latter nationality his fair complexion made manifest. His clothing was sombre in colour – unlike that of the negroes – and consisted of a blue-grey surplice-like "riga" with wide bell sleeves, richly embroidered with narrow braid-like stitching; wide drawers or "wondo" of similar material embroidered with green; slippers of yellow leather ornamented with a tooled pattern, and a turban of dark indigo blue, the coils of which were continued downwards to form a face-cloth or "litham," which completely concealed the face, leaving only a narrow space through which a strip of fair skin and a pair of piercing dark eyes were visible. As a finish to this costume, he carried a handsome brass-hilted sword slung from his shoulder by a thick tasselled cord of scarlet worsted. Approaching with the dignified carriage of his race he bowed gravely to me and Annan, murmuring a comprehensive "sanu," and held out his hand to my companion, who shook it as though it had been a refractory pump handle.

" 'Scuse me, Mr Englefield," said Annan, "dis man have some business to talk wid me." He motioned to the Fulah to take a seat beside him on the gin cases, and when his guest had seated himself – drawing up his legs and squatting tailor-wise – he fished out from his pocket a fresh kola nut and presented it to his client as a preliminary to business.

The Fulah accepted the gift with a gracious nod and drew out a small dagger, with which he cut off a piece of the nut; then pulling his face-cloth down below his chin, popped the piece of kola into his mouth and began to chew solemnly.

The preliminary arrangements being thus complete, Annan opened the negotiations with a voluble address in the Hausa language. I had not intended to play the part of eavesdropper, but in the first sentence I caught the words "Fatunan birare" (monkey skins), and surmising that I had before me one of those native hunters who "live for far bush and never come for dis country," I grinned silently and pricked up my ears.

And as I listened and watched the Fulah merchant solemnly munching his kola and spitting out the orange-red juice upon the ground before him, there were one or two things that cause me no little surprise. In the first place there was the man himself, the very antithesis of one's conception of an African; gravely self-possessed, quiet of speech, taciturn yet courteous and suave, with his long oval face, his thin aquiline nose, his delicate mouth, his olive skin – several shades fairer than my own sun-tanned hide – his black eyes, full of passion and sadness, he might have sat for a portrait of Dante or Savonarola, so ascetic and lofty did he seem beside the monkey-faced, jabbering Annan.

Then there was his speech. I have mentioned that in listening to the talk of the Hausa soldiers, I found it difficult to follow them, that their accent and pronunciation were widely different from that given by Schön and Barth in their vocabularies of the Hausa language; and I had naturally thought that the traveller and missionary were at fault. But as I listened to this man with his clear-cut European-like accent, never confusing the *l* sounds with the *r*, as the others did, I realised that what I had heard hitherto was but a debased *patois*, and that this was the real Hausa language.

But more than this. I was astonished to find how much progress I had made with the language, for now, when for the first time I heard it properly spoken, I was able to follow it with hardly a failure, although I could scarcely make out a word of Annan's jabber. Indeed, I felt confident that I could have conversed quite fluently with this stranger; but I refrained from the experiment, remembering my resolution to keep my knowledge of the language to myself for the present.

At length the Fulah, having concluded his business palaver, slid down from the gin cases, bringing his feet most adroitly into his slippers as he descended, and with another comprehensive salaam, departed, leaving his host silent and thoughtful.

The subject of Annan's cogitations being evidently monkey skins, I led the suspended conversation back to this absorbing topic.

"How do you manage to communicate with the hunters," I asked, "if they live for far bush and never come here?"

Annan gave me a quick glance full of suspicion and cunning, and then replied suavely: "Sometimes I send my clerk with some of my boys for far bush to buy de skins, sometimes I go myself. Perhaps I go dis year when de small rains finish."

"Do you have to make a long journey?" I inquired.

"Oh, long, long way. T'rou 'Shanti bush past Kumási to a country called Tánosu."

"Tánosu!" I exclaimed, with suddenly increasing interest.

"Yaas, Tánosu," he replied. "Bad country dat, bad people, but plenty black monkey live in de bush."

"Why is it a bad country?" I asked.

Annan spat on the ground in the expressive African fashion and replied, "Tánosu people no good. Too much f'tish palaver. Dem f'tish people dey wait in de bush, and when stranger men come along dey catch um. Den dey make f'tish custom" – here Annan drew his forefinger quickly across his throat and snapped his finger and thumb in the air – a pantomime that needed no explanation.

"I have often thought," I said musingly, "that I should very much like to see the far bush. It is very different from the coast, isn't it?"

"De far bush," replied Annan emphatically, "is not fit place for white man. De chop bad – bush chop only fit for bush man – de houses bad, de roads bad, de people bad – too much war palaver. No good for white man."

"Of course," I rejoined, "if one went into the bush, one would expect to rough it a little and take some risk. Still, I must say, I should like to see what the interior of Africa is like."

"P'raps you like to come with me and look for monkey skins, Mr Englefield," suggested Annan grinning.

"Why, that's not such a bad idea," said I. "How should you like to have me with your party?"

"You tink you fit to come for true?" asked Annan, now all on the alert and evidently reckoning up what he could make out of me if I came. " 'Spose you come, I get you hammock boys, I get you carriers, I speak country talk for you. I do you proper."

It was clear that Annan intended to make most of the expenses of the journey out of me, and was correspondingly keen on my society.

"Well," I said, "I won't make up my mind now. Perhaps I shan't be free to go this season, but you might let me know what it would cost me to make the trip, and then if I find I can do it, we can arrange whatever is necessary."

Annan was inclined to urge me to an immediate decision in spite of his previously unfavourable account of the interior as a pleasure resort, but as Olympio's boy at this point made his appearance to announce that "chop live for table," I broke up the meeting and adjourned for lunch.

We had hardly sat down to table, however, when the sound of a gun was heard from seaward and presently a small boy ran in to tell us that "sailing ship come from windward." Olympio and I together ran out to the compound gate to examine the stranger, and were just in time to see the *Lady Jane* swing round to her anchor, while a crowd of hands swarmed aloft to stow the sails. Already the solitary surf boat belonging to Adena was creeping out across the blue water like some huge marine beetle, so, as the brig lay out at a good safe distance from the shore, we returned to finish our meal.

The last banana fritter (a particularly greasy one) had just been flopped on to my plate by the attentive Kwaku when a heavy step sounded in the compound, and the massive form of Captain Bithery appeared in the doorway. He was clothed in white, from head to foot, and in his aspect somewhat suggested a much overheated polar bear.

"Well, Englefield, my buck," he exclaimed in his great sea voice, bringing his huge hand down with a thwack on my shoulder, "here you are then, all sound and shipshape, eating as usual – never saw such a fellow to eat. Had much fever?"

"Haven't had any," said I a trifle boastfully.

"Nonsense! No fever? and a dark man like you too! Well, you've been deuced lucky, that's all."

"Why, do dark men get more fever than fair men?" I asked.

"They seem to. It's odd, but I think it's a fact. The chap who gets let off most easily by this infernal climate is your good old sandy-headed, purple-nosed Scotchman – that is, if he doesn't get his little finger too curly. Yes, Olympio," he continued, turning to the little mulatto, "the great thing in this climate is temperance, hey?"

"Oh, certainly, certainly, Captain," replied Olympio a little shyly, setting down on the table the tumbler of gin and water from which he was about to take a sip; "no doubt of it, sir."

"Of course," continued the Captain. "Now, look at me. Did you ever see me drink a cocktail, Olympio?"

"I don't know that I ever did, sir," replied Olympio.

"Would you like to?" asked the Captain, grinning.

"Not particularly, sir," answered the little mulatto.

"Oh," said the Captain, rather taken aback at the failure of his joke, "because if you would, I see there is a swizzle stick hanging on the wall, and I'm not bigoted, you know." Here he stared stonily at the perplexed Olympio until the latter, suddenly grasping the situation, made a dive at the sideboard cupboard and handed out a black bottle with a quill stuck through the cork and a high-shouldered stone jar.

"Providence," remarked Captain Bithery, as he drew the cork out of the stone jar and sniffed inquisitively at its muzzle, "Providence must have intended the cocktail to be the special beverage of the coaster, for otherwise why should the swizzle stick tree grow in such numbers in these parts?"

This position being beyond dispute a silence ensued, which was presently broken by the musical "guggle" of the swizzle stick as it whirled round in the pink froth.

"Englefield," said the Captain, as he set down the empty tumbler, "I've got a little surprise for you. We're off in a fortnight."

"Off!" I exclaimed.

"Yes, off. I did a deal with a trader up at Bassam and cleared off the entire remainder of my stuff. So now there is only the homeward cargo to stow on board – we are half full already – and then it's 'Ho for Bristol City!' and 'goodbye' to the jolly old coast."

This was news indeed. I had not anticipated leaving Africa for several months, and had, in fact, almost abandoned my scheme of penetrating to the interior on account of my engagement with Bithery to look after the store. Now it would be necessary for me to decide at once on my future movements and make known my intentions to the Captain.

"There is a little more of Annan's stuff to be weighed yet," I said. "Shall we go out and look at it? A little rubber and about three tons of copra."

"Oh, Olympio will see to that, won't you? You come out by the beach, Englefield; it's cooler under the coconuts than in this oven."

We strolled out into the breezy palm grove by the beach, and lighting our pipes sat down in the shade on a mound of blown sand.

"I needn't ask if you are coming back with us?" said the Captain.

"Well, the fact is, I don't think I am."

"Nonsense. You're not going to take a billet out here. I wouldn't. You'll never see England again if you do."

"No, I'm not thinking of any billet here. I have an idea of making a journey into the interior."

"Great Moses!" exclaimed the Captain. "What for?"

"No special object, but curiosity. I want to see what the interior of Africa is really like."

"Don't be such an infernal ass, Englefield. 'Really like'! Pah! I'll tell you what it's like. It's like the inside of a saucepan of hot boiled cabbage. Where had you thought of going to?"

"I thought of travelling up through Ashanti, and perhaps, making for the Hausa country."

"Ho! ho!" laughed the Captain grimly, with a wry twist of his face, "you needn't prick out your course so far ahead. You'd be made into monkey soup before you were fairly out of soundings."

"Well, I mean to have a shot at it, anyhow," said I, by way of closing a useless discussion.

"Then you're a damned fool, that's all!" and the Captain angrily knocked out his half-smoked pipe on the toe of his boot.

"When will you want to be paid off?" he inquired presently. "There will be a fair little sum to come to you, you know, what with your pay and the commission on the trade."

"I shan't want much, I fancy," said I. "Perhaps you'll pay me what I want to start with and take care of the rest until I claim it."

"I'll do no such thing," he replied. "You'd better pay in what you don't want to take with you to Swanzy's agent, at whatever place you start from on this lunatic jaunt, and get a receipt for it. Then if by any chance you should come back, there'll be enough cash to take what's left of you to Europe. I suppose it's no use for me to try and persuade you to give up this tomfool's idea."

"I'm afraid not," I replied. "I've gone into the matter and made my decision."

"Well," said the skipper gruffly, "you know your own mind, at any rate; and you ought to, for there ain't many like it outside Bedlam. But I'm sorry – damned sorry," and he relapsed into silence, from which he refused to be roused during the rest of our interview.

Chapter Eight
I Make a New Acquaintance

A couple of days more saw me back at Quittáh with all my plans practically complete, for in the interval I had seen Annan and had settled to meet him at Cape Coast in a month, by which time (the end of September) the rainy season would be fairly over. I had also laid down a general plan of action, but this was of so audacious and extraordinary a character that I did not dare finally to adopt it until I had discussed it with my level-headed friend Pereira.

My reception by that gentleman, on my return, was somewhat of a surprise to me. We had been very friendly together during my stay at this house, and had got on with one another as comfortably as two people well could, but this was all, as far as I knew; so when the old gentleman met me at the compound gate and, seizing both my hands, almost wept over me, I was not a little affected, and for the first time realised how lonely was the life that he led. For Pereira, though only a trader, was in all essentials a gentleman, not only by training and education, but in manners and feeling, and was, moreover, a man of very superior intelligence; and it was easy to understand that he found the society of Quittáh – a handful of German traders and missionaries and a couple of English officials at the fort – neither sufficient nor congenial.

Still, I was a little surprised at the affectionate effusiveness of his manner, and at a certain exhilaration and excitement that he displayed as he fidgeted round while I superintended the unloading of my little caravan.

"Englefield," said he suddenly, as I was rummaging amongst the raffle in my hammock, "I've got something to show you upstairs."

"Curio?" I asked, still groping.

"No, not a curio," he laughed, "certainly not a curio. Something very pretty; it came out from England by the last steamer."

"Indeed? What is it?" I inquired.

"Come up with me and you shall see," said the old man, rubbing his hands and smiling mysteriously.

"I am coming in a moment," I said, "but I can't find my flask. Here you, headman, you look dem small rum bottle?"

"Dis ting he live for hammock," replied the headman, coming forward with the flask in one hand and wiping his mouth with the back of the other. "His lid no good; no fit proper; all de rum fall out."

I snatched the empty flask, and shaking my fist at the grinning barbarian, turned to follow Pereira who had already vanished up the stairs. As I reached the top I saw my host standing, holding the door open, his face wreathed in smiles; and I strode forward with no little curiosity as to the treasure that he had to show me. But at the threshold I fell back in utter amazement, for there advanced to meet me the very handsomest and most stately lady that I had ever seen.

"This is my daughter Isabel," said the beaming Pereira. "Isabel, this is Mr Englefield."

I am afraid that Miss Pereira's first impression of me could hardly have been a favourable one, for between my astonishment and admiration I could do nothing but stand in the doorway gaping and mumbling like a fool, until I was recalled to consciousness by becoming aware that she had shaken my hand and was speaking to me.

"It seems quite like meeting an old friend," she was saying. "For although I have only been here a week or so, my father has talked so much about you that I seem to have known you for years. I assure you that your manners and customs are as an open book to me."

"I am glad to know that," I replied, "for your worthy father has been pleased to present me at a great disadvantage. On the stage an astonished man may be picturesque and even dignified; in real life he is apt rather to resemble an imbecile."

"There, now," said Miss Pereira, smiling mischievously, "see, my father, to what frightful danger you have exposed Mr Englefield through your babyish desire to spring a surprise on him. He might have looked like an imbecile. But it wouldn't have mattered," she added thoughtfully, "I should have known it was an optical illusion."

"I am everlastingly obliged to your father," said I, "for having explained my merits so clearly beforehand. Perhaps with the artful aid of a little soap and water I may endeavour to live up to my reputation."

"Yes, a hammock journey does certainly create a necessity for grooming, as I discovered a day or two ago, when I travelled to Amutinu and back. My hair has hardly recovered yet. When I got out of the hammock, it was like a mass of coconut fibre, and you will hardly believe me, I am sure, when I tell you on my pointing this out to my father, he actually forgot himself so far as to make an unseemly and most obvious joke on the subject. You will find your room as you left it, only, perhaps, a little more tidy. *Au revoir,*" and she curtseyed majestically as I departed, followed by Pereira.

"Well, what do you think of my girl, Englefield?" the old man asked, as he made a pretence of helping me to unpack my portmanteau.

"I think she is an extraordinarily handsome girl," I replied, "and much too good for Quittáh. She is not going to stay here, I suppose?"

"It's not my doing," said Pereira quickly. "I wished her to stay in England, but she had always said she was coming to me and she came. She is a young lady with a will of her own, but she is a really good girl and a most loving and dutiful daughter. You see, she was born out here – I was living at Elmina then – and she stayed with me, after my poor wife died, until she was quite a big girl, getting what education she could from the nuns at Elmina. Then I sent her to a school in England, where she has been ever since, at first as a pupil and then as a governess; but she has always said that she would come and keep house for me when she was grown up and – here she is and here she says she means to stay, so what can I do? After all, I am the only relative she has in the world. But I mustn't stay here chattering to you or we shall both get into trouble."

Left to myself I will not deny that I bestowed an unusual amount of attention upon my toilet, and tested the resources of my very limited outfit to the utmost, even to the extent of putting on a white collar and necktie; and after three separate and fruitless attempts to produce a parting in hair which averaged one-eighth of an inch in length, I made my way back to the sitting-room, where the table was already laid for supper.

My projected discussion with Pereira concerning my journey into the interior was for the time forgotten as I sat at the table facing his daughter, for the beauty of this girl was so remarkable as entirely to absorb my attention. I have said that she was the handsomest woman I had ever seen. My experience of women, beautiful or otherwise, had indeed not been great, but there is a certain degree of beauty which is independent of comparison and which secures instant recognition by all but the most aesthetically obtuse.

Of this kind was the beauty of Isabel Pereira. Totally free from the paltry prettiness of the fashion-plate model, entirely without those conventional graces so esteemed by the modiste, she was quite in the "grand style" – a rather large woman, and in spite of the supple grace of youth, showing evidence of muscular strength and physique. In keeping with her splendid proportions was her small and shapely head and her symmetrical face with its firm straight eyebrows, clear cut nose, short full mouth, and bold well-rounded chin. As I scanned her features – which I am afraid I did with rather more enthusiasm than good manners, and somewhat to our mutual embarrassment when I was detected – I could not perceive one detail that would not, in a more commonplace setting, have been an object of admiration. In the matter of mere line and form she recalled those masterpieces that, in the Golden Age of art came forth from the workshops of the sculptors of Hellas to delight and amaze mankind for all time. But in the living face there was that which even the genius of Pheidias could not give; the sparkle of the eye, the silken softness of hair that rippled back from the rounded forehead, and above all, the gorgeous colouring of the south, the warm glow like the blush of a ripe pomegranate.

"My impression is," said Miss Pereira, as she caught my eye for the fiftieth time, "that Mr Englefield contemplates offering me for sale by private treaty to some well-to-do chiefs of his acquaintance. He has been engaged during the whole of dinner in constructing an attractive prospectus, and is now about to consider the question of title deeds."

"I am afraid I *have* been staring a good deal," I replied, considerably out of countenance, "but you must forgive me if you can. You don't realise what a rare and curious creature you are. Do you know that I have only seen one white woman since I left England, and she was an elderly German missioner?"

"And pray, Miss," interposed Pereira, "how did you know that Mr Englefield was staring at you?"

"My dear father, I saw him with my own eyes," exclaimed Miss Pereira, at which we all laughed, and I felt that the reproof was cancelled.

"Well, well," said the old man, "you need not stare one another out of countenance now, for I expect you will each see enough of the other for the next month or so. But perhaps you are going back with Bithery, Englefield? I hear he has sold out and is just filling up for the homeward voyage."

"He will be sailing for England in about a fortnight, but I am not going with him this voyage."

"Indeed! and what are you going to do? Is the store to be replenished?"

"I shall have done with the store in a few days I expect, and then I shall be paid off."

"And after that?"

"After that I have a scheme which I want to talk over with you when you have a little time to spare."

"I am not excessively busy at the present moment," said Pereira; "so, as we seem to have finished eating, you might commence your discourse."

"Won't you go and sit in the verandah to talk over your business?" interposed Miss Pereira. "I will bring your wine and see you comfortably settled before I go."

"I was hoping," said I, "to number you among my audience, Miss Pereira. If you will stay, I can promise you some amusement, for my scheme is of the most wildly original kind."

"Oh, if the matter is not confidential, I should like to stay, especially if you are going to be amusing. Besides, I am really bursting with curiosity."

"Then I will go and get my documents," I replied, and with this I retired to fetch from my portmanteau the journal of Captain Barnabas Hogg.

When I returned, a paper lantern was swinging from the roof of the verandah, and a small hurricane lamp, for me to read by, stood on the table. Three Madeira chairs had been brought out from the room, and as my host and his daughter had already taken their seats with an air of expectation, I took possession of the empty chair and unfolded my project.

"You may remember," said I, addressing my host, "a conversation we had one evening soon after I came here, on the subject of the wealth of the native kings, in which you told me of certain traditions relating to a great fetish hoard near the source of the River Tano."

"I remember," replied Pereira.

"You may remember also how on a certain Sunday at Anyáko we met an old woman leading her blind son."

"I recollect it perfectly."

"Well, my story and my project are both connected with that tradition and that meeting."

Pereira made no comment on this statement beyond a barely perceptible lift of his eyebrows.

I then went on to give a detailed account of my discovery of the ancient desk at Adena, and the finding of the old shipmaster's journal; and as I proceeded I could see that the curiosity of my auditors became more and more acute, and their attention more close; and when, at the close of my narration, I produced the aged volume and placed it in Pereira's hands, the old man turned over its musty leaves with the keenest interest and enjoyment.

"It's a most curious and interesting find," said he, at last, handing the volume to his daughter, "but I don't quite see its connection with our blind friend nor with your plans for the future."

"Of course you do not," I replied, "but when Miss Pereira has examined the book sufficiently I will read you the riddle."

Miss Pereira at once handed the journal back to me, and opening it at the now familiar page, I read to them Captain Hogg's account of the Portuguese mulatto and his strange adventures.

"What a marvellous and terrible story!" exclaimed Miss Pereira, as I finished and passed the open book to my host. "It reads like some weird legend of adventure in the underworld. It isn't possible that it can be true."

"Of its truth I feel no doubt whatever," replied Pereira, who was poring, with the deepest fascination, over the crabbed writing; "nor do I feel any doubt that this gruesome cavern still exists and is still tenanted by its terrific band of workers. But still, I do not see what this has to do with your plans for the future, Englefield."

"My dear Pereira," I rejoined. "You have answered that question yourself. You say you are sure that the cavern still exists with all its infernal machinery in full swing. So am I. And do you suppose that I can ever rest until I have seen its marvels with my own eyes, or, at least, ascertained the existence of the golden pool that feeds the crucibles on its furnaces?"

"If ever you do see it with your own eyes, it will be the last thing that you *will* see," said Pereira.

His daughter shuddered.

"Come, Mr Englefield," she said, "you have not told us everything yet. You have something more to say I am sure, haven't you?" Some scheme that you have worked out in connection with this story. Isn't it so?"

"Yes, I have a scheme," I replied rather shyly, "but it is such a wild and apparently impracticable one that I am ashamed to mention it to you."

"Oh, don't be afraid," said she, smiling. "We are prepared for anything now; I defy you to astonish us."

"Then I will tell you my plan, and you can scoff if you please. It arose from my meeting at Adena with a Fulah merchant from, I think, Sókoto. When I first saw this man I was at once struck by his extraordinarily European appearance. He was scarcely as dark as I am, his features were quite of the European type – perhaps a trifle Jewish – and, in fact, I could not help seeing that if he and I had exchanged clothing, neither of us would have appeared at all inappropriately apparelled. Reflecting upon this, it occurred to me that it might, perhaps, be not impossible for me to assume the dress and style of a Fulah, and so make my journey to Aboási without exciting remark or attracting much attention. It sounds a pretty mad scheme, doesn't it?"

"It certainly does seem a little – well, a little romantic, I think," said Miss Pereira; "but then I have never seen a Fulah, and to me an African is a black man, so I am unable to imagine you effectively disguised as a native."

"Yet it is not so mad as it sounds," put in Pereira meditatively, stroking his beard. "Englefield is perfectly correct so far in what he says. Dress him up in a *riga* and *wondo*, shave his head, wrap his face in a *litham*, stain his fingernails red, and put a streak of antimony under his eyes, and he might walk through any native market without even the Fulahs themselves suspecting him. But, my dear boy," he continued, turning to me, "there are other difficulties, as you must have seen. There is the language, for instance. You are not going to pose as a deaf mute, I suppose?"

"I know a little Hausa," I said modestly.

"A little!" he exclaimed. "You must know a great deal if you would not be detected at once. But let us see what you *do* know". He bustled away, and presently returned with a copy of Schön's *Maganan Hausa* in his hand. Opening the book at the "Story of the Prophet Jesus and the Skull," he directed me to read a passage aloud and translate it.

This I did with an ease that surprised myself and filled Pereira with astonishment.

"Why, my dear fellow," said he, "you have quite an excellent working knowledge of the language, and it seems to me, a very good accent too, although quite different from that which is spoken by the Hausas down here. With a little practice your Hausa might do. But there are yet other things – the habits of the Fulahs and Hausas, which would be quite strange to you, and your ignorance of which would betray you. Then there is Arabic; every high-class Fulah knows a little Arabic and can spell out a verse or so of the Koran. Do you know any Arabic?"

"Not a word."

"Well, I do. I lived for a year at Tripoli, and picked up a fair knowledge of it, and, as you seem to be naturally a good linguist, I daresay I can put you in the way of as much as you are likely to want. But the habits and customs seem to me the real stumbling block, you know nothing of the ways of these people, and so would be detected as a stranger before you had been in their company five minutes."

I was silent for a while.

Pereira had put his finger upon what I had seen from the first was the really weak spot in my plan, and I was left without a reply. But I had no intention of giving up my scheme.

"I admit the force of your objection," I said presently, "but I must try to get over the difficulty by learning as much of the domestic habits of the Fulahs as I can before starting, and trust to acquiring the real hallmark in the course of my travels."

"Trust in Providence, in fact. Well, you are young and hopeful. But have you settled any details as to making the start on this wonderful Sinbad voyage?"

"Yes," I replied. "I have arranged with a certain David Annan that I shall accompany him on a monkey skin expedition into North Ashanti."

"You know that Annan is a consummate rascal, I suppose?"

"I guessed it. I imagine that he will probably try to rob me and make off as soon as we are fairly in the bush, which is just what I want him to do. I shall thus disappear in a graceful and natural manner, and shall not be baulked by well-meant endeavours to discover my whereabouts."

Pereira laughed. "You are an ingenious lunatic, Englefield, and deserve to succeed, but you've not the least chance of doing so. You had much better give up this hare-brained scheme, at least for the present, and either go home with Bithery or stay here with me and make your little pile in a sane manner."

"I tell you, Pereira," said I, irritably, "that my mind is made up. I have arranged to go with Annan, and I am going."

Pereira shrugged his shoulders. "It is something for a man to know his own mind," said he dryly, "even if that mind is none of the soundest."

But he made no further objections, and we spent the remainder of the evening discussing the mysterious cavern and considering the details of the great wild goose chase. It was nearly midnight when we rose to retire, and, as Pereira shook hands with me and wished me "good night", he said with sudden warmth. "You are a romantic young idiot, Englefield, there is no doubt, but, all the same, if I were twenty years younger, you should not go on your quest alone."

"And I," said his daughter, "if I were only a man, would be proud to go with him and share his perils and adventures."

"And so there would be three of us," said Pereira, "a most glorious and undivided trinity of fools." He laughed again, and waving his hand to me went off to bed.

CHAPTER NINE
I Bid Farewell to my Friends

I remained at Quittáh some six weeks owing to various delays on the part of Annan, and so pleasantly the time sped that, as the period of my departure approached, my impatience to be gone gave way to a strong reluctance to leave the scene of so much happiness. Pereira, having once accepted my scheme, entered into it with all the fire and enthusiasm of the genuine old Portuguese adventurer, and spent all his leisure in preparing me for the difficult part I had to play. He brought out an aged Arabic grammar and dictionary, with the aid of which and of a printed Koran that he had imported for trade purposes, he instructed me in the sacred tongue. He accompanied me to the Mahommedan settlement outside the town and expounded the habits and customs of the people in it. He visited the primitive thatch-built mosque with me, and conversed in Hausa with the old Mallam or priest that I might study the vernacular and improve my accent. He took me through the camp at sunset that I might commit to memory the strange sing-song cries of the worshippers as they prayed on their mats by the roadside; and he picked up odds and ends of Hausa clothing to furnish me for my journey.

But it was not the sympathetic interest that my host showed in my project that made me look forward regretfully to my departure from Quittáh. The fact was that the fair Isabel, whose imagination had been fired by the romance of my Quixotic enterprise, had thrown herself into the scheme with an enthusiasm fully equal to that of her father, and, realising the paramount importance to me of a working knowledge of Arabic, she set herself to superintend my studies in that language; and a most exacting taskmistress I found her, as well as an indefatigable fellow student. We were thus thrown a great deal into one another's society, and there grew up between us a comradeship that was very intimate and sympathetic. It is not often that the companionship of a man and a woman is quite satisfactory, complete coincidence of interest being exceptional. But when such sympathy and community of interest does exist, it renders possible a companionship with which no other can compare. And Isabel Pereira was as delightful a companion as any man could desire.

To many men, indeed, her mere beauty would have made her desirable had her wits been far less acute than they were; but in truth, her mind was as well and justly proportioned as her body; and even as her manifest physical strength served but to render perfect her feminine grace, so her sturdy common sense and steady judgement but heightened the charm of a playful, romantic fancy and a temper entirely amiable and sweet. To me, her father's friend, she was full of frank, unaffected friendliness and good fellowship, never prudish or conscious; and yet there was with this a modesty and womanly reserve that called forth a responsive chivalrous respect on my part.

And so, as I have said, the time sped swiftly and pleasantly in her gentle companionship, and the day of my departure, ever looming nearer, was almost forgotten.

Very delightful it was in the late afternoons to walk together on the smooth wet beach, and listen to the booming surf; to watch the hideous red crabs playing peep-bo! at the mouths of their burrows and squinting at us with their goggle eyes as we passed; or to show our newly-acquired erudition by inscribing Arabic flourishes upon the smooth sand, and all the time to babble unceasingly of the mysterious cavern and of wealth beyond the dreams of avarice. Very peaceful and pleasant was the walk home in the quickly-fading twilight, with the palm trees chattering overhead, and the cicadas chirping in the distance, while the little sandpipers trotted along before us on the wet sand, and the nightjars whirled around us with ghostly flutterings. And then in the hot afternoon when the sun was high and the old merchant was taking his siesta, we would sit together in the verandah with our book between us, conning the uncouth characters and laughing over our mistakes. But in all this there was no philandering or coquetry but steady earnest work; and indeed so close was our application that it was a real relief, when Aochi appeared with the tea, to shut the book and fall to talking about the treasure in the cavern and the pool with the golden floor.

The awakening from this state of dreamy happiness came with the disagreeable suddenness of a douche of cold water.

We were sitting at table at our late breakfast, discussing – with unbecoming hilarity, I feel – the chapter of the Koran on which we had been engaged the day before, when there appeared in the open doorway an excessively dirty negro who stood and glared silently at us as he slowly masticated a chew-stick.

"What do you want, boy?" demanded Pereira sharply.

The man drew a filthy and crumpled envelope from the folds of his cloth and handed it to Pereira, who, having glanced at it, passed it to me with a grin.

"The Honourable and Reverend Mr Englefield, Esq.," I read aloud; and tearing it open, extracted a sheet of ruled notepaper covered with childish scrawl. The letter – for such it appeared to be – was headed, "Cape Coast, Friday," and commenced –

"Honoured and reverend Master,"

"With petious and mercifully I employ to thy protection – "

"Now what in the name of fortune is this?" I exclaimed. Turning the document over I sought the signature, which I presently found squeezed into a lower corner: "thy handmaidden in affliction. David Annan." I remember that, ludicrous as the thing was, none of us laughed. For my own part, I felt a sudden chill, and hastened to decipher the rest of the absurd epistle, of which I made out the contents to be as follows:

"Honoured and reverend Master,

"With petious and mercifully I employ to the protection and also the carrer man no good and he say they not fit because of susistence unless he get some pay but the Mansu brige never spoil any more and so the bush people complain the weather fine too much and the carier man they say he not fit get only his susistence because he sit down too long to wait for you. Sir I have the honour to inform you these few words to tell you if the steamer from leeward came here in few days I beg you that you came on board one time because the rain finish and carier man no good for sit down too long because he say they not fit for get sussistence unless he find some pay so I beg you not stay any longer because carrier man they say he not fit unless they get some pay.

"I have the honour to be Sir, thy handmaidden in affliction.
David Annan."

"Can you make sense of this?" I asked, passing the precious document to Pereira.

"Certainly," said Pereira; "it is perfectly clear. He means to say that he is waiting for you at Cape Coast, that the dry season has set in, that the bridge at Mansu has been repaired, having apparently been washed away by the floods, and that the carriers refuse to accept subsistence money only (threepence a day), but demand to be put on full travelling pay, so he begs you to come on by the first steamer. He also implies that he is being put to great expense in consequence of your delaying, which he will expect you to make good."

"I see. Do you know when the next steamer is due from leeward?"

"The *Benin* is due now homewards," replied Pereira, "so if you think of going by her you will have go get your things together."

He rose from the table, and, taking up a handful of biscuits from a dish, held them out to the messenger and waved to him to be gone. Then he strode up and down the room a few times, and presently halted before me.

"You had better think again, my son," said he, "whether this thing is worth doing. The chance of your really getting any substantial good out of it is, as you know, very small, and you may easily come back no wiser than you go, while the risk you run is enormous. The question is, is it worthwhile? I need not say that Isabel and I will be loth to see you go, for this will be an empty house without you – but I mustn't talk like this," he added in a shaky voice; "only, think it over again before you decide once for all."

It was a great temptation.

I had never been so happy in my life as during these last few weeks; had never known a friendship so intimate and real as that of this fatherly old man and this sweet, gentle girl. And for what was I giving up all this? For an enterprise so shadowy and vague that I could not even state it to myself.

And yet the unrest of youth was upon me and the treasure seemed to beckon me on.

"I think it is worthwhile," I said at length.

"As you will, my son," replied Pereira. "Your native clothing is in my room, so if you come I will give it to you now, and Isabel will pack it up for you."

We went to his room, where he produced from a locked drawer the garments that he had purchased as "curios" from Hausa merchants: a *riga* or gown of blue-grey cotton cloth, a pair of *wondo* – immense baggy trousers – a Fez, a *litham*, or face-cloth, and turban of dark blue cotton, a vest, and a pair of yellow leather slippers.

"Here is a knife, too," said Pereira, bringing forth a long clumsy dagger in a leather sheath, "native steel, and not much to look at, but I sharpened it myself and found it mighty hard metal. I have also got you a spearhead and ferrule – you can make a shaft for yourself – so you will be able to take care of yourself, especially if you carry a pistol, and I have made up six small packets of gold dust and a bag of cowries, so that you can start as a man of substance."

We gathered up these treasures and bore them off to my room. I had brought a small cheap iron trunk for the journey, and in this I now threw the very few things that I proposed to take with me – chiefly, for reasons which will presently appear, cast-off clothes and objects of no value. I then put aside the native clothing and weapons, placed with them the gold dust, the cowries, a pocket compass, a sailor's knife, and a small revolver with a box of cartridges, and asked Isabel to make these things into a separate package, using the *riga* as an envelope, and to stitch it up securely. Leaving her to this occupation, I went with Pereira to his office to make final arrangements as to the custody of the small remainder of my property and the money that had been paid to him on my behalf by Captain Bithery, who had sailed for England three weeks before.

"Did I show you Bithery's letter?" Pereira asked, as we took our seats at the office table; and on my answering in the negative he pushed over to me the missive in the Captain's well-known handwriting.

"Tell Englefield," it said, "that I am very well satisfied with him, and hope he is equally so with me. His pay and commission amount to a hundred and fifty-six pounds, which I enclose, with all good wishes. We have done very well this voyage, and I expect we shall be out again in less than six months, so, if he should come to his senses again in that time, he will be able to take up his berth on the *Lady Jane*."

"I am glad the Captain is coming out again," I said as I returned the letter. "He has been a really kind and generous friend to me, and I should like to have a chance of showing him that I realise it."

"Yes," replied Pereira, "Bithery is a really good fellow, and very fond of you, too. And now to settle our business. I understand you want me to take charge of your goods and this money. Is that so?"

"Yes, if you will. I will take fifteen pounds, and you hold the remainder until I come back."

"Very well." He wrote out a receipt, stamped it, and laid on it fifteen sovereigns. "You can change the gold on board ship," he said. "Is there anything more?"

"Only this," I replied, drawing, somewhat sheepishly, from my pocket an envelope addressed to himself. "It is my Will – not a very important document, but it is all regular; the Commissioner witnessed it. You can open it if you hear that anything has happened to me."

Pereira took the packet from me and deposited it in his safe. "It will remain there," said he, "with your money and the old journal until you come back; and I hope it won't be there long. Is that all?"

"That is all," I answered.

He banged the door of the safe and put the key in his pocket, and, almost at the same moment, the report of a gun sounded from the sea.

"That will be the *Benin*," said Pereira.

We both hurried round to the front of the compound, from which a view of the anchorage could be obtained, and as we turned the corner, we perceived the elegant, yacht-like steamer slowing down opposite the Fort.

"I don't expect she will finish loading today," said Pereira, shading his eyes with his hand as he peered at the ship. "I know there is a good deal of produce to go on board. But you had better have everything ready in case the Captain is in a hurry." So saying he went back to his office while I made my way slowly up to my room.

Now, it happened that I was wearing a pair of tennis shoes with rubber soles and I suppose that, walking slowly, lost in thought, I must have stepped more noiselessly than usual, for evidently Isabel had not heard me approach; and as I came to the half-open door I drew back with a start. She was kneeling on the floor before my trunk, making as if she would fold up the blue *riga* that she held in her hands, and although her back was turned to me, I could see that she was sobbing; indeed, as I stood there, she raised the blue cloth in both hands and buried her face in it.

For one moment I remained stock-still, petrified with amazement. Then I stole softly away and hurried down into the compound, looking round right and left to see that no one was about; for the choking at my throat and a fullness in my eyes warned me not to speak to anyone lest I should utterly lose control of my emotions. Slipping out by the back gate I strode down the narrow lane, breathing hard and clenching the pipe that I had thrust into my mouth so fiercely that the fragile stem crunched like straw between my teeth, and so reached the quiet lagoonside, where I paced to and fro upon the dry mud trying to collect my thoughts and to decide what I should do in these new and surprising circumstances.

For the sight of that weeping girl had been to me a double revelation. It had shown me, what I was indeed dull enough not to have seen before, that her sweet comradeship came from something more than mere friendliness; and it had made clear what I was yet more dull not to have perceived – that this lovely and gracious woman was to me more than all the world beside.

What then should I do? Should I give up my plan and settle down quietly at Quittáh? That was the course that common sense suggested. And yet that would be a heavy sacrifice, for, so strongly had this foolish scheme taken hold of me that it had become a positive obsession. And then my pride raised objections to the evident dictates of reason; not the noble pride that makes a man scorn to fall short of his own ethical ideal, but the paltry pride that makes him ashamed to repudiate an ill-formed and hasty resolution. It would seem an absurdly weak and flat conclusion if, after all these preparations, I should collapse at the last moment and go back humbly to my oil puncheons and kernel bags. The mountain that had been in labour would have brought forth such a very small mouse. And what would Isabel think of me? Might she not misunderstand my heroic self-sacrifice? It was not a noble thought; but yet it must be admitted that to a romantic girl, a lover girding up his loins for a perilous, if Quixotic, quest is one thing, and the same lover, with his sleeves rolled up weighing out rubber in the factory yard, is another and a very different thing.

That rubber decided me. My vanity came to the aid of my self-will, and I once more decided to see my adventure through.

And having reached this conclusion I made my way back to the house with a firm step and a steady lip.

She was standing in the verandah when I entered the compound, and when she saw me she waved her hand and greeted me gaily with a Hausa salutation; and when I bounded up the stairs and stood by her side she was quite cheerful and self-possessed, though rather more sober than usual.

"The ship won't nearly finish loading today," she said, "so we shall have one more evening together. I wonder how long it will be before you come back."

"Not more than a month or two, I expect," said I. "Perhaps less if I am lucky and find out what I want to know quickly. The actual distance is quite small from here to Upper Ashanti."

"Yes. And perhaps you won't think it worthwhile to stay there at all. You may find that the whole thing is a myth." I thought she seemed rather to hope that it might be so, but I did not encourage the hope.

"That is hardly likely," I said. "There must be some foundation for all those reports. But here is your father, straight from the beach, I expect, with the latest news of my reprieve."

"The Captain expects to get off between ten and eleven tomorrow," said Pereira, as he stepped on to the verandah, thoughtfully dusting his silk hat with a pocket handkerchief. "There is a lot of produce from the Bremer Factory as well as mine, so he may be later. You can go off with the last boatload."

"Very well; sufficient for the day is the evil thereof: and now let us drown our sorrows in the teapot and go for a walk."

We walked that evening along the beach towards the village of Vojé, and I was glad that Pereira made one of the party, as his presence decided the question whether I should speak to Isabel or leave matters as they were until I came back. My own feeling had been that it would be hardly fair to make any kind of declaration as I was going away on so perilous an enterprise, and I was relieved at not being left alone with her and so tempted to make confidences that I might afterwards have regretted.

On my last night at Quittáh I will not dwell. We all tried to make it as festive an occasion as possible, but with only very moderate success. Enthusiasm respecting the treasure refused to revive, and we separated at length in a quiet and thoughtful mood.

Eleven o'clock on the following morning found us on the beach watching the loading of the last boat. The time of separation had come, and we stood, with our hearts too full for speech, watching the Blue Peter flutter down from the steamer's masthead. The canoe men stood up to their knees in the water, holding on to the surf boat, which reared like a restive horse as each wave rolled in to the shore, and waving their trident-shaped paddles as they shouted their hoarse chant.

And now the last bag of kernels was flung into the boat and my little trunk laid on the heap. The steamer was hooting impatiently, and the boatswain called to me to hasten. The old man seized both my hands and prayed God to bless me and bring me back safe; Isabel and I clasped hands in silence for a moment, and then I leaped into the boat.

The keel ground upon the sand, the boat reared and swept down on the backwash, and amidst a chorus of shouts from the canoe men, and a shower of spray, we charged into the surf. I sat on the swaying thwart, with my back to the sea, watching the two figures on the shore until they had dwindled to the size of dolls, and the green waves heaved up and hid them from my sight. And even after I had climbed the ladder and stood upon the deck, my eyes turned shoreward until the surf-fringed beach had faded out of sight and the land was but a grey streak upon the sea horizon.

Chapter Ten
I Take to the Road

Soon after daybreak on the second morning after my departure from Quittáh, the fishing canoe, which had been sent to fetch me ashore, swept round the bluff into the quieter waters of Winneba Bay, and presently took the ground not far from the mouth of the little River Ainsu; and as I jumped out on to the beach, I found myself folded in the embrace of no less a person that Mr David Annan.

He seemed very pleased to see me, and not without reason, as I presently discovered, for it appeared that, relying on my assumed opulence, he had refrained from burdening himself with an undue amount of that which is vulgarly known as "the ready," and was even now in a state of some pecuniary embarrassment. The "carrier men" were, in fact, "not fit," to use his expression, and refused to lift a load until they had received tangible evidence of their employer's solvency.

A sovereign from my purse, rapidly converted into eighty "thror-pennies" at an adjacent store, revived the flagging confidence of our followers, and half an hour after landing we formed up our little caravan and stepped out briskly up the steep street of the town. I looked around me with growing pleasure and interest, for everything was new and strange. The little church with its tower of sun-dried clay, that had looked so imposing from the anchorage and now appeared so mean; the bright red walls of the houses, so different from the grimy hovels of Quittáh, built of the black lagoon mud; the steep rocky road, the strange trees, the gay and comely Fanti women, were all elements of novelty that came upon me with singular force after my long sojourn amidst the sandy flats and changeless horizon of the Bight of Benin.

Even when we descended into the wide plain the novelty was not abated, for the meadow-like expanse, with its pink soil and waving grass, was as great a change from Quittáh as the rocky upland. And so, while Isabel was mourning my absence in the dull and silent house, here was I striding gaily along the narrow track, watching the little zebra mice and the white-breasted crows and the circling vultures, with an exhilaration that I blush to reflect on.

We walked on at a good swinging pace until nearly noon, when, reaching a belt of woodland, we halted in the shade of a silk-cotton tree to rest and take our midday meal. I had left the commissariat arrangements to Annan, and now reaped the harvest of my folly, for that child of Belial had laid in, with my money, a supply of kanki — a disgusting mess of boiled maize which I had never tasted before, and hope never to taste again. It was highly satisfying, however, and its flavour encouraged moderation, so that when we resumed our march after an hour's rest I was completely refreshed.

The road through which we passed during the afternoon exceeded in beauty my wildest dreams. In the open, indeed, the prospect was merely that of a fine breezy, rolling country covered with grass and bushes; but where the winding path led through shady woodland of rustling groves of oil palms, the richness and luxuriance of the vegetation filled me with astonishment and delight. My opportunities for examining the landscape were not indeed great, for our barefooted carriers covered the rough ground at a pace that was a revelation to me, and kept it up, too, until I was ready to drop with fatigue; and when, towards sunset, we entered a straggling village, I learned from Annan, with profound relief, that this was the end of our day's march.

My trunk had been set down by the carrier against the wall of a house, so I took my seat on it and leaned back with great comfort. Soon a little crowd of women and children gathered round and stood watching me with the expectant interest that a group of rustics at home would manifest in a foreign organ-grinder. I drew out my pipe and filled it to their complete satisfaction, but my matches had become spoiled by the damp of the woodland and would not strike, seeing which, a young woman with a glossy brown baby fastened on her back, hurried away and presently returned rolling a glowing cinder in the palm of her hand. This she very adroitly laid on the tobacco in my pipe and then blew it softly until it glowed white hot and the smoke ascended in blue clouds, and when I thanked her with some warmth she laid her hands together and curtseyed prettily, murmuring "Ya wura," and then retired bashfully behind her friends.

Suddenly the calf-like voice of Annan was heard, "shooing" the children away from me, and my conductor appeared wreathed in smoke and glorious with rich apparel. For in this short time he had exchanged his rough travelling costume for the garb of ceremony, and now displayed the splendour of a velvet smoking cap, a suit of pink pyjamas, the ankles tucked into a pair of scarlet socks, and carpet slippers of prismatic brilliancy.

"You get no servant now, Mr Englefield," said he with an oily smile, "but never fear, sah, I shall be your steward and I do you proper."

"You are very good," said I. "What are we going to do about food? I have had enough kanki for today; and where am I to sleep tonight?"

"I get you fine dinner, sah – de chief's wife cook it now – and very fine bed in de chief's house. But," here he dropped his voice and pulled a most lugubrious face, "dis headman no good at all. He get a dry eye."

"A dry eye?" I exclaimed.

"Yes; he never want to give anyting unless you dash him some money first."

"Well, I don't expect him to give me food and lodging for nothing. If you pay him what you think right, or what *he* thinks right, I will let you have it back."

Annan groaned and pulled out of his pocket a gaudy purse which he opened and held upside down.

"Dose carriers take all dat you give me dis mornin' and spend it 'fore we start. Now de headman say he won't give us nutting for chop widout you dash him first."

I began to suspect that Mr Annan "get a dry eye," but it was useless to wrangle over a few shillings, so I handed him another sovereign, which he received with a gleeful guffaw and departed – ostensibly to make an advance payment to the headman – leaving me speculating curiously as to how he proposed to get change for a sovereign in this primitive hamlet. Apparently he managed to do so for I came upon him unawares shortly after, doling threepenny pieces to the carriers for subsistence; and mightily disconcerted he seemed, for some reason, at being discovered.

His account of the dinner that was in preparation was not exaggerated. It was a colossal feed. The black clay bowls came in one after another until the little rickety table would hold no more, and Annan's eyes fairly bulged with anticipation. He was indeed "doing me proper," as he expressed it, and as he was to share the meal he evidently intended to "do himself proper"; indeed, I fancy that, recollecting my inability to make headway with native dishes when we dined together at Adena, he hoped to consume the major part of these delicacies himself. If this was his idea when he ordered the feast, my appetite must have been a revelation to him; for, having decided that henceforth I must subsist on native food, and being nearly famished, I assaulted the dishes with indiscriminate ferocity, devouring yams, cassava, fowl, goat, stinkfish, palm oil and peppers with supreme disregard of their appearance or flavour until the affrighted Annan abandoned all attempts at conversation in a frantic effort to keep pace with me.

The apartment in which we dined was converted into a bedroom by the simple device of taking out the table and laying down two mattresses formed of bundles of rushes; and although, after dark, the village resounded with the shrieks of the potto calling to his unmelodious mate in the forest, and sundry scufflings and rustlings about our room were unpleasantly suggestive of rats and cockroaches, I almost instantly fell into a delicious slumber which lasted until I was awakened by Annan dragging at my arm.

"Cock-o'-peak-time, * sah," said he with a bland smile. "All de carrier men wait outside; dey say dey ready to start one time."

"But I haven't had any breakfast or bath," I objected, getting up and stretching myself.

Annan laughed. "Plenty rivers in dis country," said he, "and if you want to take chop, I get some here." He displayed a gritty-looking collection of roasted plantains in a dirty red handkerchief and moved towards the door, where a crowd of the villagers had assembled to see us depart.

It was cheerless and chilly when we emerged from the village on to the narrow woodland track. A dense mist enshrouded the landscape and made the trees look ghostly and unreal. Everything reeked with moisture. The dew pattered down from the trees, the grass and herbage was saturated and the ground sodden with the wet. Five minutes after starting I was soaked to the skin and my teeth were chattering.

"You still want a bath, Mr Englefield?" inquired Annan with a delighted chuckle as he noted my saturated clothing.

"I want my breakfast," I retorted savagely, visions of the steaming "early coffee" at Pereira's house flitting across my memory.

Annan opened his bundle, and taking out a blackened plantain, handed it to me after removing the superfluous ashes by wiping it down the leg of his pyjamas; and despite its repulsive aspect, I

---

* Cock-crow – Cock go speak.

chewed it up thankfully, cinders and all, to his undissembled joy and amusement.

"You like dis country chop proper," he remarked, as I licked my fingers and held out my hand for another plantain; but his amusement gave way to apprehension when I proceeded to eat yet a third.

We were meantime entering the fringe of the forest, and the scenery appeared to me unspeakably lovely. The trees grew more lofty and umbrageous, and their trunks were clothed in a garment of creepers and ferns. Once we passed through a grove of oil palms, and I was charmed with the delicate grace of this plant, so different from the scraggy coconut palm of the coast, so soft and feathery and symmetrical, and so beautifully adorned with the long trailing ferns that hang down in lacy streamers from the crown of the stem.

Annan's promise as to the rivers, too, was amply fulfilled, but although they were pleasant enough to look at, they were a great annoyance, as they kept my legs continually wet from wading through them; and I rather envied the carriers, whose scanty clothing made this a matter of less consequence to them.

After a couple of hours of steady tramping we entered the large village of Essekúma, where Annan decided to halt for a meal; and it was quite pleasant to sit in the open compound and dry one's clothing in the sun.

A substantial meal of oily and pungent fowl stew accompanied by a liberal allowance of tenacious plantain fufu, made me inclined to loll at my ease and quietly study the village life and meditate upon the queer sculptured ornaments on the houses; but Annan would hear of no delay, and having cleaned his fingers on the ever-ready pyjamas, gave the word to proceed. These Africans were certainly indefatigable walkers, and their powers of endurance quite remarkable – so remarkable, indeed, that I began to doubt if I should be able to keep up with our carriers, burdened as they were with loads varying from thirty to sixty pounds.

We travelled on, with rare and brief halts for rest at wayside hamlets, until near sunset, when we reached a small, primitive village called Obedumássi, at which we brought up for the night, and where our experiences of the previous evening were repeated. The headman, at whose house we lodged, kept a civet in a kind of wooden hutch for the purpose of extracting the perfume, and I had an opportunity of witnessing the operation. The animal was first poked with a stick to make it fly round its narrow cage until in the course of its gyrations it allowed its tail to project between the bars. This was immediately grabbed by the operator and pulled so that the unfortunate beast was jammed helplessly against the bars, when the perfume was scooped out of the scent gland by means of a wooden implement like a marrow spoon. This curious unctuous substance had a disgusting odour somewhat like that of a recently-extinguished tallow candle, mingled with the scent of musk, but Annan assured me that "the Hausa men find it sweet too much," so I purchased a small quantity with a view to future contingencies.

The next day was one of almost continuous trudging along a path that was far from good to walk upon. This everlasting marching would have been as monotonous as it was fatiguing but for the novelty of the surroundings, which were almost as strange to me as if I had but just come from England. Our route on this day lay through an extensive swamp, some parts of which were overgrown with bamboos, and here the aspect of nature was most singular and impressive. The bamboo could be seen as we approached it, an immense cloudy mass of moving green with mysterious cavern-like openings with led into a dim interior like that of some colossal crypt. The canes rose out of the ground in huge bundles like great clustered columns, and interlaced overhead in an impenetrable vault, so that the gloomy interior was broken up into a maze of aisles and transepts, some leading away into absolute black darkness, others showing a distant spot of bright light – the opening on the further side of the thicket.

We were treading our way through one of these passages, treading daintily on the crackling debris that formed the floor (for the mysterious twilight of the place somehow induced a silent and stealthy manner of movement), when Annan, who was leading, suddenly stopped dead, and peering down a dark side aisle began to talk in a loud, startled tone. At the same moment I noticed a group of men crouching and almost hidden in the deeper shadow of one of the clusters of canes, and our carriers, catching sight of them too, hastily laid down their burdens, and broke out into excited and voluble jabbering, so that the previously silent crypt was a Babel of noise. In a few moments the men came forth from their hiding place into the dim light of the passage in which we stood, and a sinister-looking crowd they were, quite nude, with the exception of the narrow loincloth, and each provided with a long flintlock gun with a red-painted stock and a large knife in a leopard skin sheath. They were evidently not travelling far from home, for none of them carried any baggage or provisions beyond the bottle-shaped gourd which served as a powder flask, and a bag of slugs.

A tall, elderly man, apparently the leader of the party, came forward and made a long statement to Annan, gesticulating and grimacing in the native fashion and pointing frequently in the direction in which we were going; then, after Annan had replied in a quieter tone, the carriers took up their burdens and we moved forward, while the armed men returned to their retreat.

"Who are those men?" I asked, as we came out once more into the light of day.

"Dose men," replied Annan, "is Akotádi people, and dey tell me some very bad news. Dey say all de roads shut everywhere."

"What do they mean? Who has shut the roads?"

"Because of de war palaver," replied Annan. "Dey say dat 'Shanti people fight wid Békwe, and Adánsi people fight wid 'Shanti and Akém. Plenty war palaver everywhere."

"Then it won't be very safe going through Ashanti, will it?" said I.

"Safe!" yelled Annan. "I tell you all de roads shut. Spose 'Shanti man see us he tink we Adánsis and he shoot us. Spose Békwe man sees us, he say we Akém and he shoot us. Eberybody shoot us. Shia! M'nyohum!" He shook his fist in the air and spat on the ground.

I could not help laughing at this outburst, for, apart from the highly inappropriate application of a disgusting and untranslatable Fanti expletive, the picture that Annan drew of our progress through the country was farcical in the extreme. We were Ishmaelites indeed!

"Why de debbil you laugh?" exclaimed Annan, looking as if he could have cut my throat with pleasure. "You no laugh if 'Shanti man catch you."

"No," I agreed, "I suppose not. But what shall you do? You won't turn back, will you?"

"Me, turn back!" he shouted. "I tell you, sah, I come to get monkey skin, and I fit for get monkey skin. 'Shanti man can go to hell."

I never felt more friendly to the sturdy rascal than on hearing him speak thus. I could have shaken his dirty hand – if it had been necessary. When he had spoken of the closed roads I had feared that our expedition would collapse after all, so this exhibition of dogged pluck came as a great relief.

The sun had already sunk below the tree tops, and the shades of evening were gathering fast as we came out of the forest into the open village of Pra-su. By the fading light I could see that this was different in appearance from the hamlets we had passed through, for, in addition to the ordinary Fanti houses, there were groups of beehive-shaped huts of palm thatch, such as I had seen in the Hausa quarter at Quittáh, each group enclosed by a fence of palm leaves. There were also a number of rough sheds of a larger size, and a one-storey house of European construction – the residence of the commandant. For Pra-su was the outpost of the British Protectorate, and had a small garrison of Hausa troops, commanded by an officer of the Gold Coast Constabulary, to protect the ferry across the river Pra.

We had hardly entered the village when we came upon a group of the soldiers. They had scratched upon a small patch of earth a kind of primitive chessboard, and two of them were hurriedly finishing a game by the last of the twilight while the others stood round and watched. As we came abreast of the group, I heard my name called, and an elderly sergeant stepped forward with a salute and a grin of friendly recognition.

"Welcome to Pra-su; hope you well, sah," said he.

"Why, it's Sergeant Aba!" I exclaimed, shaking him by the hand. "Well, now, I never thought to meet a friend at Pra-su."

He seemed highly gratified at my addressing him thus, and asked if he could render me any service, remarking that the Commandant had gone to Cape Coast and had left him in charge of the station.

"I should be very glad to get something to eat," said I, "and perhaps you can find me a clean house to sleep in tonight."

"You fit to eat country chop?" he asked a little shyly.

I replied that I was fit to eat anything, and the more the better.

"Den, sah, you come wid me and I give you chop, and you look my house. He be new house, quite clean, spose you like him you sleep dere."

I thanked him warmly for his offer and although Annan looked rather sourly upon the arrangement, I went off with the sergeant to inspect my lodgings.

We wandered down several narrow lanes between high fences of palm leaf and reeds, until presently, Aba halted and, separating two of the mats forming the fence, we entered his compound. The twilight had already faded into night, and I could but dimly make out the beehive-shaped houses ranged round the enclosure or the shadowy forms flitting about in the darkness, but I could see that the compound was an open space some twenty yards square. In the centre of it a dull red fire was burning, and an aged man in a turban and *riga* squatted by it on a mat and occasionally stirred it with a stick. The special object of his regard, however, was not the fire itself but a singular little fence that encircled it, which fence I found, on nearer inspection, to consist of a number of pointed sticks stuck in the earth, each stick having impaled on it several pieces of meat with a lump of fat as a crowning ornament.

Aba leaned over the fence and sniffed. "You fit chop dis sort, sah?" he asked.

I replied with a most emphatic affirmative, for my mouth fairly watered at the delicious odour of the roasting meat; so Aba fetched a mat from his house and laid it down before the fire, as we squatted on it together and watched the meat roasting.

Aba endeavoured to divert me with conversation until the meat should be ready, but the time seemed endless, and I found my famished gaze continually wandering towards the kabobs and noting the lumps of fat frizzling in the heat, and the little streams of oil that trickled over the meat and dripped upon the ground. And the way in which the old man slowly turned the skewers, sniffed critically and shook his head, and Aba's gaunt Bornu wife came forth, examined the kabobs and vanished again, wrought me to the verge of frenzy.

At last the old man seemed satisfied, for he plucked up one of the skewers, and having turned it round and round in the firelight, he sang out in a cracked voice, "Fatima! Ya karé!" and I breathed a sigh of relief and licked my lips.

To this day I look back upon that meal with a kind of greedy pleasure. After the pungent, greasy, Fanti stews, this wholesome food seemed doubly delicious, and in truth those kabobs might have raised the ghost of an alderman. Then too, there was couscous in clean wooden bowls, and flat baskets piled high with masa – little pancakes of pea-flour fried in clay moulds – and after all this a great calabash of mangoes was passed round, so that when I at length washed my hands in the bowl of water that was brought to each of the guests by Aba's youngest girl, I was a better fed man than I had been since leaving Quittáh.

We sat by the fire – new fed with crackling faggots – till far into the night, and Aba, in his halting English gave me much information and sage advice. He shook his head with grave disapproval of my journey into Ashanti, which country he said was "no place for white man," especially just now, for " 'Shanti man find blood sweet too much." He also warned me against Annan.

"Dat man bery bad man. I sabby him long time. He fit to teef your money and kill you, and den say 'Shanti shoot you. He dam rascal too much."

As a practical comment on his opinions, Annan stole into the compound just then and came and bent over me.

"Mr Englefield, sah," he whispered confidentially, "I come to beg you, sah."

"What is it?" I asked.

"De chop for tomorrow. We go to strange country; we must take plenty chop wid us because of de war palaver."

"Very well," said I, "you know what is necessary, and you have enough money to get it, I suppose."

"No, sah," exclaimed he, "dat is where you mistake. De money all finish tonight."

"Nonsense," said I. "You can't have spent all that money since yesterday."

"I tell you it finish," he declared excitedly. "De carrier chop it all. You look yourself!" He whisked his purse out with a flourish, opened it and held it upside down. Unfortunately, he had brought out the wrong purse, and as he inverted it, the two sovereigns that I had given him dropped out on to the mat; at which he was so completely disconcerted that he hastily picked them up without a word.

"Dere, what I tell you, sah?" exclaimed Aba, shaking his fist at the retreating "scholar man". "Dat man proper rascal. He teef every ting you get. I beg you, sah, you no go for bush country wid him."

I laid my hand affectionately on the honest fellow's shoulder as I got up from the mat and stretched myself.

"Never fear for me, Aba," and I; "I look him proper. If he trouble me I show him my pistol."

Aba shook his head sadly but said no more, and, as it was now late, he dragged the mat into a new thatch hut, laid a pillow on it and wished me goodnight.

CHAPTER ELEVEN
I Find Myself Among Enemies

I was aroused next morning by the bugles sounding reveille in the Hausa camp, and, as I came out of the house, I found Fatima waiting for me with a large calabash of agidi – a kind of thin porridge – to fortify me for my journey. While I was consuming this insipid but refreshing food, she went into her house and fetched a small grass bag filled with masa, which she shyly placed in my hand and then hurried away before I had time to thank her.

Down at the landing place, Annan was waiting impatiently with the carriers, and Aba, who had come to see me off, stood at a little distance, aloof and haughty, holding no communication with the Fanti merchant. As I appeared, the carriers and Annan scrambled into the long ferry canoe, and the ferryman took up his pole and prepared to push off, so Aba stepped into the unwieldy craft that he might see the last of me. I showed him the bag of masa, and thanked him and Fatima for their hospitality and would have made him a little present, but when he perceived my intention, he shook his head with such energy, repeating "Bábu bábu!" and clucking his tongue deprecatingly, that I desisted and shook him again by the hand.

As the canoe grated on the beach of the north shore, Aba addressed a few words to Annan as the latter stepped ashore.

"You hear me, David Annan, dis white gentleman my friend. He go wid you for far bush. Spose you no look him proper, den when you come back, I ask you, what you do for my friend? You sabby?"

Annan had by this time climbed the steep bank, and now, looking down at the sergeant, he made a gesture of contempt, remarking that "scholar man no fit to talk to Sálaga donkor" with which polite rejoinder he turned away along the road. The carriers followed and, with a last "goodbye" to Aba, I climbed the bank and hurried after them.

The road, as I have called it, was a narrow winding track that led at once into the sombre shadow of the forest. Before I had followed its sinuous course for five minutes, all trace of the wide river had vanished, and the bright light of day have given place to a soft green twilight by which was revealed the most amazing labyrinth of vegetation that the mind could conceive. On all hands was a confused tangle of leaves and branches, of ferns and great rope-like creepers, piled together in riotous luxuriance and shutting out alike the heavens above and the earth beneath. So indistinct was the trail amidst all this wealth of vegetation that I had to use the utmost exertions to avoid losing sight of my companions, who, more accustomed to such surroundings than I, crashed through the undergrowth at a pace that I could barely keep up with. The ground was terribly rough, too. In some places jagged masses of ironstone projected from the surface, in others the soil was sodden and boggy; the entire region was a network of small muddy streams, which here and there spread out into swamps, and everywhere great coils of snake-like roots sprawled over the ground and tripped one up at every step. I stumbled on, however, in spite of all obstacles, wading knee-deep in the swamps and vaulting over the fallen trees that constantly barred the way; but it was weary work, and I hailed with relief the sight of a small village, hoping to get at least a few minutes' rest.

When we entered the hamlet, and our carriers set down their burdens, an elderly man came out from behind a house and peremptorily ordered us to move on. Annan would have argued the matter with him, but the man – presumably the village headman – pointed to the road and repeated his command in so angry a tone that there was nothing for it but to resume our march.

After trudging on for another hour or so, we came out suddenly into the single wide street of a large village, which I found was called Attássi Kwánta. Here the attitude of the natives was but little more friendly than at the village we had passed, for, as we appeared in the street, we were met by a party of about a dozen men, several of them armed with muskets, who barred the way while they put a number of questions to Annan. Their manner was fierce and their looks sullen, and I could not fail to notice that I was an especial object of suspicion, for, as they talked, they cast frequent and highly unfriendly glances at me, and I heard the word "broni" (white man) repeated several times. Annan, for his part, entered into a lengthy and voluble explanation, and, as he pointed to me, shrugged his shoulders and raised his eyebrows; but whether he was assuring them of my harmlessness or disclaiming all knowledge of and responsibility for me, I could not make up my mind. What was quite evident, however, was that he made no particular impression on my behalf for, although we were permitted to sit down under the shade-tree to eat our food, the men stood round us with a menacing air of watchfulness the whole time, and when I went to a fire that was smouldering by the roadside to get an ember for my pipe, two of them came and rudely bustled me away from it.

The aspect of the village itself was highly suggestive of the disturbed state of the country. Not a woman or child was to be seen, and even the men were not much in evidence, although the appearance of heads now and again protruded round the corners of houses, gave the impression that the male population was not far off.

Of the men who stood guard over us, some were, as I have said, armed with muskets, and all wore powder gourds and slug bags, and in several parts of the village I could see rows of the long Dane guns leaning against the houses with their lock covers hanging loose, all ready for use at a moment's notice.

The instant we had finished our meal the chief motioned to us to go, and we wearily arose and filed out of the village to resume our march along the rough track.

This hostility on the part of the natives was extremely disconcerting, for, although up to the present it had taken only a passive form, it might at any moment become active, especially as we approached Ashanti proper, where the people would naturally associate us with their southern enemies. But still more disturbing to me was the attitude of Annan, whose manner was hardly more friendly than that of the natives. It was evident that my detection of his fraud had filled him with hatred and rage, and Aba's parting speech had not improved matters, for, since leaving Pra-su, he had maintained a sullen silence, in singular contrast to his usual boisterous garrulity, never once speaking to me except to refuse gruffly some masa which I offered him, with the remark that he "didn't eat donkor chop."

I could not help seeing, too, that my presence was an element of added danger to our party, and that both he and the carriers would very gladly be rid of me; so bearing in mind Aba's warning, I determined to keep a very sharp eye on my friend David Annan.

We pressed on during the day at a speed that was intolerably fatiguing, and must have covered fully thirty miles before sunset, which overtook us just as we reached a village called Akonsírrim. We had passed several villages during the day, but had not attempted to halt at them, hurrying through and taking our rest and food in the forest, as far as possible from any human habitation.

At the entrance to Akonsírrim we were met by a party of armed men, who appeared to be the only occupants of the place; but, although their reception of us was grim enough, they were at length prevailed upon by Annan to permit us to sleep in the village.

A little incident that had occurred during one of our halts had put me more than ever on my guard. We had seated ourselves by the side of a small stream to rest and take our afternoon meal, the packages having been set down by the roadside, and as we sat I thought I could detect the babbling of a waterfall at no great distance. When I had finished eating I rose and strolled away into the forest to look for the fall, but finding the bush impenetrable, returned almost directly. As I came near the road, I could see our party through an opening in the foliage, though I was invisible to them, and the first object that caught my eye was friend Annan busily engaged fitting a key into the lock of my trunk. He had just succeeded in unfastening it when I saw him, and having lifted the lid was about to rummage among the contents; but as I was most anxious that he should not see the bundle of Hausa clothing, I put an end to his researches by loudly snapping a twig, upon which he looked round, hastily closed and locked the box, and went back to the stream, where I found him innocently munching when I returned.

The sleeping quarters assigned to us at Akonsírrim were in one of the curious native houses, built, after the Ashanti fashion, on a platform of clay and having only three walls, the fourth side being open like the stage of a theatre. In this airy chamber I lay down on a heap of dry grass that covered the hard clay floor and composed myself as if for sleep, but although I half closed my eyes, my suspicions of my companion kept me wide awake. Presently Annan came and lay down at the other end of the hut; but he did not fall asleep as was his wont, for although he lay quite still and breathed heavily, I knew that he was listening to my breathing. I therefore simulated a gentle snore, and mumbled occasionally as though I were dreaming, and sure enough my friend began presently to crawl softly across the hut towards me. I was in doubt now whether I had not better seize him and bang his head against the wall without more ado, but perceiving by the dim starlight that his hands were empty, I decided to see what his intentions were before committing myself. He crept on silently to my side, and, rising on to his knees, examined me narrowly; then he commenced stealthily to paw me over until his hand lighted on the bulging caused by the purse and clasp knife in my trousers pocket. This was evidently the object of his search, for, having found it, he began to insinuate his fingers into the opening of the pocket; but at this point I gave a deep sigh and turned over, whereupon he scrambled noiselessly across the hut and lay down once more. He made no attempt to come to me again, and very soon his resounding snores told me that he was really sleep.

It will be readily understood that I had very little sleep that night, and in the morning I arose unrefreshed and weary; but it was necessary to get on the road at once, for the men of the village, considering that they had seen enough of us, came and conducted us out of their territory with scant ceremony, nor would they agree to sell us so much as a single plantain for food. The food question was, indeed, becoming urgent already, for I had eaten nothing on the previous day but a few plantains that I had purchased from our carriers (who had brought them from Pra-su), and one or two masa. I had still a good supply of the little cakes, but I felt that I ought to keep them for an emergency; and meanwhile the poor diet was beginning to tell on me, while the prospect of absolute starvation confronted our party if no one would sell us food.

These matters I revolved gloomily in my mind as I stumbled along the rugged path through the solemn, shadowy forest. But more grave than the food question was the conduct of Annan. Evidently he intended to rob me and, as Aba had pointed out, nothing would be simpler than for him to murder me and report that I had been killed by the Ashantis. All my weapons were sewn up in my bundle, so that I was completely unarmed, while Annan, as I knew, carried a formidable sheath knife. This state of things I determined to remedy at once as well as I could, for an emergency might arise at any moment. I had cut myself a stock on the previous day from a hardwood sapling, and now, remembering the very efficient wooden spears of the Australian natives, I proceeded to trim one end of it to a moderately sharp point, and so provided myself with a really formidable although harmless-looking weapon.

We had not been long on the march before I received a disagreeable hint as to Annan's intentions towards me. About three hours' journey from Akonsírrim the path entered a deep valley, at the bottom of which was a small stream, and when we had forded this we came to the foot of a lofty hill, the face of which was so precipitous as to form a kind of cliff. Up this the path could be traced in a series of a zig zags among projecting bosses of rock and clumps of bushes. I rested at the bottom of the cliff until Annan and the carriers had nearly reached the top, and then commenced the ascent. I was about halfway when, happening to glance up, I perceived Annan standing immediately above me and watching my progress. A few moments later I was startled by a sudden noise overhead, and again looking up, saw a ponderous mass of ironstone bounding down the cliff straight on to me. I had barely time to seize a branch and swing myself aside before it whizzed by, dislodging in its descent a shower of stones and smaller fragments. When I reached the summit, Annan was nowhere to be seen, and it was some minutes before I overtook him striding along with the carriers down the northern slope of the hill. That he had rolled the rock down on me I had not the faintest doubt, but as there was nothing to be gained by taxing him with it I held my peace.

A little further on we came upon a scene that filled me with joy and hope. In the midst of a small opening by the roadside lay the ashes of a wood fire, still hot and sending up a tiny thread of smoke, and by its side three diminutive huts built of grass and leaves fastened to central upright sticks. The still smouldering ashes told us that the travellers who had encamped here had left but recently and, as we had not met them, they must be travelling in the same direction as ourselves; while the familiar beehive shape of the huts showed that the strangers were not forest people (who always build square shelters) but Hausas or Moslem travellers from the far north.

Our carriers stirred up the embers and laid on them the few remaining plantains to roast for the midday meal, and while this simple cooking was proceeding they sat round the fire and talked earnestly with Annan, taking no notice of me; but I caught the word *broni* several times, and from this and from occasional glances in my direction I surmised that I was the subject of their conversation.

This debate received a sudden and violent interruption, for in one of the pauses in their conversation there was heard the sound of something moving softly through the underwood behind them. The startled carriers all sprang up together, and instantly the woods rang with a loud explosion and the shriek of scattering slugs, and one of our men leaped into the air with a loud yell and fell to the ground.

A perfect pandemonium followed. Annan and the remaining carriers danced about, screeching and gesticulating like maniacs, while an almost equal hubbub came from the unseen foe. After a time the yells subsided into mere shouting, and I gathered that our people were giving an explanation to their invisible assailants, for they pointed first to the wounded carrier – who lay on the ground groaning, with his hand clapped on to his thigh – and then to me; and the explanation appeared to satisfy the warriors, for presently, as the shouting ceased, we could hear the men moving away through the undergrowth, and a minute later I saw them, nine in number, cross the path at a little distance, each with his long musket muzzle downwards over his shoulder.

They had hardly disappeared when our carriers gathered round me with an angry clamour, and Annan strode up and shook his fist in my face, showing his teeth and gibbering like an excited monkey.

"You dam ogly white nigger!" he shouted. "You make all dis palaver. All dis country people want to kill us cos you come wid us to spy deir country. But you no fit trouble us much more. Soon de hasses pick your bones and den palaver finish." He spat on the ground, and the carriers, who understood not a word of this excepting that it was abuse of me, groaned in chorus.

Suddenly the wounded man, forgetting his injury, sprang up and, grabbing a lump of quartz, rushed at me, roaring and gnashing his teeth; but I received him with such a poke in the chest from my pointed stick that he dropped the stone and fell, bellowing louder than ever, with a thin trickle of blood flowing from the spot where the point had penetrated. On this the others fell back a pace or two, not liking my looks, and stood round, grinning and chattering like apes, while I paused for an instant undecided whether to charge them or remain on the defensive. At this moment Annan came to his senses and interfered.

"Dis no good," he exclaimed. "Softly, softly you catch de monkey. Finish palaver and come on."

The carriers sulkily caught up their burdens and started, but it happened that the wounded man – who was very little hurt, after all – was the one to whom my trunk had been allotted, and, as he was now not fit to carry it, Annan bluntly informed me that, if I wanted it, I must carry it myself; and angry as I was, I could not help perceiving that it would chime in very well with my plans to have the trunk in my own custody; so without more ado I clapped the head pad on top of my hat, and catching up the trunk, balanced it on my head as well as I could and followed. The ground continued to descend gently, and, as the path was a little more open at this part, we got on at a good pace, the wounded man limping along in fine style, and evidently rejoicing at having shifted his burden on to me. We presently entered a small village which appeared to be quite deserted, and our carriers halted and were just about to open an attack upon a plantation of plantains and papaw trees at its farther end, when we observed one or two men peering at us round the corners of the houses; on which they picked up their loads and hurried out of the village as if they had seen the devil.

The road continued fairly distinct, I dropped behind a little to escape from the incessant chatter that Annan and the carriers kept up, in spite of the danger by which we were surrounded, and I frequently lost sight of our little caravan for some minutes at a time, overtaking them again when a fallen tree or other obstruction brought them to a temporary halt. I had separated in this manner and was walking along lost in thought, when a turn of the path brought me in view of our party all standing stock-still and sniffing the air like dogs. At the same moment I became aware of a faint, stale and indescribably disagreeable odour which seemed to come from the forest ahead of us. As we proceeded it grew rapidly more powerful and was soon insupportably offensive, evidently proceeding from some putrifying animal matter. I surmised that some large animal had died in the bush and that the smell proceeded from its decaying remains, but my companions evidently had an inkling of the truth, for they stepped warily and fearfully along the track. Suddenly the path opened out into a large village clearing, and, as we emerged from the forest, a cloud of vultures arose and settled in the trees, from which they looked down with hoarse cries upon the horrid scene of desolation below.

In all the village there was not a single house left standing. Some were reduced to mere shapeless heaps of blackened ruins, while in others the charred skeleton of a roof yet rested on the scorched and cracked clay walls. The compound fences were reduced to lines of ashes; cooking pots stood over extinct fires; and half-burnt stools and wooden utensils lay scattered about among the ruins. And everywhere – in the streets, in the compounds, and by the ruined houses – the ground was literally strewn with corpses. In every attitude of death, in every stage of decay and dismemberment; bloated by the heat, shrivelled by the sun, hacked at by vultures, torn limb from limb by wild beasts; the loathsome harvest of war lay poisoning the air with the stale and horrid effluvium. Glossy-coated carrion beetles crept busily over them, swarms of flies hummed in the air above them, and in one place, a broad shining stream of driver ants flowed through the village like a river of jet, leaving in its track clean-picked skeletons already bleached to the whiteness of chalk.

As we stood surveying these dreadful relics, the vultures began to drop down by two and threes, watching us warily as they snapped up their grisly morsels; and when we moved up the village and came round a pile of ruins, we disturbed at their ghastly meal a troop of hyenas, which shuffled away and stood at a little distance with their shoulders hunched up, grinning at us and snarling with titters of idiotic laughter.

The village had been very completely looted by the enemy, but we found, nevertheless, in the remains of the plantation, a few bunches of plantains, and one or two half-rotten papaws; and having secured these, we stole stealthily and guiltily out of the village and hurried away along the road, not a little affected by the awful spectacle we had witnessed.

It was now past midday, and I began to consider very earnestly how and where I was to pass the night, for I had definitely made up my mind that I would not spend it in the society of Annan and his gang of ruffians. It was now clear that they were of one mind in their desire to be rid of me, and it was equally evident that Annan had already appointed himself my sole executor and legatee. This being the case, it would be obvious madness for me to trust myself asleep in their company, and I had now to settle on the manner in which I should escape from them and yet find my way to my destination.

I had turned over various plans, none of them very satisfactory, and was wondering whether the travellers whose huts we had passed in the morning were far ahead, and if it would be possible for me to put on a spurt and overtake them, when the question was solved for me by the appearance of the men themselves. We came upon them quite suddenly, for they had made a fire some little distance off the road and were sitting by it roasting plantains – the only food obtainable just now – so that we did not see them until we came opposite their halting place. There were eight of them, all grown men, and dressed in the fashion common to the Hausas and other move civilised nations of the Southern Sudan.

Our party halted opposite the encampment, and Annan stepped forward a few paces and greeted the strangers in his barbarous Hausa.

"Sanu, Sanu!"

"Sanu kadai," replied a little sharp-faced elderly man, apparently the leader of the caravan.

"Whither do you travel?" inquired Annan.

"We are journeying from Salt-pond to Kantámpo, and thence to our country, Kano, by way to Salaga," said the old man.

"This country is very unsafe to travel in at this time," remarked Annan.

"That is true," agreed the other.

"But it is more safe for a large company than a small one," pursued Annan.

"That is also true," said the Hausa.

"Therefore," continued Annan, "since we go the same way as you, it will be safer if we travel in company."

"Not so," replied the old man. "We are strangers from afar, merchants and men of peace. We have no quarrel with this people nor they with us, and so we journey in safety. But you are men of this country who have here your friends and your enemies. It is better for us to go our ways apart."

"You fear to walk with us because of the white man who is with us," said Annan.

"We do not want to travel with Nasaráwa*," rejoined the old man.

"But he is a stranger to us," Annan urged. "We will send him away to walk by himself."

"It is not good to desert a companion in the wilderness," said the Hausa coldly. "I have answered thee. We shall walk by ourselves."

* Christians

"The road is open to all!" bawled Annan insolently, "and we may walk where you may, either before you or behind, as near or as far as we will."

"That is true," said the old man drily, "but the mouse who will walk with an elephant must needs look to his toes."

Here occurred a kind of pantomimic commentary on the old Hausa's remark, at which I could hardly forbear laughing aloud, for one of the men who had been reclining by the fire now rose and stretched himself, and reaching his spear from the tree against which it rested, stirred the embers with its heel iron. There was nothing very warlike in the action, but the appearance of the actor gave it a deep significance, for the fellow stood well over six feet six inches in height and was square and massive in build, and the spear that he used thus harmlessly was a great shaft seven feet long furnished with a blade like the paddle of a canoe.

The hint was not lost on Annan who, after an astonished glance at the giant, rejoined civilly enough: "Let it be as you will, and so I wish you a safe journey and a speedy one."

The Hausas returned his good wishes in chorus, and, as we turned to go on our way and I waved my hand to them, they bowed politely, and the jolly, smiling giant called out to me to "tafia sanu" in an extraordinarily small and squeaky voice.

I had now to set my wits to work in earnest, for, by hook or by crook, I must attach myself to the Hausa caravan before nightfall. We were evidently travelling more rapidly that the Hausas, but I calculated that they would pass us the next time we halted, and would be overtaken by our party in the morning. I must therefore wait until they had passed us, before joining them, in case they should decline my company as they had declined Annan's. It now remained to invent a story sufficiently plausible to account for my appearance without companions on this perilous and solitary road, and I am free to admit that, not being an expert liar, the concoction of this fable heavily taxed my ingenuity.

It was half-past three by my watch when Annan called a halt and immediately began to make a fire to roast plantains on. He completely ignored my presence, as did also the carriers, so, as I did not choose to ask his permission to roast my plantains, and as he would probably have refused if I had, I contented myself with a couple of masa and then lit my pipe.

We had not halted more than a quarter of an hour when the Hausa caravan passed, and I noticed that each man carried a spear as a walking staff, and that three of the men had guns lashed lightly to their loads. They saluted us courteously enough in passing, but did not stop to talk, and I was glad to see that they obtained a start of fully three-quarters of an hour before we resumed our journey.

As soon as we were on the road again I began to watch for a chance to escape before an opportunity occurred. At a part of the road where the forest was densest, two gigantic trees had fallen across one another so that the way was completely stopped. When I came in sight of the obstruction, Annan had already climbed to the top, and as he stood up preparatory to helping one of the carriers to ascend, he sank in up to the middle of his thighs, for the tree had been eaten out by the white ants until it was a mere spongy mass of tinder.

I set my trunk down on the path and waited while the carriers laboriously climbed up the rotten barrier and hauled their loads up with the aid of those below, and I watched them hand the burdens down on the other side; and, when the last of them had leaped down without a glance in my direction, I clambered up halfway and peered over at them. The path ran straight ahead for some distance and they hurried along it without looking back; presently they came to a bend in the road, and, one by one, passed out of sight, and as the last man vanished, I jumped down and addressed myself to my task.

In a moment I had the trunk open and the bundle out on the road. I rummaged hastily among the other contents, but found nothing worth taking with me but an old woollen shawl; so, closing the trunk again, I locked it and twisted the key off in the lock, and then, catching up the bundle and the shawl, started back along the path at a run.

A little distance back I had noticed what appeared to be a faint track leading into the forest, and I now ran back until I reached this track, and, having found it, turned down it and ran as fast as the dense undergrowth would let me. I was surprised to find that it grew more distinct as I went on and it presently became quite a well-defined path. When I had run along it for some ten minutes, I turned off into the forest and pushed through the undergrowth until I was stopped by the great buttressed roots of an immense silk-cotton tree which towered up above me like some monumental column. In the angle between two of these buttresses I laid down the bundle, and, with my clasp knife, quickly ripped open the stitching and exposed my treasures to view.

The first thing to do was to shave, for, when I decided to make the journey, I had begun to let my beard grow, and it was now an inch and a half long and very stubbly. I had in the bundle one of those little folding pocket mirrors that are so extensively sold to the natives in West Africa, which I fixed to the tree by sticking my knife through the wire loop; and then taking my razor, mowed away at the dry stubble until the tears ran down my cheeks. But the next operation was worse, for my hair had to come off too, and, by the time I had got my scalp bare, my bald blue pate was covered with scratches and smeared with blood.

The rest, however, was plain sailing. In a twinkling I had stripped off my clothes and donned the vest, the baggy trousers and the long flowing *riga*, jammed the red cap upon my bald knob of a head and twisted round it the turban and face-cloth, and thrust my pale, naked-looking feet into the yellow slippers.

My toilet wanted now but the finishing touches, and these I proceeded to apply. A little leather flask (or stibium case) containing powdered antimony, and a slender copper rod, were among my possessions. With the rod I dipped up a little of the powder and drew it along my eyelashes, totally changing the expression of my eyes, as I discovered by examining them in the mirror. I next dyed my fingernails with some of the red stain that the forethought of Pereira had provided, hung round my neck a saffi, or amulet, that I found in the bundle, and I was complete. Lastly, I gathered up my few possessions – the compass, spear irons, mirror, revolver, cartridge box, and burning glass and dropped them into the huge pocket of my *riga* and added to them my watch and chain, purse and clasp knife.

I stood for a moment looking down at my discarded clothes, much as a toad surveys his newly shed skin. The toad, indeed, had the advantage of me, for when he has peeled off his outgrown integument, he frugally rolls it into ball and swallows it, so that nothing is wasted. As for me, I must needs leave my cast-off vestments to decay in the forest, and, as I picked up my stick and shawl and turned to go, I looked at them with a ludicrous feeling of regret. There they lay in the angle of the great root-buttresses, seeming to wait for me to come back; a pair of down-at-heel boots and toeless socks, a shabby suit of clothes, and a battered hat – a sorry enough collection, but all that was left of Richard Englefield.

CHAPTER TWELVE
I Change my Identity

When I had pushed my way through the undergrowth to the path, I did not at once turn back towards the road, for I reflected that by this time the hue and cry was no doubt raised, and Annan might quite possibly explore this very path in search of me. That he would let me go, without making an effort to detain me, I did not imagine for an instant, for he had heard the chink of the gold in my purse and had probably surmised that it represented more than the value of all the monkey skins he was likely to secure. So instead of returning to the road I walked off briskly in the opposite direction, and had not gone very far when I made a curious and very pleasing discovery; for there came through the forest, faintly but quite distinctly, the sound of voices.

I stopped and listened intently, and soon made out that what I heard was not the deep discordant jabber of our carriers, but the sharp high-pitched tone characteristic of the Hausa and Fulah races. My Hausa friends were at no great distance to the right of the patch, and seemed to be coming nearer.

The African forest roads have a peculiarity, which they share with certain rivers like the Amazon and the Mississippi – they are never stationary but are continually altering their position from side to side. When a large tree falls and obstructs the road, isolated travellers, like our party, will climb over it; but a large and heavily-laden caravan will find it easier to cut a fresh path round the obstruction, and this new path will thenceforth be used by all persons passing along. Meanwhile, the fallen tree slowly decays, but long before it has disappeared a young growth of forest has sprung up around it. Thus the new path becomes permanent and a curve of fifty or sixty yards in span becomes added to the road. By a continual repetition of this process the road becomes, in the course of time, a succession of serpentine curves, which meander far away from the original direction, their extreme sinuosity being disguised somewhat by the density of the forest growth, until some hunter from an adjacent village restores the road to its original direction by cutting a straight path across the loop, thus saving a circuit of perhaps several miles.

Now, this path upon which I had lighted was one of these short cuts, while the road along which the Hausas and Annan were travelling, was the original winding track; and I perceived that if I made haste I might come out upon the road ahead of both parties.

I therefore hurried forward as well as I could, encumbered with the various articles that I had not yet had time to make into a bundle, and in about a quarter of an hour reached the place where the path rejoined the road. Here I stood and listened for a while, but could at first hear nothing but the ordinary sounds of the forest: the chattering of monkeys, the trumpeting of a hornbill, and the squawking of parrots.

At length a high falsetto laugh came faintly through the woods, and feeling secure now that the Hausas were behind me, I walked slowly on.

By this time the sun was getting low, and it was necessary for me to be careful that I did not overshoot the mark and get ahead of the Hausas' camping place for the night; and I was just thinking of sitting down and waiting for them to overtake me, when a turn of the road brought me out into a small grassy opening, through the middle of which ran a brawling muddy stream. This, I thought, would make an ideal camping place, and here the Hausas would probably halt, so I determined to await their arrival, and set about making my preparations. First, with the aid of my large handkerchief and the thin stem of a creeper, I made my more bulky possessions into a small parcel, to which I lashed the masa bag and the remainder of the bunch of plantains that I had brought from the deserted village; then I put off my slippers and paddled in the muddy stream for a time, for I feared that the whiteness and tenderness of my feet would attract immediate attention unless I could get them well stained by the red clay. Finally I laid down my shawl on the ground and standing on it with my back to the setting sun began to pray aloud in the Moslem fashion.

I was quite disconcerted and bashful when my loudly intoned "Allah!" first broke the stillness of the forest, and I had some difficulty in giving the true falsetto turn at the end of the sentence, but a few minutes' practice improved my style and gave me confidence; and by the time the voices of the Hausas began to sound plainly through the woods, I was chanting away as though to the manner born. At length, advancing footsteps were audible close at hand. I prostrated myself on the ground as, with the tail of my eye, I saw the leader of the caravan come round the bend in the road, I rose and sent forth a howl that would have done credit to the Prophet himself.

The Hausas were evidently greatly surprised at my appearance, and looked round with a puzzled air for any signs of companions; they did not speak to me, however, but after a whispered consultation, sat down at a little distance and waited for me to finish my devotions. When at length I stepped off my shawl and put on my slippers, the old man came forward and saluted me, and the others gathered round to listen.

"Are thy companions far away, child of my mother?" the old man inquired.

"They are far away by now, my father," I replied. "They were Wongára who journeyed to Kong, and they turned off by the road to the left this afternoon to avoid passing by Kumasi and Békwe."

"I saw no road to the left," said the old man dubiously.

"He meaneth the little hunter's path that we passed this afternoon," put in a sturdy fellow with a broad, jet-black face.

"It is as thy friend sayeth," said I. "They went by the little hunter's path."

"And whither dost thou go, friend?" asked the old man.

"I go to Sálaga by way of Kantámpo," I replied.

"Thou art not heavily burdened," remarked the old man significantly.

"The camel steppeth lightly that carrieth the merchant's gold," I answered.

"It is true," he rejoined. "And how do they call thee?"

"The Hausas call me Yúsufu Dan Égadesh, but some call me Yúsufu Fuláni, for my mother was a woman of Futa."

"I am called Musa Ba-Kachína," said the old Hausa. "I go with my friends to our country through Kantámpo and Gonja. If it please thee to walk with us rather than to go alone through this wilderness, our fire shall warm thee, and our roofs shelter thee, and thou shalt be as our brother for the sake of the one God whom we all serve and who guides us through the land of the heathen."

"I will walk with thee, thankfully, my father," said I, "and thou shalt command me as thy servant while I continue with thee."

My position as a member of the caravan being thus settled, the company bestowed on me sundry smiles of friendly recognition and set to work preparing for the night. To me was allotted the task of collecting wood for the fire and staves for the huts, in which I was assisted by the giant, whose name I found to be Abduláhi Dan-Daúra more familiarly known as Dan-jiwa (child of the elephant); an amiable and joyous soul, as simple as a child, and as strong as a bull. I have myself generally passed for a powerful man, but beside this brown-skinned Titan I was like a young girl. The fashion in which he twisted off great branches and snapped them across his knee was perfectly amazing, and when I had been hacking ineffectually for five minutes at some hardwood sapling, he would come along laughing and, with a flick of his great knife, snip it off as though it were a radish.

We had soon collected a large heap of faggots and long straight poles, and these Abduláhi proceeded to tie up with cords of tie-tie into bundles proportionate to our respective sizes. I endeavoured to lift his bundle on to his head, but could not move it, on which he laughed in his soft girlish voice and hoisting it up lightly, tucked the entire collection of poles under his arm and strolled off, leaving me to follow shamefacedly with a small parcel of faggots.

When we returned to the clearing we found everyone busy and all talking at once. A large heap of grass and leaves was ready for covering the huts and making beds, and a little fire had been kindled with a flint and steel.

"We are waiting for thee, Yúsufu," said my black-skinned friend – Mahama Dam-Bornu by name. "But I see thou art an idle fellow to let the poor little Dan-jiwa carry all the wood." There was a general laugh at this, and I presently discovered that the good-humoured Abduláhi was one of the two standing jokes of the caravan, the other being a small man named Osumánu Ba-Kánu, but familiarly known as Dam-biri (child of the monkey) a sobriquet due partly to his remarkable agility and partly to his incorrigibly mischievous disposition.

Musa himself attended to the building up of the fire while the remainder of the company busied themselves in setting up the huts. And here my nautical training was of great service, for although at the outset I had no idea how such shelters were erected, yet my skill and neatness in putting on the lashings of tie-tie earned me quite a reputation as a builder, and the jocose Dam-biri christened me Yasankengwa (cat's fingers) on the spot.

The building proceeded with marvellous rapidity so that the daylight had barely gone before our little village in the wilderness was complete, and we sat down on the mats that Musa had placed round the fire, to roast our plantains and make our evening meal.

It was a strange experience, and one that, though often repeated, never lost its strangeness; to sit by the fire through the long evening, with the clamour of the forest all around, and listen to the familiar talk of my companions, and live the life of another world. It was as though by some enchantment the scene of my existence had been suddenly shifted to some remote period of antiquity, when the civilisation of the West was yet unborn.

At first the men were somewhat silent, for they were tired and hungry, and a meal of plantains involves a considerable amount of energetic eating, but as the last of the food disappeared and the diners cleansed their fingers with grass or leaves, each man settled himself upon his mat and prepared to make a night of it by talking as only an African can talk. And singularly sprightly and full of interest the conversation was, for these Hausa merchants are great travellers and, of course, make their long journeys either on foot or horseback; and a man who has walked and ridden a few thousand miles through the heart of Africa, will have gathered experiences that make his talk well worth listening to.

Presently someone suggested that Dam-biri should regale the company with a story, and accordingly, that humorist, being by no means afflicted with shyness, at once plunged into a rambling tale, far more remarkable for wit than delicacy, which related to the misfortunes of an elderly mallam who had two young wives; and with such spirit and drollery did the impish Dam-biri relate his story, standing up on his mat to impersonate the different characters, that the forest rang with our shouts of laughter until the pottos in the trees howled with alarm.

But even an African cannot talk forever, and as the night wore on, one after another rose, yawned and went off to the huts; and at last, to my relief – for I was quite spent with the fatigues and excitements of the day – Musa stood up, touched me on the shoulder and retired into one of the huts. I followed him and found the enormous body of Dan-jiwa occupying half the floor, and I had hardly spread my shawl and stretched myself out on it when I fell asleep.

We were just rolling up our mats after morning prayers on the following day when an unmelodious jabber from the woods announced the approach of travellers, and shortly afterwards my late companions appeared round the bend of the road headed by David Annan.

The latter paused to exchange greetings, which were cool enough on the part of the Hausas, and I noticed my big friend scanning the row of carriers with a frown of curiosity.

"Where is the Anazára (Nazarene) who was with thee yesterday?" he asked, looking Annan full in the face.

"The way was too rough for him" replied the latter with some confusion, "so he turned back towards the sea."

"Alone?" inquired Dan-jiwa.

"He went alone. It is not far to Pra-su," said Annan.

"I see that he has left with thee the box that he carried," remarked Musa suspiciously.

"And thou has burst open the lock," added Dam-Bornu; for my trunk, which the wounded carrier had resumed, was now closed with a band of tie-tie.

"He burst it himself. He had lost the key, and so broke open the box that he might take his goods with him." Then noting the undisguised incredulity on the faces of his hearers Annan added excitedly, "I swear it by my busum, by the great Busum-Pra. Look in my face and see if I speak not the truth," and he stared insolently at Abduláhi.

"We like better to look at thy back, friend," replied Musa drily, and turned away to tie up his mat, while the discomfited Annan resumed his journey.

We travelled on that day, with few halts, until sunset, and passed through three villages, all of which were deserted, and one partially burned; but at each of them we managed to collect a few plantains from the grove outside the clearing, as well as some papaws, the sickly-sweet flavour of which seemed to be much appreciated by my comrades. We also passed two groups of decapitated corpses, the heads of which had been carried off to decorate the war drums of the victors, and as we camped at night not far from one of these melancholy relics, we were greatly disturbed by the hyenas, whose mournful howls, mingled with imbecile laughter, made it seem as though the forest was tenanted by devils.

Early on the following morning we turned off the main road and took a bypath that led north of Kókofu through Juábin, some distance to the east of Kumasi; for Musa considered it highly unsafe to venture into the vicinity of either Békwe or Kumasi in the present state of the country. We thus gradually drew away from the active centres of warfare, and on the third day passed through a village on the borders of Juábin, where we were greeted by the welcome sight of a woman pounding fufu in a wooden mortar. We were not yet free, however, from war's alarms, for, later in the day, a body of some twenty or thirty warriors filed swiftly and silently past us, and not long after, a tremendous fusillade in the bush, accompanied by a Babel of shouts and yells, told us that they had met their foe.

About noon next day the road entered one of the large kola plantations which make this country so important to the Hausa trader; and a wonderful sight it presented, since, owing to the war, the harvest had been left ungathered, and the ground was literally covered with the great pods and the magenta-coloured "nuts" or beans.

"Here is wealth going to waste!" exclaimed Dam-Bornu regretfully. "I could pick up and carry away enough to buy me a strong slave in Sálaga or even an ass to carry my goods for me."

"There is no reason why we should not take a few nuts to chew as we go," said Dam-biri, "if we may not gather them as merchandise," and he began picking up the ripe nuts and dropping them into this pocket. Now the pocket of a *riga* occupies half the front of the garment and will hold upwards of a bushel, and Dam-biri continued to drop the nuts into his *riga* until the huge receptacle was nearly full, a proceeding that did not escape the notice of Musa.

"How wilt thou pay for all that *guru*, Dam-biri?" he asked. "I thought thou hadst spent all thy money buying merchandise at Cape Coast."

"I take but a few to chew by the way," protested Dam-biri.

"A few!" exclaimed the old man. "Thou hast nearly a slave's load," and he caught the loose gown and unceremoniously tipped the whole cargo out on to the ground.

At the further end of the plantation we entered a large straggling village, in the main street of which a number of men were filling sacks of plaited grass with kola nuts, having first lined the sacks with fresh leaves. Their master, a swaggering over-dressed Wongára, whose cheeks bulged with kola, stood hard by haggling with the head man of the village and spitting out the orange-red juice as he talked. It seemed that *guru* was cheap just now, and my companions loudly lamented their want of capital; for they had spent all that they possessed at Cape Coast, on cutlery, silk, and other portable wares, and had barely enough *kurdi* (cowries) left to carry them home.

"Come now, Yúsufu," said Musa to me, "thou art a big fellow and hast no load to carry. Wilt thou not buy some *guru* to sell at Kantámpo? It shall pay thee well."

"That I will gladly," I replied, although I wished the *guru* at Jericho, "but thou and our brethren, will not you buy, too? You have but small loads."

"We have no money," he replied.

"But I have," I rejoined, "and if you will buy what you can carry, I will lend you the money wherewith to pay, if the chief will accept the gold coin of the Christians."

"Thou art a good friend, Yúsufu," said Musa. "I will speak with our brethren and the man of the village."

He did so, and my comrades accepted the loan thankfully, but the headman made some difficulty about the sovereign that I tendered through Musa, having never seen one before. However, the kola was lying on the ground and the coin looked like gold, so he fetched from his house a little pair of scales, and placing the sovereign in one pan, laid in the other a bronze weight, formed of a tiny elephant upon a pedestal, and a few scarlet jequirity seeds: by which process one pound sterling was found to be equal to twenty-one thousand *kurdi*.

We spent that night in the village, sleeping in some stuffy malodorous houses lent us by the chief, and when we departed in the morning each of my companions carried on top of his bundle of merchandise a half load of kola, while I staggered under a full sack weighing upwards of sixty pounds, in addition to a smaller sack of cowrie shells – the "change" that had been due to me after the kola was paid for.

Chapter Thirteen
The Golden Pool

In the course of a long journey on foot through an uncultivated country one acquires the faculty of unconsciously observing and generalising from certain geographical facts. By noticing the vegetation one can detect at a distance an invisible river or a change in the soil; in dense forest, the proximity of an unseen range of hills is inferred from rapidly-flowing streams with beds of shingle, and the general slope of the country can be judged, apart from particular inclines, from the average direction of the rivers.

Now, very shortly after leaving Juábin, it became evident that we had entered a new watershed, for, whereas the streams had previously flowed mostly in a southerly direction, they now took a course for the most part towards the north-west, and were, moreover, increasing in size, the little rivulets giving place, as we travelled northward, to more considerable streams. It did not, therefore, cause me any surprise when, on the fifth day after leaving Juábin, we came to the brink of a large, slowly-flowing river.

A river of any size is, however, always an object of interest to the traveller, and as we came out into the open space on the bank, we halted and looked about us curiously. The black, sluggish waters were spanned by a rude bridge formed of a single gigantic odúm tree, and on either bank, at each end of the bridge, was a high pile of sticks, while on the farther side of the river an opening in the trees showed that the road led into a village.

As we approached the bridge, a man who had been sitting by the pile of staves rose and held up one hand, while with the other he pointed to the heap; and although he spoke not a word, our people clearly understood his meaning, for each of them who carried a stick cast it onto the pile. Then the man walked on to the bridge and, when he had passed three-quarters of the way across, halted, and tinkled a kind of primitive bell. Our men followed him, and each of them, as he reached the middle of the bridge, drew from his pocket one of the little cloth packets of gold dust that form the ordinary currency in Ashanti and, opening it, shook the gold out into the river. I was greatly surprised at this behaviour on the part of my orthodox friends, but I thought it wise to do as they did, so, laying my stick upon the wooden cairn, I took out the smallest of the packets of gold dust with which Pereira had furnished me, and very reluctantly shook out the contents into the water.

As I landed on the northern bank, I passed close to the fetish priest or wizard – for such he evidently was – and examined him with no little curiosity. He was an emaciated, shrivelled-looking rascal with a sly, sinister face, and grey hair, and was loaded with necklaces and other ornaments of cowrie shells. He appeared to resent my earnest inspection and Musa, observing this, plucked me by the sleeve and hurried me away, whispering, "Stare not so, my son; remember that he dieth early that gazeth into the eye of a wizard."

Although it was little past noon, Musa decided to camp outside the village (which I did not require to be told was Tánosu), for we were now beyond the seat of war and could not only rest in peace, but might expect to obtain some better food than plantains, of which we were all heartily sick. We did, in fact, obtain a fine short-haired ram which I gladly paid for out of my sack of cowries, silencing the protests of my comrades by stipulating that if I bought the animal, they should prepare it for eating; and having thus set them a task, I strolled away to enjoy the unwonted luxury of solitude.

And, indeed, it was necessary that I should be alone for a time, for my mind was in a veritable ferment. Here was the place just as the old journal had described it; there were the piles of staves, the wizard, the bridge, and the toll for the river god. What if this dream should turn out to be true after all?

Ah! what?

Should I be so very much forward? I had looked upon the river; I might look upon the wonderful pool; I might even trace the whereabouts of the cave itself. But what then?

I walked down to the bridge and looked at the pile of staves, which I now perceived rested on a great mound of black earth – the accumulation of centuries of decay. I turned away along by the river, and, sitting down on the bank, rested by elbows on my knees and fell into a reverie, gazing dreamily at the dark, turbid water as it crept slowly by.

What if I found the cavern? Should I, even then, be any nearer to its secret? And then, after all, what concern of mine could that secret possibly be? Was not my quest a mere wild goose chase induced by credulity, mingled with idle curiosity?

I was still turning over these questions, with my eyes fixed on the water, when I started with a pang of disappointment. There had come into view a shoal of fishes swimming leisurely upstream and snapping at an occasional insect on the surface; not such fishes as had been mentioned in the journal, huge, hideous, and ferocious, but just ordinary river fish, much like grayling in appearance, and not more than a foot in length.

Here, then, the narrative had been embroidered by the fancy of the man Almeida, or of his informants, and if one part of the story was fabulous, how much more might turn out to be mythical?

In these reflections I was interrupted by the tinkling of a bell, and looking up, saw the fetish priest approaching with a basket on his head from which steam was rising. He seated himself close to the water's edge, not far from me, and as I was on a higher level I could watch his proceedings. He laid his basket on the ground beside him, and I could now see that it was filled with eggs, which he took out one by one, and squeezing them in his hand began to peel off the shells, which he threw into the river. The bright-scaled fish gathered round, snapping at the eggshells as they sank, and crowding nearer and nearer to the bank. Suddenly the entire shoal darted off, and then there loomed through the turbid water a great dark shape, and then another, and another, until a troop of seven had come into view; and as they slowly sailed into the clear water under the bank, I could see them distinctly – huge, smooth-skinned, slate-coloured fish, fully four feet long, with great blunt heads, and grinning mouths fringed with rows of worm-like barbules.

When the priest had finished his preparations, he took the peeled hard-boiled eggs one at a time and cast them out into the stream; and as each one fell, the hideous brutes rushed at it, lashing the water into foam and snapping their jaws in a most horrible manner.

As the last of the eggs vanished the fetish man rose, shook out his basket and departed, and the fish soon disappeared into the dark depths of the river. The truth of Almeida's story was again vindicated and, in spite of my doubts, I was conscious of a feeling of elation and satisfaction.

I now retraced my steps towards the village, but, being still absorbed in thought, I missed my way and presently entered it at the farther end, where I saw a group of children gathered round a blacksmith's shop and, being in an idle frame of mind, I halted to look on. It was a primitive affair – just a thatched roof on four posts – but the work was proceeding briskly enough. A sturdy boy sat on the ground between a pair of goat skins that served as bellows, and, though the forge was but a wide-mouthed jar sunk in the ground, with a hole in the bottom for the blast-pipe, the charcoal fire in it glowed brightly. The smith was at the moment fashioning a spearhead on a flat slab of ironstone that served as an anvil, holding it with queer little tongs and tapping it with an absurd little hammer, but shaping it quickly and skilfully nevertheless.

I was about to move on, when my eye fell on the heap of crude iron fresh from some native bloomery or furnace – and I observed an object that I decided to acquire if possible. This was a rough iron bar about ten inches long by an inch and a half thick – probably a half-wrought "pig". It tapered somewhat to one end, and at the other it had an irregular cup-like hollow. The general shape – doubtless accidental – was that of a sounding lead, and for that purpose I proposed to use it, as will be seen hereafter; but it would be necessary to have a hole made in it to reeve the line through.

The smith, having finished the spearhead, put it aside to cool, and then observing me for the first time accosted me in very barbarous, but quite intelligible, Hausa.

I returned his salutation, and, picking up the bar, asked him if he wished to sell it.

"Yes. I will sell it," he replied.

"Canst thou make a hole through this end?"

"Certainly I can."

"And what will the price then be?" I asked.

He considered a moment, and then said, "A thousand *kurdi*."

"Very well," I replied. "Make the hole and I will pay thee."

He seemed greatly astonished at my accepting his price without haggling – a thing unheard of in Africa – but he promptly stuck the rod in the fire and looked out a point to make the hole with, while the boy worked the bellows.

I fished up out of my capacious pocket, the remnants of my bag of cowries, and had hardly finished counting them out on the ground before the work was done and the hissing iron plunged into a calabash of water to cool.

That night our camp outside the village was a scene of roaring conviviality, for we had passed through the starving wilderness and now, for the first time, enjoyed the luxury of a hearty meal. And, let ascetics preach as they will, there is great virtue in a good dinner "which maketh glad the heart of man," as anyone would have admitted who could have seen the beaming faces upon which the red glow of our camp fire shone that night. Now a man can smile – after a certain fashion – with his mouth full, whereas conversation under those circumstances is hardly practicable; whence it happened that the early part of the entertainment was of a somewhat silent character, communication being maintained principally by gestures and grins of satisfaction. But as the evening wore on and the remains of the ram dwindled into a "frail memorial" of clean-picked bones, and the roasted yams were scraped out to the very rinds, tongues began to wag and conversation and anecdote to buzz round the fire.

Naturally enough, the talk fell on the river god of Tano and the strange customs at the bridge.

"This is a proud god," remarked Dam-Bornu, "that will not suffer any man to carry a staff before his face."

"Say rather a proud devil," said Musa gravely. "There is no god but God."

"It is true," replied Dam-Bornu, "there is but one God, the wise and the merciful. But this Tano devil, hast thou ever seen the heathen people worship him?"

"Never," answered Musa. "How do they worship?"

"I saw them," said Dam-Bornu, "when I went to Kumasi, at a town not far from here. The wizards dressed in strange garments and wore great wooden faces with horns all painted most horribly, and the people, too, wore curious garments, and danced round the wizards in a ring, sweeping the earth with brushes and shaking rattles."

"Great is the folly of the heathen," remarked Musa, sententiously, apparently forgetting the offering he had made to the river god as he crossed the bridge.

"Hast thou heard the story that Alhassan Ba-Adami tells about the gods' treasure house?" asked Dan-jiwa.

"I have not heard it," replied Musa. "Wilt thou tell us the story, Alhassan?"

THE GOLDEN POOL

"I will tell what I have heard," said Alhassan; "but I know not if it be true or a fable."

We all settled ourselves to listen, and Alhassan, a quiet, gentle-mannered man, began, a little shyly because of the sudden silence: "It is said that in the days of old, certain Nasaráwa (Christians) came to this country to search for gold. And they came to a place called Aboási, where is a great rock and near to it a pool, in which pool the River Tano beginneth; and finding there much gold, they dug a mine which they made after the fashion of their country, not only digging a pit as the black men do, but burrowing deep into the earth as a mole doth. Now, the people of this country hated the Christians, and on a certain day, when the white men were working in their mine, the men of the country arose and took their knives and spears – for in those days the black people had no guns – and said to one another, "Let us go to the mine and take the white men and kill them; so they shall trouble us no more, and we shall have their gold."

"So they came to the mine and went into one of the burrows, but did not find the white men. Then they went to another burrow, and the white men were not there. And they went into a third burrow, which was the deepest of all, and there they saw the Christians with lamps and torches digging for gold. Then they fell upon the Christians to kill them, but the white men had guns in the mine with them, and they fired at the black people. And the voice of the guns went out through the burrows and shook the earth so that it fell in and buried them, and they all perished, both the black people and the Christians, and were never seen again. And it is said that the demon of the river took the mine for his own, and that his priests serve him there in a temple underground to this day, and heap up more and more treasure, which they hide in a strong place deep in the earth; and, moreover, that these wizards waylay and catch strangers and drag them to the mine, where they keep them to labour for the river god; but what these slaves do I did not hear and cannot guess since – so it is said – the wizards put out their eyes so that, should any of them escape, they should not be able to tell any of the secrets of the place nor guide others to the mine. This is what I have been told of the river god, but whether or not it is true I cannot tell."

As Alhassan finished speaking, a somewhat uncomfortable silence fell upon the assembly, and more than one of the men glanced round nervously towards the village whence the sound of drumming came down upon the night air.

"Where is this Aboási?" inquired Dan-jiwa.

"It is about two days' journey from here," replied Alhassan. "We pass near to it on the way to Kantámpo – that is to the pool; whereabouts the mine is I do not know."

There was another silence and them Musa said: "Well, we are ten strong men, followers of the Prophet and servants of the true God. So we need not fear the demons of the heathen. Still, I like not these wizards, and shall be glad to see the last of their accursed country."

We were preparing for a somewhat leisurely start on the following morning when there filed into the village a caravan led by a fine stately Hausa, who stalked down the street as though the entire country belonged to him, until catching sight of Musa, he ran forward and embraced him with many demonstrations of joy and affection. It appeared that Imóru (which was the stranger's name) was an old friend and fellow townsman of our leader, and had come direct from their country. So the members of the two caravans sat down joyfully together to exchange experiences and talk over the news.

I learned that Imóru was travelling first to Cape Coast and thence to Quittáh, where he had a relative who was the *mallam* or priest to the Hausa troops with whom he had formerly lived for a time. I asked him if he knew a Christian named Pereira, and on his replying that he knew him very well, I determined to make him the bearer of a letter. But I soon saw, the interest that my proposal to write a letter aroused, that I should have to write it in public and that it would be in the highest degree impolitic to display any knowledge of European language or letters. When, therefore,

Imóru produced from his scrip a sheet of coarse paper, a reed pen and a little gourd of thick brown ink, and my comrades gathered round to look on, I contented myself with writing, in my very best Arabic, a brief but affectionately-worded note stating that all was well with me so far, and hoping to see my friends again before long. When I had given Imóru this letter I felt more easy in my mind with regard to Isabel and her father, for although the missive told them little, I knew that they would learn all they wished to know by questioning the bearer.

During the next two days our road lay mostly along the right bank of the Tano River, although, owing to its windings, we only saw it occasionally; but we crossed a number of tributary streams, and the main river rapidly diminished in volume as we ascended towards its source. About noon on the second day I noticed that the river, which had now dwindled to quite an inconsiderable stream, had, from being dark and turbid suddenly become as clear as crystal and Alhassan who was walking near me, informed me that we had passed the last (or rather the first) of the tributaries, and that the clear water we saw came direct from the Aboási pool.

Soon afterwards we halted for our midday rest and meal, and I then took Alhassan aside and asked him if he knew how far away the pool was.

"It is quite near to this place," he replied. "I can show thee the little path that leads to it from the road."

"Come then and show it to me," said I.

As we were starting off, Musa caught sight of us and called out to know where we were going.

"Yúsufu has asked me to show him the little path to the pool," said Alhassan.

"What hast thou to do with the pool, Yúsufu?" asked Musa suspiciously.

"I have heard much talk of it," I replied, "and would see for myself what manner of place it is."

"The curiosity of fools is the bane of wise men," exclaimed Musa angrily. "Because thou speakest little I had thought thee a man of sense; and now thou wilt bring a mischief on us by prying into the secrets of the heathen."

"Surely," said I, "it is no harm to go and look at the water. It is there for any man to see."

"I tell thee the place is sacred and forbidden, and thou must not go near it," persisted the old man.

"I am going to see it," said I, and to save further discussion I pulled Alhassan by the sleeve and strode off.

In a few minutes we came to a small track that turned off from the caravan road into the forest.

"This is the path," said Alhassan. "Shall I come with thee?"

He was brimful of curiosity, but mighty nervous, and would not have been sorry, I think, if I had refused his company. However, I told him he might come if he pleased, and we entered the path together; but we had not gone a couple of hundred yards when we encountered an object that brought Alhassan to a dead stop.

In the middle of the path and completely barring the way was a grotesque and frightful figure with long curved horns and great goggle eyes, seated on a stool and staring stonily before it. It was nearly lifesize and was the more diabolical in aspect because it was really skilfully modelled and painted, and an additional touch of realism was imparted by an actual garment of palm fibre.

"Let us go back, Yúsufu," exclaimed Alhassan in a shaky voice, surveying the apparition with dismay, as it sat with its little heap of votive offerings before it; "this place is the abode of devils. Come away."

"Go thou and wait for me in the road," said I. "I am going to see this pool since I have come so far"; and I pushed past the image and proceeded along the path.

I could now distinguish the sound of falling water, and walking on another hundred yards, I came out on to the bank of the pool.

A brief glance round sufficed to convince me that here again Almeida's narrative was strictly veracious. The pool was a sheet of water some hundred and fifty yards across, surrounded by forest. At one end the bank rose so steeply as to form a kind of cliff, and

The Golden Pool

from one part of this a small stream of red, muddy water fell into the pool, while at a little distance from the spring there stood up out of the water a solitary mass of red rock from which two slender tusk-like fragments of quartz projected. The spring did not, however gush out of the tusked rock as Almeida had described it, but it may have done so formerly, as it now spouted from the end of a gorge which it had excavated, in the course of years, in the cliff.

The pool was evidently of considerable depth, even close in shore, and the water was very clear where I first came out on to the bank; but as I followed the path along the brink towards the spring, it became more turbid.

Before returning to the forest path I stood on the bank where the water was clearest, and attentively examined the bottom, which appeared to be of a greyish red mud; and as I stood there I was suddenly startled by the appearance of a shoal of the huge and hideous fishes such as I had seen at Tánosu. In the clear water they were horribly distinct, and as they crowded round the bank at my feet and leered up at me with their dull, glazy eyes, I felt quite a thrill of horror, and instinctively stepped back a pace lest I should slip down the bank; and as I did so, something rustled in the bush behind me. But although I turned round quickly I could see nothing, and concluded that some animal must have passed through the undergrowth.

When I got back to the road I found Alhassan awaiting me with evident anxiety, and I had no sooner joined him than he hurried me off towards the camp.

"Didst thou see the wizards, Yúsufu?" he asked in a whisper.

"Wizards!" I exclaimed. "No, I saw no one."

"They saw thee," said he, "for they came along the path soon after thee, having watched us both from the bush."

I was sorry to hear this, for not only did I not want to arouse the suspicions of the fetish men on my own account, but I should hardly have forgiven myself if I had involved my kind and hospitable companions in any trouble with the natives. It was also a little disagreeable to find the priests so watchful and alert, and I took my way back to the camp in a rather anxious frame of mind.

The meal was nearly finished when we arrived, so we had but a short rest before the march was resumed; but this turned out to be of little importance, for before we had gone more than a couple of miles, the gathering clouds and a certain chill in the air gave warning of a threatened tornado, although the season of storms had gone by. The careful Musa, therefore, called a halt, and huts were hurriedly put up to shelter our persons and merchandise from the rain; but after a time the clouds drifted away and the slanting rays of the afternoon sun shone brightly enough on our little encampment. It was however, too late to continue our journey, so our men sat about for the rest of the day chewing kola and talking.

The evening meal was prepared earlier than usual, and when it was finished we sat round the fire and talked again, until getting tired of this the men went off one by one, to rest either in huts or by the fire. I spread my own mat on the side of the fire farthest from the huts and lay down to think over the plans and wait till my comrades should be asleep.

The night was at first very dark, but as the time went on and the drowsy mutter of conversation gradually died away, the sky cleared, and presently the red beams of the rising moon began to filter through the trees. I turned out the contents of my great pocket on to the mat to make sure that I had forgotten nothing. The iron bar or sinker, a coil of the wiry stem of a creeper three or four fathoms long, a lump of shea butter wrapped in a piece of rag, a large knife, and my revolver; these formed my outfit for the night's expedition, and when I had "mustered" them I put them back. I had spent the evening in fitting a shaft to my spear irons, and the finished spear lay by my mat.

The camp was wrapped in silence except for the ordinary sounds of the forest. A potto shrieked in a neighbouring tree, an owl hooted, a couple of flying foxes whistled monotonously as though they were blowing across gigantic keys, and from the undergrowth came the squeaky bark of a genet, and the stealthy, secret chuckle of some prowling civet.

I stood up on my mat and looked round at our little camp. The fire was already dull, every man was asleep, and the big white moon now sailed high above the tree tops. I took up my spear, and picking my way softly past my sleeping comrades, stole off at a rapid pace along the road towards Aboási.

It was a most eerie walk. The brilliant moonlight made the road in parts as clear as in broad daylight, for the forest being less dense here than it had been farther south, the path was fairly open. But on either side was a wall of impenetrable shadow, and, in places where the forest closed up, the road itself was as dark as a vault, and I had fairly to feel my way with the butt of my spear. And, as I went, I seemed to be accompanied by an invisible multitude. Every clump of bush stirred as I approached it; the dark undergrowth was all in a rustle of movement: stealthy steps came to and fro on all sides, and the air was full of strange whirrings and flutterings.

Several times I was startled by some bulky creature leaping up at my feet and bounding away into the shadow, and once, as I was feeling my way along a stretch of road that was wrapped in absolute darkness, there appeared in the gloom before me a constellation of green and shining eyes that flitted and danced to a murmur of soft, snuffling growls: and when I flourished my spear and rushed at them, the forest rang out with a peal of wild laughter. It was only a pack of hyenas, and I breathed more freely when I came out again into the moonlight and saw that they had left me.

The path to the pool was not difficult to find, for a great silk-cotton tree stood at the junction and flung its huge serpent-like roots right across the road; so I strode along it with confidence, and soon came in sight of the grim idol which stood out, a hideous silhouette, against the moonlit opening. And certainly if it was frightful by daylight it now looked truly diabolical, and I half sympathised with Alhassan as I passed it in the gloom. It was quite a relief to get out into the open space by the pool; and very lovely the little lake appeared in the clear moonlight, its farther margin shrouded under the dark wall of forest and the tall monolith of the tusked rock faithfully repeated below its quiet surface.

I followed the path round the brink to a place that I had settled upon at my first visit, where a tree jutted out nearly horizontally, with its trunk partially immersed in the water. I had chosen this spot for two reasons. In the first place it was near to the spring, and I had calculated that, if there was really gold in the bed of the pool, that gold must be brought by the spring, and, as the heavy gold dust would settle sooner than the earthy sediment, the bottom in the neighbourhood of the fountain would be richest in gold. My second reason was the tree itself, which would form a kind of stage, convenient to work from.

I now hastily prepared my appliances. Passing the end of the line through the hole in the iron sinker I made it fast with a couple of half hitches. Then I took a lump of the shea butter and pressed it into the hollow at the end of the sinker to form what sailors call an "arming." Kicking off my slippers to make my foothold safer, I crept out on to the tree trunk as far as I could, and, taking the coil of line in one hand, with the other softly dropped the sinker into the water, letting the line run through my fingers until I felt the iron thump on the bottom. Then I drew it up and crawled back on to the bank to examine it. The arming of shea butter was covered by a thick layer of greyish mud, but, although I inspected it most minutely, to my deep disappointment I could not discover a trace of gold.

However, I determined to save the mud for more thorough examination by daylight, and, to this end, sliced off with my knife the top layer of the arming and laid the muddy fragment in the rag. I then crept out on to the tree and again dropped the sinker to the bottom and returned to shore to see if I had any better fortune this time; but the mud which adhered to the sticky arming was similar to that brought up by the first cast – soft grey deposit with never a trace of sparkle or colour.

I was stooping over the rag with the sinker in my hand, comparing the two soundings, when, chancing to glance up, my eye was attracted by the swaying shadows of foliage on the white, lichen-clad trunk of a tree close by; and even as I looked, another shadow appeared on the tree and slowly moved across it – the shadow of a man's head.

I remained for an instant petrified; then, as the shadow suddenly vanished, I sprang to my feet, whirling the sinker round as I rose. The heavy iron struck some hard object with a dull shock and, as I faced round, a man staggered backwards and fell, nearly upsetting a second man who was following close behind. The latter, however, quickly recovered and, as he rushed at me with an uplifted knife, I again raised the sinker; but before I could strike, he seized my wrist with his free hand and made a lunge at my chest with his dagger, which I barely escaped by grasping his arm below the elbow. So we stood for near upon a minute, holding one another at arm's length, tugging and wrenching, swaying to and fro and trampling upon the prostrate body. Then we stood stock-still for a few moments, till suddenly, with a jerk of his arm, he swept the point of his knife within an inch of my neck, and as I twisted his elbow back, he snapped at my face with his teeth, snarling like a wild beast.

Meanwhile, as we staggered backward and forward, we were gradually edging nearer and nearer to the water, and each of us struggled to back the other towards the bank. We were within a couple of yards of the brink when my assailant made another sudden lunge at me with his knife, which again narrowly missed me, but the wrench that I gave his arm to save myself, turned the weapon, so that its point pricked him in the pit of his stomach, causing him to recoil so violently that he lost his footing, letting go my wrist in his confusion. I gave him a brisk shove so that he staggered back two or three paces, and he stood for a moment on the very edge of the bank, waving his arms and striving to recover his balance; then he topped backwards and fell with a splash into the water.

He disappeared for an instant only and rose close to the tree, which he clutched at frantically, and struggled to haul himself up; but the trunk was wet and slippery, and offered very little hold, so that he continually slipped back. I debated hurriedly whether I should take the opportunity to make off, or knock him on the head with the sinker, and was inclining to the former course – for it was a repulsive idea to kill a helpless man – when the water around became violently agitated. The unfortunate wretch gave vent to a yell of agony and horror, and flinging up his arms vanished below the surface.

I stood for some moments rooted to the spot, watching the foaming eddies that told of the awful struggle that was taking place in those black depths, but, as the prostrate man now began to show signs of returning animation, I thought it high time to be gone; so, wrapping the sinker in the rag, I dropped it into my pocket, picked up my spear, and ran off down the path.

When I got back to the camp all was still and quiet save for the heavy breathing of my comrades, and my mat lay by the dull fire just as I had left it. I pushed the ends of the long faggots into the heap of embers, and as a cheerful flame leaped up, I settled myself on my mat and immediately fell asleep.

CHAPTER FOURTEEN
I am Led into Captivity

I was aroused next morning by a vigorous shaking, and, opening my eyes, found Abduláhi Dan-jiwa bending over me.

"Come, rouse up, thou sluggard," said he, giving me another gentle shake that was like to have dislocated my shoulder; "the sun is up and I have found a lovely stream of pure water. Come and bathe so that we begin the day all fresh and clean."

I rose and rubbed my eyes, yawning sleepily, for I was none the livelier for my nocturnal adventures; but I slipped off my *riga*, and folding it up neatly on the mat, followed my big friend who was frisking along with the buoyancy of a child.

The river was one of those beautiful little streams that are so plentiful in North Ashanti, whose crystal-clear waters trickle over beds of white sand between high banks carpeted with moss and fringed with lacy, delicate ferns.

Several of our people were already splashing about in the water, and when Abduláhi and I, flinging our remaining clothes down on the bank, leaped in and joined the party, a regular water frolic began; and as I watched these boisterous, high-spirited Africans chasing one another up and down the stream, sousing one another with water, and shouting with laughter and delight, my thoughts went back to the faraway Kentish shore and the sun-browned fisherboys who gambol in the pools when the tide is out in the long summer days.

The fun was at its height when a loud shouting in the camp attracted our attention.

We stopped our play and listened.

Plainly enough the sound came down the wind, and we could clearly distinguish angry voices raised in high dispute. With one accord we rushed to the bank, and huddling on our clothes, ran off at top speed in the direction of the camp.

And as we came out into the opening I saw at a glance that there was going to be very serious trouble – for me at least. A party of some thirty natives, all armed with long muskets, stood at a little distance, motionless but alert, and close by the fire half-a-dozen men, whose cowrie ornaments showed them to be fetish priests, were talking excitedly to our companions. As I appeared, one of these men, whose head was bound up with a blood-stained rag, pointed to me, and I then noticed that my *riga* lay at his feet, and that he held in his hand the sinker with its coil of line.

"What is this thing that thou hast done, Yúsufu, fool that thou art?" exclaimed Musa, furiously, as I came up. "Did I not tell thee that thy folly would bring a mischief on us?"

"What say the wizards, my father?" I asked meekly, for my conscience was mighty sore at having brought this trouble upon my friends.

"This man saith thou hast killed one of his brethren, and also hast robbed the river god of his gold."

"As to the man," said I, "he fell into the water as we struggled together and the great fishes devoured him, and as to the gold I found none."

"What, then, is this?" demanded Musa, taking the sinker from the fetish man's hand and picking up the rag with the fragment of muddy grease in it. "What hast thou to say to these? Are they not thine?"

"They are mine, my father, but they are not gold," said I.

He held out the rag with one hand and with the other presented the sinker with its arming still covered with mud.

"What is this on the shea butter, and what is sticking to this iron," he asked.

"Surely it is dirt," said I.

"It is very precious dirt," he replied. "Look more closely."

I did so, and then, to my amazement, I perceived that the mud was charged with gold dust; but so minute were the particles that it was only on the closest inspection that they could be distinguished amidst the grey deposit with which they were mixed.

"I see now," said I, "there is gold among the dirt. I was deceived in the darkness."

"The wizards speak the truth, then," said he. "Thou didst go to rob their god?"

"It is so, my father," I answered.

"Then I fear thou wilt pay a heavy price for thy folly," rejoined Musa. "The wizards say that thou must go with them."

"And what will they do with me?"

"That I know not," he replied; "but I fear they mean to kill thee."

"And if I will not go with them?"

"Then," said Musa, "they will kill thee and us also."

"It is enough, my father," said I. "I will go with the wizards."

Our people had gathered round to listen and, as the evidence of my misdoing had come to light, they, like Musa, had been highly incensed with me for thus bringing them into collision with the natives. But my frank acceptance of the responsibility for my actions mollified them considerably, and now the tide was suddenly turned in my favour by Abduláhi.

"This cannot be," he exclaimed. "What! Shall a servant of the true God be delivered into the hands of these devil-worshippers? Thou knowest, my father, how these heathen deal with their prisoners, and Alhassan hath told us what things are done by this people. Let us refuse, and then, if they will have it so, we will fight them."

Musa looked round irresolutely. His anger had quite evaporated, and he was evidently loth to let me go to what he suspected would be a horrible death.

"What say you, my brethren?" he asked. "Shall we fight the heathen?"

"No," I interrupted, "you shall not fight. For one thing, they are too many and have guns; but also the fault is mine, and if any blood is to be spilt it must be mine, too," and by way of ending the debate I walked over to the fetish men, one of whom immediately seized me by the wrist.

"Thou shalt not go, Yúsufu," cried the warm-hearted Abduláhi, bursting into tears and trying to drag me away. But I gently pushed him off, and as the armed men closed round me, Musa and Dam-Bornu held the weeping giant by the arms that he might not attack my captors.

The business was now brought quickly to a conclusion. Two of the fetish men took me by the arms, the rest of the party surrounded me, and I was marched off without more ceremony. I turned to take a last look at the camp as we moved away. Our people were all talking with furious excitement, pointing and shaking their fists at the retreating natives, and I could see the big, soft-hearted Abduláhi lying prone on the ground, rending his clothes and sobbing aloud.

As long as we were within sight of the camp no affront or violence was offered to me, for the pagans evidently had no desire to come to blows with the Hausas; but no sooner was the camp hidden from view than my captors began to give me a taste of their quality. First my arms were tightly bound to my sides with grass rope, and when I had thus been rendered helpless, the ruffian with the bandaged head dealt me a heavy blow across the shoulders with his staff. Then a halter was fastened round my neck and the end taken by one of the fetish men, who started off at a trot, dragging me after him.

We soon branched off the main road, and taking a forest path that I had not noticed before, travelled on rapidly for over half an hour in a direction which I roughly calculated would bring us to the neighbourhood of the pool. Presently we entered a large village where a crowd, largely composed of women and children, had assembled, apparently in expectation of our arrival.

Down the main street of the village I was dragged in the midst of this mob, almost deafened by the uproar of their shouting, and nearly choked by the dust, until we reached a large open space, in the centre of which stood a gigantic silk-cotton tree. At the foot of this tree, wedged in between two of the great root-buttresses, was a hut built of palm sticks, and, as we approached it, a swarm of smallish dog-faced monkeys ambled out and sat down at a little distance to watch us.

The door of the hut being removed, I was taken inside and my halter tied securely to one of the uprights, and then all the men went away with the exception of the fellow with the bandaged head, who remained behind apparently to gloat over my downfall. He came and stood before me, holding my unfortunate sinker in his hand and, thrusting his ugly countenance within an inch of my face, delivered a long and excited harangue, of which I, naturally, understood not a word. Then he held up the sinker before my face and put to me what I supposed to be a number of questions about it, and when I returned no answer, he slashed me across the face with his stick and followed this up by several blows about my fettered arms and shoulders.

This entertainment seemed to satisfy him for the present, and, with a parting cut at my legs, he went out, leaving the door of the hut open.

The space in which the hut stood appeared to be a sacred precinct, for the crowd had not followed beyond its border, and I could now see them through the doorway, a half-naked, jabbering rabble, standing some sixty yards away, pointing and gazing at the hut, just as a mob at home hangs about the gates of a hospital when an accident case has been admitted.

Presently I ascertained that my halter was just long enough to allow me to sit down in the corner, so I lowered myself with great care – lest in my helpless state I should slip and thus be strangled – and seated myself on the bare earth. I had not been long in this position when a monkey's head was thrust cautiously round the corner of the doorway. Soon another appeared, and then two more, and so on until gradually the whole troop collected, grimacing and chattering with the greatest concern and anxiety. Then they began to creep in one by one, eyeing me cunningly and suspiciously all the time, and sat down before me in a semicircle; and at length one patriarchal male reached out his hand and pinched my leg, on which I gave a sudden shout and the whole party bounded pell-mell out through the door, barking, coughing and clucking in the wildest excitement. They returned from time to time, to my excessive discomfort and somewhat to my alarm, for if they had really mobbed me, I could have made no sort of defence; but a sudden movement on my part always caused them to decamp.

When I had been in the hut about three hours, I saw one of the fetish men approaching, followed by a lad who carried a large flat calabash and an earthen jar. The calabash, I could see, contained some kind of food, for the monkeys gathered round the lad, chattering volubly and making snatches at him as he walked.

The fetish man entered the hut and sat down on the floor, and the calabash being placed beside him, he began to distribute its contents – balls of coarse meal – among the monkeys, who came forward quietly enough to receive their rations, and having each taken a ball from his hand, ambled away to a little distance, and sat down to eat it. When the monkeys were all served, the fetish man laid the calabash, which still contained a half-dozen balls, before me, and stood the jar of water beside it; but perceiving that my fetters prevented me from helping myself, he motioned to the slave boy to come and feed me, and then went away. The slave, whom I judged, by the elaborate pattern of incised lines on his face, to be a Dagómba, sat down by my side, and, breaking the balls into suitable pieces, very carefully inserted them into my mouth; and when I had finished eating he held the jar of water to my lips while I took a long draught.

This meal, rough as it was, greatly refreshed me, for I had taken no food since the previous day; but I was in a good deal of pain from the tight bands of rope round my arms, and the bruises that the fetish man's staff had produced. This did not escape the good-natured slave's observation, for, when I had finished drinking, he proceeded to loosen the bands somewhat, and soaking a corner of his cloth in water, he bathed my black and swollen bruises very gently and tenderly.

These charitable ministrations were interrupted by the approach of a procession consisting of the fetish men (who were now loaded with uncouth cowrie ornaments and had their faces and limbs painted with broad white stripes), a body of armed men, and a band of musicians, who produced appalling noises with trumpets formed of large antelope's horns and long drums, black and shiny with dried blood and elaborately ornamented with festoons of human jawbones.

When the musicians had played a few selections from some kind of devil's opera outside the hut, the fetish men entered, and having untied my halter led me forth; and I now observed that a large crowd had collected near a shade-tree in the village. Towards this spot our procession slowly advanced, preceded by the musicians and followed by the guard, and as we came near to the crowd the people arranged themselves into a long line and eventually enclosed us in a circle. I noticed that the villagers were not dressed in their usual fashion, but wore kilts or short petticoats of soft fibre and carried on their wrists and ankles a number of curious plaited bangles that rattled loudly at every movement; and that, moreover, each bore in his or her hand a long tassel or brush of the same fibre as the kilts were made of. When the circle was formed, the musicians and the guard disappeared; a wooden stool, thickly coated with dried blood, was placed in the centre of the circle, and I was seated on it with the party of fetish men behind me.

Then the people began to chant a melancholy minor air, and as they chanted, they stooped and swept the ground with their brushes, moving slowly round me, punctuating the chant by stamping their feet and shaking their rattles in unison. This strange ceremonial had an effect that was very devilish and horrid, which was enhanced by the quiet and orderly manner in which it was performed, and by the sad, plaintive character of the chant. As I sat and watched the unending line of stooping figures slowly filing past, the brushes moving softly and rhythmically to and fro, and listened to the weird song and the murmur of the rattles, like the shingle on the sea beach, I could scarcely repress a feeling of superstitious dread.

Suddenly there appeared within the circle a most horrible and grotesque figure that instantly recalled the horned image in the path by the pool.

A tall man was shrouded from head to foot in a flowing garment of the soft palm fibre, and his face was hidden by a great wooden mask, hideously painted, and furnished with a pair of long, curved horns.

This frightful apparition stalked slowly round the circle, creating no small terror in the people whom he approached. Then he slowly walked up to me, and, bending over me, thrust the hideous mask in my face and glared at me through the eye holes. When he had stood thus for a minute or so, he stepped back a few paces and began to dance very slowly and sedately, spreading out his garment on either side and wagging the great horned mask in a most horrible manner. Then he came and knelt on the ground before me, remaining perfectly motionless while the people still sidled round, chanting, sweeping, and shaking their rattles. At last he nodded the great mask at me, three times, in a slow and mysterious fashion, and in a twinkling there was slipped over my head and shoulders a leathern bag, which shut out the light and sound and nearly suffocated me. A confused din of drums, horns, and chanting voices came distantly to my ears, and I felt coil after coil of rope being passed round my body and limbs, and made out that I was being lashed to some kind of pole. Presently the pole was lifted into a horizontal position, and as I hung from it, the coils of rope cut into my flesh in the most agonising manner. I could feel my bearers lift the pole on to their shoulders, and then they started off at a brisk walk, each step causing me excruciating pain.

We left the village by a narrow forest path, as I could tell by feeling leaves and branches brushing against my body, and we travelled along this, as it seemed to me for hours. Next we crossed a wide clearing, where I could feel the hot sun pouring down upon my naked skin – for they had torn off the remnants of my clothing when they bound me to the pole – and then quite suddenly the air became dank and chilly, as if we had entered a cellar or a vault, and, in spite of the bag in which my head was muffled, I could hear that the creaking of the pole reverberated in a hollow fashion as sounds do in a tunnel. Presently they laid me on the ground, and then I was tilted over an edge and partly slid and partly hoisted down what seemed like a ladder, and again carried along the level for a time. Then came another steep descent and another stretch along the level, and of a sudden the air became hot, not with the heat of the sun but with the close warmth of a fire.

I was now laid down on a smooth, hard surface, and I felt someone unfastening the lashing that held me to the pole, although my arms and legs were still tightly bound. Then the bag was plucked from my head and I drew in a deep breath of hot, stuffy, foul-smelling air.

I was so closely bound that I was barely able to move my head, but I turned it about as well as I could and gazed round me very earnestly and curiously. But the place was in total darkness excepting for a faint red glow upon the roof above me, and I could not turn my head sufficiently to discover the source of this light. The roof itself I could barely make out, but it seemed to be formed of rough earth or rock.

That I was not alone was abundantly clear, for the place resounded with the murmur of voices, and with various noises as if a number of persons were engaged in some kind of handicraft, and all these sounds had a peculiar reverberating quality as sounds have in a vault or empty building.

The number of persons I judged to be considerable, for, although the hum of talk was loud and continuous, I could not separate any phrases or words nor distinguish what language was being spoken. Now and again I caught the clank as of a metal bucket set down on a hard floor, and the gurgle of water poured from one vessel into another; indistinct sounds of hammering came at intervals, and one or twice I thought I could hear the blowing of bellows.

The tight bands of rope which still encircled my arms and legs caused me very severe pain, and the more so by reason of the swelling caused by the blows that the ruffianly priest had dealt me, and it was intolerably irksome to lie on the hard floor unable to change my position in the slightest degree. So unbearable did the suffering become that, as hour after hour passed, I began to long for the return of my tormentors, although I felt that their arrival would be the signal for the infliction of new tortures the very thought of which made me shiver with horror.

For there was now no doubt of the circumstantial truth of Almeida's story. I had verified it step by step in every particular but one, and the time was drawing near when I should receive the last dreadful proof – when the awful secret of the cavern would be revealed to me.

At length, after what seemed a very eternity of misery, a faint flickering yellow light appeared on the roof and spread to the adjacent wall, and as it grew brighter the shadow of a man loomed vague and gigantic, gradually dwindling in size and growing more distinct as the light drew nearer, until there swept into my field of view a man carrying a clay dish on which was a conical heap of shea butter with a rush wick, forming a sort of primitive candle. He was accompanied by two others, in one of whom I recognised my acquaintance with the bandaged head.

The first man deposited the light on the floor beside me and the three fell to examining me attentively with a deal of talk and disputation; and their gestures made it easy for me to follow the gist of their discussion, which was as to whether or not my fetters required to be loosened. Two of the men were evidently in favour of slackening the cords, experience having, no doubt, taught them that when tight lashings are kept on a limb for more than a certain time, either mortification or incurable paralysis results; and as they pointed to my swollen hands and feet and the deep grooves in the flesh in which the cords were embedded, they appeared to be explaining this to my old enemy, who, for his part, was manifestly unwilling that I should be allowed even this relief. The more reasonable and humane councils, however, prevailed and one of the men set about making the change.

My feet were first dealt with.

The tight cord lashings having been cut through, a long strand of grass rope wads wound round each ankle, securely but not uncomfortably tightly, and tied, and the two anklets thus formed were connected by a short length of cord. My feet were in this manner fastened together quite firmly but without any painful or injurious ligature. The same process was applied to my wrists, which were brought together in front of my body with a play of about two inches between them, and this was a great relief after having them tied closely to my sides for so many hours.

When this welcome change had been made, one of the men produced a calabash with half a dozen meal balls in it, and a very small pot of water; but my hands were too numbed from the pressure of the cords to allow me either to feed myself or take up the water jar, so the man placed the calabash and jar on the ground by my side, and having tied the halter, which still remained round my neck, to a large peg in the ground, so that I could not sit up, they went away, taking the light with them.

I observed now that the red glow was no longer visible upon the roof, and when the fetish men with their light were gone, the place in which I lay was enveloped in total darkness. The hum of conversation continued, but the sounds indicative of labour had ceased, and I judged that the workers were settling down to rest.

After a time the talking ceased, and then a confused sound of snoring and heavy breathing told me that the other occupants of the cavern were asleep.

The numbness of my hands and feet gave place by degrees to a most intolerable tingling, but it was a long time before I could move my fingers in the smallest degree. Still it was an immense relief to have my arms partly free and to be able to draw my knees up and turn over on my side; so I rejoiced in my comparative freedom, changing my position frequently, and vigorously chafing my hands between my knees in the hope of regaining sensation and the power of movement.

For a long time I was unsuccessful in this, and my hands continued to be, to all appearance, quite lifeless except for the intense and painful tingling; but at last some signs of returning animation became evident in a slight power of still movement in the fingers and a certain amount of dull sensation, giving me the feeling of having thick gloves on my hands.

As I was suffering from intense thirst I now reached out for the water jar, and conveying it carefully to my lips, drained it to the last drop of the earthy-smelling water it contained. I then addressed myself to the meal balls, which I found gritty and tasteless but very acceptable nevertheless – so much so that I swept my fingers round the empty calabash quite regretfully when I had finished the last one.

Being thus refreshed with food and drink I endeavoured to compose myself for sleep but the novel and alarming circumstances in which I found myself were not by any means conducive to slumber. It was impossible to banish, even for a moment, from my mind the consciousness of my awful situation, or to lose sight of the terrible prospect that lay before me in the immediate future. The reflection that my misfortune was of my own deliberate seeking, so far from comforting me, but aggravated my wretchedness, and I found myself again and again cursing the perverse folly that had sent me on this fool's errand. I could not help thinking, too, with bitter self-reproach, of the suffering that I should cause to those whom I loved so dearly, by my insane foolhardiness. My imagination pictured Isabel waiting and watching for news of me, and growing ever more anxious as the months rolled by and I made no sign. Of the painful suspense, and growing dread that she and her father would feel, as doubts as to my safety merged into the conviction that some dreadful misfortune had overtaken me, and of the lifelong, haunting grief that would pursue them, when I did not come back, and they would think of me – only too truly – as a maimed and miserable wretch dragging out an existence of unvarying woe, with nothing to hope for but the merciful stroke of an executioner's sword.

These gloomy reflections were interrupted by the appearance of a dim light on the roof above me, and, as I was no longer unable to move, I turned over to see whence it came. A shaft of light was falling into the cavern from some opening that I could not see, but presumably the entrance, and it grew rapidly brighter. Presently a party of eight men entered the cavern, the foremost of whom carried a flaring palm oil lamp swinging from a chain while another bore an earthen pot from which a stick projected. None of these men wore any special garb, but I recognised among them the priests who had brought me from the camp and those who had visited me in the cavern, including the ruffian with the bandaged head.

By the light of the lamp I could make out to some extent the nature of the place that I was in. I could see that it was a large chamber or gallery, of no great width, but stretching away into undistinguishable gloom in the one direction that was visible to me; that its walls and low roof were of the rough rock, that it was divided by massive piers consisting of unexcavated portions of the rock, and that the ceiling was in places strengthened by great beams, which were supported by thick timber posts.

I obtained, too, flickering, uncertain glimpses of the objects that it contained, such as copper buckets standing here and there and piles of bowl-like calabashes; but my attention was more particularly attracted by the prostrate forms of my fellow prisoners, who lay about the floor in every attitude of weariness and repose. Poor wretches! They were at least unconscious. Perhaps some of them were even happy at that moment, living over again, in the shadowy land of dreams, the life of joyous freedom that they knew, while yet their eyes could look upon the light of heaven, and their ears were familiar with the murmur of trees and the voices of those they loved.

They were objects of interest to the priests as well as to me, for the sinister-looking band had evidently made this visit for the purpose of examining the sleeping captives. I watched them curiously as they stepped stealthily among the sleepers, lowering the lamp to let its light glare upon the sightless, unconscious faces, and gathering round like a pack of obscene carrion-seeking ghouls. They visited each prisoner by turn, and held a whispered consultation over each, and some question was evidently put to the white-headed villain who presided over this diabolical committee, for, as he shook his head, the party moved away to a fresh prisoner.

After they had inspected half a dozen of the prisoners they came to one over whom they consulted longer than usual, and eventually the old priest nodded his head. Then the man who carried the earthen pot took from it the stick, which appeared to be covered at its lower end with white paint of some kind, and with it made a mark on each of the shoulders of the sleeping man, and the procession moved on to the next prisoner.

I watched for a long time the little band of fetish men flitting about from one sleeping form to another. Sometimes they were hidden from me by one of the great piers of rock, and then by the unsteady light I scrutinised the strange interior and the dimly-seen forms of the unconscious slaves. At one time our visitors retired to such a distance down the gallery that I could see nothing from the alcove or recess in which I lay but the glare of the lamp twinkling in the darkness like some red and lurid star; but presently they

The Golden Pool

came back, having apparently made the round of the prisoners, and approached the place where I was lying.

As they appeared to be coming to inspect me, I closed my eyes and simulated sleep, and soon the glare of the light through my eyelids and the sound of muttered conversation told me that the examination was in progress.

The consultation over me was long and earnest and, although I spoke hardly a word of the Ochwi or Ashanti language, I could make out that they were debating as to who and what I was; and I gathered that they were not far from the truth, for, when someone suggested "Fulani" (Fulah), another voice, which sounded within a few inches of my face, replied very positively, "Broni, Broni," (white man), and with this the others seemed to agree.

I was very curious to know if I was to be among those distinguished by the white marking, and held myself prepared to receive it without starting; but at length the light grew fainter on my eyelids and the voices receded, and, when I opened my eyes, the party was retreating towards the entrance, where it vanished, leaving the cavern once more in total darkness.

I pondered long over this mysterious visitation and what it might portend.

That it looked no good to those eight or nine men who had been distinguished by the white markings I had little doubt, but what its meaning could be I was unable to conjecture, and I was still speculating upon the subject when, in spite of my mental anxiety and bodily discomfort, I fell asleep.

Chapter Fifteen
The Aboási Mine

When I opened my eyes I appeared to be in absolute darkness, and for a moment I could not remember where I was, but on attempting to move my hands, their manacled condition at once recalled me to my situation.

A glance upward showed me the dim red glow upon the roof, and when I turned over I looked upon a scene so strange and unreal that it might well have been but part of a dream.

Before I had slept I had seen the cavern as it appeared during the hours of rest; I now saw it in what I supposed to be its ordinary working aspect.

As I looked forth from my alcove I gazed into a formless expanse of gloom, in which shapes of deeper shadow moved to and fro. At what seemed to be the centre of the cavern was a single spot of light, and round this the strange lurid picture was grouped, and from this it gradually faded away on all sides into a black void. This one spot of light was an opening in the floor, and through it there streamed up a bright glow, as if from an underground furnace, which being reflected from the roof, lighted up the floor for several yards around quite brilliantly.

Within the lighted area were several figures, some standing against the light, mere silhouettes of black, others with the glow of the furnace falling on them, looking like statues of burnished copper, and all naked, cadaverous and horrible. One man crouched

The Golden Pool

over the mouth of the furnace and probed about it with a pair of tongs; another sat on the floor at a little distance and worked a couple of sheepskins that served as bellows. A third was filling a broad crucible with some substance that he took from a bowl-shaped calabash; and several were dimly visible in the background washing, by means of similar calabashes, some deposit that they dipped out of copper buckets, while they tipped the water into other vessels.

I could distinguish at intervals the sound of hammering, and looking about for its source, I made out the dim shape of a figure crouching in the shadow of one of the piers, beating out something on a flat stone. Presently he rose and walked over to the furnace with his hammer and a pair of tongs in one hand, and in the other one of those unjoined rings, known as manillas, which the Africans use as standard quantities of metal. He had apparently just finished the manilla, which was of gold, and had come for fresh material.

I watched him with curious interest as he stood in the light of the furnace, a tall, lean, but powerful figure with the tribal marks of the Moshi nation clearly visible on his skeleton face, and wondered how he came into his present condition; for the Moshi are among the most fierce and warlike of the inland tribes, and it was strange to see one of these bold and turbulent people meekly hammering out manillas for a parcel of pagan slave owners. The man who tended the furnace proceeded with his labours, while the Moshi stood by, grim and sullen, following the process by his ear.

The plan followed here was, evidently, first to melt down in crucibles the washings from the calabashes, and then to remelt the buttons of gold so obtained and cast the metal into bars, which were made into manillas. I was now able to watch the latter process, for the furnace man lifted out with his tongs a white-hot crucible, smaller than the one I had seen being filled, and laid it down while he felt about the floor until he found a brick-shaped block of clay. This was evidently the mould, for he now removed the lid from the crucible, and taking it up with his tongs, poured the molten metal into a cavity in the block. The Moshi then, having found the block by feeling about with his foot, turned it over, when a small bar of gold dropped out on to the floor. This he picked up with his tongs, and retreated to his place in the shadow of the pier, whence there immediately came the sound of hammering.

I was watching the furnace man prepare a fresh crucible when a light became visible from the direction of the entrance, and then two men came into view, each carrying a dish with a large shea butter candle burning on it.

With this increase of light I was able to see fresh details, and workers whose existence had been made evident by sound only, now came into view. Thus I could see two men engaged in working designs in repoussé on small square gold plates, and another apparently modelling some diminutive object in wax – probably one of the wax models from which gold ornaments are cast – and my attention was so much taken up by these that I did not at first notice that the two men who bore the light were followed by several other persons. Presently, however, the light-bearers halted to examine the contents of a calabash in which a slave was washing the gold-bearing deposit, and then the others came up, and I saw that all the fetish men who had visited the cavern were present and were accompanied by three strangers.

These latter at once riveted my attention.

They were dressed in handsome Kumasi cloths, or *ntamas*, of silk, and carried short heavy swords in leopard skin sheaths; but the most remarkable feature was their hair, which was worked up into close sausage-like ringlets that hung round their necks in a fringe, and gave them a singularly uncouth and forbidding appearance.

I regarded these strangers with the utmost horror, for I knew that this peculiar headdress is the official badge of the royal executioners of Ashanti, and the scene I had witnessed a few hours previously began to have a new and shocking significance.

I looked round to see if I could distinguish any of the prisoners who bore on their shoulders the fatal white mark, but the light was not sufficiently strong; but even as I looked, the horrid business commenced.

The executioners, evidently familiar with their duties, separated and began to examine the prisoners one by one, and as each marked victim was discovered he was led to a place some distance away from me and stood against a pier, where soon was collected quite a little party of the poor wretches who were thus entering upon the closing scene of their life's tragedy.

But my attention was soon diverted very violently from these to my own concerns, for the fetish men, bringing one of the lights with them, came and gathered round me with a dreadful air of business, and I now perceived that one of them carried a coil of stout grass rope, while another – my old enemy in fact – held in his hand an implement, at the sight of which I grew sick with horror.

It was a small iron bar, set in a wooden handle, and was flattened at the end, where it was bent over to form a sharp hook.

Without a word being spoken they set to work.

One of the men sat down upon my knees completely fixing my legs, another knelt at my head, and taking it between his knees leaned with his entire eight on my forehead, while two others sat astride upon my body, confining my arms and nearly suffocating me. Then the man with the rope passed the end under my shoulders, and was just about to draw a coil round my chest and arms, when a loud shouting arose from the further part of the cavern.

The man at my head stood up with an exclamation, and I involuntarily turned my face in the direction of the noise.

The tall Moshi was struggling in the grasp of one of the executioners, who was not strong enough to hold him, and both were shouting vociferously.

Suddenly the Moshi dragged his assailant forward a couple of paces, and stooping quickly, snatched up his hammer, and, in a twinkling, brought it down with a crash on the head of the executioner, who dropped in a heap on the floor. Then the Moshi, with a fiendish yell, rushed off, brandishing his hammer, and hitting out at everyone whom he came in contact with, and, before one had time to draw a breath, he had felled two of the prisoners and was charging straight for the condemned group, flourishing his hammer and bellowing like an enraged bull. The men who were holding me, leaped to their feet and, catching up the light, they all ran off, with the exception of one who remained standing by my side.

The disturbance rapidly began to assume alarming proportions, for the Moshi, charging in among the condemned men, dealt them such blows with his hammer that those who were not killed outright or stunned, became infuriated with rage and pain, and fell upon one another with fists and teeth until the cavern rang with their yells. They became like a pack of frightened wild beasts, running hither and thither, attacking indiscriminately everyone they came near.

The other prisoners, too, alarmed by the screams and shouts, came running from every part of the cavern, and being in their turn attacked, joined in the infernal medley.

Thus the executioners and fetish men unexpectedly found themselves involved in a seething mob of furious maniacs, all clawing, biting and tearing at one another, and growing every moment more furious and wildly excited; and to increase the confusion, the two lights were trampled underfoot and the place – except for the glow of the furnace – became wrapped in darkness.

I watched these developments with growing excitement. Already the fetish men, unable for the time to restore order, were on the defensive, and had all their attention occupied in looking to their own safety, while the man who stood over me was clearly becoming anxious, for he drew a large knife or cutlass from its sheath and played with it nervously as if doubtful whether or not he should go to his comrades' assistance.

The sight of the knife in his hand roused me to action. Reaching out my fettered hands I suddenly grasped his ankles and jerked his feet from under him, and as he came down flat on his back, his head struck the hard floor with the sound of a pavior's hammer. I dragged his unconscious body towards me and searched for the knife, which I found sticking in his back; for he had dropped it as he fell, and fallen upon it with such force that its point stood two inches out at the front of his chest.

I pulled the knife out, and jamming its wet and slippery haft between my knees, sawed through the rope that bound my hands together. With my hands free I soon cut through the cord that confined my feet, and the halter by which I was tethered to the peg, and then I rose to my feet and stretched my stiffened limbs.

The fetish men and the executioners were by this time thoroughly panic-stricken, and I could see them, by the dim, red glow, struggling frantically to free themselves from the surging crowd which hemmed them in. I stole softly to one of the piers and stood by it, knife in hand, ready to defend myself if anyone should come my way, and surveyed this astonishing scene of slaughter.

One after another the fetish men dropped, stabbed with their own weapons or felled by the hammer of the furious Moshi, whose gaunt form could be seen in the middle of the crowd like that of some avenging demon. The untended furnace died down by degrees until its glow faded away and the place was plunged into total darkness, and the swaying mass of shadowy figures grew more and more shadowy and dim until they vanished into utter obscurity.

And out of that black inferno came a din so awful and I shuddered as I listened. Howls of rage, shrieks of terror, and yells of agony, mingled in such a soul-shaking concert as might have belched up from the very mouth of Hell; and above it all rose the infuriated bellowing of the Moshi and the rhythmical thud of his hammer.

I stood rooted to the ground and fairly quaking with horror as scream after scream rang out through the darkness and told of the murderous work that was going on. Suddenly a great tongue of fire rose out of the floor and filled the cavern with a lurid glare. Someone had kicked one of the big candles into the furnace, and the melted oil had burst into flame.

And what a scene its light shone upon!

The floor was strewn with prostrate forms, some distorted and still, others yet writhing and clutching at one another, and all dabbled with blood. The few survivors were gathered into a crowd and locked together in the most inextricable confusion; and, as they swayed backward and forward, they fought like wild beasts, holding on with fingers twined in one another's hair, biting, scratching, and slashing indiscriminately with weapons that had been wrenched from the priests or the executioners.

The latter were all dead, and of the former but one remained – the man with the bandaged head – and he was on the outskirts of the crowd, struggling, with staring eyeballs, to free himself from the grasp of two of the prisoners; and at length he tore himself away, leaving his tattered cloth in the hands of his assailants, and rushed off towards the entrance.

But I was after him in an instant, and pursued him down the length of the gallery, slowly gaining on him.

Near the foot of a rude ladder he paused and looked over his shoulder, and when he saw me, he uttered a loud shriek and turned to fly up the ladder; but, before he could escape, I struck him so fairly on the back of the neck that his half-severed head fell forward on to his breast as he dropped.

I climbed the ladder and groped along the tunnel-like gallery at the top for some distance, but presently reflecting that the place was quite strange to me and that, having no light, I might fall into some shaft, or well, or might walk right into the arms of my enemies, I turned back and felt my way cautiously towards the cavern.

The flame was not yet extinct when I got back and let myself down the ladder, though the glow was growing much fainter and by its light I could see that the slaughter was nearly at an end, for two men only remained standing. One of these was the Moshi, who strode about hither and thither shouting, swinging his hammer, and battering at every prostrate body that he trod upon. The other was one of the slaves who had possessed himself of a long knife and was now hovering round with a stealthy ferocity that was very horrible to look at.

At the same moment the two men paused to listen, and each catching the sound of the other's breathing, they rushed at one another, and while the one made a vicious thrust with his knife, the other aimed a blow with his hammer.

The knife entered the Moshi's arm above the elbow, but the next instant the hammer crashed against his assailant's temple, felling him to the ground. The Moshi burst into a wild shout, and leaped about among the bodies flourishing his hammer; but presently he stopped and listened, and, as I remained stock-still and hardly breathing, the place, which but a minute ago rang with such a furious din, was as silent as the grave.

Then a curious reaction set in the mind of this fierce barbarian. The frenzy of bloodthirsty rage had time to cool, and the strange stillness evidently struck on him with a chill of fear, for he began to call out names — no doubt those of the slaves whose corpses lay around — and questions in the Ochwi language.

I still remained motionless and silent, for I feared that if I spoke he would mark my position and rush at me, and I had no wish to kill him and did not intend that he should kill me; but, as the flame was now rapidly dying out, I considered that if any fighting was to be done it had better be in what light remained, for so I had the advantage, whereas in the dark the advantage clearly lay with the blind man.

When, therefore, having received no reply to his question in Ochwi he asked in barbarous Hausa, "Is there no one here?" I replied, "Yes. There is one left."

"Who art thou?" he demanded with fierce suspicion.

"I am the new prisoner who was brought here yesterday," I answered.

"Have they blinded thee yet?" he asked.

"No," said I. "They were about to put out my eyes when the fight began."

"Where are all the others?" he inquired.

"They are lying all around, dead," I answered.

"What!" he shouted. "Have they killed all the slaves but me?"

"Many of them thou didst kill thyself," said I, "and as to the rest, they killed one another or were killed by the wizards."

"Dost thou tell me that I have killed my friends?" he exclaimed in a tone of horrified surprise. "I thought it was the wizards and the men of Kumasi with whom I was fighting, and now thou sayest I have killed my comrades. This is a dreadful thing!" and to my surprise he burst into a loud weeping, tearing at his hair and beating his breast with his clenched fist.

I took the opportunity to pick up the remaining candle and drop it into the furnace, for I had no mind to be left in the darkness with this unstable, excitable savage.

"And where are the wizards and the Kumasi men?" he asked presently.

"They are all dead," said I. "Their bodies lie around thee."

He broke out again into boisterous blubbering lamentations.

"All gone," he moaned, "and thou tellest me I have killed them – have killed my brothers who have worked by my side this long, long time. Why should I not die, too? Come, my friend, take a knife and kill me so that I may rest among my friends."

"This is folly," said I, for I felt that time was too precious to be wasted on maudlin lamentation. "The others are dead and we are alive. Let me bind up thy arm, and then let us be gone from this accursed place."

I tore off a strip of cloth from the garment of one of the dead fetish men, and bound up his bleeding arm as well as I could.

"Now," I said, "thou knowest this place better than I. How shall we go?"

"We cannot get out by the entrance," he answered, "for the houses of the wizards are there, and we shall be taken as soon as we come out."

This was manifestly true, and was as I had expected; but some move would have to be made without delay, for more of the fetish men or their armed followers might arrive at any moment.

"Is there any other way out?" I asked.

"That I know not," he replied. "There is a passage that I can show thee, but where it ends I cannot tell; only I know that some of the slaves have gone away through it, but they have always been brought back after a time, excepting two."

"And what of them?"

"They never came back from the passage, but whether they escaped, or died in their hiding places, we never knew. It was a long time ago."

I considered a moment and decided to explore the passage, for if, after all, there was no way out through it we should be no worse off. We could still try the entrance.

"Where is this passage?" I inquired.

"Show me the furnace," said he.

I put his foot against the rim of the furnace mouth, and he groped round among the corpses until he felt the bellows; then he stood up and walked off confidently, and I followed. He walked straight to a post of timber, and having felt it, turned and made for the wall.

"It is hereabouts," he said, and, raising his arms, began to feel along the wall; and when I examined the spot as well as I could in the half darkness, I could make out a shape of deeper shadow about seven feet from the ground.

"Here it is," I said. "Stand thou there and let me climb on thy shoulders and I will pull thee up after."

"Thou wilt go and leave me behind," he exclaimed suspiciously.

"Then climb on my shoulders and go first," said I, for I knew he would not go off by himself; and setting my arms against the wall I planted my feet firmly.

He climbed up actively enough on to my shoulders, gave a spring and was gone, and the next moment I felt his hand reaching down for me; but in spite of his help I was quite unable to get up the slippery wall, and, after a number of fruitless struggles, was beginning to think of abandoning the attempt and making a dash for the entrance, when I remembered the coil or rope that the fetish men had brought to bind me. Bidding the Moshi wait for me, I ran across the cavern, lighted by the now fading flare from the furnace, and found the coil lying in my alcove. Returning to the opening, I passed up the two ends to my companion, who now hauled me up without difficulty.

The passage in which we now found ourselves was a kind of tunnel about four feet high and, of course, pitch dark; and my companion being more at home in these conditions than I, led the way. We crawled along on hands and knees for a long distance until, at length, my comrade called out that the part that we had entered was higher, and I then stood up; but our progress was slower walking than crawling, for we had – or at least my companion had – to make sure of the ground before each step, lest we should fall into some shaft or pit. So we groped our way along for an apparently interminable distance until at last, to my joy, I perceived, a long way ahead, a faint spot of light. I informed my companion of this, but he seemed quite incredulous.

'It cannot be," he said, "for if there is an opening here, how could it be that the slaves were unable to get away?"

I did not think it worthwhile to argue the question, but groped on hopefully. The light grew gradually brighter, although still but a dim reflection on the wall of the tunnel, but presently a turn showed the end of the passage distinctly a long distance ahead, and evidently not opening into the outer world but into some chamber or gallery lighted by daylight.

We now quickened our pace, and soon emerged into a very singular cavern or chamber.

It was roughly circular in plan, about fifteen yards across and thirty or forty feet high, the walls gradually approaching towards the top, where there was an irregular-shaped opening through which I could see masses of foliage and a single spot of sky. The sides were of rough rock, not cut away as in the other cavern, but quite irregular and broken, like the face of a cliff, with deep hollows and large projecting bosses; but very little of the original surface could be seen, for a dense covering of moss encrusted the whole of the sides and floor, and out of this tiny, delicate, pale-green ferns sprang, while the darker corners harboured clusters of toadstools, mostly snowy-white.

Altogether there was in the aspect of the place something singularly suggestive of the unnoticed passage of time, and of solitude long undisturbed; such as one remarks on entering some ancient tomb, outside which the centuries have rolled on, while the dust has slowly deposited on the unchanging monuments of the forgotten dead within. But it was not the general appearance of the place alone that bore this suggestiveness, for the objects that it contained were yet more fraught with an air of mouldy antiquity, and these riveted my attention from the moment that my eyes fell upon them.

On one side, close to the wall, reposed a great chest of age-blackened odúm wood, evidently of native workmanship, despite the elaborate carving on its front, which, indeed, had it been seen under other conditions, would have stamped it as European in origin; for the central device showed a rudely executed square of drapery on which was a grotesque face.

But the model from which it had been copied stood opposite – a smaller coffer of jet-black oak in the last stage of decay, on the front of which could yet be distinguished a carving of the Holy Handkerchief of St Veronica surmounted by the initials J de S," and flanked by the date "1489".

Each chest bore on its lid a collection of skulls arranged with great precision, the larger chest having sixteen skulls in a double row, and the smaller chest having nine in a single row; and, even to my inexpert eye, it was easy – seeing them thus in groups – to perceive difference in type, the skulls upon the smaller chest being obviously less massive than the others, and having much less projecting jaws and smaller teeth.

As I noted these differences I understood in a flash what place this was in which I stood. It was the cavity caused by the caving in of the tunnel in which the old Portuguese adventurers had been surprised by the natives; and these skulls, which grinned at one another from the lids of the two coffers, were the remains of the men who had been overwhelmed amidst the explosions of those antique guns some four hundred years ago, disinterred from the rubbish of the fallen roof Heaven knows when, and reverently set out to confront one another in death as they had done in life.

"What seest thou in this place?" asked Bukári – for such I had ascertained was my companion's name.

I told him of the two great chests and the skulls upon them.

"Ah!" he exclaimed. "Then this is the treasure chamber of the Tano abúsum. This is where the wizards hoard the gold that we poor wretches have toiled to win from the bottom of the pool, and that the hypocrites pretend to give to the Osai of Kumasi. Let us open the chests and see if it not be so."

"No, no," said I. "Let the chests go for the present – perchance they are empty after all – and let us get out of this trap if we can. Doubtless they are searching for us even now."

This suggestion so alarmed Bukári that he instantly forgot the treasure and begged me to search for a means of escape.

I examined the place narrowly, and was somewhat dismayed to find no trace of an outlet. The tunnel by which we had come had at one time been continued on the opposite side of the chamber, and its opening was still visible; but it was completely closed with masses of rock and rubbish. Doubtless when this chamber was re-excavated, the debris of the fallen roof had been cleared away into the further tunnel, which was now consequently filled up. I walked round and round the chamber, peering into every dark corner, and glanced wistfully up at the opening overhead, where the green leaves were rustling so tantalisingly; but there seemed no more chance of escape than if we had been at the bottom of a well.

Presently I began to consider whether it might not be possible to climb up the rugged side and reach the opening. It certainly did not look very feasible, but I determined to make the attempt, so, selecting a part of the wall that presented the greatest number of projections, I began the ascent, while Bukári kept guard over the tunnel, listening intently for the footsteps of pursuers.

With a good deal of difficulty I managed to climb up a distance of some fifteen feet, but beyond this ascent was impossible, for the wall began to slope smoothly outwards. I clung to a knob of quartz that projected from the rock and turned my head to see if anything was visible from this height that could not be seen from the floor; and when I did so my heart leaped with joy and hope, for directly opposite me was the dark opening of a tunnel which had been hidden from below by a projecting boss of rock.

Perhaps my rejoicing was premature, for the tunnel was nearly twenty feet from the floor and had, as I have said, below it a great projection; but it looked like a way out and was, in any case, a safe hiding place, so I scrambled down, resolved to reach it or break my neck in the attempt. Bukári was highly elated when I told him of my discovery, and encouraged me with the suggestion that the slaves who disappeared might have escaped that way; so, throwing round my neck the coil of rope (which I had prudently brought with me) I commenced to clamber up the face of the wall under the projection.

As I worked my way up, inch by inch, I always seemed to have reached the very highest point that was possible, and as I clung, with my fingers hooked in the treacherous moss, and my toes lodged on some almost invisible projection, I looked up at the space that yet remained above me with a feeling of despair. And yet, inch by inch, with incredible labour, I crept up, slowly reducing the space, until, at length, I came to the promontory that projected forward like some great bracket or corbel. To scale this seemed an utter impossibility, for it stood out above my head with its surface at an angle of nearly thirty degrees from the vertical, and it looked as if I must fail after all within a few feet of safety.

After a brief rest I now began to edge away to one side, and in this way was able to hoist myself upwards two or three feet, but in a direction slanting somewhat away from the opening of the tunnel. Still, it was something to attain a higher level, and I crept on, streaming with perspiration and faint from the want of food, digging my fingers into the moss and taking advantage of every cranny and projecting crystal of quartz, until at last my eyes came on to the level of the floor of the tunnel.

But the tunnel was now several feet away to my left, and to reach it I must cling somehow to the overhanging rock.

The thing seemed impracticable, but yet each time I changed my foothold or the grip of my bruised and aching fingers, I came somehow a little nearer, until my shoulders overhung my feet by two or three inches. At length I lodged one hand on the edge of the tunnel floor and could look into the dark cavity; then I shifted the other hand so that it gripped the corner of the opening. After a moment's rest I managed to slide my left hand a little along the floor until it caught a projecting stone, and letting go with my right, quickly slipped it on to the same projection. Here I remained fixed, with my arms reached into the opening, and one foot holding on to a clump of moss with the toes, while with the other foot I felt about vainly for a new foothold.

Suddenly I felt my foot slipping from the moss, while the other slid down the smooth rock. At the risk of flinging myself away from the wall I gave a violent kick, digging my toes into the moss, and at the same moment tugged with all my might at the stone in the tunnel floor; and, as my legs flew from under me, I dragged my head and shoulders and chest into the opening.

I was now in an apparently hopeless position, lying across the sill of the opening with my legs dangling over the edge of the projecting rock, more than half of my body outside the tunnel, and only prevented from overbalancing outwards by my grip on the stone in the floor. Thus I remained for some minutes fixed and helpless; but at length, by dint of cautious wriggling and pulling steadily at the stone I dragged myself forward until I was able to hitch one knee over the sill. Then I crawled bodily into the tunnel and sat down with my back against the wall to get my breath.

But there was no time for rest. Our pursuers might appear at any moment, and it was necessary to get my companion out of the treasure chamber – if such it was – without delay. I uncoiled the rope, and on lowering it over the edge, found that, if I held both ends, the bight, or loop, would just touch the ground. I called out to Bukári to know if he could climb up by the aid of the rope, and on his replying very readily that he could, I directed him how to find the hanging bight. He listened intently at the tunnel for a moment, and then crossing the chamber, according to my directions, felt about for the rope; and when he grasped it he planted his feet against the wall and came up hand over hand with surprising agility, while I held on with my feet fixed against the stone.

As soon as he stood beside me, I gathered up the rope and coiled it round my neck, and without more delay we started off down the tunnel, Bukári leading as before.

This gallery extended a considerable distance, but we had not gone very far when I caught a faint glimmer of light, and presently, on rounding an angle, I saw before me a very small spot a long way off, the dazzling brightness of which left me in no doubt as to its being actual daylight. I communicated this discovery to Bukári, and we trudged along very hopefully, the light growing stronger every moment; and soon I could distinguish a mass of foliage waving to and fro across the opening. At last we came to the mouth of the tunnel, which, I was astonished to find, opened on to the face of a cliff, the foliage that I had seen being the topmost bough of a great odúm tree that grew at its foot. The cliff, however, was not so steep as to present any considerable difficulty in the descent, and its face was covered with large bushes, by which one could easily climb down to the level.

Bukári and I sat in the mouth of the tunnel, breathing in the soft sweet air – so different from the foul and noisome atmosphere of the mine – and talked over the situation. As to the geography of the mine, he knew nothing about it, but it seemed quite evident from the distance we had travelled since leaving the slaves' cavern, that the entire range of tunnels passed right through a hill, and that we were on the opposite side to that in which the entrance was situated. The tunnel that we had just traversed was most probably an ancient working that had become separated from the rest of the mine when the gallery caved in, and its existence was almost certainly unknown to the fetish men. Probably also the cliff on which it now opened had been formed by a landslip, and its original opening may have been upon a shelving hillside. At any rate, it formed a safe refuge for the present, where we could consider at leisure what our next move was to be.

But we could not give too much time to our deliberations, for the first question – and a very pressing one, too – was, where we were to obtain some food? Neither Bukári nor I had eaten a morsel since the previous day, and we had gone through a prodigious amount of mental and bodily exertion, and my own diet just lately had been of the scantiest; so that whatever we might elect to do afterwards, it was imperative that we should obtain, somehow, something to eat.

But it was equally necessary that we should not lose sight of the tunnel, which was to be our place of refuge until we decided on our future proceedings, and as Bukári exacted from me a solemn promise that I would not leave him, we must devise some plan for finding our way back to it if we left it.

From our present situation I could see but little, for the opening of the gallery was somewhat lower than the tops of the larger trees that grew on the level, so I decided to ascend to the summit of the hill in order that I might see the lie of the land. This decision I communicated to Bukári, who at once strongly objected to the proposal, being evidently afraid that I should go off and leave him; but on my solemnly repeating my promise to stand by him, he reluctantly consented, and agreed to remain in the mouth of the tunnel, so that if I should fail to find it on my return – which was quite possible since the surrounding bushes, to a great extent, concealed it – he should be ready to answer my hail.

These matters being settled, I looked about for the easiest way up the face of the cliff, and, selecting a space to one side of the tunnel where the bushes grew most densely, began the ascent.

Chapter Sixteen
I Assist in a Robbery and Become a Fugitive

The ground, as I have said, was not difficult to climb, since the surface was not quite perpendicular, and besides being rough and broken, was thickly covered with vegetation; so that without any great exertion I soon reached the top of the cliff, and landed on to a nearly level space, which I took to be the summit of a hill. From this point the view was very extensive in the one direction, although it was cut off in the other by the forest which clothed the summit. Looking back – that is, in the direction in which the cliff faced – my eye ranged over the ocean-like expanse of forest, out of which, at a distance of about three miles, rose a solitary, conical hill, while nearer – in fact, quite near – could be seen a river of some size, which I took – erroneously as it turned out – to be the Tano.

Following the edge of the summit, I walked on, each few hundred yards bringing into view a new vista, until I had gone half a mile; when I could tell, from the direction of the shadows, that I had reached the opposite side of the hill. Here I could see below me a village of some pretensions immediately at the foot of the hill, and this I guessed to be the abode of the fetish men, while at a distance of less than a mile another village was visible, which, with the large silk-cotton tree in the middle of an open space, I identified as the one to which I had been first taken – indeed, on looking carefully, I thought I could make out the very hut in which I had been confined.

Having thus made clear the position of our hiding place, I struck off across the middle of the summit, guiding myself towards my starting point by watching my shadow. I had travelled about halfway when I came to a rather deep hollow occupying, as I judged, nearly the centre of the summit; and, as it lay directly in my path, I began to descend, and had nearly reached the bottom when I was brought up with a start by the sound of voices.

Instantly I crouched down among the thick herbage and listened. There seemed to be several persons talking, but although the voices sounded near, I could not for a time make out the direction from which they came; and a peculiar hollow but muffled quality in the sounds puzzled me not a little. Presently one of the speakers laughed – a strange, hollow laugh that reverberated as if it came from the bottom of a well – and then I perceived that the noise proceeded from underground.

On this I crept forward cautiously, and after crawling a few yards, saw before me a large hole in the earth. I lay down flat on my face and drew myself softly to the edge of the chasm, and putting my head into a mass of fern, peered down between the stems. As I had expected, I looked down into the chamber that I had recently left – and left none too soon; for it was now occupied by a party of six fetish men, all armed with long knives and guns, and provided with a stinking palm oil lamp.

They were mightily excited, for they chattered and gesticulated like a pack of monkeys, and I would have given a good deal to know what they were saying. That they had missed Bukári and me I had no doubt, but whether or not they had traced our progress thus far I had no means of judging. On one point, however, and that the most important, I soon became satisfied; they clearly had no knowledge of the existence of the tunnel by which we had finally escaped.

After a good deal of talk and searching the corners of the chamber and the entrance to the filled up tunnel, they began to examine the chests, and I was now most thankful that I had not allowed Bukári to satisfy his curiosity; for I could see an old fetish man, who had been poring over the lid of the larger chest (which was immediately beneath me) pointing out to his fellows the undisturbed coating of dust on it.

In spite of this demonstration, however, they were not quite convinced apparently, for to my intense satisfaction they proceeded to remove the skulls one by one and place them at a little distance on the floor. When the top was clear, they knocked a wooden pin out of a rude hasp – the only fastening that the chest had – and raised the lid, resting it against the wall.

From my position immediately overhead I could look down straight into the chest, and the sight that met my gaze when the lid was flung back, filled me with amazement.

For that great coffer was filled almost to the top with gold. Gold masks of strange design, gold armlets, gold anklets, great dumbbell-like sword-hilts, head-plates and trinkets of which I could not distinguish the forms, were there by the score; but the great bulk of the metal was in the form of manillas – the African equivalent of ingots – of which there must have been hundreds, all tied up in bunches of a dozen or so.

Here, indeed, was "wealth beyond the dreams of avarice"!

As I looked down into the great chest I felt myself unconsciously gloating over its shining contents; and when the fetish men, apparently satisfied of the safety of the treasure, closed the lid and drove in the pin, I was conscious of quite a chill of regret, until I suddenly remembered my condition, when I almost laughed aloud at the absurdity of a naked, starving wretch like myself barely snatched from the jaws of death, and yet hankering after wealth.

When the priests had made the chest secure they replaced the skulls, and forthwith retired through the tunnel, having accomplished what was probably the principal object of their visit. The smaller chest they had not examined at all, and from this I judged that it contained nothing of intrinsic value – perhaps merely some mouldering relics of the old adventurers. When the last of the men had disappeared I drew myself carefully back on to the more solid ground, and resumed my journey across the little plateau.

In a few minutes I came out on to the edge a little to the right of the tunnel, as I could tell by comparing the positions of a large tree and the distant hill, and was about to return when I noticed some objects moving, about a third of the way down the steep slope. I stopped to observe them, and was able to make out that they were vole-like animals about the size of rabbits, with blunt muzzles and short tails, and evidently lived in a large community in burrows.

Zoophilists tell us that by nature man is a fruit-eating animal, which is possibly true – when there happens to be fruit to eat. At present, however, there was none and the sight of those rodents frisking in and out of their burrows aroused in me a very pronounced carnivorous impulse. I had noticed on the plateau a great number of nodular lumps of ironstone lying on the surface, and I now returned and gathered an armful of moderate-sized pieces, which I carried to the edge of the slope. Then I concealed myself behind a bush and waited.

Soon a little party of the rodents assembled on a small knoll immediately underneath, browsing on the herbage in leisurely security, all unconscious of the prowling carnivore above, until a lump of ironstone about two pounds in weight dropped plump on to the back of one of them, rolling him over dead; when the parliament instantly dissolved, and I climbed down to gather up my spoil.

I had not been back in my hiding place many minutes when the foolish-looking brutes reappeared and began nibbling away at the grass as if nothing had happened, so that in quite a short time I was able to secure four of them, with which I started off for the tunnel very cheerfully.

Bukári was awaiting my return with the keenest anxiety, and reproached me for being so long absent.

"I thought thou hadst gone away altogether," he grumbled. "Where hast thou been, and what has thou found?"

"I have seen many strange things," said I, "and I have found us a dinner," and I put his hand upon the dead animals, which he felt with a grin of delight.

"Grass-cutters!" he exclaimed. "I have not tasted flesh since I came to the mine. Let us cook them at once, for I am famished."

"How shall we cook them since we have no fire?" I asked.

He seemed greatly surprised at the question. "Why then, we must make a fire, of course," he replied.

This was a little embarrassing, for I had but the haziest notion of how to go about making a fire. I had, indeed, read in books of the fire drill used by the Australian natives; but I had never tried to make one, and this was hardly a suitable occasion for amateur experiments. In our camp, the light had always been kindled by Musa, who had a flint and steel and kept a supply of tinder; without these appliances I was quite helpless, and had to admit the fact.

Bukári laughed grimly. "Get me a lump of quartz," said he, "and a bit of dry bark from some dead wood, and gather some sticks. If thou canst get some clay, so much the better."

I climbed up to the plateau, and soon found a dead branch, which I carried back bodily and handed it over to Bukári to strip of its bark, while I prised out a lump of quartz from the wall of the tunnel, and I then stood by to receive a lesson in the art of fire making.

"Give my thy knife," said Bukári, and on my handing it to him he struck its back skilfully a few times on the quartz, receiving the sparks on the prepared mass of bark, and blowing gently; and in a few minutes the bark was smouldering and smoking quite briskly.

There was no time to look for clay with which to coat the animals, so when the fire was fairly alight we fixed them over it, on long, pointed sticks, and sat by patiently while they frizzled in the smoke. To while away the interval – which was really a very trying one, for, when the hair had burnt off, the animals began to emit a most savoury aroma – I recounted to Bukári what I had seen when I looked down the opening into the chamber. He was violently excited, rather to my surprise, when I described the contents of the chest, and announced his intention of helping himself to some of the gold before finally leaving the mine.

The smoke-blackened carcases were not very agreeable to look at, but they furnished exceedingly good eating, and Bukári and I lingered over our cannibal-like repast until the bones were picked as clean as if they had been destined for some anatomic museum.

By this time the sun was getting low, so I made another journey to the plateau to gather wood for the night, and with what I had collected we made up a cheerful fire some distance down the tunnel, spreading a quantity of grass upon the floor that we might sleep in comfort.

Naturally, we were very tired after all our labours and excitements, and the food had made us rather drowsy, but we sat on our beds talking over our plans for a long time before we lay down to sleep.

We agreed on the necessity for getting away from the neighbourhood of the mine without delay – indeed, we were running no small risk by staying so long in the tunnel – but on one point Bukári was resolved; he would not leave the place until he had possessed himself of some of the gold.

I could not help admiring his bold adventurous spirit, unbroken by the long years of suffering and servitude, but at the same time his obstinacy was highly inconvenient, for any attempt to remove the treasure would enormously increase the danger of our situation, which was already sufficiently perilous.

"Why not leave the gold where it is?" I urged. "We know where to find it whenever we choose to come back."

"We know where it is now," he replied, "but the wizards may take it elsewhere. Thou didst see thyself that they were uneasy and fearful about it. They may put it in some safe place."

I could not deny the truth of this; it was in fact highly probable that the priests would now look out for some more secure hiding place for their treasure.

"How much dost thou wish to take?" I asked.

"I would take it all," he replied.

"What!" I exclaimed. "Take it all! Thou art mad, Bukári. Why there is more than thirty men could carry, and we are but two."

"I know it," he answered calmly. "We could not carry it all away, but what I would do is this. I would take out the gold and bury it in a safe place, where I would make a mark to find it again by. Then I would go to my country and tell my brothers of what I had done, and they should come to this country as if to buy guru, and when they had bought the guru at Juábin, they should come back this way, dig up the gold, and take it to my country."

"Why bury the gold?" I asked. "Why not leave it in the tunnel. Nobody seems to know of the existence of this passage."

"Who knows?" he answered. "Perhaps some hunters may know of this place and come here to sleep in the rains; besides, thinkest thou that the wizards, when they miss their treasure, will not search every place? They have only to bring a ladder to the treasure chamber to find this tunnel, and then all our labour would be in vain."

I could not deny that Bukári's reasoning was sound, that is, if one admitted the desirability of meddling with the treasure at all; and as I have already admitted, the sight of the gold had aroused my own cupidity to no small extent. Moreover the treasure had really been the object of my quest from the first, although I had never dreamed of laying my hands upon the actual hoard, so, in the end I fell in with the Moshi's plan, and agreed to begin lifting the treasure at daybreak on the morrow.

There were indeed, other matters to settle, such as the proportions of our respective shares and the security to be offered to me against treachery on the part of his brother Moshis, but as the marks must necessarily be made by me, and my assistance would be indispensable in identifying the locality, I left the details for settlement at a later date.

On the following morning we were awake and on the move before daybreak, and Bukári was full of childish eagerness to commence removing the gold. But there were one or two things to be done before we could begin. First it would be wise to settle on the place where the gold was to be buried, so that there should be no delay when once the removal was begun. Then it would never do to risk carrying the uncovered gold even a short distance, for if we were observed even by a chance stranger, disaster would be sure to follow. Lastly, we must have food of some kind.

As to the first question, we agreed that the gold would best be buried near to the river that I had seen from the plateau, as we should thus have a landmark that would help in the subsequent finding of the hoard; so, as soon as the sun had risen, I set off down the precipitous hillside to examine the river, leaving Bukári to plait a couple of wicker bags out of the grass on which we had slept.

A few minutes' very easy climbing brought me to the foot of the hill by the great odúm tree, and I plunged at once into the forest, which was here rather dense, keeping a careful eye upon my shadow, that I might not lose my way. From the summit of the hill I had noted the position of the river, and I now struck out confidently in its direction.

It was very unpleasant pushing through the dense vegetation, for my unclothed condition exposed me completely to the thorns with which every bush and tree seemed to be covered, and my progress was not rapid; but at length, after walking for about half a mile, I crossed a small track, and soon after came out on to the bank of the river, which was here a rather shallow stream about thirty yards broad, whose clear water ran quietly over a bed of pale grey sand. My first action on reaching the river was to lie down and indulge in a deep draught of the limpid water, for the tiny spring that we had found on the hillside below the tunnel had given barely enough water to quench our thirst, even when carefully collected in the hollows of our hands; then I arose, and having cut a bunch of twigs and laid them on the bank for a landmark, walked slowly upstream, wading nearly knee-deep.

The river was a typical forest stream, meandering through a kind of tunnel of foliage, between high banks of crumbling yellow sandstone, clothed with moss and fern; but it was so enclosed by the forest and one part was so like another, that I could for some time find no spot that I could hope to identify on a second visit.

I had been sauntering thus for some time when my foot came in contact with some hard object in the sand, and stooping to examine it, I picked up one of the large freshwater mussels that the Adangme people call affaní. This was indeed a lucky find, for although these shellfish are tough and greasy, they are perfectly wholesome to eat; so I fell to searching with my feet for more, and before long had collected as many as I could carry in my hands.

The river, at the place that I had now reached, spread out into a wide expanse that in the rainy season was evidently a swamp, and as the foliage seemed here a little thinner, I waded across to the further bank in the hope that from thence a more extended view might be obtainable. Nor was I disappointed, for when I had crossed the river, which nowhere came above my waist, I could plainly see, through an opening in the foliage, the summit of the hill and the red patch of our cliff below it.

But more than this. The large window-like opening was bisected by the silvery-grey trunk of a lofty silk-cotton tree, and somewhat nearer to the river a tall oil palm held aloft its plumy head like a bunch of green ostrich feathers. I climbed the bank, and taking my stand upon a smooth knoll covered with thick moss, looked steadily through the opening at the hill; and now I perceived that the end of the red patch of cliff formed a nearly vertical line which appeared just halfway between the stem of the palm and the trunk of the tree. This formed a leading mark which would enable me to find the spot again with certainty, and if the soil was not too rocky, this was an ideal place in which to bury the treasure. To test the hardness of the ground I stuck my knife into the moss, which it penetrated easily up to the hilt, showing that the soil underneath was soft and deep.

Before returning, I had the curiosity to explore a little further this bank of the river, and walking away from the water, I presently made a curious discovery; for I had not gone above twenty paces when I came to the water again. I at first thought I had merely reached a sharp bend in the river, but further examination showed that the land on which I stood was a small island, about a hundred yards long by twenty wide, and that it was separated from the mainland on either side by a stretch of water fully fifty yards in width. This was another piece of good fortune, for, being cut off on all sides by water, the place was peculiarly safe from accidental intrusion and, as I gathered up my knife and the shellfish preparatory to returning, I felt that my mission had been highly successful.

I had no difficulty in finding my way back. Starting from the knoll I marked the position of the oil palm and the tree, and waded across the river towards the former, going straight through the bushes until I reached it. Then I took a new direction to where I judged the tree to be, and soon its column-like trunk loomed above me out of the undergrowth.

I sliced off two patches of bark to enable me to identify it for the present, and then taking a fresh bearing, I pushed on through the thick wood, watching my shadow attentively whenever the sunlight pierced the foliage. It was some time before I reached the track, and I began to fear that I had lost my way; but at length I crossed it, and in a few minutes more reached the foot of the hill. Evidently the track skirted the hill and diverged from the river.

I found the patch of cliff with very little trouble, and when I thought I had reached the vicinity of the tunnel I gave a shrill whistle – the signal I had arranged with Bukári – which was immediately answered by a hail from above. Looking up I could see my comrade leaning out of the tunnel, and in a couple of minutes I had joined him.

While the shellfish were roasting on the embers, I detailed to Bukári the results of my explorations, with which he was highly satisfied; and when we had devoured the affaní and taken a pair of empty shells down to the spring, to scrape up a scanty muddy draught, we set about completing the preparations for our great enterprise.

On my way back from the river I had cut two long lengths of monkey rope – not thicker than my thumb but as strong as steel hawser – and I now proceeded to hack down a stout sapling and cut it off to a length of six feet. With this, the monkey rope, the coils of grass rope and the two bags that Bukári had plaited, we took our way down the tunnel towards the treasure chamber.

We stepped silently and cautiously along the dark passage, Bukári leading, until we reached the inner opening, and I must confess that, as I lay down and, putting my head over the brink, looked down into the chamber, I felt an intense repugnance to the idea of returning to it. However, the thing had to be done, so the sooner the better.

"Shall I go down or shall I hold the rope for thee?" asked Bukári.

"Neither," said I. "We will fix the rope, and I will go down, and thou shalt pull up the gold with the small cord."

I had cut the sapling a little longer than the width of the tunnel, and I now set it across the passage a little obliquely and jammed the ends hard against the walls, so that it formed what sailors call a Sampson post, the peculiarity of which is that the more it is hauled upon, the more firmly it jams – provided one does not haul at the wrong end. To the fixed end of the post I made fast the two monkey ropes and the grass rope, each with a "fisherman's bend" so that they could not slip, and flung the ends of all three down to the floor below.

Having explained to Bukári what I wished him to do, I grasped the three ropes, gave a trial jerk to test the post, and then swung myself over the edge and easily let myself down to the floor.

It was highly disturbing and uncomfortable to be again confronted by the yawning mouth of that black tunnel that led into the terrible cavern, and I found myself continually watching it and listening at it with a nervousness that I struggled in vain to ignore. What made it more unpleasant was that strange, indefinite sounds came echoing down it from time to time, making it clear that people were stirring in the cavern at the other end; and this again suggested the necessity for silence on our part, for any noise made by us would be carried down the tunnel to the cavern as if through a speaking tube.

I therefore warned Bukári, in a loud whisper, to be silent, and set to work with all possible expedition. Quickly but carefully I laid the skulls one by one on the floor at a little distance, and with the handle of my knife pushed the pin out of the hasp and raised the heavy lid, which swung open with a dismal, protesting creak.

At the sight of the immense wealth that lay piled up within the chest I felt a thrill of greedy pleasure, and looked from one to another of the shining baubles, undecided as to which I should first lay hands upon. I passed reluctantly over a great mask of fine and curious workmanship, a parcel of delicate repoussé plates, such as the King's ambassadors wear, and a multitude of small, quaintly wrought pendant ornaments, and fixed upon the manillas, as at once the most probable and the most solid, for the first consignment. They were tied up, as I have mentioned, in bundles of about a dozen, all ready for transport, so I hoisted out a couple of bundles and carried them across to where the rope was hanging down. The weight of these insignificant-looking bundles of rings considerably astonished me, and I saw that it would take us a good many journeys to transport the whole treasure to the island.

When I had made fast the two bunches to the grass rope, I gave the word to Bukári to haul, and the first instalment of our booty went jingling up the rough wall. By the time they were unfastened and the rope dropped again, I had two more bunches ready, and when these were hoisted, two more, and so the work went on briskly for about twenty minutes, until a very perceptible diminution appeared in the contents of the chest, and I judged that a considerable pile had accumulated above.

Now it occurred to me that it would be wise to dispose of what we had lifted before taking out any more, and I suggested this course to Bukári.

"No, no," he objected. "Since we are here let us get it all up, and then we shall only have to bury it."

"But," said I, "we might be interrupted, and then we should lose it all, whereas if we bury what we have, we shall, at least, make sure of that."

"Perhaps thou art right," said he; "come up then and let us hide what we have without delay."

I closed the chest, pinned the hasp, and hastily replaced the skulls, in case the place should be visited in our absence, and hauling myself up by the ropes, pulled them up after me.

I was surprised at the quantity we had raised.

The floor of the tunnel was covered with the bunches of manillas, and I saw at once that we had a heavy day's work before us in transporting them to the island. Bukári was full of eagerness and childish glee, and was already gathering up the bunches and feverishly cramming them into the bags, but, of course, when he had filled it to the brim and essayed to lift it on to his head, he was no more able to move it than if it had been the Great Pyramid; so he regretfully emptied out two-thirds, and with the remainder he was just able to stagger.

When we reached the mouth of the tunnel with our small but ponderous burdens, we first took the precaution to fill the bags up with leaves, so that if we met anyone we might seem to be carrying loads of kola. Then we let ourselves very carefully down the steep hillside until, after a world of labour, we reached the level. I had kept the direction well in my mind, and was able to lead my companion pretty nearly by the route that I had followed on my return from the island; in fact, I managed so well that in not more than half an hour after leaving the tunnel we broke out of the undergrowth on the riverbank within sight of the island. I worked my way through the shallows until the opening in the trees came in sight, and then taking my bearings by the oil palm and the tree, I crossed the river, with Bukári in my wake, and found the moss-covered knoll at once. Here we emptied out our bags, stowing the shining spoil in a heap under a clump of bushes, and immediately set out on our return, picking up a few shellfish as we crossed the river. On our way back I cut a few sticks which, when we arrived, I laid on the mass of embers to which our fire had sunk, and set the affaní to roast, while we loaded our sacks afresh; for it was now within two hours of noon, and we were getting hungry again.

We made in all five journeys before we had cleared off all that we had raised, and as we each carried about a hundred pounds – the utmost that we could stagger under – the quantity of gold that was ultimately piled under the bushes on the island would be roughly a thousand pounds weight, or near upon half a ton.

When we had delivered the last load on to the island we set to work without delay to bury what we had brought, and this, seeing that my knife was our sole implement, proved to be no small labour. I commenced by cutting out a square of the thick moss about two feet across, which I rolled up like a turf; then I stirred the black mould with my knife while Bukári rooted with his fingers, burrowing like a mole until we had excavated a space large enough to hold the treasure. Into this we cast the manillas, packing them in as neatly as we could, and when the last of them had been crammed in, we replaced as much of the earth as there was room for, stamping it down hard with our feet, and threw the remainder amongst the bushes. Lastly, I laid the slab of moss back in its place, and when I had squeezed and coaxed it a little, it joined so neatly at the edges that the surface looked as if it had never been disturbed.

As we returned, I stopped at the tree to make a more permanent and distinctive mark, so that I might feel that the first stage of our labour was completed, and with the point of my knife I cut my initials in large conspicuous letters on the smooth grey bark. This done we resumed our journey in quite high spirits, picking out of our bags the affaní that we had collected in the river, and eating them raw as we went.

"The sun is getting low, Bukári," said I. "We shall not be able to raise much more of the gold today, for the daylight will soon be gone."

"Daylight and darkness are all the same to me," replied the Moshi grimly, "and it would seem that the night is the best time for our work, for then we know that the wizards are asleep."

I was not sure of this, but I did not contradict Bukári, who continued: "We will change places when the daylight goes. I will take the gold from the chest and thou shalt pull it up to the tunnel."

"Very well," I replied, "it shall be so; but, of course, we shall have to sleep some time."

"There will be time for sleep," he rejoined, "when the chest is empty and the gold is buried."

We had now reached the foot of the cliff, and being by this time well used to the ground, we soon climbed up and entered the tunnel. I cast on the fire a faggot that I had picked up, and we took our way, without pausing, towards the treasure chamber.

We had nearly reached the farther end, and the dim daylight was already visible, when Bukári stopped abruptly and grasped me by the arm; and at the same moment I became aware of a faint sound from the direction of the treasure chamber.

Suddenly there arose a loud and confused shouting as of several men calling out at once, and instantly Bukári turned and ran back, exclaiming: "Come away! It is the wizards! They are calling for a ladder."

I turned and fled after my companion as fast as I could in the darkness, and when I reached the mouth of the tunnel I saw him already halfway down the cliff. The sound of those voices had in an instant dissipated his reckless courage, and when I overtook him he was in state of complete panic. "What are we to do?" he gasped. "They will be out directly, and we shall be taken back to the mine. Curse the gold! Why did we ever meddle with it?" And he flung his arms about with such furious gesticulations that he struck the trunk of a tree and burst open his half-healed wound, from which the blood began to trickle down on to the ground.

I could have killed him, at that moment, without remorse, so angry was I at this childish outburst of passion, for now, as we walked, a trail of blood on the ground plainly marked the line of our flight.

"Idiot!" I exclaimed. "Is our peril not enough by reason of thy infirmity without adding to it by thy folly? Let me bind thy wound, and if thou behavest again like a child I will leave thee."

He submitted meekly to my rather rough surgery, for I meant to stop the bleeding at whatever cost to his feelings, and when I had replaced the rag as tightly as I thought safe, I took him by the hand and plunged into the forest. For a quarter of an hour we pushed and scrambled through the undergrowth, bearing towards the river; then at length we emerged on to the narrow track, and here I cut a long thin stick, and giving him one end I grasped the other, and set off at a run.

Chapter Seventeen
The Last of Bukári Moshi

When we had emerged from the tunnel the sun was already glowing crimson through the tops of the trees. As we reached the track, the short tropical twilight was beginning to fade, and before we had followed its windings for a quarter of a mile, the light had gone and the stars were twinkling through the rifts of the cloudy sky. It was fortunate that the night was not completely overcast, for had it been, I should have had no means of judging the direction in which our flight was leading us; as it was, an occasional glimpse of the "pointers" of the Great Bear told me that our average course was to the north-east.

As the darkness closed in, it became impossible to maintain the pace at which we had started, for the track, although less obstructed than many forest roads, furnished but rough travelling; but we trudged along as fast as the nature of the ground would allow us, only pausing now and again to listen for sounds of pursuit. Our long and arduous day's work had made us weary enough, but the fear of recapture was a spur that would have driven us forward even though we were dropping with fatigue; and the chance of being overtaken was not so remote either, for the path along which we were travelling appeared to be the only one that passed near to the tunnel, and its existence could hardly be unknown to the people of Aboási.

Hence it seemed highly probable that a party would be sent to examine this path as soon as our traces had been found in the tunnel, and it was not unlikely that we were already being followed; so we pressed on hour after hour, until the stars that had peeped out through the haze of the lower sky, looked down upon us from the zenith, and told us that half the night was spent.

The country hereabouts seemed almost uninhabited, for we saw no sign of any human dwelling until past midnight; when we hurried, as silently as we could, through the deserted street of a tiny hamlet, apparently unobserved except by an unseen pariah, whose high falsetto howls were still audible when we had left it half a mile behind.

There is however, a limit to human endurance, even under the stimulus of fear, and about two hours after midnight we agreed that we could go no farther without a rest; so striking off the path to the left, we pushed our way a short distance into the forest until we reached a large tree with high buttressed roots like those of the silk-cotton. In a triangular space between two of these roots we sat down and composed ourselves for sleep, half reclining with our backs against the butt of the tree; but we had scarcely begun to doze when a loud purr sounded from within a few feet of us, and as we both at once sat bolt upright, a large, dark shape moved noiselessly away.

The faint red light of the rising moon now began to filter through the trees and dimly illuminate the space opposite our resting place. Across this space there presently crept a large, shadowy form, which moved without a sound, and which I could now plainly make out to be a leopard. I rapped the hilt of my knife sharply against the tree, and the creature turned and trotted away; but in less than a minute a soft purr came from the dusky obscurity beyond, and then a half-smothered miall like the voice of a great tomcat. Bukári and I both clapped our hands and shouted, whereupon a loud rustling in the undergrowth close by told us that the brute had made off again; but it had hardly gone when the long-drawn, melancholy cry of a hyena sounded from the opposite direction, and presently as we sat stock-still and listened, a grey silhouette with high shoulders and green glowing eyes stole silently across the dimly lighted space until a low, rumbling growl from the dark bushes made it turn and shuffle away, snarling and tittering as it went.

Sleep under these circumstances was impossible, in spite of our fatigue. All night the leopard hovered round, now creeping close up with insinuating purrs, now mialling savagely at a little distance, now growling and spitting at some prowling hyena. Nor were these the only disturbers of our peace, for all the monkeys of the forest seemed to have assembled to fight and quarrel in the tree above us; a veritable parliament of pottos had foregathered close by; while shortly before dawn a measured tramp and the crashing of branches told us that a troop of elephants was passing.

So the night wore slowly and wearily away, and the first streaks of daylight found us still sitting wide awake in the angle of the root buttresses; but as the sun rose, the nocturnal beasts crept away to their lairs and left us alone, and at last we were able to lie down in peace on the soft earth and forget our miseries in sleep.

The afternoon sun was slanting through the trees when I awoke and rose, yawning and stretching my stiffened limbs. Bukári still slept, and as I was loth to wake him, I occupied myself by making short excursions, keeping always well within sight of the tree, in the hopes of picking up something eatable. In one of these journeys, as I came round the trunk of a small tree, I perceived a large hornbill on the ground. The bird's back was towards me, and it was busy tearing the skin off a plantain, which it had probably stolen from some village, so I was able to steal up behind it without being observed; and eventually with a sudden grab I seized it by the tail feathers, and in spite of its kicking, squawking, and snapping with its huge beak, I bore it in triumph back to the tree.

The noise that the creature made as I twisted its neck, woke Bukári: so without more ado, I dismembered the warm carcase, and we proceeded to devour it, and a most disgusting and cannibal-like repast it was; notwithstanding which I ate up all the flesh I could scrape off the bones, while as to Bukári, who had the advantage of not being able to see what he was eating, he gobbled up flesh, skin and entrails with a horrible relish, and seemed to have half a mind to finish up with the feathers.

When we had breakfasted in this prehistoric manner we made our way back to the path and resumed our journey, but we were both stiff and tired from the previous day's exertions, and crawled along rather sluggishly. After half an hour's weary trudging we heard the crowing of a cock, and a bend in the path showed the entrance to a small village.

I had serious doubts as to the wisdom of venturing into the neighbourhood of any human habitation, but Bukári urged me to try to get some food, and while we were debating I perceived that we were already observed; so I walked boldly into the street, leading my companion, and looked about. A single glance showed me that we were the objects of the keenest curiosity, for in less than a minute the entire population of the village had assembled, and stood about staring at us and whispering together, but keeping at a respectful distance nevertheless. Our strange appearance might, indeed, have accounted for their surprise, but there was something in their manner that filled me with uneasiness and suspicion, and I determined to make our stay as brief as possible.

As Bukári spoke the Ochwi or Ashanti language, I led him up to the group of villagers, to whom he made his appeal in a gruff, abrupt manner, but pitifully enough, eliciting, however, no more satisfactory response than an emphatically expressed desire that we should leave the village at once; but as we were turning disconsolately away, a fat, elderly woman bustled into her house, and immediately returned with a large, roasted yam, which she put into Bukári's hands, and then taking us by the shoulders, fairly ran us out of the village, exclaiming in an undertone, "Go! Quickly, as far away as you can, *and keep off the road*!"

The friendly hint was not thrown away, and, when we had thanked the good-natured soul, I ostentatiously dragged Bukári off the path and re-entered the forest to the right in sight of the whole village; but after walking parallel with the road for a quarter of a mile, I crossed it and plunged into the forest on the left. I did not, however, go far from the track, for the evening was coming on apace, and I felt that we must keep on the move through the darkness; it being evidently impossible to sleep in the forest without the protection of a fire; and whereas it was quite impracticable to attempt to walk through the forest in the dark, the road would be comparatively safe, as it is unusual for Africans to travel at night.

With what remained of daylight we sat down to make our meal off the yam, which I cut evenly into two parts, falling upon my half with the avidity of starvation; but Bukári, who usually ate like a wolf, made so little progress with his portion, that, when I was crunching the last fragment of rind, he had barely scooped out half the mealy inside.

"Is thy stomach too proud for yam now thou hast tasted meat?" I asked.

"It is not my stomach that is proud," he replied with a discontented growl. "I can hardly get my mouth open. My jaws are as stiff as the lock on a rusty musket; they have had too little to do lately."

It was dark before he had finished eating, and even then he had not cleaned out the yam; but was tucking the remainder under his arm, announced that he was ready.

By this time I was feeling quite fresh and lively, and ready for such a night march as would fairly take us out of reach of the fetish men, but Bukári plodded on in a dejected, spiritless manner that caused me some anxiety. My attempts to keep up a cheerful conversation met with but short and gruff responses, and presently he announced that his jaws were too stiff for talking, and relapsed into complete silence. So we trudged on through the darkness, for the sky was overcast and the forest dense, speaking not a word, and travelling at but a poor pace, until nearly midnight, when Bukári suddenly halted.

"What is it?" I asked. "Art thou tired?"

"I am weak," he replied, "and my limbs feels if they were made of wood. I can go no farther tonight."

He spoke in a thick, strange voice through his clenched teeth, and was evidently feeling ill. It was most unfortunate that he should break down just now, but there was no help for it, so I led the way off the road for a short distance, literally feeling my way through the thick undergrowth, until I felt the butt of a tree, and by this we sat down to wait for the approach of day. When we had sat for some time in silence – for Bukári was evidently disinclined for conversation – my companion remarked huskily that it was needless for us both to watch; and he thereupon stretched himself on the ground and appeared to fall asleep.

The forest was much quieter tonight than on the previous night; indeed, with the exception of a few civets, genets and lemurs, and one or two nocturnal birds, there was little stirring in our vicinity, and, as hour after hour passed, my watch became gradually relaxed. First I leaned my elbow on one of the roots of the tree, then I rested my head on my arm and immediately began to doze, and I must then have fallen into a deep sleep, for when I opened my eyes it was broad daylight, and I perceived two men standing at a little distance regarding my companion and me with singular and intense interest. At first I was considerably startled, but a second glance showed that they were evidently natives of the district, and by their tall lion skin caps and long guns I could tell that they were hunters. But they seemed more startled by our appearance that I was by theirs, for they stood motionless, craning forward with an expression of horrified curiosity that made me wonder what appearance I presented, until I happened to glance at Bukári, when I, too, started with a shock of horror. For the Moshi's face, forbidding at all times, was contorted with a most horrid grimace – a fixed, sardonic, diabolical grin.

I recoiled and stared in amazement as he lay, stiff and stark, with clenched fists, his eyebrows raised, his forehead wrinkled, and his mouth pulled down at the corners until every tooth in his head was visible, and I supposed that he was troubled by some frightful dream.

But even as I gazed, his features relaxed, his hands opened and he uttered a deep groan.

"What is it Bukári," I asked. "Art thou in pain?"

His lips parted, showing his tightly clenched teeth, as if he would speak, but instantly his hands closed, his limbs stiffened, and again that awful grin spread over his face, giving him the most grotesquely frightful aspect. I leaned over and took his hand, but his arm was as immovably rigid as that of a wooden image, and when I laid my hand upon his body it felt as hard and unyielding as though it were modelled in bronze. And as I looked at him more closely, at his stiffened arms and legs, his starting muscles and corded throat, I could see that every part of his body was vibrating with a fine, almost imperceptible tremor, and in a flash I realised the dreadful truth.

It was tetanus.

The subtle poison had found its way in through his untended wound, and its effects had burst with the fury of a tornado on his exhausted body.

The two hunters, who had stood staring like frightened children, drew gradually nearer, so I addressed them in Hausa; but they shook their heads, and after talking together for a minute or two, they turned and disappeared among the trees.

The paroxysm had now subsided, and my unfortunate companion lay breathing quickly, and keeping very still for fear of exciting a fresh spasm. For the same reason I was afraid to touch him, but I placed my ear close to his mouth in case he was able to speak, and as I did so, he breathed into it the one word "*rua*" – water.

I stole away softly to see if I could find any brook or stream close by – for I dared not risk going far away in that pathless wilderness – but was unable to discover any sign of water; but, as I was returning, I perceived the hunters apparently making in the same direction, and I noticed that each of them now carried something. Following them, not without suspicion, I saw them approach Bukári, and then one of them laid upon the ground near his feet a little collection of eggs and one or two roasted plantains, and the other put down a gourd shell of water.

I came up at this moment, and began thanking them in Hausa, but they merely pointed to the provisions and walked away without a word.

That day that followed was most miserable and harrowing. At first I made some efforts to give my poor comrade the drink that he craved for, but I soon found that, not only were his jaws immovably locked, but the lightest touch, or even a sound, instantly brought on one of the terrible paroxysms. Callous as it seemed, the kindest thing to do was to keep away from him, and only watch at a distance, in case he should be molested by animals.

When I had partaken sparingly of the provisions left by the kind-hearted hunters, I looked about for some occupation with which to while away the tedious and anxious time. First I cut a stout sapling of hard wood, and fashioned from it a rough spear. Then I bethought me that a fire would be necessary for the night, if I would not have my helpless companion torn to pieces before my eyes, so I gathered some bark from a dead tree, and by means of an elastic twig and some thin, twine-like creeper, made a rude bow-drill such as I had read of as being used by some barbarous races. With this primitive appliance and a pointed stick I set to work to drill the bark, and sawed away perseveringly for half an hour without any result, until at last, to my joy, the bark began first to blacken and then to smoke, and finally by vigorous blowing with my mouth, I got a large piece well aglow. The fire, once started, crackled up bravely, and I was glad to see that the smoke blew away from the direction of the road.

During these various occupations I frequently stepped over to where Bukári was lying, to see if I could do anything for him, but I usually hurried away again, sick at heart, unable to bear the sight of his suffering; for the paroxysms grew more frequent and seemed to last longer, and the poor fellow's body and limbs began to display horrid bumps and swellings where the muscles had been torn asunder by the violence of the spasms.

Things went on thus until late in the afternoon, by which time I had a good fire burning. I had been making a rather long round to gather sticks for fuel and was returning to the fire, when I turned aside to see if there was any change in Bukári's condition.

As I came in sight of him he seemed to be lying in a more easy position, for his limbs were somewhat relaxed and his hands partly unclosed. Very softly I approached, hoping he might be asleep and when I rounded the tree I saw that his head had fallen to one side, and that his mouth was open. With a quick suspicion I strode up to him and touched him. His flesh was soft and flabby, and when I lifted his arm and let it fall, it dropped limply to the ground.

He was dead.

There under the shimmering leaves, with the soft voice of the forest whispering around, he lay at last in security and peace, his long sufferings past, his perils ended.

I sat down beside him and looked into his face – hideous in death as it had been in life – and thought of all that he had suffered during the long years of his slavery, of his bold efforts to escape, and the hopes he had cherished of a life of ease and plenty when he should have brought home his share of the treasure. And now he lay dead in the lonely wilderness.

But after all it was better so, for he was at least beyond the reach of the malice of his enemies.

The fading light warned me to make what preparations I intended for the night, for although I could not bury the poor remains and must abandon the body on the morrow, I could not bear to leave it with the breath hardly out of it, to the ghoul-like beasts; so I hastily heaped together the faggots that I had collected, and built round the corpse four fires, which I lighted from the embers of the one I had already made. Within the space thus enclosed I sat at the feet of the body through the long night, often dozing with my head on my knees, and waking to tend the fire or fling a glowing faggot at the hyenas which crowded round, snuffling hungrily, and howling with anger and disappointment.

At last the faint grey of dawn glimmered through the trees, and I rose, weary and sad at heart. A small remnant of the hunters' donation remained, and having eaten this and drained the water gourd, I took my last farewell of the silent figure, lying amidst the smouldering fires, and turned away towards the road.

Although Bukári had been to me but a hindrance and a burden, yet as I took my way alone along the little path and missed the familiar pull upon my hand, the landscape grew dim before my eyes, and more than once a tear dropped down my cheek.

But as I trudged on, my own desperate condition distracted me from these sentimental regrets, and I began seriously to consider what course I was to take. Even if I escaped the pursuit of the fetish men – and I certainly did not mean to be taken alive if I could help it – I was in a position of extraordinary peril; for while I was totally ignorant of the country and without any means of subsistence whatever, my naked and destitute state must render me an object of suspicion to any person I might meet, especially as I was evidently not a native of that part of the continent.

I was yet turning over these facts in my mind when they received a very apposite and unpleasant illustration; for the path on which I was travelling suddenly joined a broad and well-worn track, and I had hardly entered this when I saw a party of six men coming towards me. I would have turned aside into the bush and hidden until they had passed, but they had already seen me, and to fly was to invite pursuit, so I held boldly on my way, and this I did with more confidence since the dress of the strangers showed them to be Mahommedans and probably Hausas.

As I approached, they all stopped and stared at me, and I heard one of them say:

"This must be the Christian. Doubtless he has left the blind man to take care of himself."

These words filled me with grave anxiety, but I pretended to have heard nothing, and made as if I would pass, giving the usual Hausa salutation.

"Whither goest thou, friend?" asked one of the men.

This was a poser. For all knew I might be steering straight for Jerusalem, but I answered as confidently as I could: "I go to look for my friends who are journeying to Kantámpo."

"Then thou art going the wrong way," said the man, with a grin, and his companions burst into loud, insolent guffaws.

"Who and what art thou?" inquired the first man.

"I am called Yúsufu Dan-Égadesh," said I, "and I am a Fulani merchant – "

"Where is thy friend, the blind Moshi?" interrupted another man, and as I hesitated, he continued: "Tell us no more lies. We know thee. Thou art the white man whom the wizards are seeking. We passed them but a little while since, and they told us how thou and another slave had run away. Now listen and take thy choice. Wilt thou come with us as our servant, or shall we take thee back to the wizards?"

I was between the devil and the deep sea, but the devil being infinitely the worse, I decided without hesitation.

"I will go with thee and thy friends," I said.

"Very well," rejoined the man who appeared to be the leader. "Give my thy knife, and let me secure thee with this rope."

"Why cannot I walk free?" I asked, eyeing the grass rope, which the man produced, with great disfavour. "I have said I will come with thee."

"It is well that thou shouldst seem to be our captive," he replied. "Thou canst walk free when we are out of this country."

"I do not see the necessity," I persisted, but my remonstrances were cut short by another of the men who had stolen behind me and now suddenly and skilfully dropped a noose over my shoulders, binding my arms closely to my sides; whereupon the others proceeded to bind my wrists and fit a halter round my neck with most suspicious neatness and rapidity.

This business concluded, we all moved off at a brisk pace, one of the ruffians leading me by the rope as if I had been a camel.

I listened attentively to their conversation as we walked, but could make out nothing from it as to who or what these men were. Nor did I care a great deal. The one vital question that excluded all others was whether or not they were going to hand me back to the fetish priests, and on this point I was full of dreadful apprehension.

We walked on quickly for a couple of hours in a northerly direction, and I noticed that the country was rapidly changing in character. The dense, shady forest opened out at increasingly frequent intervals into grassy expanses, and the great trees of the silk-cotton tribe began to give place to much smaller trees resembling the apple and pear in character.

About noon, as we were passing through a belt of forest, I thought I could distinguish a sound like the murmur of many voices, and there came through the trees the scent of green wood burning. A few minutes later we came out into a large grassy opening, where a very singular and busy scene presented itself.

A large camp had just been struck, and the caravan was preparing to get on the move. A dozen or so of beehive-shaped huts were placed in a group with a number of fires round them, and from these various cooking pots of brass and iron were being collected and made up into loads for the carriers. A party of Hausas, very formidably armed, stood lounging about the huts, and one of them was engaged in fitting a saddle with high fore and aft peaks on to a small, rough-looking horse, while several others were bustling about, allotting the various loads to the carriers. It was these latter that at once absorbed my attention. They must have been a hundred and fifty in number, of whom more than two-thirds were women and children, and their appearance was most miserable and neglected; for not only were they half-starved and dirty, but there was hardly a rag of clothing among the whole company. Each of them wore a hinged iron collar, and, through a ring in this, was passed a rope by which they were all connected together in a long line, and each had upon the right wrist a kind of handcuff, which was fastened to the collar, so that the hand was raised above the shoulder. Some of them who carried burdens had both wrists shackled to the loads, while others were allowed to steady the burden with the free hand.

As we came to a halt and I surveyed the long row of burdenless captives, each with one hand raised and the elbow projecting forward, I could not be in doubt for a moment as to the nature of this procession. It was obviously a slave caravan, and it was equally obvious that I was destined to join its ranks, to be driven to some neighbouring market and sold.

Alarming, however as the prospect was, I experienced a distinct sense of relief, for the imminent and really appalling danger – that of being carried captive back to the mine – seemed to be past, and as to the future – well, that would be provided for according to the circumstances that might arise.

My captors led me to the huts, where we found a fat, irritable old man sitting upon a mat and giving orders to some younger men, who appeared to be his sons.

"Well, Maháma," he said sharply as we approached, "thou hast kept us waiting a long time. What hast thou got?"

"The people had no slaves at all," replied the fellow who held my rope. "They say that the Ashanti king has bought all there were for fighting men and for his devil worship, but we have picked up one on the road, as thou seest."

"This?" exclaimed the old man sourly, pointing derisively at me. "Why, he looketh like a Moor or a man of Asben. No one will have him as a gift."

"He is no Moor, my father," replied the other. "He is a white man, a Christian."

"What!" bawled the old man, "an Anasára? But he looketh not like one. I thought they had yellow hair and eyes like those of sheep. Besides, who would have a Christian? They are worse than Moors; as weak as children, and as cunning as monkeys."

"This one looketh not very weak," observed Maháma, holding out my arm for the old man's inspection, "and the wizards whom we met, who were seeking him, said that he had slain I know not how many of their fellows."

"Then, thou fool!" shouted the old man, "of what use is he to us? Who is going to buy a slave that is ready to slay his masters? There! take him away, and make him secure lest he fall to killing us; and make ready to start at once, for thou hast wasted enough of our day already."

Without replying, the somewhat crestfallen Maháma marched me down to the farther end of the line, and hitched my halter on to the collar-ring of the last slave, so that as the long queue began to move, I brought up the rear. As far as I could make out, the caravan was headed by the old man, Sálifu Sókoto by name, who rode in state upon his horse, followed by a bodyguard of the younger Hausas; then came the slaves, strung together by a long rope, and last of all, a rear guard of the older and more responsible members of the caravan, including Maháma and the men who had captured me. Many of the slaves carried on their heads burdens of some kind – cooking utensils, reserves of food, and a little merchandise – a highly economical arrangement by which all transport expenses were avoided.

The country, as I have mentioned, was much more open in this part; indeed, the forest had dwindled to occasional patches, which fringed the banks of streams, and, as we marched on, we passed for the most part across grassy plains covered pretty thickly with gum-bearing wild plum trees, and the small, scraggy trees which yield shea butter. Our progress was, therefore, unhindered by the endless obstructions that are met with in the dense forest, and although the road was but a rough path, we travelled at quite a good pace, considering our numbers and the awkward way in which most of us were linked together. For my own part, beyond the ignominy of being led to market by a halter, I suffered no inconvenience, for I had no burden to carry, and I kept up very easily with the caravan. My hands were certainly bound, but not tightly or uncomfortably, and I should have been quite at my ease had it not been for the hot sun, which, as the day wore on, began to pour down unpleasantly on my naked body, and especially on my shaven head.

I noticed with some surprise that no restrictions were placed upon conversation, for, as we trudged along, a loud and continuous hum arose from the slaves, who not only talked incessantly to one another; but even chatted quite amicably with any of the Hausas who happened to be near.

This resigned and philosophical acceptance of their condition, and the tacit recognition of its legality, struck me as very odd; but it was evidently the usual attitude of the captive and the one expected; for Maháma walked close behind me for a long distance and discussed with me my later adventures – on which subject, however, I was extremely reticent – as though our relations were perfectly natural and agreeable.

With the slave to whom I was linked – a young, light-coloured Fulah woman – I became immediately quite friendly – indeed, from the moment of my arrival, we had regarded one another with mutual interest and curiosity. For my part, I was surprised to see a woman of her nationality and appearance among the slaves, of whom the rest were mostly Grunshis, Moshis, Dagómbas, Jámans, and other pagan negroes – unconsidered trifles that might have been snapped up or bought cheap from the neighbouring Wongáras; while she was still more puzzled by my appearance. For in this part of Africa the Fulah, the Hausa, and the Moor are accustomed to swagger about in fine raiment and lord it over the negroes, so that my naked and poverty-stricken appearance was highly anomalous.

"What is thy name, child of my mother?" she asked me during a momentary halt caused by some obstruction ahead.

"I am called Yúsufu Dan-Égadesh," I replied, "but some call me Yúsufu Fuláni."

"But thou art not a Fulah?" she asked dubiously.

"My father was a Dan-Asben, but my mother was a Fulah."

"Then, no doubt, thou resemblest thy father. As for me, I am called Aminé, and am a maid of Futa; my father and mother were both Fulahs."

At this moment the caravan moved on, but, the ice having been broken, we continued our conversation as we went and while Aminé furnished me with a full and detailed account of her life from birth to the current date, including her capture while on a journey, I replied with an autobiography more remarkable for careful editing than strict veracity.

"What is amiss with thy foot?" I inquired presently, observing that she limped as if in pain.

"I struck it against a rock two days ago," she replied.

"It must be wearisome to carry thy burden with a lame foot," I said, for she bore on her head a bundle of rolled-up mats.

"It is," she replied simply, and then resumed her cheerful and vivacious babble and unending reminiscences.

I was deeply touched by her stoical uncomplaining endurance of what must have been rather severe suffering, for her foot was swollen and evidently tender, and I took an early opportunity of speaking to Maháma on the subject.

"The maid is but ill fitted to carry a burden," I said. "She is barely able to walk."

"It is no affair of thine," replied Maháma, frowning.

"I would rather carry it myself than see her limping under its weight," said I. "Wilt thou set it on my head next time we halt?"

"Why dost thou wish to carry it?" demanded Maháma suspiciously. "Is it that thou art a fool, that thou wouldst carry a burden when thou mightest walk at thine ease?"

"I would help the maid who is a captive like myself," I replied. "Besides," I added with a sudden inspiration, "the sun is hot, and I have neither turban nor hat."

This explanation appeared to satisfy him, and when we next halted, while the head of the column waded through a deep stream, he transferred Aminé's burden to me, not without some protests on her part, fastening my right wrist to the cord of the bundle.

My little act of altruism had its reward, for although it was a discomfort to have my wrist tied up in this way, the bundle afforded a most grateful shade, while its weight was inconsiderable.

Our caravan travelled at a steady pace the greater part of the day, two halts being made for rest and food, which latter consisted of a miserably small allowance for each slave of a kind of porridge and some white beans plainly boiled; and as I finished my meagre ration, which barely took the edge off my hunger, I thought regretfully of the grass-cutters on the hillside and even of the affaní.

We halted for the night a little before sunset, and while some of the Hausas erected huts for the night and others attended to the cooking, Maháma and his gang prepared the slaves for their bivouac. The preparations were of the simplest. Each slave, having been relieved of his burden, if he carried one, was fitted with a pair of handcuffs or fetters, and his ankles were hobbled either with iron fetters, similar to the "bilboes" used on board ship, or with a grass rope substitute, and he was then allowed to scratch a hollow in the ground to receive his hip bone, and go to sleep. In my own case, both the wrist fetters and those on the ankles were of grass rope, for the reason, as I supposed, that the iron fetters were all in use.

In spite of the fatigues of the day, and the disturbed night that had preceded it, I did not go to sleep for some time. I was free from the galling annoyance of the iron collar that the other slaves wore, for the halter was still on my neck; but even this was an unaccustomed discomfort and helped to keep me awake, and I lay for a couple of hours dreamily looking on at the slave dealers as they sat around the fire, eating, talking, and laughing over one another's jests and stories, until one by one they disappeared. There seemed to be little, if any, watch kept; but, as the slaves had not been released from the rope, and as this was securely pegged down at intervals, the captives were pretty secure.

At length, when the camp was quiet except for the droning hum of the sleeping multitude, I huddled myself up in as comfortable an attitude as was possible, and very soon followed the example of my companions in misfortune.

Chapter Eighteen
I Again Become a Fugitive

The next few days presented little to chronicle. Life under the new conditions was monotonously uncomfortable, but not distressing to me, whatever it may have been to the less robust slaves.

We walked, with but few halts, from a little after sunrise to a little before sunset; we slept as much as our discomforts would let us, and we ate all that we could get – which was mighty little. Day after day we tramped on through what appeared to be an interminable orchard, which was so bare and shadeless that I was thankful for the burden that protected me from the sun. For at this season of the year, all the trees were leafless, and every blade of grass had been devoured by animals, so that the country had a most desolate aspect, and it was quite a relief to enter the narrow band of green forest that fringed the banks of the rivers.

It will readily be supposed that during this time I gave no little thought to my future prospects. At first I had been glad enough to be carried away so rapidly from the dangerous neighbourhood of the mine and the search parties of the fetish men; but now I began to consider whether I had so greatly improved my position – whether, if I had not actually jumped out of the frying pan into the fire, I had not at least jumped out of the fire into the frying pan. For if it was impossible for an African to escape from slavery, it might prove also impossible to me, in which case the prospect was not encouraging; and I brought all my wits to bear, as well as

Aminé's chatter would allow me, on the problem of how to get away from the caravan before I was finally sold to some private owner. I was, however, unable to think of any scheme that had the faintest shadow of feasibility. By day we were all continuously under the eyes of the slave dealers, and at night, although I was not cruelly bound, yet my hands and feet were too securely fastened to allow of my breaking my bonds.

On the third day of our march we passed a little distance from the great mart of Kantámpo, and I then observed that our conductors, no doubt for excellent reasons of their own, were avoiding the main caravan road, and travelling by a little-frequented bypath.

On the evening of the fifth day we encamped on the bank of a large and noble-looking river fully as wide as the Thames at Richmond, which one of the slaves recognised as the Firráo, or Volta; and early next morning our leaders commenced preparations for crossing.

First an advance guard of Hausas was sent over in the huge, flat-bottomed canoe that formed the ferry boat; then the rope (which consisted of lengths of a few fathoms each, knotted together) was untied, and the slaves divided up into gangs of ten, each gang being sent across separately in charge of a guard; and when all the slaves had been carried to the farther bank, the leaders of the caravan followed with the horse.

The greater part of the morning was consumed by the crossing of the river, and by the time we got on the road it was within an hour of noon. To make up for the delay, the caravan pushed on at greater speed than ordinary so that when we at last halted for the night, we were more tired that we usually were, although we had covered less ground, having travelled not more than twelve or thirteen miles. This part of the country appeared to be as thinly populated as that south of the great river, for in the day's march we passed but a single village – a queer little collection of circular huts with high, thatched roofs like candle extinguishers.

After we had consumed our meagre supper and settled down for the night, I lay awake for a long time, gloomily meditating on my position. The passage of this great river had raised another barrier between me and freedom, and every day I was being carried farther and farther into the unknown regions of the interior, from which escape would become more difficult with every mile that I travelled. Was it, after all, to be my destiny to spend the remainder of my life hoeing yams or cutting wood for some negro master far from the sights and sounds of the civilised world?

I was roused from these reflections by a soft poke in the back, and turning over, perceived that Aminé had shuffled towards me as far as the rope would allow her to, and had touched me with her outstretched fingers.

"Yúsufu!" she whispered, as I turned, "come nearer. I want to talk to thee."

"Hast thou not talked enough today, thou babbler?" I exclaimed impatiently. "Go to sleep now, and give thy tongue a little rest."

"Nay, but I have something to tell thee," she persisted. "Come near and listen."

I shuffled a couple of feet nearer to her.

"Now say what thou hast to say quickly," I said gruffly, "for the night is passing, and we have to march at daybreak."

"It is true, Yúsufu," she said earnestly. "Today we have crossed the great river. Tomorrow or the next day we shall come to Sálaga. There we are all to be sold, if any will buy us, and then we shall be taken away, who knows whither? and you and I, Yúsufu, will never see one another again."

This was rather startling and unpleasant news.

"In two days, thou sayest, we shall be there?" I said.

"Yes; or perhaps tomorrow night," she replied; and then she added in a low but emphatic whisper, "Yúsufu, thou must get thee away tonight."

"Must get me away!" I exclaimed. "It is well to talk of getting away; but how?"

"I have thought of a way," she answered. "Listen! When we crossed the stream this afternoon, I felt something hard stick in the sole of my sandal against my foot, and all the afternoon I could not kick it out. When I lay down, I picked it out with my fingers and kept it. It is a little piece of broken shell, and one edge is quite sharp like a knife. Now, thy manacles and the fetters on thy ankles are of cord, not iron like ours, and I doubt not that I can cut through them with the piece of shell. Then thou canst easily untie thy halter from the rope, and so wilt be free; and if thou goest far enough before the morning, they will never catch thee again."

I pondered. It sounded a good and feasible plan, and it was apparently my last chance.

"But what about thee, Aminé" I asked. "Thy fetters are of iron."

"Alas! Yes," she replied sadly. "There is nothing to be done for me. I must go to the market, and be sold like the rest; but I shall be glad to think that thou at least art free."

I was deeply touched by the girl's unselfish thought for me, and profoundly reluctant to go away and leave her in the hands of the slave dealers; but it would be utter folly to allow mere sentiment to influence me in so momentous a matter, especially as the caravan would be broken up in a few days, and the slaves scattered abroad like a drove of beasts at a cattle fair.

"If thou canst set me free," said I, "I shall be thankful indeed; yet I am loth to go and leave thee here."

"I am loth to stay," she answered bitterly, "but it matters less to me that it would to thee, for servitude is the lot of a woman. But perhaps the shell will not cut thy bonds after all; put out thy hands, and let me try."

I thrust forward my hands and strained the connecting cords – which were only a couple of inches long – as tight as I could, while she sawed away with the little fragment of shell. In a few minutes it began to be evident that the scheme would be successful, for strand after strand frayed out and parted, until at length I was able with a powerful wrench to snap those that remained.

With my free hands I at once set to work upon the complicated knot by which my halter was tied to the rope, while Aminé sawed at the cords that confined my ankles, and almost at the same moment that I cast off the end of the halter from its fastening, I felt the last strand of my fetters give way.

"Now thou art free!" exclaimed Aminé taking my hand for a moment in both of hers and looking earnestly into my face. "Go back by the road that we came by, and do not loiter on the way; for if thou goest far enough before the morning they cannot stay to follow thee. Now go quickly!" She pressed my hand, and then, suddenly turning her back to me, lay down and covered her face with her hands.

I rose to my feet and stretched my arms with great enjoyment whilst I took a survey of the camp.

The new moon was just setting, and by the dim light I could barely distinguish the prostrate forms of the slaves extended in a long row, and the vague shapes of the huts.

In various parts of the camp the dull glow of the waning fires was yet visible, and around the one at our end, the sleeping guards lay coiled up on their mats. I stepped lightly across to them, setting down each foot as I trod with the extremest caution, and examined them as they lay, each wrapped in a warm bernùs, and breathing heavily, keeping their vigil in the most approved African fashion, until I came to Maháma; and there I found what I was in search of, for, beside him on his mat, were deposited a fine, brass-hilted sword and the long, heavy knife that he had taken from me.

The sword was of no use to me, but I picked up the knife joyfully and crept, in the same silent, stealthy manner, back to Aminé, whom I found lying on her face sobbing silently but bitterly.

"Aminé," I whispered, "I am going to take thee with me."

She turned quickly with a gesture of impatience.

"Go away!" she exclaimed in a hoarse whisper. "It is impossible; thou art wasting precious time. Go!"

I took the rope where it was tied on to the ring of her collar and cut it through, and as she still refused to rise, I stuck the knife through the strip of rag that was tied round my loins, took her up in my arms, and hoisting her on to my shoulder like a sack, strode away out of the camp along the path by which we had approached it.

The moon had now set, and the night was pitch dark, so that although the country was moderately open, it was difficult to avoid straying from the path; and Aminé, who though but of medium height was a strapping, solidly-built woman, formed a burden sufficiently heavy to tax the strength of a stronger man than me. In fact, I had not gone a quarter of a mile before I had to set her down and rest, when she again entreated me to hurry away and leave her.

While we were resting I explored the key holes of her fetters with my finger, and finding that they were made so as to be unfastened by a key with a screw end, I determined to try and see if I could force them. For this purpose I groped among the trees and cut off a small branch, which I trimmed with my knife to a blunt point. This point I thrust forcibly into the hole and rotated it until the wood jammed into the thread of the screw hole, when by giving it a few more turns, to my delight and Aminé's amazement, the ankle clasp flew open. This manoeuvre I repeated with the other three clasps with such success that, in a short time, I was able to remove the manacles and leg fetters, and Aminé stood up, hardly able to believe the evidence of her senses, and nearly wild with joy.

We flung the fetters away among the trees, and, leaving the iron collar to be operated on by daylight, set off along the path at a run to make up for the time that had been consumed by these labours; but presently we settled down, as our excitement somewhat subsided, into a brisk walk, covering the ground at an astonishing pace notwithstanding the darkness.

It was probably near midnight when we started, and we walked on, with gradually diminishing speed but without a halt, until the first streaks of dawn began to appear in the sky behind us, and our shadows spread out before us, attenuated and gigantic caricatures.

The pale daybreak, rapidly brightening into sunlight, showed us, a little distance ahead, a small stream, and we could see that we were approaching a much-frequented drinking place, for the ground was covered with the spoor of hoofs and paws, all converging to one point.

The sight of these footmarks led us to glance back at our own tracks, and I was rather dismayed to see how extraordinarily distinct they were. In the darkness we had evidently strayed from the path which the caravan had traversed, on to one even more unfrequented, where the smooth surface left by the last rains on the light, loamy soil had not been disturbed, except by the wild beast, and the deep and sharp impressions of our feet stood out as plainly as on a sandy shore when the tide has just gone out.

Hence, if we were pursued, there could be no difficulty in tracing us, for our tracks were as characteristic as they were conspicuous, my own bare feet with the toes turned out, unlike those of a negro, and Aminé's round-toed sandals, could be identified at a glance. And that we should be pursued I had little doubt, for Aminé was probably worth as much as any other three of the slaves, and Sálifu Sókoto was not the man to let her go, within a day's march of Sálaga, without an effort at recapture. But if we were pursued we should probably be overtaken, for we had not travelled above a dozen miles in the night, and we were now spent with fatigue, whereas our pursuers would be fresh from a night's rest, and had a horse into the bargain.

It was thus clear that our only chance lay in breaking our tracks, and the stream that we were approaching seemed to offer us the means of doing this.

I stood at the edge of the little river and looked across. On the opposite side the same soft, smooth surface could be seen stretching away under the little bare trees like a level sandflat; but less than half a mile away, the rocky face of an isolated hill rose above the tree tops.

The Golden Pool

That hill would probably serve our purpose.

I led Aminé into the middle of the stream to where a large boulder stood up above the surface.

"Aminé," I said. "I am going away towards that hill, and I shall be some time gone. Sit down upon this stone, and do not move until I come back unless thou seest someone coming this way, in which case thou must walk down the middle of the stream, but do not for any reason leave the water. Now give me thy sandals, and I will go."

She sat down on the boulder and took off her sandals, handing them to me with a look of surprise, but without remark; and I at once crossed the stream and struck out through the trees towards the hill. As I strode along I selected the smoothest and softest patches of ground to walk over, and the tracks that marked my progress were as conspicuous as those in newly fallen snow.

In about ten minutes I reached the base of the hill, which was, as I had hoped from its appearance, a mass of bare rock spotted with patches of scanty vegetation. I walked round to the easiest slope, which I proceeded to ascend, and in few minutes I reached a surface so hard and devoid of soil that my feet left not the slightest impression. Here I slipped my feet in to Aminé's sandals and looking over my shoulder at the last of my tracks, began carefully to walk backwards, turning my toes slightly inwards as Aminé did, and following in this laborious and tedious fashion, the line of footprints that marked the way I had come, until I at length arrived at the stream, and walked backwards into the water. The result was perfect, for there now stretched away from the river a double line of footprints identical in character with those that Aminé and I had left on our way from the camp; and these illusive tracks disappeared in an entirely natural manner on the rocky surface of the hill.

Aminé gave a little shriek of astonishment as I came down into the stream in this unusual manner.

"What is amiss with thee, Yúsufu?" she exclaimed, "that thou walkest backwards like an ant-lion?" but when I pointed out the tracks she at once understood my ruse, and sat down again, laughing heartily.

"Thou art as cunning as an old monkey," she declared.

As we were both too tired to attempt a journey in a new direction, and were, moreover, quite ignorant of the locality, I considered that it would be safest to conceal ourselves in the neighbourhood of the stream until we judged that the search was over, and I now began to look about for some suitable hiding place.

One of the first objects that attracted my attention was a large odúm tree that stood on the bank of the stream close to the ford. It had once been a noble tree, but had either been struck by lightning or by a tornado, for its upper half had fallen, and lay, a decaying mass, on the ground, and its trunk was covered with a network of the curious little earthen tunnels of the white ants, which ran from the ground to the splintered extremity, showing that some part of the upper portion was dead. From this I inferred that there was probably a hollow space at the summit of the broken trunk, where the dead wood had been eaten out by the white ants, and if this were so, it would furnish an ideal hiding place, provided we could reach it. The latter difficulty was to a great extent solved by a large monkey rope, as thick as my arm, which had hung down from one of the top branches, and which in the fall of the upper part of the trunk, had become caught across the broken end, from which it drooped in a great bight or festoon down to the ground and again up a neighbouring tree.

The sloping position of this liana rendered it comparatively easy to climb – at least, for me – so I determined to go up and explore; and having "swarmed" up it without much difficulty, I found the upper eight or nine feet of the tree, as I had expected, little more than a shell filled with the paper remains of the wood, into which I sank up to my waist.

The tree would therefore answer our purpose admirably, but there was the difficulty of getting Aminé up to the hollow. I let myself down to the ground, and reported to her the state of things that I had found, on which she assured me that she was quite able to climb the monkey rope. However, to diminish the risk of her falling, I cut a couple of fathoms of a thinner creeper, and passed it round her and the monkey rope in a double figure of eight, so that it could, if necessary, take most of her weight, and having shown her how to manage it, I again ascended, leaving her to follow. She reached the top of the monkey rope without mishap, and when I had disengaged her from the supporting loop, I helped her over into the hollow and pulled the loop in after, so that it should not remain to give a clue to our retreat.

Once inside the hollow we were perfectly concealed from view, but by standing up we were able to look over the edge; and from our elevated position we could see a considerable distance in the direction from which our pursuers were to be expected, as we looked over the tops of the small trees with which most of the country was covered.

As it was evidently impossible that the slave dealers could overtake us for some time yet, it occurred to me to go down once more and search the stream for shellfish, for it would probably be necessary to remain in the tree the whole day, and it was necessary that we should have food of some kind. Bidding Aminé, therefore, to keep a sharp lookout, and let me know if she saw anyone approaching, I let myself down and began systematically to examine the bed of the stream.

The clean silvery sand of which it was composed did not offer a very favourable hunting ground, but, after working industriously for over an hour, I managed to accumulate a dozen or two of miscellaneous shellfish, mostly small mussels somewhat like affaní, and a kind of large water snail. These I stuffed, as I gathered them, into an empty weaver-bird's nest, which I had fortunately found hanging from a branch near the water's edge, and I had nearly filled this curious receptacle when I heard Aminé calling from the tree.

"Quick! Yúsufu! they are coming! Leave the shellfish and climb up quickly!"

I ran to the monkey rope, and, grasping the narrow opening of the nest with my teeth, climbed up as rapidly as I could; and I had hardly scrambled over into the hollow when I heard the voices of our pursuers sounding from below.

Very cautiously I put my eye to a broad crack in the bark and looked out.

The search party, headed by Sálifu himself mounted on his horse, was coming along at a rapid pace, and was now within a hundred yards of the tree. All the members of the party were armed to the teeth, and in an excessively bad humour; Sálifu at the loss of his prey, and the five men who accompanied him, at being hustled along in the wake of the trotting horse.

"We must soon overtake them now," I heard Maháma say, as he wiped the sweat from his face with his wide sleeve. "They cannot have gone much farther. Canst thou see if they have crossed the stream?"

"Yes," grunted Sálifu, standing up in his stirrups, "I can see the footmarks of the infidel pig on the other side, and the girl's too. Hast thou put plenty of slugs in thy gun?"

"It is loaded with a double charge," replied Maháma.

"It is good," exclaimed the old rascal viciously. "When we overtake them, give me the gun, and I will blow the pig-faced Nazarene ape into kabobs."

Having announced these benevolent intentions, the old gentleman urged his horse forward and splashed through the water, followed by his retainers, while I held my hands firmly over Aminé's mouth to prevent her giggles from betraying our whereabouts.

As soon as our pursuers had passed, I turned out the contents of the retort-like bird's nest, and we proceeded to breakfast on the shellfish; and while I was opening the mussels with my knife, Aminé popped the snails whole into her mouth, and crunched them up in a manner that made my flesh creep.

When we had satisfied our hunger, Aminé began to while away our vigil by pouring out an unending stream of chatter, but this I had to stop (as she could not remember to speak softly) by sternly forbidding her to speak; upon which she yawned plaintively, and presently, to my relief, curled herself up on the soft tindery floor of our cell and fell sleep.

The hours dragged on interminably. The sun rose to the zenith and glared down upon us until I was sick with the heat, and Aminé moaned and stirred in her sleep.

A belated parrot came and looked at us, and fluttered away screeching with fright; down in the plain a herd of harnessed antelopes sauntered about picking up here and there a stray blade of grass and sniffing the air suspiciously, and just below the tree a black monkey sat at the edge of the stream and dipped up little draughts of water in the hollow of his hand.

I looked on at these various occurrences dreamily and listlessly, keeping awake with difficulty, and watching the shadows slowly lengthen on the arid ground, until at last, late in the afternoon, I heard the welcome sound of voices and the noise of a horse's hoofs, and presently a splashing in the water told me that the party was crossing the ford.

"It is a strange thing," I could hear one of the men say. "I cannot understand it. They did not leave the hill, for I walked all round it."

"They were not on the hill," said Maháma, "for I searched every part of it."

"Chatter no more!" burst out the old man furiously. "They are gone. A hundred and twenty thousand *kurdi* – perhaps more – are lost. And why? Because of thy folly. Because thou must needs bring this yellow-skinned hog of an unbeliever into our camp."

"I did it for the best, my father," urged Maháma.

The old man did not reply, but, as I put my eye to the crack in the bark, I saw him kick viciously at the horse with his great spurs, and he soon disappeared at a brisk trot among the trees, leaving his followers to double wearily after him.

When they were gone I woke up Aminé, who sat up yawning and rubbing her eyes.

"Is it morning?" she asked.

"No," I replied. "It is not yet night, but they have gone back."

"Is there anything to eat?" she inquired.

"Nothing," I answered. "We ate all the shellfish."

"Then let us sleep," said she, and without further parley she curled up like a dog and instantly fell asleep again.

It seemed the best thing to do, for the night was coming on, and we had large arrears of rest to make up; so stretching myself on the soft floor, as well as the space would allow, I settled myself with an unwonted feeling of comfort, and followed her example.

Chapter Nineteen
I Make my Appearance in a New Character

The sun was well up when I opened my eyes on the following morning and Aminé had evidently been awake some time, for she was standing with her chin on the edge of the rough parapet that enclosed the hollow, looking across the country and beguiling the time by slapping at the flies that settled on the bark.

"At last thou art awake!" she exclaimed, turning her head as I rose and stretched my cramped limbs. "I thought thou wast going to sleep all day. Let us go down and look for something to eat."

My own sensations strongly seconded this suggestion, so I at once helped Aminé over on to the monkey rope, and having passed the lashing round her and seen her safely to the bottom, I slid down myself.

The first necessity being the immediate satisfaction of our ravenous hunger, we took to the stream and eagerly searched the shallows for shellfish, and I was filled with mingled envy and disgust at the indiscriminate way in which Aminé gobbled up every living thing that she encountered. Nothing came amiss to her. Water snails, queer little round-bodied crabs, insect larvae and fish spawn, all went into her mouth as soon as they were picked up, while I, more fastidious although famishing, restricted my diet to the rather scarce mussels. However, Aminé presently discovered in the forest, close to the water, a gourd-like fruit about the size of an orange, which she told me she had often eaten, and as it grew quite profusely in that spot, we were able to make a really substantial meal and a much more agreeable one than the uncooked shellfish afforded.

The question now arose, what were we to do next, and whither should we direct our steps? We could not lurk for ever in the wilderness, and yet we hardly dared to enter any town or village.

"We certainly cannot go towards Sálaga," said Aminé, "for there we should meet that old thief Sálifu and a hundred others like him. The place is full of slave dealers."

"Dost thou know anything of the road to the west?" I inquired.

"Not I," she replied. "I know that somewhere in the west is Bontúku and beyond that, Kong in the Wongára country, but how far away I cannot tell."

"We had best walk towards the west," I said, "for we shall at least lengthen our distance from Sálaga, and perhaps we may meet friends on the road."

"It is more likely that we shall meet enemies," she answered, "for anyone can see that we are runaway slaves, and if we go into any town, the first travelling merchant that we meet will claim us and say that we have escaped from him. Now if we only had a little decent clothing according to the fashion of our country, no one would notice or molest us, but we are as naked as a pair of black bush people."

This was only too true.

Had we been clothed in the Fulah fashion we should have presented nothing unusual, whereas, although we had as much clothing as most of the negroes of the district, our fair skins, straight hair, and regular features were quite out of character with our condition, and marked us at once as fugitives. However, some move had to be made, and as we were certainly not encumbered by baggage, we crossed the stream forthwith and took our way along the track westward; and I was pleased to see that Aminé, without any suggestion from me, now carried her sandals slung round her neck by a wisp of creeper, to avoid leaving any more tell-tale impressions on the ground.

We wandered on at an easy pace, browsing as we went. Some of the trees had ripe fruit on them – little sloe-like plums, very bitter and astringent, which Aminé devoured freely – and we met with a number of dwarf date palms bearing small, orange-coloured dates which we both ate although they were dry and insipid; and with these and various odds and ends of wild fruit that we picked up, we postponed, rather than satisfied, our hunger for several hours.

Towards afternoon the path along which we were travelling joined a broader track, the numerous footmarks on which showed it to be a well-frequented road. Near the junction a small hill stood a few yards from the road, and, before determining our direction, I climbed to the summit and surveyed the country. Half-a-mile away on some rising ground I could see a group of conical thatched roofs, and I was just considering whether it would be wise to venture on entering the village, when I perceived a small party of travellers advancing along the road. Before I had time to examine them they were lost to view among the trees, but I had been able in spite of the distance, to make out that they were dressed like Mahommedans, and were not natives of the district.

I communicated my observation to Aminé, and we hastily consulted as to what course we should pursue.

"Let us hide till they have passed," she urged. "If they are Moslem they may seize us and take us to Sálaga."

"But we cannot always hide," I objected. "Perhaps they may befriend us seeing that we are Moslem; and they are but few in any case."

"What shall we say to them? Shall we tell them what has happened?"

I considered, and then there occurred to me a plan which, distasteful as it was, seemed the most judicious under the difficult circumstances.

"I will tell thee, Aminé," I said, "what we shall do. Do thou go and wait by the roadside, and when the men come, bid them be silent, for thy master, who is a holy man, meditateth and may not be disturbed."

"But thou art not a holy man," objected Aminé. "Thou has not prayed once since I met thee."

"It is no matter," said I, rather taken aback nevertheless; "do as I bid thee and they may perchance think that I have cast away my clothing as a mark of my humility and holiness."

"They will think thee holy indeed to have cast away my garments as well as thine own," exclaimed Aminé laughing. "But thou art not dirty enough," she added gravely. "I remember a holy man who came to our town, who wore only one ragged cloth, but he was very dirty and had a filthy, tangled beard. My two sisters and I threw plantain skins at him, and my father beat us."

"I will rub some dirt upon my skin," said I, "if thou thinkest it necessary. And now go and wait by the roadside before they come."

She went a little distance in the direction, from which the party was approaching, and began to gather some of the scanty but tall grass stalks with which to plait a mat, while I sat myself down cross-legged a few yards off the path, and waited for the strangers.

Presently they appeared round a curve in the road – three men, a woman and a boy – and as they approached I saw Aminé come out from among the trees and hold up a warning finger, saying something to them in a low tone, on which they stopped and apparently questioned her. I sat motionless as a graven image, and, as the strangers advanced slowly along the path, I stared unwinkingly into vacancy as one who sees a vision, and totally ignored their presence.

For their part, they halted in a row opposite me and gazed at me with frank curiosity as though I were a museum specimen.

This was all very well for a minute or so, but when they all set down their burdens on the ground that they might observe me at greater ease, I felt that my position was becoming untenable. I could not maintain that wooden stare for an indefinite time, in fact, the corners of my mouth were inclined to twitch already; and as it would be fatal to laugh, it was necessary to talk; wherefore I opened my mouth and spake, as though pursuing some profound reflection.

"Moreover," I commenced, by way of encouraging myself, "have not all things their appointed places from which they depart not? Does the river leave its bed and stray up the mountain? Does the moon outpace the sun and the night tread upon the heels of day? Surely it is not so. For if the night should struggle against the day and the stars strive with the sun, then would the earth be confounded and the infidel rejoice in the pride of his heart."

I paused to observe the effect of my performance. The men looked at one another in blank amazement, and one asked in tones of awe: "Dost thou understand this, Isaaku?"

"Not I," replied the other. "I am no scholar, and his words are weighty and deep; but it is profitable to listen to the sayings of the wise."

"It seemeth to me," broke in the boy – an urchin of about ten – "that this yellow-skinned fellow talketh like an old woman that hath drunk too much pittu," whereupon one of the men dealt him a hearty cuff on the head, and he hastily retreated behind his mother, from which stronghold he silently defied me by gestures and horrid grimaces.

Seeing that my audience was eager for further samples of my wisdom, I took up the thread of my reflections.

"And if these things be so; if the hippopotamus may not soar aloft with the hawk, nor the tortoise perch upon the branch and carol to his mate; so it is also with man. The housewife shall not sit in the mosque nor the mallam fetch water from the well.

"These things are known unto the wise, but the foolish regard them not, considering only the labour of the day or the profit of the market. For the foolish pile up merchandise and *kurdi* and gold and cattle that they may grow fat with much eating; but the wise man hearkeneth unto the words of the Prophet and giveth alms of that which is given to him, shareth his plenty with the needy, and giveth shelter and raiment unto those that are houseless and naked."

If the first part of my discourse was rather out of the depth of my hearers, the conclusion enabled them, in nautical phrase, to "strike soundings," which they did with a readiness that did them credit.

The eldest man of the party beckoned to Aminé, who had been standing at a little distance listening, round-eyed and open-mouthed.

"Whither does thy master journey?" he asked.

"We journey to Bontúku," she replied, with admirable presence of mind.

"We go towards Bori," said the man, "so for the next two days we travel the same road: and if it please thy master to walk with us we will gladly share our provisions with him."

"I will ask him," said Aminé; and stepping over to me she put her mouth to my ear and gave a shout that nearly stunned me, by way of arousing me from my reverie.

I staggered to my feet in quite unfeigned confusion.

"This good man," said she calmly, "asketh if thou wilt walk with his party and rest by his fire until our ways part."

I regarded the man with assumed surprise, as if I had not noticed him before, and then said: "The companionship of a believer is good when one journeys through the land of the heathen. I thank thee for thy courtesy and will very gladly walk in thy company."

The man – whose name appeared to be Isaaku – seemed highly gratified, and assured me that all that he possessed was at my service; and, when I had again thanked him, he and his party took up their burdens and resumed their journey, Aminé and I following.

We tramped on for a couple of hours through the shadeless, monotonous orchard country, until we arrived at a small hamlet which was built in the narrow strip of woodland that fringed a small stream. Here, to my unspeakable joy, Isaaku announced his intention of staying for the night, having been on the road since daybreak and as his people piled the loads under the village shade-tree, he entered into lengthy negotiations with the headman (or village chief) with a view to obtaining the necessary accommodation for the night and permission to light a fire.

The headman, a good-natured, jocose, elderly man, readily gave permission for our party to put up for the night in his own house, and led the way into the compound, whither we removed our baggage. The house was of the type peculiar to the district of Gwandjiowa or Gonja, and quite different from anything I had previously seen. The compound or courtyard was enclosed by a low wall of clay-like mud, which connected a number of circular huts with high conical roofs of grass thatch; each hut had an oval doorway, about three feet high which opened on to the compound, excepting a larger hut in the centre of the wall, which had two doorways, one opening on the compound and the other on the street, so that this hut formed a kind of gatehouse, giving entrance to this miniature walled town.

Through this entry the chief preceded us (on all fours) and we crept through after him one at a time. There were, in all, eight huts ranged round the compound, and of these the chief assigned two to our use, one of which we allotted to the men and the other to the two women and the boy. The centre of the compound was occupied by a kind of kiln in which pottery was baked, and as we entered, one of the chief's sons was engaged in modelling a large water pot of bluish clay, which he did very dextrously with his fingers alone, the potter's wheel being unknown in this region.

Our people gathered round, as idle persons will, to look on as the workman's busy fingers rapidly shaped the mass of clay; and as I had observed that my unkempt appearance had already excited unfavourable notice and comment on the part of the villagers, I thought this a favourable opportunity to assert my character. I therefore raised my hand to command silence, and proceeded to moralise.

"Behold," said I, addressing the company in general, "how the labour of this simple workman speaketh to us admonitions to piety and good works. For this clay that he kneadeth, which under the foot is but mire and dirt, fouling the sandal of the traveller and making difficult the way, when shaped by the skilful and industrious fingers, becometh a thing of usefulness and beauty, yielding refreshment to the thirsty and making clean the body of him that laboureth.

"And what are we, my brethren, but mire and clay, until the finger of knowledge transformeth us and we become as holy vessels full of the water of wisdom? For the heathen is but the dirt that is trodden under foot, profitable to none; but when the hand of the potter hath shaped him into the comeliness of wisdom and faith, then is he fit for good works, fair to look upon, and profitable to all.

"Nor," I continued, "is any so humble that he may not be made glorious. Behold this piece of clay!" I picked up a small pellet and held it up between my finger and thumb. "It is but a mere morsel of dirt. Yet can it be made to speak the words of the book of God and sing His praise without ceasing." I took the pellet and pressed it upon the blade of my knife until it formed a smooth flat tablet, and on this, with the sharp point of the knife, I wrote the opening sentence of the Koran, "Praise to be God!" and held it aloft.

Our people and the villagers who had crowded round to listen – for all the Gonja natives understand some Hausa – stared at me in open-mouthed wonder; and when, at the conclusion of my discourse, I flung away the clay tablet, the entire assemblage made a wild scramble for its possession.

"What is written on this tablet?" asked Alla Karímu, one of our party, who had secured the treasure and was licking the dust off it.

I told him what the inscription meant.

"I thank thee, Yúsufu," he said. "I shall roast it in the fire and sew it up in a leather cover to wear for a *laiya* (amulet)."

But he was not to enjoy the distinction of being the sole possessor of an amulet, for the potter was instantly besieged by applicants for clay pellets, and for the next hour I was kept busy writing inscriptions on the little tablets, a shea butter lamp being provided when the daylight faded; and a special fire was made for hardening them, which process was conducted under the superintendence of the potter himself.

This rather absurd incident was a fortunate one for me, for by it I gained the goodwill and respect not only of our own party but of the villagers, and so far from being a burden to my hospitable host, I became a benefactor; for the gifts of fowls, yams, and fruit that poured in on me converted our evening meal into a veritable banquet.

That night, as we lay by the fire on our mats, Isaaku opened his heart to me on the subject of my appearance, which evidently troubled him not a little, for, like all Mahommedans, he had very strict ideas concerning the outward decencies of life.

"It grieveth me, Yúsufu," said he, "to see thee go so naked and forlorn. I know thou art a holy man, modest and clean in act and thought, but I fear that strangers, who know thee not, may scoff to see one of our faith, and a wise man, walking abroad uncovered as the heathen do. Moreover, it is not good that thy wife, who is young and comely, should be seen without decent raiment."

"Thou speakest wisely, Isaaku, and like a true follower of the Prophet," I replied. "I will remember thy words and buy me some fitting apparel with the first money that I earn."

Isaaku was silent for a time; then he said somewhat shyly – "I have in my pack a *riga* and *wondo* that I do not need. They are threadbare and old, and not such as are fitting to one of thy condition, but, if thou wilt take them they will at least serve until thou canst get thee more suitable raiment."

"I will take thy gift and be very thankful," I replied concealing with difficulty my eagerness and delight; whereupon Isaaku arose and, calling his wife, went with her into the house allotted to the women. Presently he came back with a bundle in his hands, which he unrolled on the mat.

"Here are the garments," he said. "They are but poor things, and little worth, but, such as they are, thou art welcome to them."

I thanked him and shook them out. They were very shabby and none too clean, and they smelt most horribly of civet; but I was overjoyed at possessing them, and without more ado I stood up on the mat and put them on.

As my head came through the hole in the *riga* I heard Aminé give a little cry, and looking towards her, saw that she was holding out a large, blue-striped body-cloth.

"See, Yúsufu!" she exclaimed gleefully; "the good Fatima hath given me a *túrkedi*."

She joyfully wrapped the cloth round her body, gave the ends a skilful little twist under her arm, and drew herself up proudly for me to see; and certainly, now that she was clothed, she appeared much more respectable if rather less handsome.

On the following morning we turned out early, and gathering up the remainder of the provisions that had been given to me, sallied forth from the village amidst the benedictions of the headman and his people. Isaaku had added to his present a cotton cap such as the Wongáras wear, so that I was completely equipped in a humble way, while, as to Aminé, she tripped along in her new *túrkedi*, as fine as a sweep's apprentice on the first of May.

As we walked, Isaaku chatted pleasantly about his experiences, and the journey on which he was now engaged, and incidentally I learned a great deal about the town of Bori, whither he was bound, and other cities of the interior.

"As soon as I reach Bori," he observed, "I shall get a *mai-tákalmi* (sandal maker) to sew up the clay tablet that thou gavest me, in a leather case, that it may not be broken."

"If I had a piece of paper," I said, "I would write thee some saying from the holy book on it, so there should be no fear of thy *laiya* getting broken."

"Perhaps we shall find some tree that shall yield us paper to write on," replied Isaaku; "then if thou wilt write some holy words on it, I shall be most thankful."

To this I made no reply, having no idea what my host meant, and not wishing to display my ignorance; but while we were taking our midday rest in a belt of forest that fringed a small stream, the boy Ali came running to his father with the news that he had found a tree that would serve our purpose.

"It is the kind of tree that the Ashanti people call Hon-ton," said he, "such as we saw the heathen in Sehui use to make garments of."

Isaaku and I followed the lad, who proudly conducted us to this treasure, a not very large tree, of a kind that I recognised as having seen in the forest.

"This will serve us well," said Isaaku; and drawing his knife he made four deep incisions in the bark, marking off a space about three feet square.

"Thou must first bruise it, father, or it will not come off," said Ali, and accordingly he fell to hammering the incisions with a heavy branch.

"Gently, gently, my son!" exclaimed Isaaku. "Beat not too hard, or thou wilst spoil it for writing. We want it for paper, not for cloth."

He tapped the marked space with the handle of his knife until the outer bark was loosened, when he peeled it off in strips. Then, sticking the point of the knife into the incision, he prised up a corner of the inner bark, and with the aid of his fingernails stripped off a square of sheet of what looked like coarse, rather flimsy, canvas.

"See, my son," he said, showing it to Ali, "if thou wantest it for writing thou must keep it smooth, but if it is for cloth, then must the pulp be bruised out of the meshes."

He rolled the bark up carefully and tied it lightly on top of his load that it might dry in the sun as we went along, and we then resumed our journey, travelling on at a rapid pace until late in the afternoon, when we entered a large village on the bank of the great river. Here, while Fatima and Aminé were busying themselves with preparations for the evening meal, Isaaku borrowed a small shallow bowl in which he ground up some charcoal and a piece of gum with water, and having obtained some fowl's feathers, laid the collection before me, with the bark, which he had cut up into pieces a few inches square.

They were not ideal writing materials, but I found that it was possible to produce with them characters sufficiently distinct to answer the purpose; so I got to work while the light lasted, and wrote, from memory, on each of the squares of bark, the short but fine and dignified introductory chapter to the Koran.

Our people gathered round and listened reverently while I read out the words of praise and exhortation, and I then distributed one of the squares to each of the men and to Fatima. The remainder, with the exception of three which I kept for my own use, I made up into a little package and handed to Isaaku, saying that perhaps he might like to give them to some of his friends. He was delighted with the gift, and most profuse in his thanks, and this being the last evening that I was to spend in his company, he directed Fatima to prepare some provisions for my use on the morrow. Then he took me aside to give me some advice as to my future proceedings.

"Hast thou any friends in Bontúku?" he asked somewhat anxiously.

"I hope to meet some of my countrymen there," I replied.

"I trust thou wilt," said he uneasily, "for thou hast more piety and learning than worldly wisdom, and art but poorly provided even for a short journey."

"Man bringeth nought into the world and taketh nought away with him," said I.

"That is true," he replied. "But while he is in the world he needeth food and raiment. Faith is precious, but it filleth not the belly. However, here is a little store to carry thee to Bontúku, and may God prosper thee and make thee as rich in the things of this world as thou art in those of the next."

He drew from the pocket of his *riga* a small wicker bag full of cowrie shells and put it into my hand.

"I like not to take thy *kurdi*," said I hesitatingly. "Is it not enough that thou hast fed me since I met thee by the way?"

"Not so," he answered. "It is thou that hast fed us; besides thou knowest that the amulets that thou hast given me shall bring a good price among the merchants at Bori."

I had not thought of this, and now rejoiced to have a fresh means of getting a livelihood opened out to me; so I thanked Isaaku and deposited the *kurdi* in my pocket.

We were up at daybreak on the following morning, and proceeded in a body to the riverside, where we found the ferryman whipping the sprung handle of his paddle with a thong of sheepskin.

Our household furniture had now increased to a grass mat and a wicker bag, in which the provisions were stored, and while Aminé was getting into the canoe with these, I laid my hand on the head of each of my friends in succession, and bestowed on them my solemn benediction. Then I stepped into the canoe and, as the ferryman had now completed the repairs on his paddle, we pushed off amidst a chorus of good wishes from our friends upon the bank.

CHAPTER TWENTY
I Join a Party of Bohemians

On the opposite side of the river we found a broad, well-worn track, along which we took our way at a brisk pace, in a very different frame of mind from that which we had experienced before we met Isaaku and his people. Indeed, it amused me to note what a difference was made in our condition by a few poor rags of clothing. No longer did we sneak stealthily along the path, hiding ourselves from casual wayfarers, but strode forward boldly, entering the villages with confidence, and exchanging cheerful salutations with all whom we met on the road. And it was well that our affairs were in this improved condition, for we were now on the main road from Bori to Bontúku; and not only were the travellers numerous, but villages and hamlets occurred at pretty frequent intervals.

We trudged on steadily for a couple of hours, meeting small parties of travellers – mostly travelling Wongáras – and passing through two or three villages, until we came to a small stream with the usual fringe of shady woodland; and here Aminé proposed that we should halt and breakfast.

"I know not why we should push on so fast," said she, "seeing that one place is as good for us as another," and she sat down on a moss-covered bank and began to rummage in the provision bag.

"Is it true that thou lookest for friends in Bontúku?" she asked presently, as she pulled a leg off a spare and ascetic-looking fowl.

"I look for friends everywhere," I replied with a grin. "Perhaps we may meet thy father there" – for she had told me that she had been kidnapped while accompanying her father on a journey to Kong.

"There is little fear of that," she rejoined. "He will have gone back to his country long since."

"Little fear!" I exclaimed. "Dost thou not wish to meet thy father then?"

"Not I," she answered, "for if we should meet him he would take me back, and since thou hast not the wherewith to pay my dowry, he would perhaps give me to some other man."

As the conversation appeared to be drifting into an undesirable channel I changed the subject.

"What hast thou in that little bag that is hanging round thy neck?" I asked.

"This?" exclaimed Aminé, taking it in her fingers. "Surely it is the little clay tablet that thou didst write the holy words upon. Thou didst not write me a *laiya* upon the bark as thou didst for the others," she added, a little reproachfully.

This was a sad oversight. The fact was that I had not reckoned on her taking my performance seriously, seeing that she was more or less of a confederate, and I had forgotten how little she really knew about me. However, I hastened to retrieve the situation.

"I have kept three," I said, taking the bundle from my pocket, and spreading out the documents before her. "Take the one that thou likest best."

She fingered the squares of bark with childish pleasure, comparing their merits, and then handed them back to me, saying: "Do thou choose for me, Yúsufu; thou knowest better than I which is the best."

I selected one and held it out to her.

"Keep it for me in thy pocket," said she, "until I can get a leather case to carry it in;" so I replaced and resumed my assault upon the provisions.

"I wish I was able to write words as thou art, Yúsufu," said Aminé presently, when, having finished our meal, we sat dreamily watching the little stream as it pursued its noiseless course.

"Why dost thou wish that, Aminé?" I asked.

She crept closer to me and laid her cheek against my shoulder, regarding me with an expression that filled me with vague uneasiness.

"Thou didst tell the people," said she, "that the written words speak ever without ceasing. If I could write, I would make thee a *laiya*, and I would write on it, 'Aminé loveth thee,' and thou shouldst wear it always round thy neck."

"It needeth no *laiya* to tell of thy faithfulness," said I. "Thy deeds speak more clearly than words written on paper or clay. Ever since I met thee thou has been to me even as a dear sister."

Aminé sat up with a jerk.

"God hath given me as many brothers as I want," she said shortly. "As for thee, thou art not my brother, nor am I thy sister, of which I am truly glad, for if I were, then could I not be thy wife."

"That is true," said I helplessly; for this frank avowal, with its implied proposal, left me fairly dazed with astonishment, and I had barely enough presence of mind to turn the conversation into a new channel.

"Thou art a good girl, Aminé," I said, rather irrelevantly, "and thou art very patient with our poverty and hardship. Perhaps we shall meet with some better fortune at Bontúku. At any rate, we have enough *kurdi* to keep us for a day or two."

"Thou must keep thy *kurdi* as long as thou canst," said she, coming back reluctantly to the prosaic realities of our life. "For my part, I shall gather these yellow caterpillars that swarm upon the trees. If I cannot sell them in one of the villages, we can eat them ourselves."

I made an involuntary grimace at the suggestion, which did not escape her notice, for she exclaimed somewhat severely: "Thou art a very dainty man, Yúsufu. Thou wilt not eat snails nor crabs nor the little black plums, and now thou makest a wry face at the good, fat caterpillars, although we have but a handful of *kurdi* to buy us food. Thou canst teach wisdom to others, but thine own actions are full of folly."

"He who giveth much alms leaveth his pockets empty," said I, laughing, whereupon she slapped me smartly on the shoulder, and emptying the provision bag into my pocket, went off to collect caterpillars.

We walked on at a more easy pace for the rest of the day, for we learned from some travellers, whom we met, that the large village or town of Táari lay at no great distance ahead; and as we journeyed, Aminé's bag became gradually filled with a writhing, squirming mass of the large, yellow caterpillars, which she persisted in thrusting under my nose at frequent intervals, by way, I supposed, of awakening in me a less fastidious appetite.

The afternoon was well advanced when we entered the village of Táari, and sat down for a brief rest under the enormous shade-tree that graced the middle of the principal street. This tree was the most wonderful specimen of vegetation that I saw in all my wanderings – more wonderful even than the colossal silk-cottons of the forest, for whereas the latter towered aloft to an immense altitude, this great banyan-like shade-tree spread abroad over an area that was almost incredible. In shape it was like a giant mushroom, the flat undersurface supporting multitudes of dangling bunches of aerial roots, and the shade that it cast was as profound as that of a yew tree. We sat in the deep twilight on a pile of fantastically twisted roots, and looked out into the dazzling street on to a scene of life and bustle that was new and strange to me. Hausas, Fulahs, and Wongáras in their gay *rigas* strode to and fro; strangely-dressed natives of unknown regions came and went, and now and again some wealthy merchant rode by upon his horse; and as we watched, a caravan, which must have followed us long the Bori road, entered the town, led by three men mounted on white, humped oxen.

"Let us go and look for the market," said Aminé. "There are many people here; perhaps I shall be able to sell my caterpillars."

We rose and walked down the street, which at the farther end opened out into a wide space in which the market was being held, and which was filled by a dense and motley crowd in which all the nations of Africa seemed to be represented, from the grave and dignified Fulah, richly clothed and looking out secretly through the narrow opening of his face-cloth, to the half naked natives of some neighbouring villages.

We pushed our way into the throng, and sauntered past the rows of open booths, in which well-to-do merchants from Hausa, Bornu, Kong and even Jenne and Timbuktu, sat presiding over a rich display of clothing, leather work, arms and jewellery.

"Look, Yúsufu!" exclaimed Aminé, halting opposite a booth where a venerable Hausa sat on a handsome rug in the midst of his wares, "what a beautiful *riga saki* this old man has. I wish we could buy it for thee, so that thou mightest throw aside thy old ragged *riga*." She pointed to a splendidly embroidered gown that hung on the partition of the booth.

"But a day or two ago I had no *riga* at all," said I, and I led her away from the tantalising spectacle.

We passed between the double rows of booths and entered the produce market, where rows of countrywomen sat on the ground behind their little stalls, with their goods spread out on mats or in baskets or calabashes. It was late in the afternoon, and many of them, having sold out their stocks, were rolling up their mats preparatory to going home. One old woman who was thus preparing for her departure, had left upon the ground one circular basket tray, on which there yet remained a couple of heaps of the identical caterpillars that formed Aminé's stock in trade, and as we stopped before the stall, a Hausa woman came up, and, after some haggling, laid down a dozen *kurdi*, and gathered up the two piles of insects.

As the old woman picked up the empty tray, Aminé stepped into the now vacant space and spread out her mat, on which she began to arrange little heaps of the caterpillars, the corpses of which she disinterred from the "black hole" of her bag. When she had set out the stall to her satisfaction she seated herself at the end of the mat to wait for customers, and I strolled off to see the "fun of the fair". There was plenty to see, and as I looked at the strange and novel spectacle I almost forgot my forlorn and destitute condition.

I elbowed my way through the crowd, and joined the other idlers and sightseers around the more entertaining stalls. Here was an old Hausa busily writing *laiyas* or amulets, and I watched him with a special interest, noting his methods and materials and the prices his trumpery fetched. Then I came to a man roasting kabobs over a pot of charcoal, and the aroma they diffused around made my mouth water, so that I hurried on. There were drinking stalls, where a kind of crude sherbet was dispensed in little calabashes from a great jar, and a stall where a man was frying *masa*; and the little cakes looked so tempting that I invested twenty *kurdi* in half a dozen for supper. From a specially dense part of the crowd came a Babel of talk and shouts of laughter, and, on pushing my way to the front, I beheld a barber plying his trade; and as he mowed the stubble from the head of a kneeling client, he kept the bystanders in a roar of merriment by an unceasing flow of jests and anecdotes.

I was absorbed in one of the barber's not very proper stories when my ear caught the strains of what sounded like an aged and infirm piano or a spinet, and turning with the rest of the crowd, perceived a party of musicians advancing up the market. The leader of the band was hammering a rude dulcimer; one of his two assistants sawed away at a preposterous little fiddle, while the other kept time with a drum, and all three bellowed out their songs as though they were fresh from the Borough market with a cargo of broccoli.

As they came opposite the barber's stall the musicians halted, and the drummer advanced, holding out a small calabash for contributions. The pitch was well chosen for the crowd was in high good humour, and the *kurdi* rattled into the calabash merrily, the barber contributing half his recently earned fee. When the drummer came to me I shook my head, for my means did not admit of my making presents, but the man was persistent, and stood before me with the calabash thrust under my nose.

"Wilt thou not give the poor musicians a few *kurdi*?" asked the barber, confronting me with a saucy leer. "They who swagger about in rich apparel should be generous to the needy."

This delicate satire on my ragged appearance was greeted by a shout of laughter.

"I am but a poor man, and must needs feed myself before I give to others," said I gruffly, rather nettled at the barber's impudence.

"Feed thyself!" ejaculated the barber. "What need to feed thyself when thou art bursting with fatness already? Give alms to the poor, and let thy belly have a rest."

Fresh shouts of laughter greeted these exhortations, for my late experiences had left me as emaciated as a Cape Coast chicken, and I felt strongly disposed to pull my tormentor's nose; but, apart from the unsuitability of the organ – which was as flat as a monkey's – I saw that it would be the height of folly to lose my temper, for the crowd was growing every moment.

"Let the Moor sing us a song if he will not pay," suggested a broad-faced Bornu.

"Good!" exclaimed the barber. "I have never heard a Moor sing. Sing us a good song, and I will shave thee for nothing – and not before thou needest it either."

The suggestion was received with acclamation by the crowd, including the musicians, so I determined to fall in with their humour.

"Very well," said I. "Give me thy instrument and I will sing."

I took the dulcimer from its owner, and slung it over my shoulder, and with one of the rubber-tipped hammers banged out the scale to try the range of the instrument and find the sequence of the notes. It had twenty notes, and was tuned sufficiently well to produce an intelligible air upon, and as I had been used to strum a little upon the piano in old days, this simple instrument presented no difficulties.

I struck out boldly the opening phrase of "Tom Bowling" as a prelude, and then burst into song with a roar like the hail of a Channel pilot.

I had expected to be stopped in the first bar, but, to my astonishment, as I proceeded, the grins of derision on the faces of my audience gave place to an expression of wondering admiration; and when I had let off the final yell and thumped out a brief postlude, I was overwhelmed with congratulations. The sherbet merchant ran off to fetch me a bowl of his muddy, sour beverage, and the barber dragged me on to this mat and commanded me to kneel.

"Art thou going to shave me then?" I asked,

"Shave thee!" he exclaimed. "I would shave a porcupine to hear a song like that thou hast sung."

He whisked off my cap, and set to work on my scalp with a clumsy little razor, but very skilfully and easily, while the crowd pressed round the mat until I was nearly suffocated.

"Thou singest sweetly," said the barber, as he mowed away, "and thy song was most tuneful, but I could not understand thy words. Was it a Moorish song?"

"No," said I, "it is a song that I heard a Christian sing when I was at Ogúa (Cape Coast)."

"It is true," broke in the Bornu. "I have been to Ogúa, and there I heard the *masu-bíndiga* (soldiers) of the Christians play much fine music, and this song I heard also."

An earnest discussion on the white men and their customs followed, and was still going on when I arose with smooth and tingling head and chin, and, thanking the whimsical barber, made my escape. I was hurrying away when I felt someone pluck me by the sleeve, and, turning, found the dulcimer player at my elbow.

"That was a good song of thine," said he, "and right well sung. Dost thou know any more of the songs of the white people?"

"Yes. I know a few," I replied cautiously.

"Then perhaps thou understandest their language?" said he.

"I speak it a little," I answered. "why dost thou ask?"

"Because," he replied, "I and my brothers think of journeying to Ogúa. I have heard that the white people are rich and generous, and we think we might earn enough there to buy some of the Christian's merchandise, and bring it back to our country. Now, if thou canst sing their songs and speak their language, we would be glad to have thee with us, and would share our earnings with thee if thou wouldst come."

This was an offer not to be lightly rejected, for it promised immediate subsistence and an escort and guides to the Coast, whither I desired to journey as quickly as I could.

"It is a long journey," said I. "I should like to think about it."

"Where dost thou stay?" asked the musician.

"I have but just arrived," I replied, "and have yet to find a place to sleep in."

"I stay with a countryman of mine, a man of Kong, and I doubt not he will let thee sleep in his house. Come, and I will take thee to him."

"I must first go to my wife, whom I left in the market," said I.

"Shall I come with thee?" he asked.

"No," I replied. "I will come back to thee anon."

"Very well," said he, "I will wait for thee at the corner here by the mosque."

I found Aminé sitting patiently on her mat with a row of little heaps of caterpillars spread before her, and I feared that her speculation had failed. She brightened up when she saw me, and beckoned me to her side.

"Thou hast been a long time, my Yúsufu," said she, laying her hand fondly on my arm. "My caterpillars are nearly all gone. See! we are quite rich," and she proudly displayed a pile of *kurdi* that was hidden beneath her bag.

"I shall not sell any more now, I think," she continued, "for it is getting dark, and the people are going home. Hast thou found us a place to sleep in, where we can get some food?"

I told her of my appointment with the musician and the proposal he had made, on which she pursed up her lips rather doubtfully.

"We can hear what the fellow says," she said; "and thou knowest what is best to do better than I. But these minstrels are a worthless set of vagabonds as a rule."

However, she put the caterpillars back into her bag, and, bidding me take up the heap of *kurdi*, rolled up her mat and followed me. We found the minstrel waiting by the door of the mosque, looking out for us with some eagerness, and when we came up he regarded Aminé with undisguised admiration.

"Thou art a lucky fellow to have such a handsome wife," said he. "Not but that thou art a proper fellow thyself. But come and let us see if we can find thee a place to sleep in."

I noticed that Aminé appeared to relish the man's compliments as little as I did, but we walked after him, as there seemed nothing else to do.

Our conductor, who seemed to know the place well, led us through a maze of foul-smelling alleys until we came to a high mud wall, in which was a doorway closed by a gate of palm leaf. Entering through this, we found ourselves in a spacious but dirty compound, in the middle of which a Wongára woman was attending to some cooking pots, assisted by her two daughters. The women rose from the fire and stared at us inquisitively, and when our acquaintance had explained who we were, the elder woman shouted gruffly to her husband, who at that moment emerged from the house.

"This is my countryman, Osumánu Wongára," said our friend, introducing us, "a most excellent man and my trusted friend."

"Spare thy compliments, and tell me who these people are," growled Osumánu, looking at us sourly enough.

"They are friends of mine who would lodge in thy house, most worthy and respectable people, my brother," replied the minstrel suavely.

"Then they are not like most of thy friends," retorted the other; "but they can have a room if they are able to pay for it."

"I should not come to the house of a stranger if I could not pay," said I stiffly.

"Thou wouldst not remain long if thou didst," he replied pleasantly. "How much wilt thou give for a room?"

"Show me the room," I said.

He fetched a shea butter lamp and led me into a filthy little cell with black mud walls and smoke-blackened rafters, the rustlings and cracklings from which hinted broadly of mice and cockroaches. There was no window nor any opening but the unguarded doorway.

"Pooh!" exclaimed Aminé, turning up her nose in disgust, "it is better to sleep in the wilderness than in this stinking little hole."

"No doubt thou art more used to the wilderness," replied Osumánu drily.

"How much?" I asked.

"Fifty *kurdi*," answered Osumánu.

"I will give thee twenty," said I.

"*Albérika!*" replied mine host, using the courteous stereotyped form of refusal.

"Give him twenty-five," suggested the minstrel.

"That is five for the smell," said Aminé, sniffing disdainfully. "Thou wilt get plenty for thy money, Yúsufu."

"Thou saucy jade!" exclaimed Osumánu. "If thou wert my wife thou shouldst know the feel of a hippo hide whip."

"If I were thy wife," retorted Aminé, "I would put something into thy soup that would make me a widow, and go and look for a man."

The Wongára raised his fist as though to strike Aminé, but I caught him by the wrist.

"If thou layest a finger on my wife I will stick my knife into thy belly," said I.

"These are pleasant friends that thou hast brought Ali," grumbled the Wongára, licking his wrist where I had gripped it.

"Give him a price and have done with it," said Ali, as the minstrel appeared to be named, grinning with secret enjoyment.

"Very well. Thirty-five, and I will no take one less."

I pulled out my bag and counted out thirty-five shells into Osumánu's hand, whereon he departed.

"If thou wilt sup with us we can share our provisions," suggested Ali.

"We will sup by ourselves," Aminé put in quickly, evidently suspecting that we should not be the gainers by this arrangement. "We have just enough for ourselves, and no more."

Accepting the hint, Ali took himself off, and Aminé immediately set about preparing our supper. With some trouble she obtained the loan of a flat cooking pot from the uncivil Wongára woman, purchased a little shea butter and other materials, and took temporary possession of the fireplace, while I spread the mat on the ground and sat looking on.

"What hast thou in thy pocket?" she asked, as she rose from the frizzling pot.

"I have the remainder of what Fatima gave us and some *masa* that I bought in the market."

"Then we shall do well for tonight," said she gleefully, "and tomorrow we can think of when it comes."

And, in fact we supped royally. A substantial remnant of Fatima's gift was yet unconsumed, and I had brought quite a little pile of *masa* from the market. But the crowning glory of the feast was the product of Aminé's cookery, which she turned out of the pot with a flourish on to a flat basket tray, and laid before me all crisp and smoking. I knew that the brown, whitebait-like objects were caterpillars, and tasted a few with shuddering trepidation, but I ended by greedily devouring more than half of the pile, to Aminé's joy and pride.

During our repast Ali came to our quarters, and we thought he had brought us some additions to our meal; but he had only come to beg a couple of *masa*, and when I had given them to him, we saw him go and devour them in a corner before going back to his comrades.

We sat for a long time after supper discussing our future movements.

"I like not these new friends of thine, the Wongáras," said Aminé; "nor does it seem good that a wise man as thou art should be seen abroad with a pack of ragamuffin minstrels. Still, thou knowest best."

"I like them not myself," said I, "but they go to the settlements of the Christians, where I have many good friends, and I see no other means of getting a livelihood."

Our talk was interrupted by Ali, who came over to us with his clumsy-looking instrument, which he set down upon the mat before me.

"I have brought thee the balafu that I may show thee how to play on it, since I know not thy songs," said he. "Although thou didst very well today, and hast, no doubt, played on one before."

I made no reply, but taking up the instrument, and examined it curiously. It consisted of a light framework of sticks fastened together with lashings of fibre, which supported twenty rods of hard wood, suspended above the frame on two tightly stretched strings; these diminished progressively in length from two feet at one end to six inches at the other, and under each rod was hung a flask-shaped calabash of a corresponding size, to act as a sound box. The whole contrivance was about a yard long, and the ingenuity with which it was constructed, and the musical knowledge that its design displayed, filled me with surprise and admiration. I took the two hammers – carved sticks with knobs of native rubber at the ends – and struck the rods in succession, eliciting the clear, wiry, dulcimer-like tone that I have described, and now found the range of the instrument to be two octaves and five notes, the order of succession being similar to that of European keyed instruments, and the tuning remarkably correct.

Having thus made my acquaintance with the balafu, I placed myself under Ali's tuition, and, as the vagabond minstrel was a really skilful player and a musician of some taste, I made such progress that, when the lesson was finished, I could accompany one of my simple English airs in quite a proficient manner.

CHAPTER TWENTY-ONE
I Meet With Some Old Acquaintances

We were up betimes on the following morning, and shaking off the abundant dust of Osumánu's inhospitable abode, sallied forth with our companions. It was Ali's plan to give an entertainment in the market before leaving Táari, that we might start with replenished purses, but the people were now busy with the commencement of the day's work, and no strangers had yet arrived; whence the performance – in which I took no part – fell rather flat, and was brought to a premature close; so, having invested the meagre collection in a small stock of provisions, we took to the road.

It had been our original intention to pass through Bontúku on our way south, but the fiddler, Osman, who knew the country well, urged us to turn south-east by way of Banda, as we should thus considerably shorten our journey through the forest; and, as my recollections of the horrors of forest travelling were most vivid, I supported Osman in his contention that we should keep as long as possible in the orchard country. We therefore turned off from the Bontúku road and took a smaller path, which led through Banda to Ashanti.

Along this road we met but few travellers, and, although the villages were pretty numerous, they were small and poverty-stricken. We gave a performance in one of them, but the result was not encouraging. It is true that there was no lack of an audience, for every person in the village attended; but when Baku, the drummer, went round with his calabash, the people merely peered into it, and not a single shell was forthcoming. Baku pointedly suggested that a few plantains or beans would be acceptable, but the hint was received with surly derision, and, when at length the minstrels assumed a bullying manner and Osman attempted to snatch a stray fowl, the woman and children vanished as if by magic, and the men, marshalled by the chief, assumed such a threatening attitude that we were glad to take ourselves off.

It being thus pretty evident that we should not make much profit out of the villages, we pushed on at a rapid pace towards Banda, which town, I gathered, was about forty miles distant from Táari. As we went along, my companions enlivened our journey with an unceasing flow of talk, but like many public performers, they were a little disappointing in private life, and their conversation was often of a kind that would have deeply shocked the serious and patriarchal Isaaku; indeed, the more I saw of my new associates, the less I liked them; and I could not but admit the justice of Aminé's estimate of them. They had all the faults of the strolling Bohemian, with perhaps some of his virtues, for they were certainly gay, careless fellows, taking little thought for the morrow, and making light of present discomforts; but they were greedy though extravagant, grasping though improvident, coarse in their manners, lax in morals, and very obscure in their pleas of honesty.

When we came to prepare our evening meal at the village in which we intended to sleep, Ali spread out a mat, and the three minstrels, to Aminé's astonishment, and mine, began to unship from their enormous pockets various odds and ends of food – one or two plantains, a few sweet potatoes, a couple of red yams, loose handfuls of beans, millet and maizemeal; and Osman produced a large lump of fufu wrapped in leaves.

"Where didst thou get all these things?" Aminé asked the latter as he laid down the fufu. "I did not see thee buy anything."

The three men looked at one another and laughed long and loud.

"Didst thou not see Osman go a-marketing at the last village we passed?" asked Ali with a sly leer.

"I did not see him at all there," replied Aminé.

"Then thou mightest have known that he was gone a-marketing," rejoined the balafu player, and the minstrels all roared with laughter again.

"I like not these Wongáras," said Aminé to me when we had retired that night to the hut that the headman had lent us. "They are but a party of thieves, and will get us into trouble; and that old ape, Ali, trieth to make love to me when thou art not looking. As though I would look at a black, monkey-faced Wongára, who have a husband like thee!"

There was much truth in these observations, and the conduct of our companions caused me some anxiety. But what troubled me much more was the attitude of Aminé herself. Her calm adoption of me as her husband was beginning to be a very serious matter. Of course, her position was a perfectly reasonable one from an African point of view. A Mahommedan is not restricted to one wife, and certainly no countryman of Aminé's would have hesitated a moment to snap up such a prize as this handsome Fulah girl. Nevertheless, the position was a very awkward one, for while, on the one hand, my acceptance even of the outward appearance of the relationship was an affront to Isabel and a reproach to my love and fidelity, on the other it was unfair to the poor girl herself, a fact that was impressed on me anew by every fresh instance of her simple faith and devotion. Yet I could not bring myself to the point of dispelling her delusion, and when my conscience rebuked me, as it often did, I was apt to put myself off with the hope that when we arrived at the Coast, Aminé's fancy might be captivated by some gaudy sergeant-major or native officer of the Hausa force.

As we marched along next day I kept a sharp eye upon our companions, and soon had an opportunity of observing the manner in which their "marketing" was conducted; which was characterised by masterly simplicity. As we neared the first village, Osman began to lag behind, and I presently noticed the handle of his fiddle sticking out of Baku's pocket. On entering the village street Ali and Baku began to thump their instruments vigorously, and both the rascals burst into song, shouting at the very tops of their voices. As an inevitable result, the people came running from every part of the village, and crowded round us as we sauntered slowly down the street; and when we halted near the end, we were surrounded by a mob that, no doubt, included every living soul in the place. Here we stood for some minutes with drum and balafu in full blast, until Osman strolled up and began to beg from the bystanders; on which Ali and Baku shouldered their instruments, and we all moved briskly out of the village.

This performance was repeated at every hamlet through which we passed, each of the rascals taking his turn at the "marketing," so that as they day went on, the pockets of each became more and more portly. For my part, as I had no intention of sharing the plunder, I gave Aminé my cowrie bag, and told her to buy what was necessary for us from the villagers.

It was already dark when we reached Banda, and as we had covered in the day considerably over twenty miles, we were all very tired. Fortunately we had no difficulty in finding lodgings for the night, and our good-natured landlady even agreed to prepare us a meal, so that we spent the remainder of the evening pleasantly enough; and as we learned that the market day was on the morrow, and that many strangers had already arrived in the town, we turned in betimes with the intention of making an early start with our business in the morning.

Nevertheless the sun had been up a long time when we strolled out into the street and looked around at the scene of bustle that it presented. The market women were already streaming into the town in long files, and many had taken their places and were setting out their stalls, while the strangers roamed about in little groups, chattering, laughing, eating, and examining the wares of the market people. We had joined the throng of idlers, and were slowly making our way up the market place, when our attention was attracted by a person who was approaching from the opposite direction. This was a small and powerful elderly man, who stalked along at the head of small party of followers, pausing now and again to bestow on them a few words of abuse. His aspect was fierce and forbidding, and one blind eye, white and opaque, did not increase his attractions. Although he wore but a single cloth or *ntama* after the fashion of the pagans, he was evidently a person of consequence, for he was followed by a stool-bearer, a pipe-bearer, and numerous other dependants, on two of whom he leaned heavily – for early as it was, he was considerably the worse for liquor.

As he came up to us he stopped and regarded us with drunken stare.

"Who are you, my fine fellows?" he asked gruffly in very bad Hausa, "and what do you do in this town?"

"We are the musicians, most mighty chief," replied Ali in his oiliest manner, and bowing to the ground before the old reprobate, "and we have come to sing to the people in the market, if it please the valiant chief graciously to permit us."

"We want no wandering vagabonds here," exclaimed the old man fiercely. "More likely ye have come to thieve than to sing. Still, I will hear your singing, and if it please me not I will fling this bottle at your heads. Now! begin! Do you hear me?" he shouted, "Sing!"

The stool-bearer planted the seat upon the ground, and the old ruffian dropped upon it heavily, and sat swaying from side to side, scowling at us, and holding a square gin bottle poised ready to throw.

My companions were in such a hurry to obey that they all commenced simultaneously with different songs, but perceiving their mistake before it was noticed by the chief, Osman and Baku stopped, leaving Ali to sing alone; which he did with surprising spirit, pouring out a torrent of extemporised ribaldry of a foulness beyond belief. He had, however, hit off the taste of his audience to a nicety, for, as the performance proceeded, the old chief lowered the gin bottle and shouted with laughter and enjoyment.

"Thou art a proper singer," said he, as Ali struck out a few concluding flourishes. "Now let us hear that long-nosed Moor who is with thee. He looketh as sour as a monkey-bread; if his song is not more pleasant than his face he shall have the bottle at his head. Come, sing, thou yellow-skinned baboon, before I smash thy ugly face."

"Sing, in the name of God!" exclaimed Ali, tremblingly slinging the balafu from my shoulders. "He is the chief of the town, and will certainly kill us if we cross him."

I was much disposed to consign the old savage to Hades or its pagan equivalent, but I smothered my wrath as well as I could, and hammered out a flourish on the balafu, while I decided on a suitable song. After a moment's consideration I hit upon the "Leather Bottél" as being specially appropriate to the old rascal's condition, and began forthwith to bellow it out. The crowd rapidly increased, and gave manifest signs of approval, for the melody had in it just that swinging rhythm that is so grateful to the African ear; but the old chief evidently found it a dull performance, for in the middle of the second stanza he staggered to his feet, and roaring out, "I understand not one word of thy gibberish!" lurched off. However, I did not allow his departure to interrupt my performance, for Baku was already busy with the calabash, and I could hear the *kurdi* rattling into it; so I worked my way through stanza after stanza until I reached the last; and I was just considering the advisability of beginning over again when I was startled by the apparition of a man's head and shoulders standing up above the heads of the onlookers. For an instant I supposed that it was some idler who had raised himself upon a stool or case that he might get a better view, but at a second glance I recognised with a thrill of astonishment my old friend Abduláhi Dan-Daúra. The recognition was mutual, and in a moment the genial "child of the elephant," with a cry of joy, pushed his way through the crowd, and folded me in his enormous arms.

"And is it indeed thou, Yúsufu, child of my mother!" he exclaimed, almost weeping with delight. "Little I thought ever to set eyes upon thy face again. We had given thee up for dead long since, and now here thou art, all alive and singing like a cricket in a meal pot! Musa will rejoice to see thee, and so will the others."

"Are they in this town then?" I asked, rubbing the hand that he had pressed in the exuberance of his affection.

"That they are," he replied, "and here is my friend Mahámadu Dam-Bornu, who has travelled with us from Kantámpo. Mahámadu, this is Yúsufu of whom we have told thee, who hast come back to us from the land of the dead."

"They do not appear to spend much on clothing in that country," remarked Mahámadu with a grin, "nor on food either, for that matter."

"No, indeed," agreed Abduláhi; "thou lookest but poorly in body and in pocket. But that matters little, for Musa hath all the gold that thou didst leave behind as well as thy good clothes and the money that we owe thee."

I was sorry that he had mentioned this matter publicly, for the musicians, who had pressed forward to listen, pricked up their ears mightily at his words, and I caught a greedy glitter in the eyes of my friend Ali.

"Come with me now to our house that our brethren may see thee," said Abduláhi, and taking me by the hand, he marched off, leaving Dam-Bornu and my companions to follow with the gratified Aminé.

He led me to a large, prosperous-looking house in the Mahommedan quarter, and entering a gateway, we found ourselves in a wide compound where numerous packages of merchandise were piled under a thatched shed. Through an open doorway I had a view of Musa, Dam-biri, and several other of my friends, seated upon a handsome rug, holding an animated discussion. They uttered a shout of surprise when they saw me, and leaping to their feet ran forward to greet me.

The Golden Pool

"Now God be praised," exclaimed Musa, holding both my hands, "That thou art delivered from the hand of the heathen. We had thought thee dead long since, and have spoken of thee as one cut off from the land of the living. But God is merciful and wise, and thou hast come back to us."

"I thank God truly that thou hast come back to us," said Alhassan, "for it was I that showed thee the accursed pool. Often in my dreams have I seen the horned devil devouring thee, but now I trust I shall see him no more."

"Thou wilt come and stay with us, Yúsufu," said Musa; "there is room to spare in this house. But who are these minstrels and the young woman who have come with thee?"

"We," said Ali, coming forward with a greasy smile, "are the friends of Yúsufu, who have stood by him in the hour of adversity, and whom I know he will not despise in his prosperity."

"Assuredly," said I, "my good fortune shall benefit you as well as me, but go now, for I have to speak to my friends of matters which concern them alone."

"Very well," replied Ali. "We will see thee tomorrow, Come, Aminé."

"I stay with my husband," said Aminé haughtily, taking hold of my hand.

"Yes; she will stay with me," I said. "*Sei gobé*" (*au revoir*), and the three minstrels, returning my adieu, swaggered out of the compound.

"Thou hast better taste in women than in men," said Musa drily, as he gazed at Aminé who wriggled shyly at the implied compliment.

"Yes, truly, those minstrels seem but sorry knaves," agreed Danjiwa. "Where didst thou pick them up?"

"Thou shalt tell us all thy adventures tonight," said Musa. "Now, we must go and look at the market, but first let me give thee back thy goods and pay our debt to thee."

He fetched from his own chamber a bundle securely sewn up, which he proceeded to rip open before me.

"Here are thy clothes," he said, "and thy purse with the gold coins in it. Here is the strange gold *laiya*" (he meant my watch), "and the *laiya* of leather, and the other things that we found when thou left us. Also I have put in this little bag the gold dust that we owe thee – for we sold all the *guru* quickly at Kantámpo, and are even now going to Bontúku to trade with the profits before we set out for our country. See that all is right; thy spear standeth there in the corner."

I checked the articles and handed the more bulky ones over to Aminé (who was all agog to see me put on the fine clothes), thanking Musa most warmly for his scrupulous care and conscientiousness.

"It is nothing," he replied. "If thou hadst not come back we should have divided thy goods amongst us when we got back to Kano. But we like it better to give thee back thine own. Now, come and I will show thee thy room."

He led the way across the compound to an unoccupied room or hut, which he assigned to my use, and here Aminé deposited my property.

"Now go in and put on thy fine clothes," said Dan-jiwa, who had followed us, "for thy wife longeth to see thee fitly dressed, as, indeed, do I also."

I retired and rapidly made the change, while Aminé remained outside babbling ingeniously to the amiable giant. When I came out resplendent in *riga saki*, embroidered *wondo*, in turban and face cloth, and yellow slippers, the former gave a shriek of delight and clapped her hands.

"Now thou has a fine husband, Aminé," said Dan-jiwa, laughing. "I see thou hast put on thy *laiya*," he added, taking in his hand the leather-cased amulet that Pereira had included in my outfit. "We have often wondered about the writing on the back of it, which seems not to be Arabic, for even Musa could not read it. Dost thou know what it is?"

I turned the *laiya* over and looked at the back, and there, as Dan-jiwa had said, was an inscription, done with a lead pencil, and so inconspicuous on the black leather that it had escaped my notice. It was a good deal rubbed, but I made out without difficulty the words, "Open this case when you are alone."

"It is certainly not Arabic," said I. "Perhaps some Christian has written upon it. It was given to me in one of the towns where there are Christian merchants."

"No doubt that is so," rejoined Abduláhi, and the subject dropped.

It will readily be understood that I was now consumed with impatience to be alone that I might probe the mystery of the leather case, but Abduláhi stuck to me like a leech, and I had no heart to shake the affectionate fellow off. Then it was necessary that Aminé, who had shared so cheerfully my poverty and hardship, should be made to partake of my good fortune, so I invited the pair to come with me and look at the market.

There was not so fine a display as at Táari, but I managed to buy Aminé a fine new *túrkedi*, a silken *zenné*, or veil, a handsome pair of sandals, and a coral necklace, and with these purchases she tripped homeward, chattering with joy. Abduláhi I presented with a pair of finely-worked slippers, and for myself, I bought of the sandal-maker some of the slender thongs with which leather is sewn, and at another booth a few large-eyed needles.

Having diplomatically sent Aminé and Abduláhi home with their presents, I made my escape from the market and hurried out into the country.

It was near noon, and there were few people stirring on the road, which was moreover but a bypath leading to a neighbouring village, so that I was no sooner fairly out of the town than I found myself in complete solitude. I looked before and behind, and seeing that no living being was in sight, I drew out my knife with a trembling hand and slipped the cord of the *laiya* from around my neck. It was sewn, as was usual, with fine thongs of skin, but the stitching had evidently been renewed, and that by a hand less skilful than that of the Hausa leather-worker. With the point of my knife I cut through one stitch after another until three sides were unfastened and I could lay the case open. As I did so, a mass of wadding fell out, in which was a small paper packet which I opened with feverish haste. Inside it was a plain gold locket, and on the paper was written in Isabel's handwriting – "May God bless you and keep you and bring you safely through all your perils. Think sometimes of us, who have you constantly in our thoughts."

The flutter of anticipation with which I unfastened the clasp of the locket merged into a thrill of intense emotion as my eyes fell upon its contents. From one side of it looked out the old-world cavalier-like visage of Pereira; from the other the calm and lovely face of Isabel.

I cannot describe the feelings which surged through me as I gazed at those beautiful and beloved features. For months – long months filled with peril and suffering that made them seem like years – I had not looked upon the face of a European; I had not even seen my own face since the day on which I fled from Annan. Gradually my standard of human beauty had become accommodated to my surroundings, until Aminé – by far the handsomest African woman I had ever seen – had come to represent a quite satisfying type of feminine comeliness. And now this vision of beauty burst upon me, dispelling in a moment the bias of recent experience, and I stood, in my turban and *riga*, the same Richard Englefield who had looked upon the setting sun as it sank in a crimson glow behind the palms of Jella-Koffi.

I sat down upon the spreading roots of a baobab that stood by the wayside with its squat colossal trunk, like some weird Hamadryad, grown elderly and stout, and with the open locket in my hand, fell into a brown study. Straightway the present vanished and was forgotten. The bare and dismal orchard land with its meandering trail; the vultures wheeling in the blue, the stealthy antelope, the brown baboons, watchful and inquisitive, and the hollow-voiced secret cuckoo: all faded out of my consciousness, and I looked upon a flat seashore where the surf fretted upon shining, pearl-tinted sands; I heard the ripple of girlish laughter mingle with the murmur of the sea; I felt again that gracious presence that had stolen into my lonely life and filled it with beauty and romance. Often in the strenuous, eventful life of the last few months had my thoughts turned to that quiet house by the lagoon, that held all that I really loved in the world; but I had rarely been alone, and my harassing circumstances had left me little opportunity for reflection, so that this vivid message, coming as it were direct from another world, gave substance and reality to what had begun to appear but a dream.

"Here he is! I have found him! What? Art thou meditating and seeing visions again?"

It was the voice of Aminé, and it jarred on me like the jangling of discordant bells. Back in an instant I was dragged from my reverie of peace and love into this hurly-burly of savagery, with its sordid unrestfulness; back from the sweet domestic calm to the clamour of barbarism. I hastily closed the locket and secreted it, and dropping the open leather case through the neck hole of my *riga,* stood up.

"We heard thou hadst taken this road," said Dan-jiwa, who had accompanied Aminé as bodyguard, "and so came to meet thee. Musa is roasting a sheep that we may rejoice at thy return."

I turned and sauntered regretfully towards the town, still thoughtful and abstracted; but as we entered the street Aminé stole up and shyly took my hand.

"Thou hast not looked at my new *túrkedi* or my *zenné,*" she said plaintively.

I stopped, deeply ashamed of my unsympathetic egotism, and looked at the girl.

She was indeed transformed. In her dark blue *túrkedi* with the darker blue silken *zenné* dropped hoodwise over her head, the scarlet beads upon her shapely neck, and the dark line drawn under her eyelashes with the stibium rod, she made a most striking figure, and might have been some princess of the house of Judah. It was not the most auspicious moment to have chosen in which to bespeak my admiration, but I told her that she looked fit to be the wife of the Sultan of Sókoto, and this seemed to give her pleasure.

"I want no Sultan for my husband, if I have thee," she said simply, at which Dan-jiwa patted her on the shoulder approvingly, saying: "Thou art right, Aminé, and art a wise girl not to leave it to other women to find out thy husband's merits."

The feast given that evening by Musa was a magnificent affair, for the well-stocked market of Banda had been ransacked for dainties, and the cooking operations had been on a portentous scale. It was my friends' last evening at Banda, and they intended that it should be a memorable one. Accordingly the feasting commenced early and went on until the town was wrapped in silence, and even then was only brought to a close by the extermination of everything eatable. Yet it was not a scene of gluttony, for as soon as the edge was worn off the appetites of the revellers, conversation and anecdote took the place of steady eating, and very soon a demand was made for an account of my adventures; to which I responded with perfect frankness, giving a true and detailed account of all that had befallen me, excepting the incident of the treasure. I had for a moment thought of confiding this secret to them also, and of engaging them to help me to remove the gold, but on reflection I resolved to speak of the matter to no one until I had consulted Pereira, with whose aid I had no doubt I could organise an expedition for lifting the treasure with safety and certainty.

When we were about to separate for the night I took out my purse, and setting on the mat five sovereigns, pushed them towards Musa.

"At daybreak tomorrow," I said, "you all depart for Bontúku. Before we part, I wish to give you a little present that you may buy something to take back to your country."

"Nay," replied Musa, pushing the coins back, "put up thy money. Thou wilt want all that thou hast on thy journey."

"Not so," I rejoined. "I have enough for my needs, and it will be a pleasure to me, if it please God that we meet no more, to think that my friends have taken with them to their country some little thing, which when they look on will bid them think of their old comrade, Yúsufu Dan-Égadesh."

"It shall be as thou sayest, and we thank thee, my son," said Musa, taking up the coins; "but it needs not thy gifts to make us remember thee, and we shall at least all meet again where there is no buying and selling nor long journeys, nor weariness of the feet nor hunger and thirst."

At daybreak Musa and his people were up and ready to start. Aminé and I walked with them for half a mile along the Bontúku road, and we then took leave of them with many expressions of affection and goodwill on both sides.

"God be with thee, my son," said Musa, "and may we meet again soon. One thing I would counsel thee, and that is that thou walkest no more with those vagabond minstrels. Either go thy way alone or wait until some men of reputation will journey with thee."

"I will remember thy words, my father," I replied, and pressing his hand once more I turned back. I was strongly disposed to abide by the old man's advice and cut myself adrift from the good-for-nothing musicians, and had, indeed, almost made up my mind when, on reaching our house, I found them waiting at the gate.

"Thou hast not gone with thy friends, then," said Ali, with evident relief at seeing me.

"No. I think of remaining at Banda for a while," I replied.

Ali's face fell. "That is a pity," said he, "for we had intended to start at once for Ogúa. Osman knoweth the way well, and he sayeth he can take us thither in eighteen or twenty days."

My heart gave a bound. Eighteen or twenty days! In three weeks I might, with reasonable good fortune, be on board ship, or even at Quittáh. The thought was intoxicating.

"To speak the truth," I said, "I like not the way in which thou and thy brethren pilfer from the country people."

"We will do so no more," replied Ali persuasively. "We are not now so poor, for we have earned a little here, and thou hast enough for thyself. If we promise to steal from no one wilt thou come with us?"

It was a great temptation.

If I went with them I should be in Cape Coast in three weeks, with all my troubles and hardships behind me, whereas if I waited at Banda it might be weeks before I met with any travellers bound thither, for I had learned that most of the European trade was conducted not with Cape Coast but with Kinjabo (Grand Bassam).

I pondered for a minute, while Ali softly thrummed upon the balafu, and at length succumbed to the temptation.

"Very well," I said. "I have thy promise to pilfer no more. Wait here while I put my things together, and we will start."

It was a fateful resolution.

Chapter Twenty-Two
A Catastrophe

In less than an hour we were on the road, stepping out briskly towards the south. A good store of provisions was in our scrip, and we had that comfortable feeling of being independent of the vicissitudes of the hour that accompanies a well-lined purse.

The musicians strode on ahead, Osman leading, and as they went they chattered gaily, and broke out from time to time in snatches of song. Aminé and I walked some distance behind that we might talk more freely, for neither of us felt any desire to increase our intimacy with the minstrels.

"Yúsufu," said Aminé suddenly, when we had left the town behind, "what was it that thou hadst in thy hand when Abduláhi and I came upon thee sitting under the tree?"

"In my hand?" I repeated, considerably disconcerted by the question.

"Yes. Thou didst hide it when I spoke, so I said nothing, because Abduláhi was there."

I was surprised at her discretion, and after a moment's reflection decided to get the explanation over at once. I therefore drew out the locket (which I had not yet sewn up in its hiding place) and opened it. Aminé gazed at the two faces in blank amazement, and for a time spoke not a word.

"What is it?" she asked at length; "is it witchcraft?" and then with sudden suspicion, "who are they? Who is the woman?"

"She is the maid who is to be my wife," I replied, feeling about as comfortable as a polar bear might in a Turkish bath, and perspiring almost as freely. "The old man is her father."

"Thy wife!" exclaimed Aminé hoarsely. "Thou toldest me nothing of this!"

She made a sudden snatch at the locket, which I narrowly evaded, and hastened to stow the precious bauble out of harm's way.

"I will get that thing and fling it in the fire," Aminé declared in a voice husky with anger, "and as to the woman, I will kill her when I meet her."

I made no reply, being not a little distressed at the turn things were taking.

"Why didst not thou tell me?" Aminé continued passionately, "that thou hadst a beautiful wife, one far more handsome than me? I would not have come with thee. Abduláhi would have taken me gladly."

I wished most fervently that he had, but held my peace.

Suddenly she burst into a storm of sobs, beating her breast and moaning aloud, and tearing the coral necklace asunder, she flung it down in the road.

I feigned not to see this, and presently she went back and picked it up, but she did not again overtake me but continued to follow some twenty or thirty yards behind.

Throughout the day she maintained an attitude of sullen aloofness, never coming near me nor speaking unless under actual necessity, and when she was compelled to address me she spoke with a gruff curtness in extreme contrast to her usual soft and winning manner. Her altered behaviour was viewed with but ill-concealed amusement by the musicians, and Ali took the opportunity to adopt a highly insinuating and sympathetic manner towards her; but his attempts to fish in troubled waters met with no better result than a vehemently uttered threat on her part to break his skull with a large stone.

The Golden Pool

Late in the afternoon we turned off the road on which we had been travelling, and took a small and indistinct track, which Osman informed me would shorten our journey by a couple of days, and which presently brought us to a tiny hamlet on the bank of the River Tain – a large tributary of the Firráo or Volta. Here Aminé obtained for herself and me a house which stood in a small compound of its own, and she commenced to prepare our meal, leaving the minstrels to make their own arrangements. When the meal was ready she took it into the house, and set it before me in silence; but instead of sitting down with me to share it, she went out into the compound and supped alone by the fire.

By the time I had finished eating the night had closed in and the hut was in darkness, but presently Aminé brought in a large shea butter lamp or candle and set it on the floor; then she cleared away the remains of the food, and again left me in solitude.

For a long time I sat cross-legged at the end of my mat, watching the shadows dance upon the walls as the unsteady flame flickered in the draught, meditating gloomily upon this new complication in my affairs, and wondering what the end of it would be. My reflections were at length interrupted by the entrance of Aminé, who walked straight up to my mat, and, kneeling down upon it, laid her head upon my feet.

"Wilt thou forgive me, Yúsufu?" she asked meekly, "for the wrong that I have done thee? I was vexed when thou didst show me the face of thy wife, and I saw that she was so fair to look upon, for I feared that thou wouldst love her only and not me. I will trouble thee no more, my husband, nor make strife in thy house, and the beautiful woman shall be as my sister, and I will even be subject to her, and serve her as her bond-maid if it please thee, so that thou shalt love me too. Wilt thou not forgive me, seeing that I am but a woman, and that my folly ariseth out of my love for thee?"

She raised a piteous face to me, and her big eyes were swimming with tears as she made her humble appeal. As to me, I was too much overcome to be capable of any reply, and giving way to a natural, though insane, impulse, I took her head in my hands, and laid her cheek against mine. She uttered a sigh of profound content, and presently rose, and, spreading her mat near mine, curled herself up upon it and there lay, not sleeping, but watching me like some devoted terrier basking upon a rug, with one fond eye fixed upon its master.

I was deeply affected, and very angry with myself, for by thus weakly yielding to my emotion, natural though it was, I had made the situation far worse than it was before, and the bitter disillusionment had to be begun all over again. And then how pitiful it was to see all this noble and faithful love running to waste in a world where it is so precious and so rare; when so many have to pass through life uncared for and alone.

When I came out of the hut in the morning I found Aminé dressed in her old *túrkedi,* holding a review of our household goods, which were spread out on her mat.

"I have been thinking," she said, "that it seemeth a pity for us to be wearing our fine clothes on this rough journey through the forest, so I have put on my old *túrkedi*. Wilt thou, too, not wear thy old *riga* and *wondo,* and let me put the fine ones in a bundle and carry them?"

It seemed a reasonable suggestion, so taking the old clothing into the hut, I made the change.

"It would be well," said she, as she folded my embroidered *riga,* "to put in the bundle all that thou needest not for use on the road, so that thou shalt walk more easily."

To this I also agreed, and laid on the mat my watch, pistol, and cartridge box, my purse with the remaining money in it, the bag of gold dust that I had received from Musa, and a few other odds and ends. I kept out a bag of *kurdi* for our immediate wants, and I wore my two knives – my original knife and the one I had obtained in the mine – stuck through the waistband of my *wondo*. The locket I had already hastily stitched into its case, and this hung round my neck.

As Aminé was putting the finishing touches to the bundle, I strolled towards the gate of the compound, and was just stepping out, when Ali strode up hurriedly and with an air of confusion for which I could not at the moment account.

"I have come to look for thee, thou sluggard," said he boisterously. "Wilt thou keep us waiting for ever?

"I am going to find our landlord, that I may pay him for our lodgings," I replied, but at that moment the man himself appeared and saluted me civilly. I thanked him (in Hausa – which he did not understand) for the loan of his house, and presented him with a handful of cowries, which he received with lively tokens of gratitude, and as Aminé was now waiting with our entire effects upon her head, we made our way to the river, picking up Osman and Baku on the way.

We forded the Tain without difficulty, for there was barely four feet of water in the middle, the river being now at its lowest; but the high, steep banks showed us what a volume it swelled to in the wet season, and we saw that, had we been a month later, it would have been quite impassable. For we were now at the very end of the dry season, and, indeed, one or two showers had fallen while we were at Banda.

The track along which we travelled became more and more obscure as we went on, but Osman picked his way along it with the confidence of a skilled pathfinder. I noted, however, with some concern, that in spite of his promise that we should keep to the more open orchard country, we were already entering the outskirts of the forest. Another thing I noticed before we had been long on the road, and that was that we had evidently crossed a water parting, for the brooks and little streams that we forded in the early part of the day all ran towards the north-east, evidently going to join the Tain, but about midday we began to meet tiny streams meandering away to the south-west; and in the afternoon we crossed a more considerable – though still small – river, three times in rapid succession, after which it turned westward, and we saw it no more. About an hour after we had crossed this river the sky became suddenly overcast, and the chill of approaching rain was sensible in the air, while the forest was filled with the strange continuous murmur of moving leaves that foretells a storm.

We had passed no village or sign of habitation since leaving the Tain, and Osman assured us that we should meet with none until late on the morrow.

"Wherefore," said he, "we had better make ourselves a shelter against the storm as quickly as we can."

On hearing this we lost no time, but forthwith set about collecting the necessary materials, the minstrels and I cutting long sticks for the framework, while Aminé, armed with one of my knives, mowed down the high elephant grass of the opening in which we were to camp, thus at once clearing a space for the huts, and accumulating a pile of cut grass with which to thatch them. We worked with such a will that in less than an hour we had two tiny wigwam-like huts erected in the middle of the opening, where, if they were more exposed to the rain, they were safe from the principal danger – that of falling trees.

We had just finished the huts and piled inside one of them as many dry sticks as we had been able to find, when the storm burst and the rain fell in torrents. But in spite of the threatening signs of its approach, it was but a small affair after all, and in half an hour the sun was shining again, and there was every promise of a fine night.

"That is well over," observed Ali, putting his head out of the low doorway of his hut. "We can make us a fire outside now, and cook us some food."

"There is mighty little to cook," said Baku, following his leader into the outer air. "It is a pity that we did not stop to catch some of the fish that were swimming about in the river. There were plenty of them, and fine, large ones too."

"For that matter," said Osman, "we might go and catch some now while Aminé tends the fire. I have some hooks that I bought at Táari."

"It is a long way back," I objected.

"We need not go back," replied Osman. "The river is not far from here; I can show thee quite a short way. It should be good fishing after the rain."

"Then we should have to leave Aminé all alone," I said.

"I do not mind being left," said she. "You will be back by the time it is dark. Go and catch some fish while I get the fire ready to cook it."

I at length agreed to "go a-angling" with the musicians, and in a few minutes had made the necessary preparations. A wicker bag – Aminé's original caterpillar bag, in fact – fitted with a sling of creeper, answered as a creel; a ball of cotton yarn from Aminé's private bundle would serve as a line, and Osman had a dozen or so of large, coarse hooks. With these appliances, and such bait as we might pick up, it would be possible to capture some of the fish, provided they were of an unusually unsophisticated and confiding nature.

Osman's short cut to the river turned out as disappointing as short cuts generally do. We scrambled through the thick undergrowth, pushing through thorny bushes and tripping up over the sprawling roots of great trees, but making very little headway, and the manner in which we twisted and turned and altered our course made me fear that Osman had lost his way.

"We should have done better to go by the road," I grumbled, as I extricated myself from the grapnels of a climbing palm; "we should have been there by now, and with less labour."

"The way is rough, indeed," Osman admitted, "but we are nearly there."

He pushed on ahead and disappeared among the trees, and sure enough in a few minutes we heard his cheery announcement: "Here we are; here is the river at last, and here are the fish too, swarms of them."

The conditions were certainly favourable enough for sport, for the river, swollen by the rain, was now swift and turbid, and even through the muddy water we could see the fish snapping at the floating insects and debris that had been swept into the stream.

Nor was there any scarcity of bait, for snails, large and small, crept upon every bush, and caterpillars and grubs could be collected by the dozen.

Osman served out to each of us four hooks, while I furnished the others with lengths of cotton yarn, and soon we were fully equipped, with the spare hooks stuck in our *rigas*. A fat, green caterpillar served me for bait, and with my spear as a rod I proceeded to make a trial cast.

The fish were truly most confiding. Quite unsuspicious of the thick white yarn and the great hook, they proceeded to gorge the wriggling bait and came up spluttering on to the bank in the greatest astonishment. It was magnificent, but it was not sport; however, the basket soon began to wax heavy, and visions of broiled fish floated across my mental horizon.

"Where are Ali and Osman?" I asked of Baku, who was fishing a few yards away from me.

"They are farther down, just by the bend," he replied.

"If they have been as successful as thou and I, they will have nearly enough," I said, for I had seen Baku hooking the fish out even faster than I was doing. "We must not stay too long, or we shall have the darkness upon us."

"That is true," he answered. "I shall go and collect a few more caterpillars, and then when I have caught three more fish I shall angle no more."

He wound up his line and began searching the bushes, among which I soon lost sight of him. I had just stowed a specially large fish in my basket when, looking up, it seemed to me that the light was beginning to fail.

"Come, Baku," I called out; "here is the evening closing in, and we have to get back. We must start at once."

He did not answer.

"Where art thou, Baku?" I called again, raising my voice, as I wound up my line and stuck the hook in my *riga*.

There was still no answer.

"Ho, there!" I shouted. "Ali! Osman! Where are you all?"

I listened, but not a sound came back but the cry of a hornbill that had been startled by my shout.

With a sudden pang of suspicion I ran along the bank looking in all directions and shouting at the top of my voice, but no sign of my companions was to be seen nor did my shouts evoke any answer. They had gone, and the stealthy manner of their departure filled me alike with anger and anxiety. For when I would have followed them I realised that I had but the vaguest idea of the direction in which the camp lay. The devious manner in which we had approached the river had completely bewildered me, and I dared not trust myself to plunge into the pathless forest in search of so small a point as our opening. There was only one thing to be done; I must work my way up the river and endeavour to identify the place where we had crossed it, and this would be difficult enough, for, as I have said, the path on which we had been travelling was but an obscure and unfrequented track, and it was now rapidly growing dark. Moreover, I had no means of judging how far I was from the ford, whether it was but a few hundred yards away or a dozen miles; I could not even be certain that this was the same river, although I felt very little doubt that it was.

I at once commenced a systematic examination of the banks, working my way slowly upstream – for the ford undoubtedly lay in that direction – and the more I searched, the more hopeless did the task appear. The night came on apace, and soon I could barely see the ground without stooping. Once or twice I struck off on what I thought looked like a trail, but after following it for a hundred yards or more, found myself in impenetrable bush. And every moment my anxiety grew more and more intense.

As I recalled the incidents of the day the evidence of a settled plot became so manifest that I marvelled at my blindness. I remembered Ali's confusion when I encountered him at the compound gate, where he had without doubt been watching through the fence as Aminé packed the valuables in her bundle; I perceived that Osman's pretended short cut to the river through the trackless bush was but a device to prevent me from finding my way back; and again the sinister question presented itself: "What was their object in all this?" That they intended to make off with the gold was obvious, but what about Aminé? Would they drag her off with them, or would they leave her alone and helpless in the wilderness? With these questions I continued to torture myself, cursing my folly in having associated myself with these villains after what I had seen of them, and still searching with a sinking heart for any trace of our trail on the banks.

It had been dark more than two hours, during which time I had toiled painfully along the brink of the river, now wading in the shallows and now climbing the rugged banks, oblivious alike of the stampede of startled antelopes and the angry growls of beasts of prey, when the rising moon threw a shaft of pale red light through the trees; and at the same moment I seemed to recognise something familiar in the surroundings.

I gazed at the banks and perceived that they shelved in the same manner as I remembered them to have done at the ford. Trembling with mingled hope and anxiety, I eagerly examined the ground by the wan moonlight; and suddenly my heart gave a bound, for there in the soft earth was a familiar little oblong depression, and near it a footprint. The depression was the mark of the heel iron of my spear, as I now made certain by fitting the iron into it, and the little track, indistinct as it was, could yet be made out, meandering away into the forest.

Having definitely ascertained that this was really the path, I hurried forward as fast as I dared in the dim moonlight – for the track in places almost completely disappeared – my anxiety becoming keener with every moment that passed; but with all my haste, a full hour passed, and yet no sign of the camp appeared. A dreadful fear that I had strayed from the track began to be added to my other troubles, and grew momentarily more acute.

Suddenly a breath of wind in my face brought with it the scent of burning wood, and a minute later I perceived through the trees the glow of a fire. In a tumult of excitement I broke into a run, and almost immediately came out into the opening by the two huts.

The large untended fire and the silence of the camp struck me with a chill of foreboding. I rushed forward, calling loudly to Aminé, and, receiving no answer, dragged aside the thatch of our hut and crept in trembling with fear, and reaching out my hand touched a soft, chilly arm.

"Who is it?" I gasped. "Is it thou, Aminé?" and then, receiving no reply, I dashed out of the hut, and snatching a great faggot from the fire, ran back, blowing it into a flame.

Great God! What was this?

It was indeed Aminé!

Aminé with limp disordered limbs, and blind, staring eyes, with a little pool of blood by her side, and a gaping wound in her breast!

For a full minute I knelt transfixed, holding the shaking brand over her face; then with a hoarse cry I rushed from the hut and flung myself on the earth.

I thought my last moments had come, and that I must die where I lay. My head seemed bursting; a roaring was in my ears, and lights danced before my eyes.

As I slowly recovered, the shock of overwhelming horror and grief became mingled with an access of fury that threatened my reason. I stalked up and down before the huts, shaking my fists and cursing aloud like a maniac. If I could have laid my hands at that moment on the murderers, there is no act of ferocious cruelty of which I should not have been capable. Merely to tear them limb from limb or hack them into pieces would have seemed too merciful, in the passion of hatred and rage that now possessed me, and I have since been thankful that I did not then encounter them, for I should certainly have disgraced my civilisation with some horrid act of barbaric vengeance.

Presently I grew calmer, and setting a cotton wick – torn from my *riga* – to one of the balls of shea butter that lay in her brass cooking pan near the fire, I made a lamp and carried it into the hut.

Poor child! Poor faithful heart! Was it for this that I had brought her through so many perils and hardships, away from the promise of a home in some far away Hausa city, where she might have shared the love of some husband of her own race and seen her children grow up around her? In a passion of sorrow and bitter regret I stooped and kissed the cold cheek of the sweet barbarian, and knew for the first time how dear she had become to me with her simple faith and love, so childlike and yet so womanly.

As to the details of the foul deed, they were now obvious and plain. The fishing excursion had been deliberately planned to get me out of the way, and Osman's devious wanderings to and fro in the forest were doubtless designed to confuse me as to our direction (for probably the river was really close at hand, as he had said). When we arrived at the river, Ali and Osman must have hurried back almost immediately, while Baku remained for a time to occupy my attention. No doubt the two villains had endeavoured to persuade Aminé to accompany them in their flight (for Ali had ever cast a greedy eye on the handsome Fulah girl), and on her refusing and retreating to the hut to protect our valuables, they had followed her and silenced her resistance by stabbing her to the heart. As to which of them was the actual murderer I had little doubt, but any that I had was quickly resolved, for one of the hands of the poor dead maid was closed and seemed to grasp something, and on my gently opening it I took out a wisp of hair and a couple of red glass beads. Now, the three musicians wore, after the Wongára fashion, a plait of hair on each side of the face. Osman's plaits were plain, Baku's were ornamented with threads of coloured cotton, while Ali had decorated each of his plaits with a bunch of red glass beads.

If curses could have killed, the villainous balafu player would never again have looked upon the daylight, for I heaped upon him every malediction that my lips could frame or my heart conceive, and I swore that if ever I met him, even though it were under the very walls of the castle, he should not escape until he had paid his debt to the uttermost farthing.

Curses, however, could not undo the dreadful deed nor bring back life to the poor chill body, and there remained the last sad offices to be performed for the lost companion of my wanderings. These I set about with the tears streaming down my face, and many a choking sob, as I recalled the little incidents of our comradeship, and especially the affecting scene of the previous night; reverently I composed the contorted limbs, and closed the eyes that had looked on me with such fond devotion, and with my broad spearhead began to turn up the earth in the floor of the hut.

It was but a shallow grave that I could dig with my imperfect appliances, for the soil was gravelly and hard, and the greater part of the night was spent before the narrow trench was hollowed out. By that time the last of the shea butter was burnt out, and I was faint from want of food, so I went out, and, laying a few of the fish upon the red embers, waited for the dawn, unmindful of the hyenas that prowled, moaning and snuffling around the camp.

As the first pale glimmer appeared above the trees, I went back to the hut. The little clay tablet that the poor child had so prized still hung in its bag around her neck. I untied the string and transferred it to my own neck, and having cut off one of the long soft plaits of which she was so justly proud, I lifted the dead girl and tenderly laid her in her narrow bed, spreading her *túrkedi* over her and tucking it around her that I might not see the cold earth fall upon her body. Then I filled in the grave and piled the little mound of earth over her, and going out, securely closed up the doorway of the hut.

The rest of the day I resolved to spend collecting stones with which to build a cairn over the grave, for I could not bear to think of her resting place being desecrated by the ghoul-like beasts of the night.

I had for a moment had a wild idea of going in pursuit of the murderers, but the futility of this was so apparent that I immediately abandoned it; for apart from the fact that they had many hours' start, I could not tell whether they had gone forward or backward, and it was quite certain that they would take effectual means to avoid being overtaken. I therefore broiled the remainder of the fish, and when I had eaten it and piled up the fire with green wood, I took my mat into the vacant hut to sleep awhile before resuming my labours.

I did not sleep more than two or three hours, notwithstanding my fatigue, for the sun was near the zenith when I arose, and as I wished to complete my task before night, I set to work without delay. There are plenty of large stones to be picked up in most parts of the forest, for the heavy rains lay bare the rocky subsoil wherever there is much slope, so I had little difficulty in finding the material for the cairn, although it was heavy work carrying what I had collected to the camp.

In one of my excursions I took my way, with the wicker bag, down the path that led from the camp, as I had observed the ground to be more stony in that direction, and I had walked barely half a mile when I came to the river, which here made a sweep to the east and then turned away westward again. At this point there was a small rapid, and the bed of the stream was full of water-worn fragments of rock, most of them of considerable size. With these I filled up my bag, but before returning to the camp I baited a couple of my hooks with fragments of snail and secured the lines to overhanging branches so that the baited hooks nearly touched the bottom.

I made several journeys to the river, returning each time with a bag of stones on my head, a number of others in my pocket, and a big one under each arm, and in the course of the afternoon I caught four good-sized fish. The day's wants being thus provided for, I proceeded with my melancholy task, and before nightfall I had built up a cairn over poor Aminé's grave that nearly covered the floor of the little hut, and had moreover strengthened the hut itself with a number of thorny branches, which I hoped would effectually prevent the beasts from tearing it open. The short remainder of the daylight I spent in making more secure the hut in which I was to sleep, and in collecting an abundance of firewood; and when the darkness at length closed in I cooked my frugal meal and then made up the fire. I did not turn in for a long time, but sat by the fire, in the blackest dejection, gazing at the crackling sticks, meditating upon my forlorn and hopeless condition, and thinking of the poor murdered girl who lay under the cairn, whom but yesterday I was so anxious to be rid of, and whose cheerful prattle I would have given so much to listen to again.

At length, as I felt that I was becoming sleepy and the prowling beasts were stealing up on all sides, I again fed the fire and banked it up with grass and sods of earth, and retiring to my hut, secured the doorway with strong lashings of creeper.

But I spent a miserable and unrestful night, for as soon as the fire burned low the camp was filled with the most hellish uproar, and several times a vigorous scratching at the frail wall of my hut had to be stopped by a thrust of my spear between the frame poles. Towards morning, however, the hubbub subsided, and I fell into a sound sleep from which I did not waken until the sunlight was streaming in through the chinks in the thatch.

Chapter Twenty-Three
I Make a Curious Discovery

When I came to review my situation as I raked together the almost extinct embers of last night's fire, and coaxed them into life with dry twigs and charred fragments, I could not but be dismayed at the difficulties and perils with which I was surrounded.

Here I was, alone in the wilderness, without a morsel of provisions, totally ignorant of the locality, quite unacquainted with the speech of the forest peoples, and with but a hazy idea of the direction in which I should turn my steps. True, I knew that far away to the south lay the Gulf of Guinea and the European settlements; but between me and the coast lay the whole width of the forest and the kingdom of Ashanti.

I might perhaps succeed in making intelligible to the forest villagers an inquiry as to the way to Cape Coast, but my judgement urged me to give all villages a wide berth in my solitary and unprotected condition. Then I might – taking the sun and stars as my guide – strike due south, when sooner or later I must reach the sea – if I were allowed to pass unmolested; but my experience of the treatment of solitary strangers was far from reassuring, while the stories I had heard of the sacrificial customs of Ashanti – stories that I had largely verified – made a journey through that country seem a forlorn hope indeed.

On the other hand I might, of course, retrace my steps, and endeavour to overtake Musa and his people; but this would be to renew and extend my wanderings into the interior of the continent, of which I was by this time heartily sick. Besides, my mission was accomplished; I had found the treasure and tested the truth of the narrative in Captain Hogg's journal, and now I yearned for the sight of a white face, longed to hear the voices of my friends and to be among people of my own race.

No! However great the dangers, and however many the obstacles, the passage of the forest must be made. The sea was my goal, and I must keep my face resolutely towards the south. But how to reach the sea was a problem that I found myself utterly unable to solve. In the deepest perplexity I turned over the various alternatives that presented themselves without hitting upon any feasible plan of action. The obvious thing, however, being that I must obtain food without delay, and the river furnishing the only means of my doing so, I took my way thither, pursuing my reflections as I went.

Having found a comparatively deep pool some distance below the rapid, I baited my hooks, and flinging them into the water, sat down on the bank to wait for a bite.

Angling has been described by its immortal exponent as "the contemplative man's recreation." Its contemplative character is perhaps apt to be interfered with if the possible catch stands between the angler and starvation; nevertheless, as I sat and watched my hooks, I found myself again picturing in detail the various possibilities of the immediate future. I saw myself, without fire or shelter, slowly starving to death in the wilderness; or, once more bound and captive, borne off to grace some funeral sacrifice at Kumasi or some infernal fetish rites in a forest village. Perhaps I might encounter another slave caravan, or be murdered by wandering natives, or devoured, whilst sleeping, by wild beasts. These things were all possible, and not so very improbable.

I was pursuing my meditations in this cheerful fashion when my attention was arrested by a small object that was floating slowly past. It was an empty achatina shell, buoyed up by a bubble of air in the spire; and as it drifted along on the surface of the quiet, clear water, turning round and round or bobbing up suddenly when some inquisitive fish smelled at it, I found myself watching it with a strange wistfulness, and speculating upon its destination and the incidents of its voyage.

Down the river, ever downwards, it would pursue its noiseless journey; through the lonely forest, past noisy waterside towns and villages; hurrying through blustering rapids, lingering in silent pools, turning in many an eddy and backwater; on, till the river grew broad and the crocodiles basked on the bank; on, till it met the mangrove, and heard the roaring of the bar; and so out into the dancing waters of the ocean where the dolphins were at play, and the great ships spread their sails in the sunshine.

The shell drifted out of sight, and I sighed disconsolately. Where should I be when it reached its destination on the surf-beaten shore?

Suddenly there came into my mind a new thought. Why should not I also make the river my highway? It led to the sea, I knew. Why should I not make myself some raft or coracle and drift down the stream, too, like the infant Moses or the Lady of Shalott? I grinned sardonically at the whimsical idea – and yet it was less impracticable than any other plan that I could think of. Indeed, the more I thought about it the more did it commend itself to me, and my imagination soon began to fill in details of the scheme. The river would not only be my guide to the sea; it would carry me without fatigue on my part, and furnish me with food – for I could fish as I went. Then the approaching rains, which would flood the forest lands and make the roads impassable, would fill the river and make it safer by covering rapids and shallows. Finally, I could build a little shelter on my coracle, and thus take my house with me, and so could even travel in the heavy rain, when walking would be impossible.

So strongly did the idea begin to take hold of me, that my excitement made me restless, and as I had now caught two fish, and was secure from immediate starvation, I arose, and winding up my lines, began to wade through the shallows, searching the banks for a suitable place to take up my abode in while the coracle was being made.

The river was, as I have said, but a small stream, formed by the confluence of a number of tiny brooks; but its banks rose pretty steeply for fully seven feet above its present level, showing that in the rains it carried a large body of water. I had wandered down nearly half a mile when I found the banks receding on either side as the river grew rapidly wider, and then the stream appeared to divide into two. At first I supposed that a tributary had entered it, but on going to the fork and observing that the water flowed down each side, I perceived that the river had really divided, and I had no doubt that the central portion of land was an island. In order to ascertain if this was the case I took the left-hand division, scanning the banks closely as I went, and as I proceeded the stream continued to widen out forming a lake-like expanse, the appearance of which impressed me with a strange sense of familiarity. Presently I set my foot upon a hard, smooth body, the feel of which I knew at once. It was an affaní, and as I picked the mollusc up and dropped it into my wicker bag, the chain of association was complete. I felt certain that this was the very place where Bukári Moshi and I had crossed with the bags of gold upon our heads.

With my heart thumping with excitement and anxiety, I splashed across the stream to the bank of what I believed to be the island, and wading along the shore looked for the landing place. Presently I came to a spot where the bank shelved down more gradually, and running up the incline, found at the top a wide stretch of level ground covered with soft moss. Surely this was the place; there could be no doubt about it; but yet so intense was my excitement and my fear of a disappointment that I hardly had the courage to look for the crucial proof. At length I summoned up my nerve, and casting my eyes across the river, at once made out a tall oil palm rising out of the undergrowth, and near to it a lofty silk-cotton. Between the two stems was an opening in the foliage, through which I could see some high ground in the distance. I drew off a few paces to the left, but the two stems approached and came into one line. Then I stepped away to my right, and as the stems separated, the hill became more visible, until suddenly there appeared through the opening a patch of red cliff on the hillside. It was the cliff on which the tunnel opened.

Inch by inch I shifted my position until the red patch appeared midway between the palm and the silk-cotton. Then I stooped, and began frantically driving my knife into the soft moss; and I had scarcely made a dozen stabs when I felt the point arrested by something hard. With a hasty glance around to make sure that my solitude was undisturbed, I cut out a square slab of the moss, and thrusting my hand into the hole, dragged out a bunch of the gold manillas.

Very absurd was the triumph with which I gloated over the precious trash and dusted the black mould from their shining surfaces. Indeed, I could not but be struck by the irony of the situation. Here I was, sitting upon a fortune of some seventy thousand pounds, of which the whole was mine – or, at least, I considered it to be – with death from starvation or exposure staring me in the face! It was a fine commentary upon the worthlessness of riches, to which my gnawing hunger gave a special point; and as my momentary exultation flickered out, I sadly poked the manillas back into the hole, and replaced the moss, carefully pinching the cut edges together.

The treasure was mine indeed, but should I ever possess it? Through what perils and miseries must I pass before I could finally lay hands upon it? I had yet to creep like some belated ancient Briton in a wretched coracle of wicker and skin down an unknown river, through a land swarming with savage beasts and peopled by savage men. Should I ever reach the coast? and if I did, would even this great fortune tempt me again into this loathsome wilderness? Or even if I did come with trusty companions, if the natives permitted us to pass, could I make sure of finding the treasure again? To none of these questions could I give a confident and satisfactory answer, and my short-lived triumph was succeeded by black despair.

Suddenly a new idea flashed into my mind, and although I put it away at once as preposterous, it returned again and again with such insistence that I presently began seriously to entertain it.

It was this.

I had resolved that the river should not only be my guide to the sea, but should actually carry me to my destination. Why should it not carry the treasure, too? If I were lost, then it would matter nothing that the treasure should be lost with me; while if I could succeed in navigating the river, the presence of the treasure need not materially add to the danger. Of course, it would be no wicker-built coracle that would carry half a ton of metal. A really stout canoe would be required, and the construction of this was the main, and almost the only, difficulty. Now, given the materials and appliances, there was no doubt of my ability to build a canoe or boat, since I had both built and rigged the canoe-yawl in which, as I have mentioned, I used to sail around the Thanet coast; but my sole appliances at present were my knives, my spear, and a few needles, and as to materials, they would have to be gathered in the forest.

The question was, therefore, whether it would be possible, with the means at my disposal, to build a canoe of the necessary strength. At the first glance the thing appeared impossible, but I determined to give it careful consideration, for if it could be done, and I could successfully navigate the river, then I could say goodbye, once for all, to the inhospitable forest.

Meanwhile I resolved to shift my residence to the island at once, for whether I built a large canoe or merely a small coracle, this would be a most suitable place in which to carry out the work, not only because of its being actually on the river, but also on account of the improbability of any person visiting it.

The country round, indeed, appeared to be almost uninhabited, for I had not seen a human being since we left Tain-su; but on the mainland there was always the possibility that a chance stranger might appear, whereas the island was almost completely secure from intrusion.

Before returning to the camp I looked round for an "eligible building site". The island was about a hundred and fifty yards long by fifty broad. It was mostly above the level of the banks of the river (and therefore above the flood level), but at the end near which the treasure was buried there was a central hollow or miniature valley, and this I pitched upon as the site for my hut, as the higher ground on each side would conceal it from anyone walking by the river. As a first instalment of furniture, I carried a number of stones to the spot, and laid them down as a hearth in readiness for the fire. Then, having collected a dozen or so of affaní, I made my way back to the camp, which I found to be little over a mile distant.

While the fish and affaní were roasting, I occupied myself in taking down the hut that the musicians had built, for it would be quicker to carry the materials to the island than to cut and collect fresh ones. Then I ate my all too frugal meal, and, having devoured the last morsel, even to the fishes' heads, I made preparations for the removal.

My first care was the fire – for although I had once kindled a fire by means of the drill, I might not succeed a second time, and I meant to take no risks. I therefore scooped up all the red embers and charcoal into Aminé's brass pan, piling up as much as it would hold, and gathered up the faggots into a bundle with their glowing ends together. Then, setting the pan upon my head, which I protected with a pad of grass, and taking the bundle of faggots in my hands like a huge torch, I ran off towards the island like some African Solomon Eagle.

The faggots were still alight, and the embers in the pan still glowing when I reached my new abode, and I at once proceeded to build up my fire after the fashion that I had learned from the Hausas. The art of making and maintaining a fire with green wood is a very simple one, but requires to be practised with method. The important thing is to place the faggots like the spokes of a wheel with the burning ends at the centre. Thus each faggot becomes dried by the heat, and the fire slowly spreads outwards, becoming more and more dull as the burning ends become more widely separated; but built in this way it will burn without attention for an incredible time, and when almost extinct, it can be revived in a moment by simply pushing the faggots forward until their ends meet in the central heap of embers and hot ashes.

I tipped out my pan of charcoal on to the hearth, and arranged the faggots in the way I have described, and soon had the satisfaction of seeing a well established fire in my new camp. It took me two more journeys to transport the poles and thatch of the hut, and as I came away with the last load, I looked round sadly at the little grassy oasis in the forest. It was now to be left desolate and deserted. A large white patch of ashes and poor Aminé's primitive mausoleum alone remained as memorials of the dreadful tragedy that it had witnessed.

The remainder of the day was spent in fishing, collecting firewood, and re-erecting the hut, which I did not build in its original beehive form, but in a conical shape like that of a bell tent. I constructed it without a centre post because, as my stay on the island might be a prolonged one, I intended to build a larger house for permanent use, and this conical hut would then serve to make the fire in, so that it might not be extinguished by a night's rain.

Through the long evening as I sat by the fire I considered and reconsidered my wild scheme of carrying away the treasure, and as I turned it over, its difficulties – so insuperable at first sight – began to melt away, while its attractions grew upon me, and, when I at last banked up the fire and turned in, I had made up my mind not to abandon the plan until I had tried it and found it impossible to carry out.

Daybreak saw me hard at work on my new residence, a building of much more ambitious and extensive design; for in a tropical country with nearly twelve hours of darkness out of the twenty-four, life would be intolerable with no better shelter than the tiny conical hut afforded, and I could not at present judge how long my labours might detain me on the island. A reasonable amount of comfort and convenience was indispensable, and with this view I decided to build the new house in the square Ashanti style – a much more commodious form than the conical or beehive shape. As to the dimensions, the floor space was to be, roughly, ten feet by eight, the height to the ridge of the roof six feet six inches, and the height to the eaves three feet. This was a very different affair from the little temporary huts that I had hitherto made. The mere cutting of the poles and the creepers for lashings was a work of some hours, and I had not completely finished setting up the framework when the light failed, and the long evening's idleness commenced.

While I had been at work I had left my baited lines pegged down near a spot which I had ground-baited with the offal from my meals, visiting them from time to time, and so had a fair supply of fish for my supper; but this diet was both scanty and monotonous, and I felt that some better arrangements would have to be made in regard to board as well as lodging.

When I came to survey the result of my day's work on the following morning, before recommencing my labours, I was not a little pleased to see how much was done. The frame was nearly complete, and looked like a huge wicker birdcage, but it stood firm, and was stiff and strong, and the interior seemed very large and roomy. Half an hour's work sufficed to finish the framework, and then came the tedious task of clothing the skeleton. I did not propose to use thatch, for grass was scarce in the forest; but leaves were abundant enough, and it seemed to me would answer the purpose better. I had noticed, in particular, a creeper that shrouded almost every tree trunk, and bore stout, glossy leaves nearly a foot long. These – of which I could gather as many as I wanted – would be almost as good as shingles for the roof, while the flexible stems could be split to furnish lashings. I accordingly collected a quantity of this creeper, and fastened the broad leaves in overlapping rows on to the roof and gables; but although I worked steadily from daybreak to sunset, with but short intervals of fishing and firewood cutting, when the darkness closed in I had only the roof and gables finished. However, as the night looked threatening, and I was uneasy about the fire, I moved into the unfinished house, and transferred the blazing faggots to the interior of the conical hut; and it was well that I did so, for that night the rain fell for a short time in such torrents that, had the fire been exposed, it must inevitably have been put out.

Another hard day's work saw my house completed, and not only completed, but furnished; for in addition to a door – three feet high by two broad – which could be firmly secured by a lashing, it boasted a bedstead – a structure of sticks much resembling a wooden gridiron on eight small posts, on which I could spread my mats, and sleep clear of the damp ground.

In this palatial residence I took up my abode in state as soon as it was dark, and by way of making it more cheerful, kindled a fire in the middle of the floor, by which I got not only light – and a great deal of smoke – but a warmth that was most grateful, for the nights were now damp and very chilly.

Here, upon my new bed, I sat through the long evening, with the door shut and fastened, and the flickering flames lighting up the little interior, uncommonly elated at finding myself so comfortably housed, and full of enthusiasm for the work that the morrow was to see begun. For now that I had a comfortable home, the building of the canoe must be pushed forward with all speed, so that I could make my dash for the coast as soon as the river was full.

Long that night I sat cogitating upon my scheme, and as it took more definite shape and details suggested themselves, I covered my dirty white *riga* with figures and diagrams scrawled on it with a stump of charcoal from the fire. The problem to be worked out was simple enough. The weight of the gold I estimated at half a ton; it could hardly be more, for Bukári and I had carried it from the mine to the river in five journeys, each carrying, of course, a tenth part of the whole treasure. My own weight was eleven stone – probably less now – or a hundred and fifty-four pounds, making, with the gold, a total of twelve hundred and seventy-four pounds. This weight added to the weight of the canoe itself, represented the displacement of the vessel when fully loaded, that is to say, the loaded canoe would displace, in floating, this weight of water. Now a cubic foot of water weighs sixty-two and a half pounds, or a little less in the Tropics. Calling it sixty-two, to be on the safe side, the gold would displace eighteen cubic feet of water, and my body would displace two and a half, a total of twenty and a half cubic feet without reckoning the weight of the canoe.

This was not in itself an alarming amount. A canoe twelve feet long by three wide, and drawing one foot of water, will displace about twenty-four cubic feet, and these dimensions were considerably less than those of the canoe-yawl that I had built at Ramsgate. But there was the weight of the vessel itself – which must be strong to carry this weight, and withstand the rough usage that it would certainly meet with – and this I could hardly estimate until I had decided on the materials of which it was to be made. Reckoning it, however, provisionally at three hundred-weight (which was probably excessive), a canoe twelve feet long by three and a half wide, and drawing one foot, would answer the purpose, for a vessel of these dimensions would displace twenty-nine cubic feet of water, or three cubic feet more than was necessary.

The question of materials had next to be considered. Of what was the canoe to be made? A "dugout" or hollowed log I at once rejected, for not only is such a vessel clumsy and very heavy, but the making of one involves the felling of a tree, the shaping of the log, and the digging out of its interior – a task quite beyond my powers, seeing that my entire outfit of tools consisted of two knives, a spear, and the packet of large needles that I had bought at Táari.

Evidently the canoe would have to be made on the principle of a coracle – a framework of wicker or lashed sticks with a covering of some sort, and this covering was the real crux of the situation. As to the frame, I felt confident of being able to build that without difficulty, but the covering gave me pause.

The Britons covered their coracles with hide, but it was tanned hide, which I could not procure. The Eskimo cover their canoes with untanned skin; but they navigate frozen seas, whereas the tepid waters of the Tropics would reduce such skin to putrefying pulp in forty-eight hours. Suddenly I bethought me of the birch bark canoes of the Redskins, and with a thrill of exultation I felt that the difficulty was solved. For the forest abounded in the Honton tree, to the tough, canvas-like bark of which Isaaku had introduced me; and this material, easy to obtain and to work, would form an ideal covering or skin for my canoe. It was true that the bark was rather porous, and so not very watertight, but it would be hard if I could not devise some means for filling the pores. At any rate, the main difficulty was disposed of, and with a sigh of satisfaction I lay down upon the mat that covered my bed, and drawing Aminé's mat over me by way of bedclothes, settled myself for the night.

Chapter Twenty-Four
I Return to an Old Trade

As I took my way into the forest soon after daybreak I felt that sense of exhilaration that accompanies a settled purpose. The building of the house had been a necessary labour, but it had delayed me and hindered the execution of my plans. Now I was to begin the actual building of the canoe, and with the commencement of this work my deliverance seemed to come within measurable distance.

The forest is a boat-builder's paradise. Whatever kind of timber is required, whether large or small, curved or straight, it is to be had for the cutting. The great trees – which did not concern me – tower aloft and spread their crowns of foliage like flat-topped umbrellas, two hundred feet from the ground; and towards the chinks of sky between their giant canopies, multitudes of saplings of all sizes crane up, as smooth, as straight, and as slender as fishing rods, while lianas or creepers, varying from the thickness of a pack-thread to that of a man's thigh, hang from tree to tree in great festoons, twining around trunk and branch, and twisting round one another in every conceivable curve and contortion.

If a spar or a straight timber is wanted, all that is necessary is to select a sapling of suitable thickness and cut off the length required, while for a curved timber a liana of the requisite size can be selected and the portion cut out that presents the curve required. On the present occasion I contented myself with the cutting of a good bundle of stout straight rods and a quantity of thin liana to serve as cordage, devoting myself especially to a critical examination of the trees viewed in the light of boat building material; and I was relieved at meeting with no less than three specimens of the Hon-ton tree, any two of which would, on a pinch, have yielded sufficient bark to cover my canoe.

My first labour, on returning with my load of poles, was to erect a set of four trestles, forming a rough staging on which to build the canoe and from which to launch it when it was finished; and in order to render the launch more easy I made the ways with a slight slope towards the water. The place where the staging was erected was by a small bay at the bottom of the valley in which my house was situated – indeed, the ways were only a dozen yards from the door of the house. Here the ground was somewhat swampy and was evidently submerged during the rainy season, so I felt secure against the attacks of the white ants, which, in a drier situation, might have come up in the night and devoured both staging and canoe.

This work, with the necessary intervals for attending to my fishing lines, cooking the fish, and preparing firewood, took up most of the day, and I determined to devote the remainder to felling a young odúm tree that I had noted growing near the middle of the island. It stood some fifty feet high, and was nine or ten inches in diameter at the base – a considerable thickness to hack through with a knife, especially as the wood is very hard and tough; but it had a fine crown of branches at its summit, which would furnish nearly all the straight wood that I should want, so the labour of felling it would be well spent. However, the darkness came when I had hacked but half through the trunk, and I had to leave it to finish on the morrow.

That night, as I sat by the firelight in my house, I continued to perfect the design of my canoe; but also I gave some serious thought to the question of food, for the diet of fish was becoming excessively distasteful, to say nothing of the shortness of the supply. I was loth to waste my precious time in seeking provisions, but I must be fed or I could not work; so at last I reluctantly made up my mind to give up the ensuing day, or part of it, to a search for fresh food.

Accordingly, on the following morning, after setting my lines and making up the fire, I sharpened my spear upon a slab of sandstone that I had picked up in the bed of the river, and crossed the shallows to the side of the river that was most distant from the hill. Plunging at once into the forest, I went forward softly, peering in all directions and keeping a careful eye upon the shadows so that I should not lose my way. It was a most tantalising place to a hungry man, for it abounded in game, and fruit was fairly plentiful; but the game – mostly hornbills and parrots – was up in the far-away treetops, and the fruit was all strange, and I dared not taste it lest it should be poisonous. Presently, however, I had a stroke of luck, for I came to a tree the trunk of which was covered with a trailing vine bearing numbers of globular fruit somewhat like oranges. I was much tempted to try one of these, and was standing before them irresolute, with watering mouth, when a pair of Diana monkeys came down the creeper, hand over hand, and each picked one of the fruit and retreated to the top regions, where I saw them seat themselves on a branch and nibble off pieces of peel which they spat down on to me. Concluding that what was wholesome for a monkey could not be poisonous to me, I cut off a couple of branches, each bearing a bunch of the fruit, and dropping one bunch into my pocket sat down among the roots of a tree to breakfast off the remaining bunch. As I proceeded with my meal I noticed that a thick milky juice was exuding freely from the cut end of the branch, and before I had finished eating, this sap had begun to grow thicker and more tenacious. Much interested, I was examining the sticky exudation more closely when my attention was diverted by the sound of something moving among the bushes.

I listened. Something – beast or human – was certainly approaching, and was not far off. Very silently I rose to my feet and stood close against the tree, stealthily peeping round the shaded side. As I did so I saw, on a patch of bare earth, a shadow, the appearance of which startled me considerably for the moment, for it exactly resembled the head of the horned image near the Aboási pool. It was not the Sakrobundi devil, however, as I immediately realised, but an antelope with curved horns – probably the demon's prototype.

I stepped back a pace and stood with my spear poised ready to throw. The shadow came nearer, vanished for a space, and then reappeared on the other side of the tree. A second later the animal's head appeared, and instantly I flung the spear with all my strength.

The startled beast leaped into the air and bounded away among the bushes with the spear hanging from its neck. I darted after it, and a few paces forward picked up the spear, while I could hear the wounded animal crashing through the undergrowth ahead. The pursuit was not difficult, for the track was marked by great pools of blood, and I had not gone much more than a quarter of a mile when I came upon my victim lying upon the ground dead.

Very fortunately for me, the animal in its flight had gone straight towards the river and had fallen within fifty yards of the bank, so that, when I had ascertained my position, I was able to drag the carcase to the water and tow it down to the island, where I eventually got it ashore close to the staging.

The skinning and cutting up of the antelope was a formidable task, for the beast was nearly as large as a red stag, and I was considerably exercised in my mind as to how I should dispose of so much meat; for the flies had scented it already, and in the damp heat of the forest it would hardly keep twenty-four hours. At last it occurred to me to hang the joints up in the fire hut, which was always full of smoke and very dry, in the hope that they would become cured, and this plan I adopted, to the disappointment of the flies. In the afternoon I finished felling the odúm tree, and selected two of its stoutest branches to form the inside keel or kelson of the canoe. These I cut off, so as to leave each one with about two feet of the main stem attached to it, forming an L-piece, which I intended to make into the stem-post and stern-post respectively.

That night I made an interesting discovery. I had dined sumptuously off a lump of grilled venison, and was clearing up the debris, when I bethought me of the fruit with which my pockets still bulged, and endeavoured to pull out the bunch. But it would not come out. A quantity of the milky sap had exuded and, solidifying, had cemented the branch so firmly to the inside of the pocket that I had to turn the latter inside out and cut the stalk free; and when I came to examine the cut surface of the cement I found, to my joy, that it was rubber. My hunting expedition had been a fortunate one indeed, for here was an ideal material with which to make my canoe watertight.

During the following week I worked steadily at the canoe, cutting and shaping the sticks for the frame, and lashing them together by the daylight, and reserving for the evening such tasks as could be done by the light of the fire. These included the making of a few simple tools; for instance, finding that lashings alone would hardly make the frame sufficiently rigid, I determined to fasten the larger timbers together with wooden pegs or "treenails" in addition, and to this end I took my smaller knife out of its handle and sharpened its tang to make a boring tool. Then the tree-nails themselves had to be cut and shaped, and a mallet made to drive them in with, and in addition, the sticks for the ensuing day's work had to have their bark peeled off, which bark I tore into narrow strips and twisted into cord for lashings. Finally, I had to make a measuring rule, which I did by marking my own height upon a long rod, adding two inches to make it six feet, and then dividing it up into equal parts with the aid of a piece of cord. So that my evenings were as busy as my days, and I usually turned in early, thoroughly tired.

My well-stocked larder relieved me of any immediate anxiety on the score of food for the meat became admirably dried and cured in the smoky fire hut; but I made few demands on my store, since, in the course of some experiments upon the rubber vines, I produced an elastic cord with which I was able to make an excellent catapult, a weapon with which I had been very skilful as a boy; and as pebbles were plentiful in the river bed, I was able to supply most of my wants by this means.

Every morning, as a rule, I made a short journey into the forest for the purpose of marking the position of any rubber vines or Hon-ton trees, so that when I was ready to use them there should be no delay. The vines were fairly abundant, and I found also several other rubber-bearing trees and creepers, so that I did not anticipate any difficulty in obtaining as much rubber as I should want; while as to the Hon-ton or bark trees, a couple would have been enough, and I had marked at least a dozen. From these expeditions I generally brought back a parrot or two, a hornbill, turakow, or other bird, and sometimes a small animal such as a squirrel or a pangolin, and one day I speared a porcupine. Monkeys I could have knocked down with my catapult by the dozen, but I had conscientious scruples (for blood is thicker than water), and avoided any nearer approach to cannibalism than the killing and eating of a potto.

At the end of the week's work the canoe had made considerable progress. The keel was laid, the stem and stern-posts shaped and strengthened with angle pieces, and the principal ribs or timbers of the midship portion fixed to the keel with tree-nails and strong lashings. The gunwales were also in position, the ends of the ribs joined by crossbars or deck beams, and on either side of the main kelson (or inner keel) was another, rather lighter one at a distance of twelve inches, so that the floor of the boat would be very strong and rigid.

Before the close of the second week the frame was finished, and very shipshape it looked. I had at first had some misgivings as to the strength of a boat put together in this way, but I had none now, for although the separate timbers (excepting the kelson) were light and flexible, their number made the construction immensely strong. There were twenty-four ribs on each side, those of the midship portion being in one piece from gunwale to gunwale, and made of curved pieces of tough, springy liana; and the ends of all of them were joined by transverse bars or deck beams, excepting where the opening of the well would be. The ribs were fixed by eight stringers of hard wood on each side, in addition to the gunwales, running from stem to stern and fastened to the stem and stern posts. The fittings, too, were now nearly complete, for the long hours of darkness gave me plenty of time to work at them. The rudder (of the drop pattern like that of a lifeboat) was ready to fix on; four anchors, or rather grapnels, had been made from the hard stem of a bush which bore its branches in whorls of four, and now, with their shanks weighted with stones and their cables of liana secured, were ready for use. Two leeboards of framed sticks covered with bark, a seven foot mast, and the yard and boom were completed, and the fashioning of the paddle – the most arduous task of all – had been commenced. And besides all this, I had accumulated a quantity of liana cordage and a good length of rope made by plaiting strands of fibrous bark.

The most difficult part of the work had now to be attacked – the covering of the frame with its "skin". The method by which I proposed to do this was to turn the frame bottom upwards and lay the sheets of bark upon it, cutting them to the shape and sewing their edges together with an overlap. Then, when the entire shell or skin was made, I intended to bring the edges together upon the deck with a lacing that I could tighten as the bark stretched until the covering was strained on tightly enough to be permanently fastened.

I spent two whole days tediously stripping the white canvas-like bark from one of the trees that I had marked, and after this I usually devoted half the day to collecting the bark, and the remainder to fitting it to the frame; until I found I had accumulated more material than I was likely to use, and was able to give up the entire day to the work of fitting.

During all this time I had seen but a single human being – a hunter whom I had espied in the forest one morning without being observed by him – and I had marvelled more and more at the absolute desolation of this out-of-the-way corner of the wilderness. But the sense of security that had, in consequence, grown up in me now received a severe shock; for one afternoon, as I was stitching away busily and whistling cheerfully over my work, I was startled by the unmistakable sound of voices. Quickly dropping my needle, I crept up on to the higher ground and peered through the bushes, when, to my horror, I saw two men – apparently hunters cautiously wading across towards the island, and looking about them very warily. No doubt they had heard my whistling, and had come across to investigate.

For a moment I was doubtful how to act, but as their manner showed hesitation and a little alarm, I thrust my fingers into my mouth and blew a loud shrill whistle; whereupon they turned about, and waded back without any hesitation at all, and disappeared quickly into the forest.

For the time, then, the situation was saved, but the incident caused me very grave anxiety. These men had been easily enough frightened away, but they would talk of what they had heard, and some bolder spirits might come – probably would come, in fact – and in more formidable numbers. With my imperfect weapons I could hardly keep an armed party at bay, and "war palaver" was the very last thing to be desired; besides, the visitors might call in my absence.

In great perplexity I pondered upon the problem as I paced up and down before my house. At length I received a suggestion from an unexpected quarter. In a moment of idleness I had taken the skull of the antelope from the river, where the fish had picked it clean, and fixed it as an ornament above my door; and happening now to glance at it in passing, and again being struck by its resemblance to the image by the pool, I suddenly conceived the idea of sheltering myself behind the superstitions of these forest natives. I remembered the effect the encounter with that hideous effigy had had upon Alhassan – Mahommedan as he was; doubtless upon an actual worshipper of the river god the effect would have been even greater.

Then why should I not turn river god myself? No place of residence could be more appropriate to such a deity than the island on which I lived.

I sniggered a good deal at the notion, which nevertheless commended itself to my judgement; and as the light was waning, I hastily collected the materials for manufacturing a suitable "make up," and took them into the house. They consisted of a length of curved timber, left over from the canoe frame, a quantity of odds and ends of fibre that had been cut off in sewing the bark together, and one or two furry skins of animals that I had eaten; and with these I spent a busy evening by the firelight preparing for my apotheosis on the morrow.

But when the morrow came, and I looked at the absurd productions of my labour – which appeared for all the world like the properties from some amateur pantomime – I was inclined to pitch them into the river, so preposterous did the whole thing seem. The "make up" included a cap or wig of mixed fur and rubbed fibre, very flowing and dishevelled, to which was attached a pair of curved horns of hard wood and a beard that concealed the fastenings. I had also made a kilt of the same materials, as I should have to discard my clothes – which, indeed, would be little loss, for they were by this time a mere archipelago of holes.

Presently I summoned up courage to try the ridiculous things on, and when I had tied the wig securely in its place and exchanged my rags for the kilt, I went round to the little bay, and stooping over the bank, examined my reflection in the still water. The hideousness of my appearance quite startled me, and I realised for the first time how haggard and emaciated I had become with all this hard work, anxiety, and low diet; and as the wig caused me little discomfort and the kilt none at all, I decided to keep them on for the present.

I had hardly made this resolution when I caught the sound of voices, and on mounting the ridge, I could see through the bushes a party of six men on the opposite bank. I thought I could recognise two of them as my friends of the previous day, and these were pointing at the island and talking in loud, excited tones. Then the whole party began to wade slowly across the shallows, each man manifestly endeavouring to be the last of the procession.

As I saw that they must land under a high bank, I crept along the ground to receive them on my domain, and when the leader was within a dozen yards of the island, I slowly reared my head above the bank and fixed him with a stony stare. He did not see me at first, having turned to speak to his comrades; but when he suddenly met my eye, he stopped dead, and stood with mouth agape as though turned into stone. In a few seconds he recovered himself, and turning about, splashed wildly across the river, screeching like a terrified child and followed closely by his five companions. When they reached the farther bank they paused to look back, and I took the opportunity to let myself be seen for a moment as though flitting from one hiding place to another. A single glance was enough for them, for the instant I appeared they made off at a run.

My visitors, then, were disposed of, at any rate, for some time to come, and, as I returned to my work, I congratulated myself on the brilliant success of my ruse. But yet the old sense of security was destroyed. and I pushed on my labours with anxious impatience. For although it was pretty certain that these men would not again venture near the island, and that all the villagers would give a wide berth to a place haunted by so dreadful a presence, yet the story of the apparition would inevitably become the talk and wonder of the district, and others besides the villagers would hear it. There were the fetish men in their settlement not two miles away. They might resent the intrusion of an unofficial demon into their jurisdiction, and their expert acquaintance with performances "in character" would probably make them highly suspicious and sceptical, while if the reports represented the island *abonsam* as having a white skin, they would be likely to connect him with the runaway slave who had cost them so dear. This last consideration was especially disquieting, and it kept me in a continual state of apprehension and watchfulness.

During the afternoon of the day following this incident I put the finishing touches to the covering of the canoe, and slipping it on to the frame, fastened the lacing by which its edges were to be drawn together on the deck. It was not a perfect success, for although it fitted fairly well, there were slack places in which the skin bulged away from the frame. After it had been on an hour or so and the bark had stretched a little, I was able to draw in the lacing somewhat; and this, with some judicious rubbing and stroking, reduced the bulgings appreciably, but still it did not set as smoothly as I had hoped. In the night, however, several showers occurred, and, when I came to examine the canoe in the morning, its skin was as tight as a drumhead, and fitted the frame perfectly; and all that was necessary to maintain this condition was to draw in the lacing as the skin relaxed in drying.

I had now reached the last stage in my labours – the coating of the bark skin with rubber to render it watertight; and if I failed in this, then all my previous work would be wasted, for the canoe would not float ten minutes in its present state.

It was therefore with no little concern and anxiety that I sallied forth into the forest to collect the material for the first trial. I made my way straight to a place where I knew the vines grew in some abundance, and, dragging down one of the long stems, cut it through just above the ground, and hurried back to the island. By the time I arrived, the sap was already becoming thick and sticky, and I had to cut a fresh surface, from which the milky juice exuded freely; and as it oozed out, I let it drip upon the skin of the canoe, spreading it out with a small rag of bark. From time to time as the flow diminished I had to cut away fresh portions of the stem, until the whole was used up, when I ran off to my collecting ground for a fresh supply. It was a tedious and slow business, for after almost a whole day's work, I had covered not more than nine or ten square feet; and as I estimated the surface of the canoe at from seventy to eighty square feet, this was a painfully small beginning.

However, on coming out the next morning to inspect my work, I was consoled to find that, little as there was done, that little had been done effectually, for the part that I had smeared with the juice was now covered with a moderately thick film of rubber – enough to render it watertight beyond all question. The method was therefore practicable, and the accomplishment of my object was only a question of time, and I set about my day's task with renewed courage and spirit.

The slowness of the process I managed to remedy materially during the first day's work by rigging up a light scaffolding over the canoe, from which I could suspend three or four vine stems at once; and as they dripped much faster when hanging vertically, I could cover the surface with comparative rapidity. The vines, too, turned out to be even more plentiful than I had supposed, so that the work of coating the canoe progressed briskly.

Meanwhile, the evenings' labours were being carried forward with such goodwill that the last of the fittings was well advanced. This was the sail, and a terrible business the cutting out and stitching it had been, for I had had to make it of odd pieces of bark left from the covering of the canoe, and my needles penetrated the tough material with difficulty even when I had made myself a sailmaker's palm with a plate of bone for a thimble. Still, in spite of all difficulties, the sail had been put together, and now only required to be roped round with a cord of plaited bark fibre to be complete. It is true it was clumsy and ill-shaped, but it was strong and rather large for the size of the canoe – having an area of over thirty square feet – for I reckoned that the great weight of ballast would enable me to carry a good spread of sail.

At length, after six days of unintermitting labour, the coating of the canoe was complete. From stem to stern, from deck to floor, she was covered with a continuous sheet of rubber, smeary and uneven, but unquestionably watertight. Even this, however, I did not intend to take for granted, but proposed on the morrow to ladle some water into her with my brass pan – for I finished the coating just as the light was failing – a proceeding that was rendered unnecessary by a heavy shower in the night. It had been my custom to cover the vessel, when I was not at work, with some thatched frames or hurdles that I had made for the purpose to protect her from the increasingly frequent rain; but this being now no longer necessary, I left her uncovered, with the tilt or apron off the well, and when I came to look at her in the morning she contained two or three inches of water. By hoisting her with levers, and rolling her from side to side, I made this water wash all over the inside, but not a drop came through anywhere. She was as tight as a drum, so I rolled her over, and let the water run out.

I now entered upon the last task of all – the fixing of the outside keel and the fitting of the rudder; and this would be but a short day's work, since these parts were finished, even to the tree-nails, and ready for fitting.

There were three outside keels, one central and two lateral or "bilge keels," corresponding to the inside ones, to which they would be fixed by long tree-nails passing through both keels and timbers. They were highly important, as they would protect the skin of the canoe if she ran aground or had to be pulled over an obstruction, and were made accordingly pretty stout and deep. It took me but a short time to fit them on, for the holes were already made in the wood, and it remained only to carefully perforate the skin, lay on the keels, and drive the tree-nails home. The fixing of the rudder was even a simpler matter, for there was nothing to do but to pass the long wooden bolt or pintle through four hardwood eyes – two on the stern-post, and two on the rudder – and fix it there; and when I had done this I stepped back and triumphantly surveyed my handiwork.

The canoe was finished, and ready to commence its voyage. My work was done; the time of waiting was past, and I could, if I pleased, launch my craft, and set out upon my journey this very day. And, indeed, my impatience rather urged me to adopt this course; but, on sober reflection, I resolved to defer the start until daybreak on the morrow. My first day's journey must needs be a long one, that I might at once get clear of the dangerous neighbourhood of the mine and the fetish priests; and to make possible a long day's paddling, a good night's rest was essential. So

I commenced in a leisurely way to make my preparations and survey my resources.

On overhauling the contents of the fire hut, I noted with satisfaction that I had enough provisions to last me a week or ten days, for not only was the antelope practically intact, but I had made small additions to my store from the surplus of my meals. The smoked meat was nearly black, and most unsavoury in appearance, but it was quite sweet, and would now keep as long as I should want it.

Having inspected the provisions, there next arose the question of unearthing the treasure. It ought to be dug up by daylight, for otherwise some portion of it might be overlooked and left behind; but unfortunately, the place in which it was buried was visible from the opposite bank, and my confidence in the solitude of the place had been quite destroyed. Yet there was no help for it; the only thing to be done was to get it over as quickly as possible, and keep a bright lookout.

I made my way to the spot – familiar enough by this time – and taking once more the bearings by the oil palm and the tree, stuck my knife deep into the moss. After one or two probings I felt the blade strike the buried metal, and looking sharply up and down the river to make sure that there were no observers, cut out a large square slab of moss, and turned it back. The ends of a manilla stuck up through the earth, and passing my fingers through the ring I hooked up the first bunch, weighing about twenty pounds. In less than a minute I had three other bunches out of the hole, and with the four I went off to the house, where I deposited them on the floor. The work of disinterring the gold was not a long one, owing to the convenient way in which the manillas were fastened together; in about an hour I had removed the entire treasure, consisting of fifty-seven bunches, and stacked them in a heap at the farther end of the house. Returning after carrying the last load, I probed the ground in all directions to make sure that I had left none behind, and then kicking the earth back into the hole, flung the slab of moss down on to it.

At this moment a loud shout rang out from down the reach, and looking up, I saw a sight at which my heart seemed to stand still. A procession was slowly making its way along the bank towards the island, and the leader, who had already sighted me, was pointing to me, and talking excitedly to his followers. There were ten men, including the leader, all armed with long muskets, and most formidable to look at; while the leader himself was, to me, the most terrifying figure of all, for even at this distance I could see the broad, white bands of his cowrie necklace and amulets, which told me that he was a fetish priest. Almost choking with rage and disappointment, I rushed to the house to arm for the fray, resolved to compel my foes to kill me rather than submit to capture. There lay the heap of gold, a mere mocking illusion, turning to dust and ashes at my touch. There it would presently be found by the fetish man, while I… Bah! I was too infuriated to pursue the thought. With an oath I snatched up my spear and catapult, and the bag of pebbles that I used when hunting, and rushed out of the house with set teeth, as unpleasant an enemy as any man might desire to meet. I was still wearing my horned wig and kilt – indeed, I had worn them continually since my last encounter, and had become so accustomed to the former, that I ceased to be conscious of it – and murderous as I felt, I was yet determined to make the most of my appearance before resorting to mere carnal weapons. I therefore laid down my spear, as being out of character, and commenced a few preliminary blandishments.

The party had by this time reached the bank opposite the island, where they halted for a few minutes to reconnoitre. I now introduced myself to their notice by peeping furtively from behind a tree until they observed me, when I drew back my head, and taking advantage of the ridge, suddenly appeared in a different place, while they were still staring at the tree. These sudden eclipses and reappearances, together with my uncanny aspect, seemed to have a highly disturbing effect on their nerves, for when the fetish man at length took up his musket and stepped into the water, they were very reluctant to follow. However, the priest, who seemed in no way alarmed, would not listen to their objections, and presently the whole party began to advance across the shallows. The river had risen considerably of late, and the men were soon immersed above their waists; and as the current ran rather swiftly, they had to step cautiously.

As soon as the advance actually commenced, I got ready my catapult (which, by the way, I had gradually improved from the form that I first devised, into a most formidable weapon, in the use of which I had indeed become very expert), and waited behind the ridge until they should come within easy range. They came forward slowly in single file, holding their muskets up clear of the water, the fetish man leading by a few paces.

When the priest had reached the middle of the ford, and paused for a moment to reconnoitre, I considered that he had come far enough, so, taking careful aim at his chest, I let fly a good-sized quartz pebble, which went home with a sharp thud. With a piercing yell the fetish man spun round, and fell plump into the water, discharging his musket as he fell, right over the shoulder of the man behind him. He was up again in a moment, spluttering and choking, brandishing his dripping musket, and roaring to his followers to avenge him. But they were in full retreat. They had not seen the missile, but only its effects; and three of them had been hit by the slugs from the priest's musket. Therefore they were executing a rapid strategic movement to the rear.

The fetish man stood in mid-stream bellowing for them to come back, but as they took no notice of him, he seemed inclined to follow them. I helped him to make up his mind by discharging another pebble, which struck him in the back; on which he uttered such a terrific screech, that the warriors all broke into a run, and scrambling up the bank, vanished into the forest, followed closely by their leader.

I breathed again as the last man disappeared; but it had been a tight squeeze – and it was not finished yet. I owed my escape, or rather my respite, entirely to the superstitious fears of the armed villagers, for as to the fetish man, he evidently was not imposed upon by my "make up." He would now be, no doubt, excessively annoyed with me, and I very strongly suspected that he had recognised me. In any case it was practically certain that he would return, and more efficiently supported this time; and the only question was, how soon might I expect the next attack? The settlement was barely two miles distant, so that it would be possible for him to return in an hour if he could collect a suitable party; yet I hardly expected this, for the sun was just setting, and night attacks are not much in favour with African strategists.

But while I was turning over these matters, I was making active preparations for my departure. The staging on which the canoe was built was originally close to the water's edge, but I had afterwards extended it, forming "ways" (i.e. a launching slipway) right into the water; and as the river had risen several inches since then, there was depth enough at its end for launching the loaded canoe into. I determined, therefore, to load the craft before launching her, as this would be quicker and more convenient than carrying the loads out to her as she floated in the stream. First I made the canoe fast to a post with a stout liana, which I belayed to a cleat in the well. Then I levered her up with a pole, and rubbed her keels with some fat that I had saved from my meals and stored in the brass pan, and the remainder I spread upon the transverse bars of the slipway.

She was now ready for her cargo, and I began forthwith to stow the bunches of manillas on either side of the inside keel, tying each bunch in its place with ends of lashing that I had left for the purpose, so that the cargo could not shift during the launch. This took me a considerable time, and it was dark long before I had finished.

After the cargo came the stores – the tarry-looking joints of smoked meat, my two mats, the brass pan, fishhooks, needles, anchors, and a quantity of spare cordage. The leeboards, mast, sail, paddle, and pole were already on board, as well as a sinker or drag – a log of hard wood weighted with stones, and fastened to a long, stout liana, which I intended to use for trailing along the bottom where the current was swift, to retard and steady the canoe, and hold her bows upstream as she drifted, thus enabling her to be steered with the rudder. When everything was on board, I placed an anchor, ready for dropping, on one bow, and the sinker on the other, belaying their respective cables to cleats in the well; so she was now fit to launch at a moment's notice, and the tightness of the cord that held her to the post showed that she was ready to slide down the ways as soon as it was let go.

During all this time I kept a sharp and anxious lookout, but there was no sign of any fresh invasion; and as it now began to rain heavily, I drew the covering over the well of the canoe, and retired to the house.

Chapter Twenty-Five
I Set Out Upon my Voyage

The night dragged on wearily and miserably. Inside the house a chill discomfort reigned, for I had lit no fire this evening, and every article that I possessed, even to the sleeping mats, had been stowed in the canoe. The rain thundered upon the flimsy roof and oozed through in places with unpleasant tricklings, while from outside came the continuous hissing roar of the deluge as though some giant locomotive were blowing off steam. At long intervals there was a lull, and then I ran out to see that the canoe was not washed away, and that no enemies were approaching my stronghold.

So the night wore on, full of unrest, anxiety and bodily discomfort. Each time that I visited the canoe I found the water farther up the slipway, and each time that I went to the bank to look out across the river, the murmur of the rushing water seemed louder.

About an hour before dawn (as I judged by observing a group of stars through a rift in the clouds) there came a more decided lull in the downpour, and a few patches of starlit sky appeared overhead. I had been sitting on my bedstead dozing, but the sudden quiet aroused me, and I went forth once more to see that all was secure. The air was brilliantly clear, and although there was no moon, I could distinctly see the dark shapes of the trees on the opposite bank. And as I looked, I could see something else; in the dark space under the bank was a spot of blacker darkness which began to move slowly out into the stream, growing smaller as it did so. It was soon followed by another, and yet another, until there was a line of black spots on the dim surface of the river, like a row of corks above a driftnet.

A night attack was being made, then, despite the unfavourable weather.

I waited until the leader had reached mid-stream, when I could make out his head and shoulders just emerging from the water, and his arms held up, grasping either a musket or a spear; then I turned and softly ran to the canoe.

As I passed along the rear of the island, I was startled at observing a party of men approaching from that side of the river also. The water, I knew, was now too deep there for them to get across, but this second party suggested yet others and made me anxious to be gone. Excepting my spear, which was in my hand, all my goods were on board, so when I reached the canoe, I silently pushed back the cover, climbed into the well, and unfastened the mooring line from the cleat.

I stood for a moment with the taut line in my hand, looking out across the little bay to see that no one was approaching from that direction; then I let go, casting the end clear of the stage, and immediately the canoe began to move. There was a soft rumble as her greased keels slid over the slippery bars, and as she gathered momentum, her stern dived into the still water, deeper and deeper, until for one horrid moment I thought she was overweighted and was going right under; then her bow dropped with a gentle splash and she rode on an even keel, gliding away into the quiet backwater at the end of the island.

I drew a deep breath as the rapidly widening space of water appeared between me and the land, and, putting the helm over, guided my craft towards the swift stream that swept between the island and the shore. In a few seconds the canoe emerged from the backwater into the flood stream, and on this began to drift rapidly down the river.

At this moment the rain came on again and poured down in such torrents that I was glad to take shelter under the waterproof apron or well-cover. I had rigged two curved sticks on cord pivots so that they could be drawn over the well, thus supporting the cover and forming a hood like the tilt of a wagon. This tilt I now fixed in position, and found it a perfect protection from the rain; and as the opening was at the after end, I could look out over the stern, although, of course, in the direction of the bows the view was obstructed. When the tilt was up I let go a fathom or so of the line attached to the sinker, and found that I was able to feel, by the vibration of the cord, to what extent the weight was dragging on the bottom, while the noise of the water rushing past the canoe enabled me to judge roughly how much her drift was retarded by it.

I was just belaying the cord of the sinker when a tremendous shouting arose from the direction of the island, and was answered from the banks. My good friends had apparently realised their loss, but by what means I could not judge. Perhaps the empty house had told the tale, or possibly they had found the slipway and guessed at its purpose. If the latter were the case I might expect a hot pursuit, especially if they should come across the empty hole, for of the significance of this they could have no doubt whatever.

As the shouts re-echoed from the banks I was tempted to take to the paddle and forge ahead at full speed, regardless of the rain and the darkness; but my judgement told me that it was better to go cautiously at reduced speed than to risk dashing on to some obstacle and either wrecking the canoe or becoming so involved that I must wait for daylight to extricate myself. Indeed, had there been any choice at all, I should certainly have anchored until the darkness was past, for I might even now, for all I could tell, be drifting straight on to an impassable rapid or even a waterfall. But there was no choice. If I anchored, I should be overtaken and totally lost, whereas if I were wrecked on a rapid or fall, I might save myself and even ultimately recover the treasure. So there was nothing to be done but crouch in the shelter of the tilt and hope that the river hereabouts was free from falls and rapids, and that my good genius would carry the canoe clear of sunken rocks and snags.

Let me, once for all, make clear to the non-nautical reader my mode of progression. The canoe was being carried along by the swift current of the flooded river, but over her bow hung the line with the weighted log attached, which by trailing along the bottom created a resistance to her progress, which was great or little according to the length of line paid out, and kept her head pointing up stream. She thus drifted down the river stern foremost, but as she moved more slowly than the water, the current acted on her rudder as though she were moving against it; so that if the tiller were put over to the right her head would turn to the left and she would be carried by the current obliquely across the river to the left bank, and vice versa.

Consequently, the vessel was far from being out of control – in fact, this is the safest method of descending a rapid river; but, of course, the canoe's obedience to her helm was of little avail at the moment, for the darkness was profound, and I was being carried on into unknown regions. Yet even so, the trailing sinker was of service, for it naturally rolled down into the deepest parts of the riverbed and thus guided the canoe clear of the banks and shallows.

And all this time the deluge descended with a roar like that of some great cataract. My frail shelter trembled with the impact of the falling torrents, and the water around was lashed into seething foam.

It cannot have been much above an hour (although it seemed a very eternity) that I had sat crouching in my shelter, peering out into the grey void, my ears stunned by the uproar and my heart in my mouth with the momentary expectation of being flung into some fall or rapid or being dashed against a rock, when the dimness around began to lighten and I knew that the dawn had come. A cheerless dawn it was, with the sombre grey pall overhead, a sheet of dirty yellow foam around, and on either side a dim and shapeless shadow that I knew to be the wall of forest on the banks. Yet it was better than darkness, for I could see far enough to steer clear of visible rocks and snags; and now and again, when the canoe swung in towards one bank, some tall shape would start out of the void and encourage me by the speed with which it passed. There might be dangers ahead, but there also lay safety, and my pursuers must needs be fleet of foot to overtake me at this rate.

Not long after daybreak, as the canoe was slipping along pretty close inshore, the wall of forest suddenly came to an end, and for a little space neither bank was visible; then the tall grey shadow reappeared, first on one side and then on the other. By this I judged that the river had joined some larger stream – probably the main stream of the Tano – and this surmise was confirmed by the fact that the current was now noticeably stronger, although the river seemed no wider than before.

The cravings of hunger had been making themselves felt for some time past, and as my anxieties were now somewhat allayed, I thought it time to pipe all hands to breakfast; so I looked up the hind legs of a ground squirrel, which, being the latest addition to my store and therefore the least perfectly cured, required to be consumed without delay, and made a barbaric but refreshing meal.

There was one feature of my voyage that had all along caused me some uneasiness, and had recurred to my mind more than once since I had left the island.

This was the Tánosu bridge.

I remembered that it hung very low – so low, in fact, that at the middle, where it sagged a good deal, its lower surface was immersed even when I crossed it in the dry season, while the ends were hardly high enough then for the canoe to pass under. The river had risen considerably since the rains began, and it was certain that the bridge would be partly submerged. If it should be deeply submerged all would be well, but if it were only awash I should have to unload the canoe before I could drag it over. But Tánosu was a mighty unpleasant place at any time at which to execute a manoeuvre of this kind, and now, with the possibility that the hue and cry had already been raised there, it would be a veritable hornets' nest. True, I might not be on the Tano after all, but this was highly improbable, as that river drained practically the whole of north-western Ashanti, and the island was but a mile or two from its source.

I was still cogitating upon the matter, when the rain, which had been decreasing in violence for some minutes, ceased altogether, and as the banks came clearly into view, I swept round a curve into a long straight reach of the river, and there, hardly a quarter of a mile away, was the bridge itself.

It presented a most formidable obstruction.

The ends, on a level with the tops of the banks, were just clear of the water, while the central part was quite submerged; but I could see by the way the water foamed over it that its surface was not many inches under.

Directly I saw the bridge, my decision was made. I would try to jump the obstacle without unloading.

To this end I began rapidly to unfasten the bunches of manillas from their lashing and push them down towards the bows, keeping an eye upon the trim of the canoe, that I did not either swamp her or strain her timbers in the process. Less than half the metal had to be moved, for when this change had been made in the stowage, her bows were nearly under, while her stern was almost out of the water.

By the time these hasty preparations had been made the bridge was less than two hundred yards ahead, so having steered the canoe into mid-stream, I pulled up the drop rudder by its cord and hauled in the sinker, letting the craft go at the full speed of the current. Straight, stern on, she charged at the middle of the bridge, over which the water was roaring and foaming as if on a weir; her stern passed on to the bridge and over it and for a moment I hoped that we should float clear, when, with a shock that flung me on to the floor of the well, her keels ground against the massive timber and she stuck hard and fast, turning nearly broadside on to the current as she brought up.

This last circumstance alarmed me terribly, for the water poured over the bridge with such force that I feared every moment that the canoe would be capsized and sunk; besides which the water was now washing right over the forward half of the vessel and threatening to come into the well. However, I was relieved to find that the rudder was well clear of the bridge, so that as soon as I could get the weight back into the stern I could bring her head to stream again.

I was about to dive into the bows to bring back the cargo, when a shout from the bank attracted my attention, and I saw a man running away from the river towards the village, apparently giving the alarm.

There was no time to be lost.

Letting the rudder drop down, I crawled into the bows and hauled for dear life at the manillas, dragging bunch after bunch aft of the well, yet stowing the weight carefully so as not to break the back of the canoe. I had got all the cargo back into its place and was beginning to trim it farther aft, when I saw a party of men running furiously from the village towards the river; and, before I could move more than a single bunch, they had reached the end of the bridge.

In sheer desperation I put the helm hard over, and getting out of the well, crawled right out on to the stern, sinking it nearly flush with the water. This caused the current to lay hold of it so that the canoe swung round head to stream; and just as the foremost of the men was ankle deep in the rushing water that poured over the bridge, the keel slowly grated down the edge of the great timber, the bow slipped down with a splash, and she floated away on the current.

The men who were on the bridge instantly turned about and began to run along the bank, but finding that they could barely keep up with the canoe (for the current was sweeping along at fully five miles an hour), they struck off into the bush, evidently taking a short cut for some bend in the river.

This was highly unpleasant, for I had noticed that some of the men carried muskets, while others wore the familiar garb of the fetish priest; probably they intended to wait for me at some promontory farther down, and as they were on the right bank, I at once took my paddle and steered well under the left, urging the craft forward with all my strength. The combined effect of the current and the paddle drove the canoe along at fully seven miles an hour, and I had some hopes of outstripping my pursuers, which I was most anxious to do, for their behaviour clearly showed that they had received news from Aboási and intended to stop me at all costs.

The river now made several abrupt turns, which compelled me to keep nearly in mid-stream; then it entered a long straight reach like that at Tánosu, and I was beginning to congratulate myself on the chance this afforded me of drawing ahead, when I caught the white glint of broken water at the far end. I was approaching a rapid.

That this was the trysting place selected by my friends was now made clear, for I could hear the shouts of the advancing party and even the cracking of the branches as they pushed through the forest.

It was a terrible dilemma.

If, as I strongly suspected, the rapids were impassable it was useless to rush blindly at them, and yet it would be impossible to unload the cargo and ease the canoe down, with a squad of ruffians peppering me from the bank.

As I neared the critical spot and the roar of broken water was borne to my ear, I stood up and hastily surveyed the rapids. A broad band of yellowish-white foam stretched across the river almost from bank to bank, broken here and there by projecting masses of rock. In one place only was the water unbroken – a narrow space quite near to the right bank.

There was little time to consider, for the voices of my pursuers grew rapidly nearer, and I was being swept down towards the rapids with increasing velocity; so as the passage seemed clear at the one place, I decided to take the risk of what lay beyond. I therefore pointed the head of the canoe at the smooth space, paddling in towards the right shore, and at that moment a chorus of yells from the bank almost abreast of me announced the arrival of the enemy. As I charged at the narrow passage a loud explosion rang out, and the air was filled with the screams of flying slugs; but to these I paid no attention, for I had enough to do to keep my bark in the little alley of smooth water.

The next few bewildering moments were passed in a whirl of noise and confusion. The water roared on both sides, great hummocks of rock whizzed past, muskets boomed from behind, slugs howled through the air, and the canoe flew forward with a velocity that left me breathless.

Suddenly a great rock loomed up right ahead, halfway down the rapid. I flung down the paddle, and snatching up the pole, lunged wildly at a passing ledge. The canoe swerved imperceptibly and swept on, as it seemed to inevitable destruction; but her bow missed the rugged monolith by a hair's breadth, and her side flashed past its rough face, but so close that the paddle, which projected a couple of inches, was caught by the rock and flung into the water. Once past this obstacle, the dangers of the rapid were over, although the heavily-weighted craft almost buried her bows as she plunged into the smooth water below; and a sharp turn of the river carried me out of the range of the muskets.

As the firing ceased I looked round to see if the men were following or taking measures to cut off my retreat, when I observed that a stream of some size, and very full and swift, joined the river just below the rapid. By this my pursuers were most effectually stopped, at any rate for the present, and almost certainly for good; for when I remembered the network of rivers by which the forest is intersected – rivers which just now would all be flooded – I felt that I had nothing to fear from a pursuit overland.

It would not do, however, to lose my paddle, for as the water was too deep for poling, I was rather helpless without it; but it could not be far away, and must certainly come along presently on

The Golden Pool

the current. So I let go two or three fathoms of the drag line, and as the canoe slowed down, I presently saw the paddle come round a bend in the river, floating nearly in mid-stream, and slowly overtaking me. When I had recovered it I hauled up the sinker, and paddled ahead in a leisurely fashion. There was no need to exert myself, for the current was already taking me along as fast as was safe in so tortuous a river; but I had to use either the paddle or drag to keep the canoe under control, and I grudged the trifling delay that the latter caused. The river hereabouts seemed pretty free from obstructions, although the overfalls or eddies upon the surface told of jagged rocks at the bottom; indeed, it is probable that in the dry season, this part of the river was an almost continuous series of rapids. But now a good depth of water covered the rocks, and snags, and the whirlpools plainly pointed out those that approached the surface, so, by keeping a bright lookout, I was able to keep on my course.

And now that there was a lull in the excitements of the voyage, I had time to examine the bark that was carrying me so bravely on my way. A very staunch and sturdy little craft she was, and fully up to my expectations, and I was gratified to notice how accurately my calculations had worked out. She showed a good seven inches of freeboard amidships, and a foot at either end; was quite dry inside, and so stiff and steady by reason of her breadth and the weight of ballast, that I could stand up without in the least affecting her stability. She was certainly very heavy to paddle, but as the whole voyage was downstream this mattered little, and I had no doubt that she would sail moderately well.

For several hours I pursued a very uneventful journey, steering with the paddle rather than propelling the canoe. Once I encountered a fallen tree which stretched almost across the river and was rather difficult to pass without damaging my vessel; I also met with two or three small rapids, but as I was now unembarrassed I had no difficulty in steering clear of the rocks.

As I went on, the river widened out very perceptibly, the tributaries being very numerous, and many of them of large size, so that by the afternoon I found myself upon a really fine and noble-looking stream; and as I looked upon its yellow, unruffled waters, rolling on majestically between the lofty, forest-clad banks, it seemed strange that it should be so desolate and silent. Yet for hours I had passed no village, nor seen any sign of human occupation, and only the familiar forest sounds – voices of bird or beast – disturbed the death-like stillness.

The afternoon passed away, not tediously, though with little incident, for the leafy banks that slipped by so quietly, but swiftly, were so many milestones on the road to freedom; coming from ahead with friendly greeting, and passing astern with a silent God speed! And when the dull grey of the western sky turned to a duller crimson, I began to look about for an anchorage with a cheerful and thankful heart.

For some reasons I would rather have drawn my canoe up on the shore for the night, but the overhanging banks were crumbling and unsafe, and the beasts of prey might prove dangerous. So I decided to anchor in the slackest water I could find, sufficiently far from the bank to be secure from nocturnal visitors.

With this object I dropped the sinker and drifted down until, just round a sharp bend, I found a sheltered spot out of the main current. Here I was about to let go my anchor when I noticed a tall odúm tree on the very edge of the bank – a highly undesirable neighbour at this season of the year – and remembering the tree I had passed earlier in the day, I let the canoe drift another fifty yards down; when, as the current was comparatively slight, I dropped anchor, and paid out a good length of the stout liana cable. It was with some trepidation that I checked the outrun of the cable, fearing that the prongs or flukes of the hardwood grapnel might snap off; but they held quite securely, so I belayed the cable to its cleat, and hoisted the sinker, and, for the first time, my little ship rode to her anchor.

There were but a few minutes of daylight left, and these I employed in critically watching the bank to see if the anchor dragged at all; but there was no sign of movement, and when I pulled on the cable, it seemed as firm as though there had been a fifty-pound Trotman at the end of it. So I set up the tilt, in case it should rain in the night, made a frugal supper of smoked meat, and, having spread the mats, lay down between the two rows of manillas.

It was an odd sensation, but very pleasant and peaceful, to lie in that tiny cabin and listen to the water gurgling past outside the thin bark skin. But I did not listen long, for I had had no sleep on the previous night, and was tired out with the day's exertions; and my head had rested but a few minutes on the pillow that I had hastily extemporised by wrapping an antelope's ham in my *riga*, when I fell asleep.

I cannot tell how long I had slept, when I woke with a violent start and the feeling that something had happened. The canoe was rocking slightly, and the rain was pounding upon the deck and tilt. At first I thought my bark had broken adrift, but the trickle of the water past her run was still audible, and on giving a pull at the cable, I could feel that the anchor was fast. I put my head out of the opening of the tilt, but, of course, nothing was to be seen in the black obscurity, so, as the canoe was now motionless again, I concluded that some floating object must have struck her and aroused me; and with this I lay down again, and was asleep directly.

The dull light of a wet morning was streaming in through the companion hatch (as I may magniloquently call the tilt opening) when I next opened my eyes, and as I was ravenously hungry, I commenced the day by breakfasting off a portion of my pillow – it is needless to say which portion – after which I piped all hands to heave up the anchor. But before beginning to haul on the cable, I put my head outside the tilt to see that all was clear; and immediately the cause of last night's disturbance was apparent. The lofty tree that had aroused my misgivings on the previous evening lay sprawling across the river, its flat base of roots at the top of the bank, and its crown of branches in mid-stream. It had fallen just over the place where I had first intended to anchor, and even now, some of the topmost branches were barely ten yards from the canoe. My caution had not been superfluous, and as I hauled in the cable – very gently, so as not to strain the anchor – I congratulated myself on my escape.

I examined the anchor anxiously as it came up out of the water, and was much relieved to find it none the worse for the night's work. Two out of the four flukes had been deep in the sandy bottom, and had manifestly held fast, for the canoe had not dragged an inch in the whole night.

As the rain still fell slightly, I kept the tilt up, and drifted down, trailing the drag. My spirits were very buoyant, for I had succeeded beyond my expectations in this enterprise; one day of my voyage was gone, and I must have travelled well over sixty miles in the thirteen or fourteen hours that I had been underway. And not only had I left far behind the most imminent and alarming dangers, but I had met with far fewer obstacles and difficulties than I had anticipated. None of the rapids had been impassable, even to the loaded canoe, and the river had been most unexpectedly open and free from snags.

But it was not all to be such plain sailing, for even as I was thus complacently reviewing the previous day's exploits, my ear caught a new sound – an even, continuous murmur, faint and distant, but unmistakable – the sound of falling water.

As I drifted on, the murmur grew louder, but with a slowness that was ominously suggestive of a great volume of sound travelling a long distance, and several reaches were passed before it seemed much nearer. Gradually, however, it waxed in intensity, until it rose clear above the hiss of the rain, and I began to look ahead with keen anxiety at each turn of the river's tortuous course.

At length, creeping along inshore on the shallow side, I rounded a rocky promontory, and met the full roar of the cataract, which appeared to be halfway down the next reach. Yet there was little to see. The river seemed to break off abruptly, and its continuation at a lower level was visible through a steamy haze.

I ran the canoe inshore where a small, stout tree grew close to the water's edge, and to this I prepared to make fast. The canoe was fitted with a painter (or mooring rope) of plaited bark, the strongest piece of cordage I possessed, twenty feet long, and fixed to the stem-post with an eye-splice; so there was no fear of her breaking away from her moorings. Having hitched the painter securely to the tree, I tied on my wig, and taking my spear and catapult, stepped ashore. There was no one in sight on either bank, so with a cautious look round, I made my way along the shore towards the rapids.

When I reached them their aspect filled me with despair. They commenced with a sheer drop of seven or eight feet; but this was only the beginning, for the water poured down into a chaos of rocks, amidst which it boiled and spouted, only to dash onward into a new labyrinth. I wandered dejectedly downstream, eagerly looking for the end of the rapids, but at each few paces a fresh stretch of foaming water came into view, tumbling boisterously among great blocks of stone, and filling the air with noise and spray.

I walked on for about half a mile without seeing any sign of the river resuming its ordinary course, and then, growing uneasy about the canoe, turned back, terribly disheartened, and at my wits' end how to proceed.

It looked as if my voyage must end here, for it seemed as impossible to carry the canoe this distance on land, as it was to navigate her through the cataract. And how much farther did the rapids extend? That was a question I could not answer, and yet until it was settled I could form no plan.

As I turned my face upstream, I noticed with no little surprise that the fall was out of sight, for my attention had been so fixed upon the water that I had not observed the way in which the river curved, and I now found that I had traversed nearly a quarter of a circle, and that the curve below continued to turn in the same direction.

I found the canoe just as I had left it, and stepping on board, cast off the painter, and paddled a little way up in the slack water; then turning her head offshore, I drove her at full speed obliquely across the river, and secured the painter to a tree on the opposite bank. Once more taking my weapons, I climbed up on to the level and entered the forest, and had gone but a short distance when I struck a path of the usual narrow and tortuous type. Proceeding briskly along this, I had walked two or three hundred yards when, quite suddenly, I came in sight of a party of six men sitting round a small fire. They looked like Ashantis, and were evidently travellers, for their narrow, canework trays piled with produce lay hard by; and I observed with envy a goodly bunch of plantains lashed to each tray.

As I was standing taking in these details, one of the men turned his head and observed me, and for a moment seemed paralysed with astonishment; but he presently rose slowly, still staring at me, and reaching out for his tray, snatched it up, clapped it on his head, and bolted precipitately down the path. His companions looking round for the cause of his alarm, also perceived me, and with one accord grabbed up their loads and fled.

The fact that they had taken their goods made it clear that they had no intention of returning, so I sauntered up to the fire and examined it. More than a dozen peeled plantains lay on the embers roasting, and two or three with the skins partially removed had been dropped close by. Evidently I had frightened the poor fellows away from their breakfast, and if my conscience reproached me a little, I allowed the recollection of the bunches on their trays to allay my qualms, and licked my lips at the prospect of a meal of cooked food. Pursuing my way along the track I soon distinguished the murmur of water ahead, and presently came to the place where the path divided into two. Following the left-hand branch, a few paces brought me to a shelving hard or landing place – possibly a ford in the dry season – apparently at the foot of the rapids, for above this spot the water came foaming down among scattered rocks, while below the channel was almost clear.

I walked some distance along the bank to make sure that there were no more rapids below, and having ascertained that the river seemed to have resumed its normal course, I made my way back towards the canoe, gathering up the roasted plantains as I went. But the existence of the ford below suggested the probability of another farther up, so before returning to the canoe, I explored the road in that direction; and to my unbounded satisfaction came presently to a side path leading down a gentle incline to the water.

The problem of the portage was now considerably simplified. The river, it was clear, made a wide, horseshoe sweep, the whole of the curve being occupied by impracticable rapids, enclosing a peninsula across the isthmus of which the canoe would have to be dragged, that it might be again launched in the smooth water below. The difficulties of the task were enormously reduced by the existence of the road, and especially of the landing places; for, of course, the portage was a contingency not unforeseen nor unprovided for, and it was only the steepness of the banks and the denseness of the forest that had made it seem so impossible. The distance across the isthmus was about a quarter of a mile – a long way to haul so heavy a weight; but with sufficient time and labour the thing could be done, and I could start once more on my voyage.

The first thing to do was to unload the canoe, and on reflection, I decided to carry the gold at once to the lower landing place, where it would be ready to put on board without delay as soon as the canoe was launched.

But this required circumspection, for the track was evidently used by travellers, and might possibly lead to some neighbouring village, and it would certainly be unwise to carry the gold uncovered, in case I should meet any strangers.

The plan I adopted was to wrap three bunches of manillas in my old *riga*, and two more in my *wondo*, and passing the connecting cords over my shoulders (which I protected with pads of grass) I was able to stagger along pretty well, the weight being only about a hundred pounds.

I had made eight journeys (depositing the manillas among some bushes at the water's edge, where they were hidden from view, and yet were easy to get at for restowing), and was returning for a ninth load when I heard someone talking at no great distance. Hastily stepping off the path, I retired a little way into the bush, and took up my position behind a large tree; and I had but just hidden myself when I heard the strangers coming down the path. They were a small party of Wongáras (as I ascertained by peeping at them when they had passed), heavily laden, and apparently in a great hurry, for they strode along at a swinging pace, all talking together, without even stopping to look at the fire by the roadside.

I followed them to make sure that they were not going down to the river, and when I had seen them take the right-hand turning, I went for a fresh load.

The transport of the gold was completed in three more journeys, but on the last two, to save an extra journey, I had to carry six bunches, which I found very heavy; and when I had deposited the last of the manillas by the launching place, I fetched the uncooked plantains from the canoe, and rested by the fire while they roasted. The hot, cooked fruit seemed very delicious after my monotonous animal diet, and I was soon sufficiently revived to attack the main difficulty – the portage of the canoe.

The arrangements I had made for this purpose were not very satisfactory, but were the best that I could manage with my limited appliances. I had brought with me four rollers about three feet long, and four poles each eight feet, which I carried lashed on the deck. The latter were to serve as rails for the rollers to run on if the ground should be rough or soft. I also had a hardwood eye, through which I could reeve a rope, and so make a primitive purchase tackle (or "handy Billy," as sailors would call it), but I was badly in want of an efficient tackle or a small windlass.

Poling the canoe with some difficulty against the swift current that ran past this shore, I brought her to the upper landing place, and made fast; then having hoisted the drop-rudder, I went ashore and laid down the lines on the easiest part of the slope. Setting one of the rollers on the lines, I lifted the stern of the canoe on to it, and made fast with a spare rope to a neighbouring tree while I cast off the painter, which latter I brought aft and lightly lashed to the stern-post, so that in hauling on it, the weight would be principally borne by the strong bow timbers. I next fixed the tackle on to the painter, and, having rubbed the eye with a piece of fat to make it run easily, secured one end of the tackle to a tree some distance up the slope, and hauled steadily on the other. The canoe ran on to the roller more lightly than I had expected, and I soon had her out of the water and the other rollers in position, with small pegs stuck in the ground to prevent them from running back down the slope when they were released. The slope was but a short one, as the river was nearly full, and with a few hearty pulls at the fall of the tackle, the canoe came up on to the level. Here there was no difficulty at all, for when the lines were laid and the rollers placed, she ran along quite easily.

All the time she was on the road I was in mortal dread of meeting some of the natives; for one cannot hide a canoe at a moment's notice, and my "make-up" might have failed to produce its customary effect. But nobody appeared along the path, and I worked with such a will, that in less than half an hour her stern was overhanging the slope of the lower landing place, and the tackle fixed ready for letting her down. Here the rollers were not really necessary, but were used to save her keels from chafing; with their aid she ran down the incline in fine style, and I had the satisfaction of seeing her once more afloat and sitting on the water, without her cargo, as light as a bubble.

It took but a short time to put the gold on board again, and when this was done I pushed off without stopping to distribute the weight. As the rain was still falling, I let go a length of drag rope and put up the tilt; and as the canoe drifted downstream, I gradually trimmed the cargo into its proper place.

For some miles the river continued to be slightly obstructed by jutting masses of rock, and here and there small rapids occurred; but towards afternoon the stream wider, and its channel quite clear and open.

The loss of speed entailed by the use of the drag was a constant source of regret to me, and as the river was for the present easily navigable, I grudged it the more, and began to consider if it could not be avoided. It occurred to me that, as the water at the bottom of a river flows more slowly than at the surface, perhaps it would be sufficient if I let the sinker hang just clear of the bottom; and on making the experiment I found it to answer perfectly, the slower bottom current checking the canoe just enough to enable her to be steered.

I drifted on for several hours without any incident, making very good progress as I took my ease inside my shelter, and rested after the morning's exertions. I passed two villages, but saw none of the inhabitants, who were probably sheltering indoors from the rain; on the bank, however, by the second village, I noticed a long, flat-bottomed dugout canoe, probably a ferry boat (for the river was already too wide to be spanned by the ordinary single-log bridge), and I noted the fact with interest, as showing that I was entering a more populated region.

About the middle of the afternoon the rain cleared off and as the river was wide and open, I lowered the tilt and took to the paddle, so making up somewhat in the latter part of the day for the delays of the morning; and I continued my voyage thus until the sun began to dip behind the trees. Then having found a secure anchorage on the slack side of the river, I made all snug for the night, and turned in soon after the darkness had set in.

Chapter Twenty-Six
I Put Out Into the Darkness

As soon as the daylight appeared, I put my head out of the tilt opening to take a look at the weather. But I very quickly drew it in again; for within a yard of my face was the massive and unlovely snout of a hippopotamus.

Recovering somewhat from the start he had given me I cautiously peered out again. The huge brute was standing in the shallow water, gazing at the canoe with a fat, stolid smile of conscious superiority that I found highly offensive, and I wished he would go away. Such, however, did not seem to be his intention; he had never seen a canoe like this before, and apparently he was making the most of the experience, for he stood motionless, with his absurd little eyes fixed on me, breathing softly like a blacksmith's bellows, with an exasperating air of contentment.

If I hoisted my anchor, the canoe would drift right on to him, and a sudden movement on his part would be enough to send me to the bottom. It was excessively awkward, for I was anxious to start, and equally anxious to get away from his immediate neighbourhood. I thought of trying the effect of a sudden shout, but I could not tell how he would take it, and he was so very large. Presently he yawned, offering for my inspection a most remarkable collection of very yellow teeth, and I hoped he was becoming bored; but when he closed his cavernous mouth, he resumed his consideration of the canoe with unabated interest.

As he was apparently a fixture, I set about extricating myself from my unpleasant position. Putting the helm hard over and lashing it, I began slowly to haul in the cable until the canoe swung round across the current, clear of the hippopotamus. Then I dropped the sinker and pulled up the anchor, and immediately my bark began to move obliquely downstream and out into the main current.

The hippopotamus gazed regretfully at the retreating canoe, and when it had passed some distance, to my dismay, he walked into the deeper water and began to swim slowly after it. It was not long before he came abreast and passed, when he turned his head upstream and floated down with his eyes fixed on the canoe, from which he maintained a distance of a few yards. Clearly his intentions were not hostile; but, although prompted apparently by mere curiosity, his proceedings caused me considerable uneasiness, and I continued to watch him so closely that I had drifted into a new danger without observing it.

Halfway down the reach that I had just entered, a long canoe was putting off from the bank, and the eight or nine men in her had evidently noticed my canoe, for they were standing up, staring in my direction and pointing, while they shouted to some people on the shore. As I came nearer I could see quite a considerable crowd on the bank, and it was manifest that my vessel and its strange companion were the objects of keen curiosity, for the people on the bank as well as those in the canoe gazed steadily at the approaching phenomenon. The hippopotamus floated on, stern foremost, all unconscious of the spectators, while I, crouching inside the tilt (although the rain had ceased), was concealed from view; but, as the native canoe was being poled up on the shallow side of the river, apparently with the object of intercepting my vessel, I thought it time to make my appearance. I therefore tied on my wig (the horns of which rendered it highly inconvenient inside the tilt), and as the canoe pushed off to meet me, I thrust my head out through the opening.

The first person who saw me was a man in the bow of the dugout, and he announced his discovery by upsetting three of his companions in a frantic attempt to get to the other end of the craft, and finally falling on top of them yelling like a maniac.

For a short time, the dugout was a scene of wild confusion, every man endeavouring to seize a pole or paddle; but she soon reached the bank and was empty in a twinkling, and when I drifted past the landing place not a soul was in sight.

At the first outburst of noise, the hippopotamus had dived, and I now saw him near the top of the reach going upstream at a speed that filled me with envy.

The remainder of the day passed with little incident. When the rain fell, I set up the tilt and lowered the drag, and when it was fine I lowered the tilt and paddled. Once I had to unload the canoe to take her down some rapids, but this caused only a trifling delay; and by the time I let go my anchor for the night in the shelter of a sandbank, I reckoned I had travelled over sixty miles since daybreak.

The next two days saw a repetition of the experiences I have recorded above. One or two unloadings and restowings, one actual portage of a couple of hundred yards, a little paddling, and a great deal of drifting in the heavy rain, would be the principal items in my log. I saw surprisingly few people, a fact that was probably accounted for by the almost incessant rain – for the African is not more partial to getting wet than other people; nor was I troubled any more by animals until the latter half of the fifth day, when the crocodiles began to be unpleasantly numerous and of portentous size. Even these reptiles did not actually molest me, but they were very disagreeable objects to look at, under the circumstances, as they lay on the bank with their enormous jaws agape, while the little spur-winged plover ran round them and peered into the yawning cavities in search of leeches.

I turned in that night with much less feeling of security than I had hitherto experienced, for I felt that if one of these immense brutes should take it into his ugly head to climb on to the canoe, he would either capsize it or scratch a hole through the skin. But nothing untoward happened in the night, and I woke in the morning in high spirits and full of hope.

Indeed, the greater, and by far the most perilous, part of my voyage was over, for the great width of the river, as well as the time I had been on my journey, told me that the coast could not be far off; and once on the coast, was I not in the protected territory of Her Britannic Majesty? In a land of incorruptible police and district commissioners without spot or wrinkle?

Up to the present there had been no opportunity for using the sail, for the river had been so shut in by the forest that the air was nearly motionless; but now the great width of the stream allowed a light breeze to steal up from the south. This was a headwind, it is true, but with my leeboards down and the swift current running to windward I could afford to sail very close, and if I gained little in speed, it was more amusing to sail than to drift. So I stepped the mast, bent the halyard on to the yard and hoisted the sail. Even in that gentle breeze the grey, wrinkled sail gave quite an encouraging pull on the sheet; and when I let down one leeboard and sailed the canoe pretty full across the river, I was delighted to see the way in which the floating rubbish slipped past her side.

Having made this trial of her speed, I put her as close to the wind as she would go, and tacked to and fro across the river; and thus made nearly as much headway as if I had been working with the paddle.

The weather was very pleasant on this morning – the sixth of my solitary voyage; showery, but bright and sunny in the intervals, and as I sat lazily grasping the tiller, I could not but note with admiration the beauty of the scene. On either bank the rich, soft foliage crowded down to the very water's edge, an impenetrable mass of living green, while the slender trunks and branches of the great trees, snow-white in the sunlight, soaring away above the lesser vegetation, spread abroad their leafy canopies. Fantastic lianas drooped in strange festoons from tree to tree, orchids blossomed on the boughs, ferns nestled in the undergrowth, and at the margin of the river, its form faithfully repeated in the still water under the bank, the oil palm lifted its plumy head with indescribable loveliness and grace.

It was wonderfully beautiful, this exuberant life and warm luxuriance of the forest; but I was tired of it – tired of its silence and gloom, its steamy, humid air, its vastness and its loneliness; and I longed for the hum of human life, the bustle and clamour of men at work, and the familiar voice of the sea.

Meditating thus, I tacked my little bark across and across, down the wide reaches by wooded promontories and shady bays, for a couple of hours. And then, as if in obedience to my unspoken wishes, there came a change in the scene. The lofty forest began to recede from the river, and at the water's edge there appeared scattered clumps of bushes of a colourless sagy green. At first they were few and wide apart, but soon they drew together, creeping out into the shallows and hiding the banks, while the forest retreated farther and farther, until it vanished behind their summits.

Then all the beauty of the river was gone, and I looked upon a bare expanse of yellow water, bounded on each side by a low wall of sage-green foliage, monotonous and ugly, but yet to me most welcome.

It was the mangrove.

As I coasted inshore, peering into the gloom among the hideous, skeleton roots of this amphibious forest, I passed, now and again, the mouths of little creeks or channels that appeared to penetrate the swamp. Presently I encountered an island of mangrove, separated from the main swamp by a comparatively broad channel, and reflecting that this creek must open again into the river lower down, I thought I might take this opportunity to examine the interior of a mangrove swamp. So I lowered the sail and mast, and putting the canoe into the channel, allowed her to drift along on the current, which I now noticed had grown quite sluggish, while I tied on my wig, in case I should unexpectedly meet any of the natives.

Soon the channel grew much narrower, but as it was still open ahead, I let the canoe drift on while I looked about me and marvelled at the strangeness of the scene. The trees – if I may call them by that name – appeared to be mere confused tangles of branches, without trunks and standing upon high stilt-like roots that arched and twisted in the most astonishing manner. Moreover, fresh roots appeared, springing from the most unexpected places, some even from the very highest branches, and these dropped down as straight as a plumb-line with their round ends pointing at the water like attenuated fingers.

Before I had drifted very far, the foliage closed completely over the creek, converting it into a dim and gloomy tunnel, and producing a most extraordinary illusion; for the stillness inside the swamp was so absolute that the surface of the water was invisible, the reflections of the trees being quite continuous with the trees themselves, and the one indistinguishable from the other. Overhead was a tangle of branches and leaves, and a similar tangle appeared at an equal distance underneath, while the strange, contorted roots merged above and below into the branches. Thus, as I drifted along, I appeared to be suspended in mid-air in the axis of a large tube of foliage, and the weird, fantastic effect was not lessened when I looked overboard and was confronted by a hideous, horned apparition peering up at me from below.

Such animal life as there was, was in keeping with the ghostly unreality of the scene. Big, piebald kingfishers sat motionless and silent on the roots, with an inverted duplicate perching on the inverted roots below; and purple-bodied crabs crawled along the branches overhead, squinting horribly and seeming to grin with secret amusement at their incongruous position.

I was so much engrossed by the strangeness and novelty of my surroundings that I hardly noticed the passage of time; and I had been drifting along near upon half an hour before I realised how great a delay had been caused by my entering this creek. Then indeed I suddenly became anxious, and even thought of turning back, but reflecting that I should have to return against the current and might possibly miss my way, I decided to push on. So I took my paddle and struck out vigorously, covering the mirror-like surface with ripples and shattering the reflections into a labyrinth of waving zigzags. The canoe now slid through the tortuous tunnel at a good pace, and after traversing a half-mile or so of devious windings, I came in sight of a wide opening; and as my little craft shot through this out into the light of day, I could have shouted for joy, for straight ahead was no forest-clad bank or dingy mangrove, but an ocean-like expanse of grey water, stretching away to the horizon and beyond.

At last I was out of the river and on the great Eyi lagoon; beyond that grey horizon were the sand dunes of Appolonia; behind the sand dunes was the sea!

My exultation received a check at the outset, although not a serious one, for I had barely emerged from the creek when I felt my paddle strike the bottom, and a minute later the canoe ran aground. The explanation was at once obvious: the still water of the mangrove swamp had allowed a mud-flat to form, and the waves of the lagoon, striking the edge of this, had enclosed it with a chain of sandbanks. No doubt there was a passage out, but as the sandbanks were but a little way ahead and I could see the small waves breaking on the farther side, it would be simpler to pull the canoe over the banks and launch her into the deep water beyond. So, taking a look round to see that no small crocodiles were lurking in the shallows, I stepped overboard and took hold of the painter. Relieved of my weight the canoe floated again, and I was able to tow her forward thirty or forty yards, when she once more took the ground. I hauled with all my strength on the painter, but could not drag her more than a few feet, and it was clear that she must be, at least, partly unloaded before I could pull her over the banks; so without more ado I lifted out a couple of bunches of manillas and ran forward with them to the nearest sandbank, where I laid them down.

As each instalment of the cargo was removed, the canoe floated higher and could be drawn nearer to the sandbank, and by the time she was half-empty I had pulled her near enough to get her on to the rollers. To lay down the lines and set the rollers was but the work of a minute, and I now found that on the very gentle slope I could haul her along without further unloading.

The distance was quite short, and as the lines stood well on the hard sand, I soon had her over the bank and launched her into the little popple of waves on the other side. The heap of manillas – only half of my treasure – looked very precious and shining as they lay on the sand at my feet, and I realised their immense value now in a way I had never done before. But this was no time for gloating over my riches; more than half the day was gone, the broad lagoon lay before me, and I had yet to find some secure haven for the night. So I picked up the jingling bunches and stowed them in their places along the floor of the canoe, and sitting on the deck washed the mud and sand from my feet before getting into the well.

At this moment I experienced a terrible shock, for there came to my ear a single, distinct splash; and looking in the direction whence the sound seemed to come, I noticed a small creek penetrating the mangrove. It was very dark inside, but, looking at it attentively, I could just make out the blunt end of a native canoe a short distance from the entrance.

Here, at the end of my journey, my customary caution had forsaken me. I had spread out the heap of shining gold in the broad daylight in such perfect confidence of there being no onlookers, that I had taken not the slightest precaution. And there could hardly be any doubt that my treasure had been seen, although the occupant of the canoe was invisible to me. It was more than provoking, for it might mean disaster, and as I stepped the mast and pushed off from the shore, I cursed my folly in making so unpardonable a slip.

But when once the sail was up and the leeboard down I felt more comfortable, for a fine fresh breeze blew in from the sea, and the canoe thrashed through the water at a pace that gave me confidence in her powers. In a few minutes the shore was well astern, and I began to hug myself with the belief that the occupant of the native canoe was only some harmless fisherman gathering oysters from the mangrove roots. But, from time to time, my eyes wandered uneasily to the opening of the creek, until presently I saw the canoe emerge and, coasting rapidly down inside the sandbanks, pass through some opening out into the lagoon.

There was one man in the canoe and, oyster-gatherer as he probably was, his appearance suggested something less unsophisticated than a common fisherman, for he wore a velvet smoking cap and a jacket and trousers of coloured cotton – habiliments that seemed to savour of the native trader or "scholar man".

As soon as he had gained the open lagoon, he headed his craft straight into my wake, and the energy and purpose with which he plied his pole left me in little doubt that he was following me; from which two unpleasant corollaries might be deduced, *viz.* that he had seen the gold, and that he cared not a fig for my horns and beard, having detected the white man under the disguise.

Soon the water grew too deep for his pole and he had to take to the paddle, much to my satisfaction – for the paddle is a comparatively feeble appliance for driving a large heavy dugout – and as a result, he soon began to fall astern; but he worked with a will, and soon I saw that I should have great difficulty in shaking him off.

The behaviour of my canoe gave me unbounded satisfaction. She bore her sail well, and would have carried more with ease, even in this fresh breeze; her speed was fully up to my expectations, and, with her leeboard down, she made hardly any leeway. She was quite dry, too, although the lagoon was very choppy, and the sharp, hollow waves struck her with great force; but I was glad I had put a high coaming round the well, for the water splashed freely across the deck.

It was greatly against me in the race with my unknown pursuer that I knew next to nothing of the locality and that I had no settled destination, for had I only had some refuge to make for, I could have drawn ahead of him without difficulty. As it was, my goal was the south shore of the lagoon, which I knew ran parallel to the sea shore, but how wide was the strip of land separating the lagoon from the sea, I could not tell. It might be a few hundred yards or it might be several miles.

I had not been sailing very long before a few scattered coconut palms appeared above the horizon ahead and soon the south shore was well in sight, running apparently due east and west; and as the wind blew from the south-west, I had to sail pretty close-hauled to head due south, in which, however, I was assisted by the current from the river, which ran sluggishly to the west.

As I approached the shore, I rapidly turned over the alternatives it presented. I could go about and sail due west towards Assiní, where there was a European Station – French, I believed. But Assiní was a long way off – from twenty to thirty miles – and I should have to sail all night in unknown waters to reach it, while my pursuer would certainly follow with reinforcements. Then I could go straight on shore and investigate; or lastly, I could sail eastward with the wind and look for a suitable place to land.

I chose the last plan, as it gave me the advantage of a fair wind, and when I had come within a few hundred yards of the shore I turned sharply to the east and ran along at fine speed in the smooth water, with my sheet well out.

The appearance of the shore was not encouraging. The longed-for boom of the surf was indeed audible, but it sounded a long way off, as if a wide stretch of land lay between me and the sea; and straight ahead, at a distance of a few miles, a headland jutted out far into the lagoon.

Just as I was beginning to despair of getting to the sea, I opened a small bay, at the head of which a rather wide creek could be seen, winding away in a southerly direction. Without a moment's hesitation I put down my helm and, heading up the bay, entered the creek. It appeared to be a temporary or recent opening through the land, probably caused by the overflow of the lagoon at the first burst of the rains, for its banks were destitute of vegetation and covered with shingle; and I was in momentary dread of coming to the end of it, especially as I noticed that the water was quite still and stagnant.

Finding the creek too narrow to sail in, I lowered the sail and mast and took to the pole, with which I drove the canoe rapidly through the sinuous channel, my hopes rising as reach after reach was passed. But the banks gradually closed in, and the water grew shallower until presently an ominous grating sensation told me that the keel was on the bottom, and the next moment the canoe stopped dead.

I was now among a range of old grass-covered sand dunes, and the hollow throb of the surf seemed close at hand, so, leaping ashore, I ran up one of the dunes and looked south. But a few hundred yards away was a bare and open beach with the snowy surf and the blue ocean beyond; a mile to the west a small cluster of huts marked a fishing village, but not a creature was in sight.

Turning my gaze northward, I swept the wide expanse of lagoon. On all that great stretch of water I could see but a single human figure – that of my pursuer, poling furiously (for he was now in the shallows), and just entering the bay.

I ran quickly along the dwindling creek to its termination among the sandhills. From the foot of the dunes a level space of loose, blown sand extended for a couple of hundred yards, then the actual beach sloped down pretty steeply right into the surf.

If it had not been for this fellow who was dogging me so suspiciously, my task would have been simple enough – until I launched into the surf; and for a moment the idea of ridding myself of this enemy by a thrust of my spear crossed my mind. But instantly dismissing it, I set about unloading the canoe with all speed. There was no time to make any arrangements for carrying the gold; I could only take up a pair of bunches in each hand and stagger off with them to the foot of the sandhills, drop them there and return for more. But this took up a considerable time, besides being very fatiguing, and I had only made five journeys when, as

I returned, I saw the velvet-capped head of my pursuer over the land, zigzagging along the next reach but one.

By this time my canoe was well afloat again, so catching the painter I ran off, towing her after me, and got her nearly a hundred yards before she went aground again. As she did so, the dugout suddenly appeared round the bed of the creek, and the man, pole in hand, jumped ashore and ran up into the sandhills, where he disappeared.

Whether he was hiding to spy on me, or was preparing to take me unawares, it was evidently impossible to continue the unloading, and I was inclined to take the offensive and pursue him; but time was pressing, for the afternoon was well advanced, so I got out my lines and holding two of them on the bottom with my feet, pushed a roller under the canoe's forefoot. With some difficulty I dragged her forward a little distance, and then slipped another roller under, and so managed to haul her right on to the rails, and when she was fairly on the rollers, I drew her along quite easily, a good deal of the weight being still borne by the water. I had pulled her along some distance when I noticed a large shell on the bottom, and thinking this might cut her skin, I stooped quickly to pick it up. As I did so, a big stone whizzed past, a few inches above my head. Had I been standing upright I should have been knocked senseless.

This sort of thing would not do, at any rate, I thought, so snatching my catapult, stone bag and spear from the canoe, I ran to a sandhill opposite the one from which the missile had appeared to come, and creeping up it, crouched behind a high tussock of reedy grass. For nearly a minute my antagonist remained invisible. Then a head was warily advanced from behind the shoulder of the hill and slowly followed by the body.

I fitted a good sized stone into my catapult and waited. Finding that I made no sign, he crept farther forward, and I saw that he held a large stone in one hand and a reserve of similar ones in the other. Suddenly I perceived that he was about to fling a stone at the canoe, possibly to draw me from my concealment; which it did, for I instantly let fly the pebble from my catapult, hitting him on the bone of the elbow; and as he leaped to his feet with a howl of rage, I caught up my spear and charged down the slope at him. Before he could recover himself I was so near that further dodging was out of the question, and he turned tail and ran for his life down the sandhills and out on to the sandy flat, while I followed at his heels shouting like a Bedlamite. But I could not waste time in pursuit, so I stopped and taking careful aim, sent another pebble after him, which struck him a very audible rap on the back of his head, making him run even faster; and I continued to take shots at him (lest he should irresolutely turn back) until he took to the wet beach, and was evidently going off for assistance.

Returning to the canoe, I continued the work of hauling her along, and managed without much difficulty until I came to the end of the creek, and laid my lines on the soft, blown sand, when I found it necessary to lighten her further.

A little more than half the gold was now unshipped, and in this trim I was able to haul the canoe, foot by foot, across the level sand flat; but it was slow work, since the lines and rollers had to be continually shifted forward, and it seemed a long time before the shore was reached. At last, however, I had the satisfaction of giving the final push that sent the canoe's bow clear of the little cliff where the blown sand was undermined by the wash of the surf, and was able to set a pair of lines on the hard sand of the beach.

What little tide there is on the West Coast of Africa seemed to be full, for when the canoe had rolled down a single length of the lines, her forward half was on the wet sand, and washed by the edge of each wave that rushed up the steep slope of the beach. Further than this I could not lower her until she was loaded, as the breaking water would have lifted her and thrown her broadside on to the shore.

All this time I kept a sharp lookout up and down the beach, but the solitude was still unbroken save by the solitary figure of my assailant, which had now dwindled to a mere speck in the distance, and seemed to be close to the fishing hamlet.

Having removed all the rollers but the middle one (so that the canoe should not run away down the beach), I made my first journey to the sandhills, bringing back with me four bunches of manillas, which I stowed and tied in their places – for it would be madness to venture into the surf with this ponderous cargo unsecured. Then I returned for a fresh load, and as I crossed the flat, noted that my enemy had disappeared into the village. The transport of this quantity of gold over so great a distance was a rather formidable task, and could not be got over quickly. Four bunches of manillas represented about eighty pounds, and there were some thirty bunches on the sandhills.

As I toiled over the soft, blown sand with my fourth load I observed with some alarm, but little surprise, a number of black specks issuing from the village. My friend was returning with reinforcements.

The village was but a mile distant, and I had yet four more loads to carry. It looked as if I should have to leave some of my spoil behind, and as I ran panting to the sandhills and tottered back, sweating under my burden, I watched with growing anxiety the increasing size of the spots of darkness on the yellow beach.

By the time I had stowed the seventh instalment, the spots had clearly resolved themselves into figures advancing at a rapid run, and I debated for an instant whether I should not abandon the three bunches that remained. Only for an instant, however. Greed and reluctance to leave sixty pounds weight of good yellow gold to these thieving rascals settled the question, and for the last time I raced across the loose sand. Catching up the three bunches, I set out for the beach at a kind of stumbling trot, and as I appeared from behind the sandhills, the approaching party saw me, and burst into a shout. Then followed a mad race for the canoe.

The natives came on, kicking up clouds of sand in their furious haste, shouting and brandishing long knives; while I, panting and sweating, with my heart pounding like a steam-hammer, staggered forward jingling like a team of sleigh-horses.

At last I reached the canoe, and, flinging in the manillas, threw down the second pair of lines ahead, stood on them that they should not wash away, and slipping a roller under the forefoot of the canoe, dragged her on to it. Instantly she began to move forward with such weight that I could hardly hold her back. But the waves were, for the moment, small, and barely reached over my ankles; so I slipped another roller under her stem, and eased her slightly forward.

A glance to seaward showed me a great comber just about to break. A glance ashore revealed a dozen men, not a hundred yards distant, racing wildly forward, shouting and flourishing knives and hatchets. A boom from the sea and a yell from the land came simultaneously to my ears. The wave had broken, and its shattered fragments came driving forward in a snowy, roaring avalanche, but so slowly, that the men were almost upon me before I felt it boil up around my feet.

Then I let go, and the canoe rumbled down with gathering momentum, and as her bow plunged into the foam, I leaped into the well and snatched up the paddle. With such weight did she fly down the slope, that she hardly checked when she met the onrushing flood, but swam clear into the seething brine, and moved steadily forward. The men were close behind, and I could hear them splashing into the water as I wildly plied my paddle.

The water paused in its movement for a few brief seconds. and I waited to know my fate. Then, with a resounding roar, the great mass swept back in the undertow, hurling the canoe forward with breathless velocity. I had just time to pull the apron round me when there came a crashing shock, a thump on my chest, and a blinding cataract of spray. She had dived into the recoil wave, and for a moment I thought she had gone under, but as the water streamed off my face, I saw that her weight had carried her through the wave.

Breathless as I was, I plied my paddle vigorously to avoid being flung back on to the beach, and steered cautiously towards the surf.

Another great comber had rolled in, and the pile of foaming water was sweeping inshore, looking very high and threatening from my position. I put the canoe straight on to it, and got up what speed I could, expecting such a sousing as I had just had; but she was now on an even keel, and her weight was mostly stowed amidships, so when the great mass of water struck her she merely flung her bows up into the air, and sent a fountain of spray on either side. I continued to paddle cautiously forward towards the line of breaking waves until I was as near as I dared to go; then I waited for the interval that comes periodically in the surf, and only paddled enough to hold my ground, whilst the broken water struck me blow after blow, and tended to sweep me inshore.

At length, as a great wave curled over and burst with a dull explosion, I looked over the wall of foam, and could see no following crest.

Now was my time, while the brief lull lasted, and digging the paddle deep into the water, I charged straight forward at the advancing wall of foam. As I met it, the canoe nearly stood on end, and the spray flew up in a cloud, but the ballast prevented me from being thrown back, and as the bubbling water swept past, I paddled for my life. If I failed to dodge the surf now I must inevitably be swamped.

As I drew near the main line of the surf, the brief lull came to an end, and I saw a huge wave sweeping towards me, growing higher as it approached, like a moving mountain. Onward it came, all in a tremble, rearing its colossal bulk above me until I could see the sky through its green crest. Then a spot of white appeared on its summit with a hissing murmur; the edge began to turn over, and as the canoe soared upward, the murmur swelled into a roar. In the midst of a blinding cloud of spray I felt the canoe check and begin to turn, and with the energy of despair I plied my paddle to keep her head to the sea.

For an instant my fate hung trembling in the balance, but a moment later the full explosion of the bursting wave boomed from just astern, and the canoe sank into the rear hollow.

But I was not yet safe, for my bark had been thrown back some distance, and I dug my paddle viciously into the water as I struggled to regain my place. Another immense wave came rolling in shorewards, and as the canoe flew upward with a velocity that took away my breath, the crest crumbled into foam, and blinded me with a shower of spray. But it held the canoe only for a moment, and then I slid down the back of the wave. A dozen more strokes of the paddle carried me out of immediate peril, for the next wave, though it towered above me in a most terrifying manner, only whisked me up into the sky, and dropped me on its farther side, without so much as a sprinkle of spray. I was safely through the surf, and when I had paddled for yet a few minutes more, to get a proper offing (for this was a lee shore), I ventured to look about me, and to see how my late pursuers were faring.

I could only see the beach at intervals, when I was lifted on the shoreward face or summit of a wave, and when I looked at the place whence I had put off, my pursuers were nowhere to be seen. It was only when I turned my gaze westward, towards the village, that I made out a constellation of black specks on the beach near to it. And then I saw something else. Another group of moving specks surrounded some larger object, with which they were moving towards the sea. The villagers were launching a fishing canoe, and I could have little doubt of their object. The pursuit was not over yet.

As soon as I realised this, I lost no time in getting my mast stepped, and the halyard bent on to the yard. and, having done this, I lowered the port leeboard and the drop-rudder, and hoisted the sail.

The breeze that was blowing outside here was fresher than that on the lagoon, and, although the high waves partly becalmed the sail at times, the sheet pulled sturdily, and I could tell by the pressure of the tiller that my craft was slipping through the sea at a good pace. In spite of all her buffeting, she had taken in practically no water, thanks to the apron, and now she was going perfectly dry, for the big ocean waves on which she rose and fell were far easier than the quick, choppy waters of the lagoon.

When she was fairly under sail, I turned the canoe's head obliquely out to sea, heading in a south-easterly direction, thus keeping the wind a little free; and having put her on her course, again turned my attention to my pursuers. From time to time I could catch a glimpse of them, and noticed that they looked smaller each time. I saw them launch their canoe from the beach, and watched its protracted struggles as it dodged and waited for the dangerous surf. But at last, after several trials and failures, it shot through, and fairly started in pursuit.

Meanwhile the afternoon had merged into evening. The cloudy horizon took on a coppery glow; and I had hardly seen the pursuing canoe head into my wake before the brief twilight faded, and left the sea in darkness.

Chapter Twenty-Seven
Ship Ahoy!

To a small craft like mine, a passage by sea on a dark night is ordinarily an adventure full of peril and anxiety, and eye and ear must be constantly strained to catch the gleam of approaching lights or the warning throb of a propeller.

But in the lonely waters of the Gulf of Guinea there is – at any rate at this season of the year – only one great danger – the surf-bound shore; and the navigator who keeps a good offing and attends to the lead, has little to fear.

Hence, as I crouched in the well with my few rags drawn round me for warmth, I steered forward quite confidently, although I could not see a hundred yards ahead, for I had laid my course obliquely off the land, and, even making a liberal allowance for leeway, I must be drawing pretty rapidly out to sea.

I had, indeed, no compass, nor was any star visible in the black vault, but I could feel the wind and the run of the sea, and these I knew to be constant enough to steer by quite safely. So I sailed on, rising and falling easily on the great round swell, enjoying a strange and novel sense of security; for ahead of me were no unknown rapids or cataracts, no sunken rocks or hidden snags, but only a waste of waters on which the morning light might show some friendly sail.

As to my pursuers, I had almost forgotten them. They had certainly put off to follow me, but I had so long a start that I felt no fear of their overtaking me, and thought it probable that they had already given up the pursuit and put back.

When I had been sailing — as I judged — a little over an hour, the moon struggled faintly through the clouds in the west, illuminating the sky around and throwing a broad, unsteady wake of light. And right in the middle of the wake, far away and small, but quite sharp and distinct, I could see the black silhouette of the pursuing canoe, and could even make out the paddles, rising and falling with machine-like regularity.

My confidence was shattered at a blow, for, far away as the canoe appeared, it had shortened considerably the distance that at first separated us. The chase bid fair to be a long one, and I might even tire out my pursuers; but I knew the strength and endurance of the Gold Coast canoemen, and my hopes declined once more.

The moon soon sank below the horizon, and the pursuing craft was again invisible in the darkness; but I knew she was there and that she was creeping slowly up to me, and I looked often and anxiously into the obscurity astern, although, of course, I could see nothing. I turned over several plans of escape, but rejected them all. I thought of changing my course by going closer to the wind on the chance that the canoemen might miss me in the darkness, and I even considered lowering my sail to render my vessel still more difficult to see, and then paddling straight out to sea. But I had so often had proof of the amazing keenness of eyesight of African natives — especially of their ability to see in almost complete darkness — that I did not trust either of these plans, and they would both greatly diminish my speed.

On the other hand, if I turned more off the wind I should sail faster, but then I might easily run ashore in the darkness; so, in the end, I decided to hold on as I was going, and trust to tiring out the canoemen before they could overtake me, or fighting them when they did.

Some little time had elapsed since the setting of the moon had hidden my enemies from my sight, when a faint sound from astern made me prick up my ears. Presently it was repeated, and I now clearly distinguished voices – probably raised in altercation, but too distant to be intelligible. Clearly the canoe was overhauling me, and I listened intently to try if I could make out the thud of the paddles. It was not yet audible, and the voices had now died away; but even as I was listening, I was startled by a new sound that broke out loud and clear in the stillness of the dark sea – a sound that instantly revived my drooping hopes.

It was an accordion, raucously blurting out the rollicking air of "Finnigan's Wake."

I peered about me in astonishment, but the darkness around was impenetrable, until I lifted the boom and looked out under the foot of the sail; then my heart bounded with joy, for out of the obscurity shone a bright red light that sent a wavering thread of reflection along the surface of the water.

A sailing vessel was approaching me on the opposite tack and the glimmer of her port light must have been visible for some time (for she was quite near now) but had been hidden from me by my sail; and but for that unmelodious instrument I might not have seen her until she had passed out of hail.

I instantly put up my helm and sheered down towards her, and as the light shone straight over my bows, I raised my voice in a mighty shout.

"Oh! the ship ahoy!"

The accordion stopped abruptly and I listened for an answer, but, as none came, I hailed again.

"Ship ahoy!"

"Hallo!" shouted a voice in return.

"Heave-to and pick us up," I sang out.

"Who are you?" demanded the invisible speaker.

"Shipwrecked seaman!" I bellowed at the top of my voice.

"Where away?" inquired the other.

"On your port bow," I replied; and immediately I heard the voice – presumably that of the lookout – repeating my answer to the officer of the watch.

In a few seconds a new voice hailed me.

"Boat ahoy!"

"Hallo!" I roared.

"I'm going to heave-to. Come alongside as sharp as you can."

"Aye, aye, sir," I answered, and I certainly felt no temptation to dawdle under the circumstances.

The red light grew rapidly brighter, and soon there loomed above it in the darkness a great shape of deeper shade, which, as I approached, took on the definite outline of the masts and sails of a brig. She was hove-to with the foretopsail aback, but was moving slowly forward.

I lowered my sail and ran alongside just as a rope ladder was tumbled over about amidships, and to the rope side of this I immediately made fast my painter with a "fisherman's bend" so that the canoe should not pull adrift.

"He's alongside, sir," a voice reported to the officer, who immediately sang out, "Swing the yards and sheet home the foresail."

There was a tramp of feet followed by the squeak of parrel and sheave, and the flapping of canvas, and then the voice of the officer sounded from above: "Come, tumble up, my man; I've got underway."

"One moment, sir, while I make all fast," I replied, for I was just lowering and securing my mast.

When I had done this, I lashed the tiller over a little to give the canoe a cast off from the vessel, so that she should tow clear without bumping, and then I secured the well cover, as she would splash a good deal while towing, and might take in a serious amount of water.

"Now then!" shouted the officer impatiently, "are you going to be all night there? Here, give me the lantern and let's have a look at him."

I hauled on the painter and got on to the ladder, up which I ran nimbly. As my head came above the bulwark rail, a lantern flashed full in my face, and a startled voice exclaimed – "Jesus!"

The lantern was slapped down on the deck, there was a stamping of feet, and with a simultaneous bang, the forecastle scuttle and the doors of the companion hatch were slammed to. When I recovered from the blinding glare of the lantern and looked around, the deck was deserted.

I was struck dumb with amazement, but there was no time to marvel at this astonishing conduct of the ship's company. The pursuing canoe must be close up by now, and I must look to the safety of my treasure.

Running across the deck, I looked out over the lee rail. The fishing canoe could be dimly seen a little distance away on the leebow, turning round and evidently making ready either to cross our bows or run alongside under our lee, and her crew were hailing the brig lustily. Now my canoe was towing on the weather side, so it was important that the pursuers should be prevented from crossing our bows, or they might dash alongside, cut my painter, and be off with the freighted canoe towards the shore, whither we could not follow them. So I took hold of the deserted wheel and put the helm a little up, bringing the brig back on her course (for she was nearly broaching-to); I then kept it up so that she fell off a little more, and so headed straight for the fishing canoe.

By this manoeuvre I not only ascertained beforehand which side the fishermen intended to board us, but left myself the means of dodging them on either side; for if they crossed our bows I could up helm and run before the wind, leaving them on the weather quarter, and luffing back gradually as they fell astern; while if they tried to run alongside under our lee, I could luff suddenly and leave them on the lee quarter.

As soon as the brig headed towards them, they backed a stroke or two, showing that they intended to board us on the leeside, as is usual. I kept the helm a little up, edging imperceptibly more off the wind, and they continued to back their paddles to keep clear of the advancing vessel. As the brig approached them, they began to paddle forward to run alongside, but at this moment I jammed the helm hard up, and the brig swung round and charged straight at the canoe. The terrified fishermen, howling with fear, backed frantically for their lives to escape the onrushing bows that towered above them, and in the midst of their confusion, I spun the wheel round in the opposite direction, putting the helm hard down. The brig immediately came round on to her course, presenting her stern to the fishermen, who must now have grasped the object of the manoeuvre, for they paddled furiously in a wild effort to get alongside. But they were too late. They were now dead astern of the brig and travelling only half as fast, and before I could fairly get my breath, the darkness had hidden them from view.

All this time I had been conscious of confused noises and smothered mutterings from the companion hatch, and now the doors cautiously opened, revealing a huddle of heads standing black against the light that streamed up from the cabin.

"Mother of God!" exclaimed a hushed and awe-stricken voice. "He's steering the ship! and phwhere will we be bound for, I'd like to know?"

Suddenly a loud familiar voice broke out from below: "Now, what's all this damned nonsense you're talking. Here, let me come." And as the heads were withdrawn, the companion doors flew open and a bulky form arose from the hatch.

Halfway up, however, it stopped abruptly, and I heard it hoarsely ejaculate: "Great snakes!"

"Isn't it the truth I was tellin' ye, sorr?" asked a voice from below.

There was silence for a moment, and then the man in the companion demanded in a stern but shaky voice: "Who's that at the wheel?"

"Shoore anny fool can see who it is," murmured the voice from below.

"It's I, Captain Bithery," I replied. "Your old purser, Richard Englefield."

"Englefield!" exclaimed Bithery incredulously. "Then all I've got to say is that you've most damnably altered for the worse since I saw you last."

He emerged slowly from the companion and stepped sideways across the deck, keeping his face towards me, until he came to the lantern, which he picked up and held above his head, advancing towards me with the extremest caution and a singular scowl of terrified suspicion on his face.

I gazed at him in blank amazement until it suddenly flashed upon me that I was still wearing my horned wig; when, with a shout of laughter, I untied the beard and, tearing off the hideous adornment, flung it down upon the deck.

"Good God, Englefield!" ejaculated Bithery, "what an awful start you gave me. What, in the name of fortune, induced you to come aboard in these devil's trappings? You've frightened the ship's company into fits."

"I'm really very sorry, Captain," said I, wiping away a tear with the back of my hand. "The fact is, I have only just escaped from the natives, and I had quite forgotten my character costume."

"Well, Moloney's not likely to forget it in a hurry," responded Bithery, with one of his dear old familiar lopsided grins. "He was going round his rosary like a sprinter at Lillie Bridge when I came through the cabin. Here, Moloney!" he shouted, "it's only Mr Englefield. Come up and have a look at him."

"Oi'll see the gintleman in the morning," replied Moloney faintly from the cabin; on which the skipper chuckled and invited me to come below.

"We can't leave the wheel," said I.

"No, that's true," replied Bithery, and catching up the lantern, he ran forward and pushed back the forecastle scuttle.

"Come up out of that, you infernal fools!" he bawled.

A man popped his head up through the opening and looked round the deck.

"Is he gone, sir?" he asked anxiously.

"Gone!" roared Bithery. "Why, you confounded idiot, it's my old purser come aboard."

"Damn funny-looking purser," remarked the man, without offering to come up any farther.

Hereupon the Captain entered into a brief explanation, and the men emerged one by one and reluctantly followed him down the deck.

"Whose trick at the wheel?" demanded Bithery.

"Bob Gummer's, sir," replied the men cheerfully, in chorus, and they immediately retreated forward, leaving the unfortunate Gummer standing alone.

"Take the wheel, Gummer," said the Captain, and, as the man seemed unwilling, he added sharply: "Catch hold of it, man! It won't bite you."

As I let go the spokes, and the alarmed Gummer took charge (on the opposite side of the wheel), Bithery again suggested that we should go below.

"I must unload my canoe first," I said.

"Oh, hang your canoe," replied the Captain. "Come and have some grub."

"But I've got about half a ton of gold in her," said I.

"Half a ton of gold!" ejaculated the skipper. "Are you mad or are you joking?"

"Neither," I replied. "The fact is, I struck a fetish hoard and got off with part of it, and that's the reason I appeared in that striking make-up."

"Do you really mean it, Englefield? Half a ton! My eye!"

He ran to the bulwark and looked over at the canoe towing alongside; then he lifted up his voice in a lusty shout: "All hands stand by to bout ship!"

That shout broke the spell that had lain upon the brig since my arrival. The afterguard came bundling out of the companion, the seamen ran to their stations by sheets and braces, and the steersman spun the wheel until its spokes were invisible.

"Helm's a-lee!" roared Bithery.

The thunder of flapping canvas, mingled with the stamping of feet, filled the deck with noise and confusion, above which presently rose trumpet-like the voice of the skipper: "Topsail haul!"

More thumping of sails and squealing of blocks, until the main-topsail filled and the brig drew off on the starboard tack.

"Shorten sail and heave the brig to, Mr Jobling," said the skipper. "Mr Englefield has some heavy stuff to unload from his canoe; and we shall want a dozen kernel bags."

"Very well, sir," replied Jobling; and recognising me for the first time, he exclaimed, "How d'ye do, Mr Englefield?" and then added, "Good Lord! You *are* an ugly-looking beggar!"

The remark, if over-candid, was not, I fear, without truth; for as I stood there, naked but for my kilt, emaciated, dirty, with a half-grown heard and a bristly poll, my appearance must have been unprepossessing in the extreme; and perhaps Bob Gummer was less unreasonable than I had at first thought him.

As soon as the canvas had been reduced and the brig hove-to, I took a couple of kernel bags and went down the ladder. Throwing back the well cover, I crawled in under the canoe's deck and dragged a pair of bunches of manillas from the forward part of the cargo into the well; and as I was stuffing them into a bag, the skipper came down the ladder with a rope having a pair of sharp hooks spliced into an eye at the end.

"I've passed this through a snatch block above," he explained; "but you had better follow each bag up the ladder, in case of accidents."

I stuck the hooks through the neck of the strong canvas bag and gave the word to hoist, and as the first instalment went up I followed, holding on to it, until it swung in over the rail.

The skipper soon reappeared and was evidently greatly excited, for he came scuttling down the ladder, and leaning over the well, exclaimed, "It's all right, Englefield, they're the right stuff. By gum! But you've struck it rich this time, and no mistake. It pays to be a lunatic."

I had another bag ready by now, and the skipper convoyed this to the deck, sending down a couple of empty bags on the hooks.

So the unloading went on, the skipper's wonder and delight increasing as bag after bag went aloft.

"You ought to see the stuff, my boy," he chuckled when twenty-four had been transshipped. "I've stowed it on the lower bunk in the spare berth that you are to have. It's a sight, I can tell you; reminds me of the Arabian Nights or the vaults of the Bank of England. Are these hooks secure? All right; heave up!" and away went number twenty-five over the rail.

The twenty-ninth was a light load with only one bunch in it, and this was the last of the cargo. As it vanished inboard, I drew up the drop-rudder and ascended the ladder.

"Is it all out?" asked the Captain, popping up out of the companion like a Jack-in-the-box.

"The cargo is all out," I answered. "There is only the canoe to hoist in."

"You don't want the canoe, do you?" said Bithery.

"Why not send her adrift?"

"I couldn't do it, Captain," I replied. "She's as much to me as the *Lady Jane* is to you. You'll understand when I spin you the yarn."

"Very well," said the skipper. "Get the canoe hoisted on deck, Mr Jobling;" and the mate, with a gang of hands, got to work with such will that, in a few minutes, I had the satisfaction of seeing the trusty little craft, that had brought me through so many dangers, reposing peacefully on the deck.

"Where did you get this canoe, Englefield?" asked Bithery, sniffing round her with a puzzled air. "I didn't know they made this sort of craft in these parts. I've seen nothing but dugouts."

"I built her myself," I replied; "built her of bark and branches in the forest;" whereupon the skipper seized me by the arm and dragged me to the companion.

"Come below and pitch us the yarn," said he. "I am in the humour to believe anything, and my flesh is beginning to creep in anticipation."

So I went below, and having been furnished with a country cloth, put it on toga-wise, when I looked, as Bithery remarked, "like a Roman Emperor – rather dirty one," and thus sat down at the table.

How sumptuous the cabin looked, with its polished wood, its red silk curtains, its swinging lamp, and the white cloth, and glittering table appointments! Quite spacious, too, after my tiny lair on the island. But I am afraid my attention was principally concentrated on the eatables – the ox tongue, the boiled fowls, the yellow Canary potatoes, and other unfamiliar delicacies, at which I found myself glaring with wolfish enjoyment.

"My eye, Englefield," exclaimed the Captain, as I sent up my plate for the fourth time, "you've got a pretty good twist on you. You won't be long filling out at this rate."

"How are the Pereiras?" I asked, disregarding his remark.

"Mister or Miss?" he inquired, eyeing me sideways, like a parrot examining a doubtful banana.

"Both," I replied.

"Why, the fact is," said he, "they have been worried to death about you. You see, there were all sorts of unpleasant rumours that seem to have reached them, I don't quite know how, and made them very anxious and miserable; and then, only last week, we all got a very nasty knock. A fellow at Cape Coast (one of Miller Brothers' people) bought a gold watch from some natives from the interior and he showed it to me. I noticed a Ramsgate jeweller's name on the dial, and what I took to be your initials on the back – but you know what these infernal monograms are, all scrolls and flummery – so I bought it and showed it to Pereira, and he knew it at once. We couldn't find out where the natives got it from, but there it was; and it so upset the Pereiras that they made up their minds to fit out an expedition and go up country to make inquiries."

"You don't mean that Pereira was going himself?"

"My impression was that they were both going. They seemed to think that you might be hung up somewhere in the interior, and that it might be possible to get you away by purchase or ransom. However, you seem to have ransomed yourself pretty completely."

"Where are you bound now?" I asked with some anxiety.

"I *was* bound to Grand Bassam (I left Axim late this afternoon), but I was only going to look for chance cargo. I shall give up the trip now, and as soon as we have got enough offing to clear Cape Three Points, I shall put her nose straight for Quittáh. Mr Jobling!" he bawled through the open skylight.

"Sir!" said the mate, taking a bird's eye view of the cabin through the opening.

"How's her head, Mr Jobling?"

"South by east a quarter east, sir," replied the mate.

"Put her east by south and set the stu'nsails, and let me know when you see the light on Cape Three Points."

The mate repeated the order and vanished, and I could soon feel by the altered motion of the vessel that we were heading east.

As soon as the table was cleared, and the spirits and cigars set on it, the Captain mixed a glass of grog, lit a cigar, and settled himself in a corner of the cushioned locker with the air of a man who is about to be entertained. The second mate had turned in and the mate was on deck, so we had the cabin to ourselves.

"Now, my boy," said the Captain, "let's have the yarn from the beginning."

After all my exertions and the enormous meal I had made, I should have preferred to idle away the evening and turn in early; but the skipper's curiosity had to be satisfied, so I plunged into the narrative of my adventures without preamble.

The account which I gave him was necessarily sketchy and condensed, but even so, eight bells had been struck and the watch changed before he rose to see me to my berth.

"You see I've covered the gold up for tonight," he said, as he shook me by the hand. "Tomorrow morning I will let you have an empty chest to stow it away in."

I turned back the covering and gazed complacently at the glittering mass spread out on the bunk, and putting no little strain on its stout oak bottom. Fortune had favoured me at last. I was a rich man, and if only I prospered as well in the adventure that lay before me, I felt that I should indeed be a happy one.

The whole of the next day we sailed parallel to the coast, and some twenty miles off the land; and as the brig sped on with all her flying kites abroad and the good Guinea current helping her along, I paced the deck with a buoyant heart, resplendent in one of Jobling's white drill suits, and washed and shaven as became a civilised man of fortune.

By sunset we were well past Winnebah; before I turned in, the lights of the shipping in Accra roadstead were visible; and when I came on deck at daybreak, the low shore was full in sight and the roaring surf of Adda was under our lee. I looked shorewards at the spouting breakers with solemn interest, for that snowy surf marked the mouth of the great Firráo (or Volta) River, whose upper waters I had crossed so recently, a fettered captive, fresh from the horrors of the mine. And then I thought of the rascally Sálifu and of honest Isaaku and his family, friends and foes now scattered abroad in the great continent; and of poor Aminé, so tender, so loving and so true, sleeping under her cairn in the lonely forest. And so I grew pensive and sad, while I watched the dreary shore of the Bight of Benin creep along the horizon until Cape St Paul lay well on our quarter.

Then indeed I roused from my melancholy with a sudden burst of joyous anticipation; for the skipper had turned every rag out of the flag locker and was covering the brig from deck to truck with bunting.

A German steamer tugged at her anchor ahead; busy surf-boats crawled to and fro like many-legged beetles; and plain on our port bow were the white roofs and soft green palms of Quittáh.

Chapter Twenty-Eight
In Which I Bid Farewell to the Reader

The *Lady Jane* glided up the bay, taking in sail as she went; and as square after square of creamy white canvas was gathered up into wrinkled festoons, the men began to crowd out on to the yards, and the hoarsely-carolled strains of "Old Horse" and "Paddy Doyle" mingled with the music of running rigging. As the brig opened out the whitewashed fort from behind the trees, she slewed up into the wind; the report of the little brass gun on the poop rang out sharply, and the chain thundered out through the hawse-pipe.

No sooner was the anchor fairly down than the Captain commenced to spy inquisitively at the shore through his telescope, which he steadied against a shroud; nor were his observations long without result, for after about ten minutes' spying he suddenly beckoned to me.

"Pereira's boat has put off," said he; "I know her by her white paint."

"Is anyone coming with her?" I asked nervously.

"I can't see yet – Yes I can, by Jove! – Yes, the old man's on board; I can make out his black coat and topper."

"No one else?"

"No, I can't see anybody else. No, there's only one chair in the boat, and the old man's sitting in it."

I drew a breath of relief.

I should have been sorry for my first meeting with Isabel to take place in public, for my position with regard to her was one of some delicacy and difficulty. That she loved me I had little doubt; but yet, since I had spoken no word to her, I could not take her love for granted, especially after so long an absence, and I looked to our first meeting to put an end to my suspense.

Bithery handed me the telescope, which I levelled at the approaching surf-boat. Already the quaint figure of my old friend was clearly distinguishable in his queer habiliments, and I could see him scrutinising the brig with the aid of a binocular. As the boat came nearer, I leaped on to the rail and stood holding on by a backstay and waving my cap – or rather Jobling's. He recognised me almost at once, for I saw him stand up and wave his hat in response, sitting down again with some suddenness as the boat gave a lurch.

As the surf-boat swept alongside he made a snatch at the ladder, and was on deck in a twinkling, fairly falling into my arms as he came over the rail.

"Now God be praised that I have been spared to see this day!" he exclaimed, in a voice that shook with agitation, "this blessed day that I had ceased to hope for."

He stood, holding both my hands, while the tears chased one another down his sunken cheeks, though his face beamed with delight.

As for me, I was too much affected by the old man's emotion and my own to be able to speak, until the skipper created a welcome diversion by loudly stigmatising the bystanding deck hands as "a pack of grinning apes," and hustling them away forward.

"How is Isabel?" I asked, when I had recovered my composure a little.

"She is well, my dear boy, very well, thank God. Ah! and that reminds me; she must share our happiness at once. Captain, would you kindly fire the gun twice? It was to be the signal. We saw the brig come in all gay with flags, and I promised, if she brought good news, we would fire the gun once, and if our dear friend was on board, we would fire it twice. She is on the beach with the telescope now."

Twice the little gun sang out its joyful note, and then Captain Bithery executed a diplomatic move, the brilliancy of which I have never ceased to admire.

"Look here, Englefield," said he, "there is no need for you to stay here while I am pitching Pereira the yarn and letting him finger the gold. Yes, my friend, gold; good, yellow gold by the hundredweight; you cut ashore, and send the boat back for us, and tell Miss Pereira that we are all coming to breakfast."

I glanced at my old friend to see how he took the proposal, and as he beamed approvingly, I lost no time, but dropped into the boat forthwith.

"Shove off," I said to the boatswain, as I took my seat in the Madeira chair that was lashed to the thwart; and as the big boat sheered off, I caught a glimpse of Jobling's face looking over the bulwark, wistfully regarding his best drill suit as it moved shoreward.

The canoemen glanced at me curiously as we went along, having apparently gleaned some particulars from the natives on board, and presently they broke out into the classical Gold Coast boat song, "White man cummygain" – which was so apt to the circumstances, that I would have rewarded them with a substantial "dash," but Jobling's pockets were empty.

With a glance round, to make sure that Isabel was not on the beach, I ran across the sandy flat, and down the narrow streets, until I came to the compound gate. Here I paused a moment to get my breath; then I pushed open the creaking gate and entered.

She was standing on the verandah waiting for me, looking in her soft white dress, with its single spot of scarlet blossom, more daintily lovely even than the visions my memory had conjured up. I hurried across the compound, and ran up the stairs, at the head of which she met me with outstretched hands and a radiant smile of welcome.

In a moment all my fine speeches were forgotten; all my resolutions to consider the delicacy of our position vanished before the ingenuous love that sparkled in her eyes; and without a word I took her in my arms and kissed her.

She did not resent my bluntness, but only murmured some broken words of joy and relief at seeing me alive and well, till growing more conscious, she made as if she would gently disengage herself, and this with a very pretty confusion.

But possession is nine points of the law, and I would not give up my advantage.

"Isabel," I whispered, "this is what I have thought of and longed for in all the long months of my wanderings – this, and to hear you say that you love me, that there is to be no more parting for us until the end."

She looked up into my face with grave frankness.

"You may hear me say it now," said she, "as you might have heard me months ago. When you went away my heart and my world went with you."

"If I had, I should never have gone," I said.

"Then would there have been saved a world of sorrow and heart-sickness in this house," she replied; and with a sudden burst of emotion she exclaimed: "Oh! my dear! how long the days have been! How dark and full of sickening dread, and hope dying into despair!"

Her eyes filled at the recollection, and laying her head on my shoulder, she wept silently.

I was touched with remorse at the thought of her sufferings, but yet my heart was singing with joy.

"Come, my dearest," I said, "this is no time for weeping or thoughts of sorrow and sadness. Let us dry our eyes and rejoice; 'for, lo! the winter is past, the rain is over and gone, and the time of the singing of birds is come.' "

Epilogue

I am writing these last few lines, telling of the end of my youthful wanderings, by an open window that looks out across the sunlit sea, where the Goodwins sleep peacefully amidst the summer blue, and the idle shipping lingers in the Downs by the hazy Sandwich shore.

Down in the garden I can see a white-haired old man sitting on a bench enjoying a cigarette which the deft fingers of Isabel have just rolled and lit for him. The pair are watching a burly old man who is rigging a flagstaff with the help of a tall, sturdy boy; and as the former turns to his assistant with a wry, genial smile, I see that the brown, wrinkled face is that of my old friend Captain Bithery.

My papers lie upon the ancient desk that my father-in-law brought with him when he left Africa for good – the desk on which good Master Barnabas Hogg was wont to write up his "Journall" when Charles the First was King; and I look around upon other mementoes of the stirring days of my youth. And especially upon a little cotton bag that hangs on the wall hard by. In it is a tablet of baked clay, on one side of which is scratched in rough Arabic characters, "Praise be to God," while the other bears the inscription, in my wife's handwriting, "Aminé loveth thee."

R Austin Freeman

The D'Arblay Mystery

When a man is found floating beneath the skin of a green-skimmed pond one morning, Dr Thorndyke becomes embroiled in an astonishing case. This wickedly entertaining detective fiction reveals that the victim was murdered through a lethal injection and someone out there is trying a cover-up.

Dr Thorndyke Intervenes

What would you do if you opened a package to find a man's head? What would you do if the headless corpse had been swapped for a case of bullion? What would you do if you knew a brutal murderer was out there, somewhere, and waiting for you? Some people would run. Dr Thorndyke intervenes.

R Austin Freeman

Felo De Se

John Gillam was a gambler. John Gillam faced financial ruin and was the victim of a sinister blackmail attempt. John Gillam is now dead. In this exceptional mystery, Dr Thorndyke is brought in to untangle the secrecy surrounding the death of John Gillam, a man not known for insanity and thoughts of suicide.

Flighty Phyllis

Chronicling the adventures and misadventures of Phyllis Dudley, Richard Austin Freeman brings to life a charming character always getting into scrapes. From impersonating a man to discovering mysterious trap doors, *Flighty Phyllis* is an entertaining glimpse at the times and trials of a wayward woman.

R Austin Freeman

Helen Vardon's Confession

Through the open door of a library, Helen Vardon hears an argument that changes her life forever. Helen's father and a man called Otway argue over missing funds in a trust one night. Otway proposes a marriage between him and Helen in exchange for his co-operation and silence. What transpires is a captivating tale of blackmail, fraud and death. Dr Thorndyke is left to piece together the clues in this enticing mystery.

Mr Pottermack's Oversight

Mr Pottermack is a law-abiding, settled homebody who has nothing to hide until the appearance of the shadowy Lewison, a gambler and blackmailer with an incredible story. It appears that Pottermack is in fact a runaway prisoner, convicted of fraud, and Lewison is about to spill the beans unless he receives a large bribe in return for his silence. But Pottermack protests his innocence, and resolves to shut Lewison up once and for all. Will he do it? And if he does, will he get away with it?

OTHER TITLES BY R AUSTIN FREEMAN AVAILABLE DIRECT FROM HOUSE OF STRATUS

Quantity		£	$(US)	$(CAN)	€
	A Certain Dr Thorndyke	6.99	11.50	16.95	11.50
	The D'Arblay Mystery	6.99	11.50	16.95	11.50
	Dr Thorndyke Intervenes	6.99	11.50	16.95	11.50
	Dr Thorndyke's Casebook	6.99	11.50	16.95	11.50
	The Eye of Osiris	6.99	11.50	16.95	11.50
	Felo De Se	6.99	11.50	16.95	11.50
	Flighty Phyllis	6.99	11.50	16.95	11.50
	The Great Portrait Mystery	6.99	11.50	16.95	11.50
	Helen Vardon's Confession	6.99	11.50	16.95	11.50
	Mr Polton Explains	6.99	11.50	16.95	11.50

ALL HOUSE OF STRATUS BOOKS ARE AVAILABLE FROM GOOD BOOKSHOPS OR DIRECT FROM THE PUBLISHER.

Internet: www.houseofstratus.com including author interviews, reviews, features.

Email: sales@houseofstratus.com please quote author, title and credit card details.

OTHER TITLES BY R AUSTIN FREEMAN AVAILABLE DIRECT FROM HOUSE OF STRATUS

Quantity		£	$(US)	$(CAN)	€
☐	Mr Pottermack's Oversight	6.99	11.50	16.95	11.50
☐	The Mystery of 31 New Inn	6.99	11.50	16.95	11.50
☐	The Mystery of Angelina Frood	6.99	11.50	16.95	11.50
☐	The Penrose Mystery	6.99	11.50	16.95	11.50
☐	The Puzzle Lock	6.99	11.50	16.95	11.50
☐	The Red Thumb Mark	6.99	11.50	16.95	11.50
☐	The Shadow of the Wolf	6.99	11.50	16.95	11.50
☐	A Silent Witness	6.99	11.50	16.95	11.50
☐	The Singing Bone	6.99	11.50	16.95	11.50

ALL HOUSE OF STRATUS BOOKS ARE AVAILABLE FROM GOOD BOOKSHOPS OR DIRECT FROM THE PUBLISHER:

Hotline: UK ONLY: **0800 169 1780**, please quote author, title and credit card details.
INTERNATIONAL: **+44 (0) 20 7494 6400**, please quote author, title, and credit card details.

Send to: House of Stratus
24c Old Burlington Street
London
W1X 1RL
UK

Please allow for postage costs charged per order plus an amount per book as set out in the tables below:

	£(Sterling)	$(US)	$(CAN)	€(Euros)
Cost per order				
UK	2.00	3.00	4.50	3.30
Europe	3.00	4.50	6.75	5.00
North America	3.00	4.50	6.75	5.00
Rest of World	3.00	4.50	6.75	5.00
Additional cost per book				
UK	0.50	0.75	1.15	0.85
Europe	1.00	1.50	2.30	1.70
North America	2.00	3.00	4.60	3.40
Rest of World	2.50	3.75	5.75	4.25

PLEASE SEND CHEQUE, POSTAL ORDER (STERLING ONLY), EUROCHEQUE, OR INTERNATIONAL MONEY ORDER (PLEASE CIRCLE METHOD OF PAYMENT YOU WISH TO USE)
MAKE PAYABLE TO: STRATUS HOLDINGS plc

Cost of book(s): ———————— Example: 3 x books at £6.99 each: £20.97
Cost of order: ———————— Example: £2.00 (Delivery to UK address)
Additional cost per book: ———————— Example: 3 x £0.50: £1.50
Order total including postage: ———————— Example: £24.47

Please tick currency you wish to use and add total amount of order:

☐ £ (Sterling)   ☐ $ (US)   ☐ $ (CAN)   ☐ € (EUROS)

VISA, MASTERCARD, SWITCH, AMEX, SOLO, JCB:

☐☐☐☐☐☐☐☐☐☐☐☐☐☐☐☐☐☐☐

Issue number (Switch only):
☐☐☐

Start Date: **Expiry Date:**
☐☐ / ☐☐   ☐☐ / ☐☐

Signature: _____

NAME: _____

ADDRESS: _____

_____

POSTCODE: _____

Please allow 28 days for delivery.

Prices subject to change without notice.
Please tick box if you do not wish to receive any additional information. ☐

House of Stratus publishes many other titles in this genre; please check our website (**www.houseofstratus.com**) for more details.